When the War Is Over...

by

Agathe von Kampen

PublishAmerica
Baltimore

First printing

ISBN: 1-60441-761-7
PUBLISHED BY PUBLISHAMERICA, LLLP
www.publishamerica.com
Baltimore

Printed in the United States of America

When the War
Is Over...

by

Agathe von Kampen

Agathe von Kampen
Rom 8:28

Dedication

This book is dedicated to my daughters and grandchildren who had no choice but to take part in my life's journey with me and, in spite of, or because of my part in their lives, turned out to be upstanding citizens and loving human beings. They gave me a reason to live when many times I wanted to give up. I love you.

Acknowledgments

In appreciation of all my friends, old and new, you know who you are, for supporting me during the hard times and celebrating the good times. Especially, De Etta who so graciously typed every word of the manuscript with enthusiasm and returned them with tear stains on the paper. Pat, whom I could always count on to give me honest criticism. Aurilie, who always offered coffee and cookies—and her time to listen to me vent. My spiritual advisor, pastor Carl, who is an answer to my prayers, and his wife, Irene, who's special gift of friendship sustains me daily. My husband, Bunk, for patience during my "computer madness" phase of getting this manuscript to the publisher. But most of all to my niece—my soul daughter—Tina, who made herself available as my literary agent and worked tirelessly to get this book published. Tina, you have my love, admiration and gratitude.

All names except those of the original family have been changed to protect the privacy of certain individuals.

Chapter 1

The clear tones of the soloist rang through the mortuary as a last tribute to the woman who risked death to give me life. As her daughter, she expected me to be a copy of herself. I spent a lifetime trying to meet that expectation but I failed miserably.

Nothing in our relationship was bland: as an adult I disagreed with her on almost every issue. We had frequent verbal fights, hurting each other deeply. But always our love for each other was total.

Now I sat alone in the family section of the funeral home, listening to the eulogy delivered in a monotone by the minister. I fidgeted with the pleats In my navy blue skirt, the only dark piece of clothing in my closet. I had always taken pride in dressing meticously for the occasion. Now, due to having spent all my free time in caring for my Mother's needs, I'd found no time to shop for the proper black dress. For that I blamed my brother. At first his decision not to attend the furneral had astonished me, but now the tears that welled up under my lids were from bitternes and anger. He failed me when I desperately needed his strength and counsel. He left me alone. Alone.

How could I cry when I had no shoulder to lean on? Bitterness and anger slowly took the place of sorrow. It was a familiar emotion in which I had come to feel safe. I had learned long ago that anger was a more constructive way to deal with my emotions than sorrow. Anger created energy, and I used it to function. With it I could survive this ordeal, too.

It was July 1, 1981, a holiday in Abbotsford, a suburb of Vancouver, British Columbia, Canada. I stopped first at the hospital where Muttie (this is what I called my Mother in our native German tongue)—had died. There I signed the necessary papers after which a nurse handed me a paper bag containing my Mother's belongings: a purse and the clothes she had worn to the hospital. Also, she handed me my Mother's cane that I recognized as the cane used by Oma, my grandmother twenty-nine years earlier, when as war refugees we traveled from the Ukraine through Germany and then finally, as part of the displaced persons re-settlement program of the late forties, on to America—the "Promised Land".

"Promised Land?" Ha! My physical pain due to hunger, disease, and filth during the war in Europe wasn't half the hell that I experienced since arriving in this country. I simply exchanged physical deprivation for psychological torment. I didn't blame America; and I didn't blame God. Nor did I blame myself. Who, then, should I blame? As I looked toward the casket in which Muttie's body now lay, I was tempted to blame her. Was it her conditioning that from my childhood had set me up for all the traps into which I had fallen? A resounding "Yes" wanted to jump from my throat. I wanted to hate this woman who gave me life, but she was dead and within the hour she would be lowered into the ground. She was gone. She could no longer withdraw her love as she used to do to punish me when I was a child. She could no longer blame me for her pain.

Did I really want to blame her for my sorrows? In spite of the pain I suffered—through it all—I loved her. I had loved her longer than anyone else in my life, but at what cost? Was it worth it? Sometimes I think that even the wrong kind of love was better than nothing. Or was it?

What difference would it make now anyway? She was gone, and I missed her already. Who would I go to now? Who would know exactly how to comfort me when no one else could. I was alone—truly alone!

* * *

My Mother, Anna, was born in 1905 to a Dutch-German Mennonite family whose ancestors had immigrated to the Ukraine, Russia, during the reign of Catherine The Great. As a child, I listened to the stories of my heritage often during the long winter evenings after the family had finished their chores. Burning kerosene lamps was considered a luxury, so in the dark evenings there was nothing else to do but entertain each other with stories of the past. I remember clearly, sitting on Oma's lap, her gentle arms enfolding me safely against her ample bosom, allowing me to entwine my fingers in the hand crochet lace shawl that always covered her shoulders. Feeling the wrinkled skin on the top of her work-worn hands—looking into her kind blue eyes and watching the last rays of light play in her silvery hair pulled tight in a bun. Oma seldom spoke, but often hummed favorite hymns softly, making me feel secure whenever she was near. My brother, Gerhard, who was five years my senior, considered himself too mature to snuggle up to anybody, but instead claimed his spot on the wooden bench, handcrafted by Papa, next to the open fire. He was proud that he was trusted to treat the fire with respect. It is difficult to recall ever seeing Muttie without a sewing project in her hands—even in the dark she seemed to be able to do the necessary mending and endless altering of old clothing to be made into new outfits for us children since nothing was available for purchase in the stores. She had Oma's blue eyes and full figure, but that's where the similarities stopped. Muttie had a volatile nature and was given to mood swings that always kept me somewhat off balance. I was happiest when I was with Papa—in his presence I felt safe and protected. His handsome features of dark hair and black eyes made him somewhat mysterious, drawing me to him in a strange exciting way. He liked to tickle my face with his mustache. He was somewhat shorter than Muttie, and to Muttie's constant dismay, was able to eat whatever he chose and remain thin. In contrast to Muttie's round body I remember Papa as being a very small man.

As the evenings would come to an end and before Papa would play his violin to accompany Muttie's high soprano voice as she sang lullabies to Gerhard and me until we would fall asleep, our heritage was reminisced over and over again, lest we would forget.

The Mennonites were a fairly large religious body in the Dutch, German, and Netherlands regions of Europe who followed the teachings of a religious leader named Menno Simons. Believing in pacifism, their refusal to bear arms brought persecution.

During this time, Netherland-born Catherine the Great secured the Russian throne by forcing her husband-emperor, Peter III, to abdicate and later by permitting his assassination. She not only realized the agricultural potential of the Ukraine but also witnessed the reluctance of the Russian peasants to put forth the effort and hard work required to make it productive. When the plight of the unfortunate Mennonites came to her attention, she saw an opportunity to develop the Ukraine. She promised these honest and hard-working people that they would be exempt from serving in the armed forces as long as they would cultivate the land and pay higher taxes.

I heard many stories of the hardships endured by my ancestors as they settled into their new homeland, but they persevered and by the time my Mother's parents were born, they had managed to become an affluent German society in Russia. They operated their own private schools where only the German language was spoken.

My grandparents were productive farmers in Rosenthal (renamed Chortitza after the Bolshivick Revolution,) raising a large family at the turn of the century.

Sitting in a cozy corner of our home, her knitting needles clicking, Oma would tell of the good days when she raised her family in a spacious three-story brick house with a maid and nanny. Muttie, her youngest, had only faint memories of that house. By the time Muttie was old enough to remember clearly, the Czar had been exiled and the revolution was in full force. These were the experiences Muttie related to me, which was quite a contrast to the pleasant scenes my grandmother painted.

The government changed so rapidly, people didn't know who to salute. According to the supporters of the Revolution, the common people would have a better life because riches would be taken from the wealthy and distributed to the poor. Muttie remembered the day the soldiers broke into her house, destroyed all the furniture, killed the farm animals, and took the whole family captive, relocating them in shacks fit only for animals. All this was done in order to equalize everyone. Bricks of cow manure and clay mixture were dried in the hot summer sun and used to build small one-room huts, covered with straw roofs, using the natural clay found so abundantly in that area as a floor. Amazingly, they did have glass windows. During the winter, straw was stacked around the outside to protect the manure bricks from the heavy rains during the Fall and Spring. The men worked in a collective farm system, referred to as simply a "collective." The only wages was enough food and fuel for the family, and free "housing." If anyone objected, food was withheld until they submitted.

A drought devastated the wheat crop, and by winter starvation spread nationwide. Adding to the suffering, an epidemic of typhoid fever broke out, killing hundreds. There were not enough healthy people left to bury the dead. Bodies left on the frozen ground, had to wait until the spring for burial. Those who survived were left emotionally and spiritually scarred, grieving for their loved ones. After such a difficult winter, the citizens naturally submitted to the collectives for just a crust of bread.

During this time, Muttie, a teenager, dreamed of a far off land: America. Food had been sent from there during the drought, and many Mennonites had sold everything—quickly and cheaply—before the soldiers had taken it away, in order to pay for passage to North America. For a time, the Russian government allowed the exodus in order to continue American help so badly needed. Muttie stood at her fence, watching friends and neighbors go by in their wagons, heading toward Moscow for the necessary processing to exit Russia.

Without warning, the government revoked all exit visas, and many people trying to escape returned as fugitives. The government seized the churches and beautiful cathedrals, turning many into stables and army headquarters. My family began to practice their religious faith in secret.

Life goes on, even in the worst of circumstances, and children grow up, fall in love, get married, and thereby continues the cycle. My parents were engaged just before Papa had to report for duty in the red army. Release from the armed forces for the Mennonites was a thing of the past. Some staunch young men were sent to Siberia for refusing induction, but most went to war.

* * *

My parents had their first child in 1926, a boy they named Gerhard after Muttie's father. Bright, beautiful, with an endearing disposition, he was everything two parents could hope for.

A housing, fuel, and food shortage forced several families to live together in the small huts in the villages and two-room flats in the cities. My parents lived with Papa's youngest brother and his wife and child. Because of the sub-standard living conditions, poor nutrition and lack of medical care, contagious diseases like tuberculosis and malaria were common. My uncle suffered from tuberculosis and died just before his wife gave birth to their second child.

Gerhard developed a cough. For two years the young parents watched their beloved baby become weaker until he finally died in Muttie's arms at the age of three. Grief turned Muttie cold and bitter, and her defiance extended beyond the family. The threat of Siberia to anyone who practiced independent thinking meant nothing to her; without her baby, she didn't want to live.

Actually, at this time the communists didn't send women to Siberia. That came later after imprisoned man-power built the cities. Many citizens were arrested on charges of being enemies of the state. For that, the government needed documentation which was obtained from forced confessions of innocent people held captive for this purpose. Because of Muttie's careless attitude, Papa, (the head of the house) was arrested. Many years later, I heard him tell of the tortures he had endured until he finally signed whatever papers were set before him. A few days after his release, my uncle who lived up the hill from us, was taken away by the N.K.V.D. (later the KGB) during the night, leaving my aunt with two small children and one on the way. We never heard from my uncle again. Papa realized that he had signed papers condemning his brother-in-law, and the guilt of this act weighed heavily on him as the years went by.

By the time my parents' second son was born, life had become so intolerable that they could only feel deep sorrow for their child who would grow up facing life in this hostile country. They named him "Gerhard" to replace their lost firstborn, and he soon proved himself to be everything they had lost. With dark hair and flashing eyes his handsome features took after my father's family. He was also intelligent and in the years to come exhibited a delightful sense of humor not displayed by his deceased brother.

Muttie had a difficult birth. Early in her pregnancy she developed toxemia, and that along with an attack of malaria resulted in convulsions during delivery. Her physician advised her not to have any more children and urged her to have a sterilization. She refused. Her religious convictions allowed only for total abstinence as a means of birth control.

Life became more grim every day, and were it not for the sunshine their "little happy-go-lucky" boy brought them, there would be no reason to live. But the worst was yet to come.

After four years Muttie found she was expecting another child. Her doctor insisted on an abortion to save her life. Papa agreed. But again my Mother refused and for nine months she had to deal with feelings of guilt, self-pity, and fear—the fear of death and the fear of leaving her precious little boy motherless. At first she blamed herself for making this decision, but as time went on, she shifted the blame to her husband. Compounding the problems, food was in short supply, they lived in a shack, and they did not have sufficient fuel for heat through the long cold winter, and rumors spread that war with Germany was imminent. Muttie resented the fact that Papa continued to work on the collective which provided little. They were always hungry and always the threat of Siberia hung over his head. Then there were the never ending quarrels and resentful silences between herself and Papa.

17

November 15, 1935, on her 10th wedding anniversary while battling another malaria attack, Muttie went into labor. Winter had come early that year, and a storm raged outside. Papa walked to the collective office, borrowed a horse, and went to get the doctor.

Many hours later he heard the doctor exclaim, "It's truly a miracle," as he held up the healthy baby. Both mother and child were doing fine. For Papa, it was instant love for this tiny little girl. He had his wife, alive; a five-year-old son; and now a daughter. He had a complete family circle. It was a miracle, Papa agreed. Maybe a sign that things would get better. Maybe Russia wouldn't enter the war against Germany. Maybe the communist government would improve with time. Maybe, just maybe, good times were ahead. Wasn't it a good omen that a healthy daughter had been born? All would be well. God was still in control. For now, Papa was content to sit in his chair, holding me, his little miracle. I remember being held in his strong arms many times, feeling safe as bombs exploded and sirens howled.

* * *

After all the anxiety Muttie experienced during her pregnancy, her joy now was complete. She had her little girl. I was a miracle baby. I was perfect, at least she believed I should be—God's gift in uncertain times. In the years to follow I tried living up to her expectations, God knows I tried. But sadly, I disappointed her, and failing her, I failed myself because my goal was to be perfect—to be Muttie's miracle child.

"The first couple of years," my Mother said when I had grown older, "you were everything a mother could wish for, but I knew you were in for a difficult time. Gerhard was a boy, it wouldn't be too bad for him. But you, you're a girl. It's unfortunate to be born a girl in a war." Then she would rock me to sleep, singing a lullaby she had composed herself:

"Kleines Maedchen
Armes Kind,
Siehst noch nicht
Die Not I'm Wind."

"Little girl, poor child, can't see yet the trouble in the wind." Not able to comprehend the meaning of the words, Muttie's whispered lullaby comforted me even as she pressed me against her soft bosom.

Germany attacked Russia, and within a short time things became critical. Anyone speaking German or with a German ancestry was suspect. Attempting to blend in, we discarded our German names. At birth I was named Agathe after my grandmother, but now I became Gatel. My brother was called Jehorka. My father, Julius, became Jils; and Muttie, Anna, became Annuschka.

As men were pressed into military service, a shortage of farm workers developed, and women, including mothers of young children, had to report for work in the collectives. All children from the smallest infants on were to be raised in child care centers where the proper communist training would take place. This was a difficult development for our family. We were converted to a faith restricting us from many government requirements. To resist meant Siberia and already the word brought dread to any heart. Even though I was only two years old, I can still remember clinging to Muttie's neck in terror as a Russian-speaking day care attendant pulled me away from her arms. Following orders, my Mother walked away without coming to my rescue.

Muttie worked as a wet nurse in the nursery. The facility was a large room divided with something similar to a chain link fence. I was on one side with other children my age, and Muttie was on the other, holding and nursing some of the babies. I couldn't understand why she wouldn't hold me. I clung to the chain fence and cried. Still she didn't come. An attendant slapped my mouth in an effort to quiet me, but I screamed all the louder. Finally in desperation, the attendants enlisted the help of my Mother with strict orders to find a way to make me behave. When she held me, of course I stopped crying and there was no need for punishment—I had what I wanted and needed. But when she sat me down to leave, I resumed my hysterical wails.

"Gatel, you have to stop crying," she yelled over my screams. It seemed to me I was being abandoned. How could Muttie with the soft voice that put me to sleep now sound so harsh and bitter? Of course it must have been unbearable for her to see her baby abused in this way, but in my childish mind I saw my Mother loving strange children and rejecting me. Every day this routine repeated itself. I would hang onto the fence, watching Muttie love other babies, and I would scream until my throat hurt and my lips bled from the slaps I received. Every morning Muttie admonished that I shouldn't cry. Every day I cried. I got the message that Muttie went on loving other babies as long as I was a "bad" girl and kept on crying.

At times we were allowed to go outside for playtime. The pre-schoolers and the first graders played together. My brother seemed to be happy, playing with these children who talked a language I could not understand; indeed, he even talked like them. Isolated from the children and from my Mother, I cried. While crouching in the corner of the play yard, tears streaming down my face, Jehorka came over to me and whispered in German, "Gatel, you must stop crying and do everything they tell you, then they won't be so mean to you." So, that was it: It was my fault that I was treated so harshly. I would oblige. I couldn't do what I was told because I couldn't understand them, but I could stop crying, then everything would be all right. I would be a "good" girl and Muttie would take me home and love me again.

This she did, but not because I was good, but because I was sick. The mixed emotions my poor Mother must have felt, when once more she was able to take care of me, but fearing that she would lose me permanently through a dreaded childhood illness.

It started with another malaria attack, followed by a mild case of diphtheria, which Jehorka had simultaneously—only more severe. While everyone was busy trying to save Jehorka's life, I contracted measles. As Jehorka's condition improved, mine worsened and was now complicated by an infection. Congestion made breathing difficult and a high fever brought convulsions and hallucinations. Visions of black ravens on my bed pecking at my sores left by the measles, are still vivid memories.

None of the doctor's treatments or medicines seemed to do any good. My grandmother finally spoke up, suggesting some folk remedies she had practiced in the past. The doctor shrugged off her suggestion saying, "You Germans think you know everything. If you make use of this steam therapy you're talking about, I'll report you to the authorities." This spelled out "Siberia" for my parents. Nothing could be done. They could only pray and even that had to be done in secret.

My condition continued to worsen over the next several days. Finally the doctor said there was nothing more that could be done. With my family sitting around the room, the doctor filled out my death certificate and handed it to my parents, instructing them to fill in the date when I died. He was sure I wouldn't live through the night.

After his departure, my mother and grandmother decided to take a chance on the home remedy. They draped a blanket over a chair, fashioning a tent. My Mother then sat under the blanket on the chair and held me in her arms, while my grandmother kept a tub of water (with herbs) steaming under the chair. This created a soothing mist. For hours Muttie sat in this heat, holding her limp child, watching thick ribbons of pus ooze from my nose, mouth, ears, and eyes. My fever continued to climb.

Sometime in the middle of the night they changed the treatment from moist heat to a cool wrapping in order to bring my fever down. By morning the crisis had passed, and I slept peacefully. As Muttie was holding me tenderly, I could feel the tension draining from her body, indicating a glimmer of hope that she would keep her little sunshine— she wouldn't have to sign the death certificate. My first thought after regaining consciousness was, would I have to go back to the day care center now that I was getting well? I hoped to stay sick.

The German army advanced rapidly through Russia, disrupting village life. While Muttie tended to my recovery, the government organized refugees, German and Russians alike, into wagon trains and evacuated them toward Siberia in order to keep them out of the German's hands. Droves passed through our village; the Russians happy to escape capture and the Germans sad not to be freed by the advancing German army.

To make matters worse, another drought parched the land. Water, first doled out by the cup, then by spoon, soon gave out altogether. Sickness spread due to a combination of spoiled food and the lack of pure water. Soon the main job for the men working on the collective was to bury the dead.

When the rumble of gunfire could be heard from the distance, the Russian soldiers increased their efforts to keep the refugees moving by driving them like cattle with whips. I remember sitting by the window listlessly watching a young mother holding her infant, kneeling before Muttie and begging for just a drop of water. Muttie told her that the baby was already dead and that water must be saved for the living. Several men finally took the baby from her for burial. The mother's screams pierced the hot, dry air. The scene added fear of thirst, hunger, and gunfire to my fear of the day care center.

I listened to my parents talk during the night when I was supposed to be sleeping. "If we can just manage to stay here until the Germans come, we will be saved," Papa said. I also heard how some of the Germans from other villages tried to hide with friends and relatives in our town. When they were found, Russian soldiers tortured them to death. I had forgotten how to smile, but no one noticed; smiles were a thing of the past.

* * *

We lived in Chortitza, located near the Dnieper River. The German army had to cross this river to continue making advances into the Ukraine. The Russians were retreating through Chortitza, driving the refugees ahead of them. We knew that once the Germans crossed the Dnieper River, it would be our turn to be evacuated. Because the Russian soldiers were busy stalling the enemy armies and controling the vast mob of refugees, less time was spent observing our activities. My uncle had somehow managed to secure an old radio that was taken into our "basement"—really just a small hole under the house where we had secretly hidden Papa from possibly being picked up on nights when the NKVD had recruited "prisoners" this way. My uncle and Papa would then climb out and report to us the German's possible location. If only we could hide when our turn came and the Germans would enter Chortitza before the Russians would find us, we would be saved. We became bold enough to gather in small groups secretly to pray to God for deliverance. Oma, who was now living with us, was talking about how we needed faith. Just then the door was knocked open and soldiers burst in with rifles aimed. Orders were given for us to hurriedly pack warm clothes, wear felt boots, and take whatever food we had that wasn't perishable. We recognized immediately our destination. It was summer, we wouldn't need felt boots—only in Siberia. It was too late now to plan any strategies. Paralizing fear gripped us. The Russian soldiers were just as scared of being taken prisoners by the Germans if the escape wasn't fast enough as we were of Siberia. The fear of Siberia was so great that some people purposely defied the soldiers to provoke them to shoot them on the spot instead of dying a slow death in Siberia.

We were now taken with our meager belongings to the Collective where most of our neighbors and relatives had gathered, already waiting in wagons with horses ready for departure. We looked around anxiously for relatives. My uncle and aunt had secretly been digging a shelter covered with earth and garden debris and stocked with some food. His decision was to hide with his wife and three children, and if found, to have the whole family die together rather than to be taken to Siberia. We could not see them anywhere. We were loaded into one of the wagons that needed a horse. Several of the wagons were still unoccupied. Women and children were crying. Men were trying to negotiate with the soldiers. "Look," they said, "you can see that you will be overtaken. If you're captured by the enemy, all our fates will be doomed. Why don't you just ride up ahead and tell your superiors you barely escaped; they'll never know the difference. With the Germans already across the bridge, so save your own lives."

I was about five or six years old and for the first time I noticed the difference in my parents from most of the other families. In the midst of all the other men stood my Mother, tall and erect, with her hands on her hips trying to negotiate with the soldiers in a bravado voice, fearless in the face of danger while my Father cowered in the background, afraid of the consequences. Returning to ourwagon she turned on her husband, "Jils, a lot of good you are—while the other women are being protected by their husbands, I have to wear the pants in the family while you hide behind Oma's skirts." I watched my Father shrink in size as Muttie ended her tirade with "I should have known better than to marry a man shorter than me." Papa was a small man indeed, but endowed with physical strength matched by few. Unfortunately, Muttie could only judge him by the lack of brawn he displayed in times of need.

The soldiers were visibly afraid. They did not shoot the dissenters any more. They needed to save what little ammunition they had for their own protection so our men were silenced with the butt of their rifles and whips.

The remaining wagons were loaded except for two—on their list were two families names; one of them was my uncle. Anyone informing on their whereabouts would be given the fastest horse. No one spoke up. Oma prayed silently for her daughter with husband and children. Would they be found?

Gunfire was coming closer and orders were given to move the wagon caravan out. We still didn't have a horse. Two soldiers had to stay behind to find the two missing families and a horse for the wagon. Finally, a crippled old horse was produced for our wagon. The other wagons were quite a ways ahead and a whole company of Russian soldiers were coming in the other direction to fight the frontlines—replacements—that meant the Germans were gaining on them. We were so close to freedom. The horse laid down and refused to get up despite the brutal beating with the soldier's whip. Among a string of curses, the soldier told us to stay there while he would hunt up another horse. Now was our chance. Would we dare try an escape? The decision had to be made instantly.

Papa hoisted me on his shoulders. He grabbed a couple of bags with food. Muttie, Oma and Jehorka did the same. Not a word was spoken as we made our way through heavy wooded areas and deserted houses to Uncle Abram's dugout. We scratched our way through the leaves covering it to the inside. It was dark and smelled of earth. No guests ever received a more heartfelt welcome, not only that hopefully we would be saved together, but also that it was us—not the Russian soldiers as expected. Once inside, we sat there, afraid to breathe lest we would be heard. Before long we heard the Russian soldiers outside, looking for us. Finally we heard more voices joining them. They were told to stop looking for this handful of dissenters and join the army on the front lines. "They'll never survive the crossfire when the Germans get this far anyway," we heard them say as they rode into the distance. Is that what would happen to us? Must we die in the crossfire?

* * *

For days we hid in this cave, burying our human waste with a shovel provided for this purpose, listening to the sounds of war. Bombs were exploding in the distance, coming closer; cannons going off with their deep heavy sound. Finally, heavy tanks moving across the earth, mowing down shrubs in their path. Then machine gunfire and rifles with human screams scattered. We covered our ears. Would it ever stop? Who was winning? Suddenly it was still—an occasional rifleblast, then nothing. We waited. Repeatedly we children were told to be very quiet. My cousin, Dori, who was the same age as me, was crying. My aunt was holding her, muffling her cries. No one had to stop me from crying—I had learned my lesson well at the day care center.

In terror, we waited to hear any sounds of German-speaking soldiers, which would mean freedom for us or the all-familiar sound of Russian cursing which would mean certain death for all of us; but we heard nothing; absolute silence. From exhaustion, we eventually fell asleep. Jehorka and my cousin, Heinz, woke up first. In their boyish bravery, (they were about ten or eleven years old), they decided to sneak out and scout out the situation. When the adults discovered this, the agony of waiting to see what would happen was indescribable. Fortunately, it wasn't long before we heard their loud, clear, happy voices at the entrance of our shelter—"The Germans are here, the Germans are here. They've already knocked down Stalin's statue, only his boots are left." One by one, we crawled out. It was hard to tell who welcomed whom. The German soldiers were as happy to find German-speaking people as we were to see them. A lot of embracing took place, followed by us taking some of them to our home, (my uncle's family doing the same), and preparing a meal. We sat late into the night, exchanging stories of our experiences. From then on, our home and yard was filled with German soldiers.

For the next couple of years, we were living on the dividing line of war, the Russians on one side of the Dnieper River and the Germans on the other. Amidst the slaughtering of soldiers daily, I spent the happiest time of my childhood.

With the Communist oppression lifted, we were free to think and speak and act according to our conscience—or so we were told. Our men did not have to work at the Collective any more, and were able to pursue their professions and trades again. Our next door neighbors whom I called aunt and uncle though they were actually not related, opened a photography studio. Uncle Willie had to do some practicing with various films, etc., and asked Muttie if he could use me along with his own little girls as models. Great preparations were made. My new dress—the first I ever owned—my cousin had embroidered and Muttie sewn, was freshly starched and ironed. I had a little blue basket filled with fresh violets to hold and even got a satin ribbon in my hair. I remember the excitement I felt to be receiving all this attention. As we were walking out the door, Muttie knelt down in front of me and very sternly said, "Now, Gatel, don't embarrass me again with your bashfulness like you always do. I want you to smile and act like a normal, happy child." A string of admonitions followed until, by the time we arrived at Uncle Willie's, I was in tears; but she told Uncle Willie to go ahead with the preparations, that I would behave myself. The longer this fuss went on, the more I cried, wanting to go home. Muttie refused, commanding me to smile. I still have the photo of me smiling with tears running down my cheeks.

Papa had opened his carpentry business again and was working at his bench when we returned. I ran to him for comfort with Muttie's voice sounding behind me, "Ya, Ya, go run to your Papa. You know, Jils, if you wouldn't give her all that sympathy, maybe she would act more like a normal child; you have no idea how she just embarrassed me in front of Willie." Papa, who had scooped me up in his arms, now put me down with a heavy sigh. "You expect too much from her, Annuschka."

Muttie recounted my behavior in every detail. Papa told her she expected too much of me. I slunk into the kitchen and sat quietly listening to them argue, with me being the cause. I had failed again. After a while, Muttie came inside, crying; telling me to get out of her sight, I was such a disappointment to her. I went out to the shop to see if Papa didn't want me either. He picked me up in his strong arms and held me till my sobs subsided, never saying a word. I felt that I was still bad, disobedient and stupid, but he loved me anyway. Wasn't he wonderful to be able to love someone as unlovable as me. I had to hold on to that love.

From that time on, I spent much of my time sitting at the back of Papa's workbench, playing with the wood-chips that fell from his tools, enjoying the security of his love. I didn't talk much, I was too afraid that he would be disappointed in me also if I said or did the wrong thing. So, I was content just being with him.

I heard Muttie tell him often how he spoiled me and didn't spend enough time with his son, whereupon he would accuse her of giving Jehorka too much attention, and another argument would take place. Why couldn't I please her so we could all be happy together? I would just have to try harder. I would have to become perfect.

A lot of changes took place as we slowly accepted our new freedom. All the red flags with the hammer and sickle, so familiar and dreaded, were replaced with the black swastika on red. Once more we were able to speak our native German language with pride. We listened to the radios to hear Adolf Hitler, our Fuehrer, give speeches, promising freedom and affluence for all. There was music and laughter heard from the adults visiting in the streets and the children playing. The war was still taking its toll, but it was farther away now. We were surrounded by German soldiers—that spelled safety. Whatever happened, they would protect us. Life took on an almost comfortable routine. After supper we would all sit around with the soldiers, talking about everything except what was on their mind, which was that in the morning they would all roll out to take their place in the front lines, knowing that only very few would return. Like lambs to the slaughter, they were moved out with new shipments coming to take their place daily. They were as young as fourteen years old, not even old enough to shave. As it got dark, someone would always produce an accordian, my father his violin, my Mother her guitar, a few mouth harmonicas, and we would all sing sad, sad songs. At sunrise we heard the familiar requests, "Come, Mamutchka, give me a kiss for good luck." We children were hugged mostly by the soldiers who had a child at home that they missed, and the tanks would move out with the foot soldiers following, knowing this would probably be their last march. After shedding some tears for these young men, preparations would have to be made for the new shipments. Sadly, all the changes taking place in our village were not for the better.

One day all the Jews in our village were arrested. We did not understand. These were our friends and neighbors—we protested. Word came to us to stay uninvolved or we would be considered sympathizers and receive the same fate. Since my family had separated from the Mennonite faith and observed Saturday as their day of worship, we were told we would have to be especially careful not to be identified as Jews. So once more, we had to meet in secret. Some of us, including Papa, stopped worshiping altogether. What Stalin had been unable to accomplish with torture, Hitler was able to do with promises. Life was just too good after the long years of hardship to throw it all away. The young men were drafted into the army and some even joined voluntarily. Some of our young Mennonite women married the soldiers who were stationed there who were considered worldly men by the elders. The older people worried about it all, but again we were learning to smile and pretend out of fear.

One day orders were given at a town meeting for all the villagers to assemble at a local Lye-pit a short distance from the village. All kinds of stories circulated as to what was to take place there. When we arrived, we were forced to watch as these poor Jewish villagers were stripped of their clothes and line up at the edge of the pit. An officer gave a short speech as to what would happen and for this to be an example for all those who would in any way sabbotage the Third Reich. The soldiers opened up machine gun fire and the bodies fell into the Lye-pit to save the trouble of burial. After that, all persons with a biblical first name like "David," for instance, had to get their names changed to a non-Jewish sounding name. My cousin, David, became "Willi." Aunt Esther became "Elsie," and Jils, Anushka, and Jehorka once more used the German name of "Julius, Anna and Gerhard," but for some reason I stayed "Gatel." All this was very confusing, but I had learned not to question things but just to accept and endure, if necessary. Besides, I had Papa home to be with me whenever I felt insecure, so everything would be all right. I spent all my time trying to do things just right to gain Muttie's approval and became very adept at pleasing her. I learned to sew, embroider, knit and crochet, and enjoyed some pleasant times sitting next to her at the sewing machine doing the same thing she was doing. I listened to her sing. Sometimes I would try to sing along, but was told I better just listen since I hadn't been blessed with a singing voice, (although I later sang in a choir). I cherished those times, for before long I would always manage to do or say something to make her angry, then I would quickly find my way to Papa's workbench, but there were times when escape was impossible.

I listened to many arguments between my parents regarding religion: "Julius, by your refusal to attend worship service you will bring damnation to all of us," was Muttie's favored accusation. Papa's reply was usually one that sounded like he had reasoned out his decision with much consideration. "Anna, if I get caught worshiping on Sabbath like the Jews and they send me to the concentration camp, how is that going to help us?" I decided to accept Papa's viewpoint on the issue of religion.

My first test came the following Sabbath morning. The atmosphere was tense as we prepared to go to one of our fellow believer's home for worship. I would somehow manage to stay home with Papa—I had a strategy. At breakfast when he asked the blessing, it was customary for everyone to say "Amen." I was silent. Now, I thought, I would be asked the reason and I would explain my decision; Papa would be happy about it and I would be excused from worship service, but no one asked. Muttie sternly said, "Gatel, say 'Amen' silence; again I was ordered to comply. By now I was scared, and when fear took a hold of me, I had learned the only defense mechanism I knew at the daycare center was to be quiet and not cry. Now Muttie angrily ordered, "Gatel, if you don't say 'amen' I will have to spank you—no response. She took the leather strap from the hook on the wall, laid me across the chair and let the blows fall on my backside. I ground my teeth and endured without making a sound. The blows kept coming with an occasional pause to wait for me to say "amen." By now I was paralyzed with fear. Would Papa ever come to my rescue? Oma tried to reason with Muttie that it was enough, that I was too young for this kind of punishment. Gerhard started crying, "Please, Muttie, don't hit her anymore, hit me instead." This was of some comfort to me since Gerhard had paid very little attention to my existence so far, leading me to think that he would have preferred if I had never joined the family. Finally Papa stepped in and took the strap away from Muttie, but she had worked herself into such a frenzy that she turned on Papa—poor Papa. I had gotten him into trouble again. Breathless, she was shouting accusations at me: "You are the most insensitive child I have ever known. You don't care how you hurt your Mother. I'm trying to bring you up as a God-fearing human being but you insist on having your rebellious way; well, I'll teach you—say amen, Gatel, say amen." When I continued with my silence, she dissolved into tears: "You can't even act normal when you get punished; most children would at least cry and beg for forgiveness but your heart is made of stone—look at you sitting there, glaring at me—me—your Mother who saved you from the measles—I do everything for you. I would sacrifice my life for you, and what do I get in return—rebellion." Her tirade subsided as she sat down next to me limp and defeated. She pulled me close to her, her tears washing my face as she repeated over and over—first in a demanding, harsh voice, then quietly, plaintively, "Why couldn't you at least cry, Gatel; can't you at least cry?"

* * *

The execution of the Jews was fading somewhat in our memory and except for having to worship secretly, life was quite pleasant. I spent most of my time in cold weather at Papa's workbench or with my dolls that Muttie had sewn for me out of scraps of material. I was very creative in fashioning doll clothes and would spend hours playing with them, treating them as live friends. I realize now that the love and care I bestowed on them is what I wanted from Muttie.

The summer was spent outdoors, enjoying the warm sunshine and running free. The soldiers were delighted to have us children divert their attention from what lay before them, which made for quite a variety of activities. Then suddenly, September arrived. Back to school for Gerhard but this year I was going on seven years old and was told that I would be expected to start first grade. After my attempt at making my own decision not to worship on Sabbath had failed so completely, I did not even protest although I was terrified of spending long hours surrounded by strangers, unable to go to Papa for protection if necessary.

On the walk to school the first day with Muttie holding my hand, I felt as though I was going to my execution. When we arrived, I recognized the building; it was the same place I had been left by Muttie years before—the daycare center. I stood glued to the spot where she left me, paralyzed. The teacher finally picked me up and put me in the chair I was to occupy. The hours drifted by. How long would this last, I kept thinking. During recess the other children played games outside, but I wouldn't move from my seat. I guess the teacher reasoned that if she left me alone long enough, I would get tired of sitting there. Lunchtime came and this time she dragged me to the lunch table and gave me strict orders to eat. The menu was borscht (a kind of thick cabbage soup). I obediently tried to eat. When I got a big piece of meat that was all gristle, I chewed on that for what seemed forever but it would not reduce in size for me to swallow. My eyes filled with tears but I could not possibly allow myself to cry. In trying to choke back the tears, I swallowed the meat and started to choke. Several teachers came to my rescue and dislodged the meat and proceeded to shout at me about how stupid I was to try to swallow that gristle, and that I better behave the rest of the day.

The other children had used the restrooms during recess, but since I hadn't left the room all morning, I now was in need of the restroom, but of course speaking up to ask to be excused was out of the question under the circumstances, so I would just have to endure the discomfort. The teacher was asking students to participate in the lessons by having them stand up to answer questions, since everything had to be done orally because of the unavailability of paper or slate boards. When my name was called, I decided I better obey so as not to get into more trouble. When I stood, my bladder failed me. I now was the laughing stock of the class, and worse yet, the teacher excused me to go home which meant that I would incur Muttie's wrath—but maybe that would excuse me from attending school altogether. Oh, I hoped the punishment I expected at home, I might be fearing needlessly. This time Muttie had nothing but sympathy for me. "Poor Gatel," she said, "I'm afraid you are going to have a hard time all your life; you're such a misfit, I should have let you die from the measles but I loved you so much I just had to save you and now you have to pay for my selfishness."

Since we had to do all our practicing of letter and number writing on the blackboard in front of the class, I did not even attempt to try. The anxiety of being up front to make a fool of myself was so great, it took all my energy, and so the days went by in a fog, each one worse than the day before. Finally, the teacher had a conference with Muttie in my prsence, telling her that I was mildly retarded; that I would never be able to learn the things necessary to progress in society as was expected and that my parents could keep on trying for a while but she didn't hold out much hope. At home I practiced my letters outside in the sand with a stick to prove to myself that I could do it. I was doing advanced work on the sewing and knitting; I could calculate how many stitches I needed on a knitting needle to come up with the right size for a given doll, etc. Why couldn't anyone see that my problems were emotional? Anyway, I silently accepted my label as being stupid.

Christmas was approaching, the first for me with actually a tree and cookies and presents. (In Communist Russia, Christmas was outlawed as a religioug holiday and the first year of the German occupation was too full of turmoil for any celebrations). I received my first store-bought doll, the head was made of some type of paper mache. Muttie had made her several outfits and a little blanket. I was so thrilled I was afraid to touch her; just to sit and hold her was ecstacy.

We had dinner next door at Uncle Willie's. They had two daughters, Irene and Elsie. Elsie was quite a bit younger than Irene and me, and a brat—(probably because she was usually excluded from our games.) Irene had received a table game for Christmas and we wanted to try it out. I laid my doll on Irene's bed and covered her for a nap. When we finished the game and I went to retrieve my precious doll, I found Elsie sitting on the floor with a pair of scissors, just finishing cutting a big hole in the doll's forehead. All my usual bashfulness left. I screamed at her, hit her and pulled her hair. My parents took me home and I spent a long time listening to them point out my shortcomings as a human being. "Anna, please go easy on her; after all, it was her first store-bought doll," Papa pleaded as they took me home to face the consequences. "You can't be happy, Gatel, unless you cause problems for me." Muttie's voice shrieked—the voice I had heard in laughter and merriment only moments before at Uncle Willie's. "You should have known better than to leave your new doll unattended, that only goes to show how ungrateful you are; and then, to show your violent temper by hitting little Elsie who doesn't know any better yet; it's no wonder you don't have any friends in school if this is how you behave. And Julius, you are standing there helpless, leaving all the disciplining to me." Then I was left alone to grieve for my broken doll. Finally, in my privacy, I could hold the tears back no longer. I don't know how long I cried, but it seemed I was unable to stop once I allowed the hurt emotions to come to the surface.

Evening came and we were scheduled to go to a Christmas program in the town hall with all kinds of entertainment and refreshments. I sat between my parents, feeling numb. I wanted to be home with my broken doll—how she must be hurting all alone. The music stopped and everyone stood up to applaud. The noise was deafening. I could see stars in front of my eyes, the whole room started spinning. Darkness enveloped me and the next thing I knew, cold water was thrown on my face and I came back to reality—I had fainted. The family had to go home early on my account—I had failed again.

* * *

As we sat in the waiting room, I listened to Muttie explain, "Now, Gatel, don't you worry about a thing. The doctor will find out what made you faint. Whatever your sickness is will probably turn out to be the reason why you are so bashful and unable to comprehend what you're learning in school. He will give you some medicine and you'll become my sweet little girl again—the way you were before the measles changed you."

The doctor seemed to be a friendly, kind old man who took an instant liking to me which was very unusual because after all, I was a very unlovable little girl. People didn't like children who didn't talk or smile, except your parents and they had to love you, at least Papa did, and of course Muttie would if I'd just learn to be good. The doctor examined me and told Muttie that there was nothing physically wrong with me but I seemed to be an unusually nervous child at such a young age. Muttie became very upset and told him all about my stubborn, disobedient and insensitive behaviour, ending with a description about my not even crying when she had used the leather strap on me. "It's like she has no feelings at all," she said. He quietly asked her to leave the examining room to question me alone. She left, which was a total surprise to me. Muttie didn't obey orders, she gave orders to others, so this was a new experience.

I immediately had great respect for this man who could silence the most powerful person I had known, with a few quiet words. He sat me on his lap very gently and started asking me questions. To my amazement the answers started pouring out of my mouth—I could talk, and be listened to. No one had ever asked me why I didn't want to do some things, I was only given instructions and told to obey. This man seemed to understand my reasons, and he still liked me. It was instant love on my part. I didn't want to leave. I wanted to stay in his arms forever.

Afterwards he talked to Muttie privately and then Muttie had a private discussion with Papa after which I was told I would not have to attend school anymore until I was older. What joy! I could be happy. I would make everybody happy, even Muttie—especially Muttie. I would obey her every word. I would smile. I would even try to say funny things like Gerhard and everyone would laugh and hug me and I would become a normal person. Happy days were here, even for me.

* * *

Now that I didn't have to attend school anymore, I was free to play outside with the younger pre-school children all day. With my newfound confidence, I was able to make friends with a little girl in the neighborhood. I was even bold enough to invite her to have lunch with us a few times and Muttie even seemed to approve; in fact, I was able to please Muttie quite often. Even though on the war front things were getting more serious, the German army was forced to retreat more and more, and the bombs started to fall closer to home again. At home, peace seemed to be in our family. Now I was really convinced that all the problems had been caused by my misbehavior in the past. With my new resolve to be totally obedient at all times, it was not hard for me to promise my parents never to pick up or play with guns or hand grenades, or anything suspicious-looking that littered the surrounding fields. These things held no interest for me anyway; I was busy finding wild flowers which bloomed in profusion to pick for Muttie. Her smile for me was what I lived for, and now they were available in abundance,it seemed.

One day I was roaming around outside with this little neighbor girl when we saw a hand grenade under a bush. She wanted to pick it up for a better look, but I sternly admonished her not to go any nearer to it but rather for her to stand still and mark the spot while I would fetch Papa. We had wandered quite a ways from home and I started running. Suddenly I heard this terrible explosion. I turned around and saw pieces of my friend's clothes floating to the ground. I was paralyzed with fear and shock, and my usual reaction was to do nothing. I just stood there, frozen to the ground—no screams, no tears, no feeling. People started running toward the scene, Papa and Muttie among them. Some of the women were crying hystericily. I watched everything through a thick fog, like I wasn't part of the scene at all. The little girl's mother ran over to me and grabbed me by the shoulders and started shaking me. "You're so much older than her, why didn't you stop her; haven't you got any sense at all. Now she's dead. It's all your fault. If you had been in school where you belong, none of this would have happened."

Papa tried to comfort the woman, saying he was sure there was an explanation, turning to me. "Gatel, tell us what happened?" No words could be pried from my lips. I was glued to the ground and kept seeing the stars in front of my eyes. Would I faint and everything would be all right again? No—no oblivion to rescue me this time. Everyone was busy taking care of that poor mother. Finally Papa carried me home and no one paid any further attention to me. Everyone was busy with the funeral. I heard the grownups talking about how I surely should have had more sense at my age than to leave that little girl to play with a hand grenade. But then, what could be expected from a seven-year-old who couldn't even manage to stay in school. Papa kept insisting that there was a good explanation if he could only get me to talk about it. But Muttie said, "Well, here is good proof that something is wrong with her; normal children don't act like this." She held me in her arms and rocked me, weeping softly: "My poor little girl, the measles sure damaged you; maybe it would have been better for you if I hadn't saved you. I just loved you too much to let you go. It's just lucky for you that you have a mother who loves you enough to sacrifice her whole life to take care of you."

* * *

The German troops were retreating rapidly. The men spent most of their time digging shelters, rescuing people trapped under bombed out buildings and extinguishing fires caused by bombs and explosions. No day or night went by without the sounding of the dreaded sirens signaling another air attack which meant we had to drop everything and go to the shelters. We hated the shelters—all they were were holes dug under the earth with some crude boards or pipes holding a piece of plywood up to keep the earth from caving in. It was totally dark in these places; it smelled of wet dirt, and worms, mice and spiders were crawling all over.

One day as we were just sitting down to have dinner, we heard the planes far off even before the sirens sounded. Muttie said, "We're not going to the shelter this time. If we die we die, but at least we'll die while we're eating a hot meal for a change." So we sat there eating our meal while things kept exploding around us. No one said a word. All of a sudden the window shattered and a piece of schrapnel with part of a human finger fell right into the pot of borscht. Muttie calmly removed it with a spoon, disposed of it, and we kept on eating. I remember thinking someone ought to be saying something, but the only sounds we heard was the shooting as it faded away. The gruesome incident was never mentioned again. Was this what it was like to be grown up—not to show what your feelings were? Then why was I being criticized for being insensitive? Strange world!

The war front was so near now that everything was in a constant turmoil. The grownups had no time for us children; the talk was only about our possible fate when the Russians would push the German troops back far enough again to take control of our village. The women were busy preparing food of the type that would not perish easily in case of the necessity for flight. I was preoccupied with Peter. Peter was a gray-striped kitten who had come from nowhere and attached himself to me.

He loved me unconditionally. He followed me around everywhere and slept in my bed. I was fiercely protective of him and somehow felt dependent on him for affection—only when I was holding him, feeling his warm little body purring in my lap did I feel safe.

I heard Muttie talking to Papa one night: "Julius, I'm really concerned about Gatel. She seems to have totally withdrawn into herself. She's too attached to that darn cat. It's unnatural for her not to play with any of the neighbor children, or even show fear at the sounds of exploding bombs."

"Anna, can't you ever just accept that child as she is? She's probably still in shock over the hand grenade accident. It's obvious she's capable of feeling. Look at all the love and tenderness she's bestowing on

Peter." Muttie's reply surprised me: "Well, you can just ignore the problem if you want to but I'm going to love her back into reality."

In Mutties attempt to cheer me up, she somehow managed to borrow a doll one of the old ladies in a nearby house had been able to save. Muttie came in where I was playing with Peter and held up the most beautiful china doll I'd ever seen, with real hair and a ruffly satin dress. I had never seen shiny material like that with lace on the edges. Muttie said, "Poor Gatel, you've been so sad lately, I promised Greta that you would not break the doll or get her dirty; that you took very good care of your things and would be careful with her if you could just have her for one day, so here she is. Tomorrow night we'll have to take her back but you can enjoy her for a little while." I could hardly believe my ears. Muttie had confidence in me not to disappoint her. I would make her proud this time.

Until the next day I did nothing but sit and hold that doll, admiring her clothes, touching her hair, laying her down to watch her eyes close and then open with beautiful long lashes. Her lips were slightly parted to display tiny little teeth. How could anything look so beautiful! The time came to take her back. We walked to Greta's house slowly. Muttie asked me very lovingly if I would please forget about being so shy and say thank you to Greta. I didn't answer her. I didn't want to promise something I might not be able to do, but when we arrived there, I summoned all my courage and not only thanked Greta but even told her how beautiful her doll was. After all, Muttie was so kind and loving; if I could please her by talking to Greta, maybe she would continue to love me. And I was right! All the way home she told me how proud she was of me and that I hadn't even cried when I had to give back the doll even though she knew how much I wanted to keep her. Strange, I thought; one time I'm good for not crying and the next time I'm bad. Maybe when I get a little older I will know exactly when to cry and when not to, and then Muttie will love me always.

* * *

The air attack was a surprise on this particular night. The bombs were falling heavy-and very close before even the air raid sirens sounded. This one was close enough that we all ran for the shelter in fear of our lives. People were shelled on the way to the bunkers. Several of the people who were assigned to our shelter were missing. People were crying all around me. I always sat on Papa's lap during an air raid. I kept groping for him but could not find him. Finally Muttie made contact with me and pulled me close with Gerhard on her other side. I asked where Papa was and was told the men had stayed behind to tend to the injured, even during the bombing. Oma said we needed to pray for their safety.

We did, and before long someone was leading out in singing hymns. Everyone felt there was no danger in doing this since we could not be heard. Somehow that made me feel very safe and protected. The bombing kept on all night. Explosions were very near by. Now there was machine gun fire. That meant the enemy had penetrated our village. Slowly it seemed to fade away into the distance again. Were the Germans able to push them back again? By early morning there was silence and someone came to open our shelter. The devastation we saw was unbelievable. Most houses were nothing but rubble. Fires were everywhere. Dead and injured soldiers were laying in the streets, moaning. Everyone was working feverishly, bringing the fires under control and tending to the injured. Even the children had to help.

I moved in a fog, doing what I was told. It was the smaller children's job to take the tags and other I.D. off the dead bodies before they were buried. Some of these were the soldiers who had visited with me and told funny stories only the day before. I wanted to release the screams inside of me but somehow I was convinced that if I opened the door to my emotions, I would surely die too. I kept looking for Papa—he was no where to be seen. "Oh, God, please keep him safe. I need him so," I prayed silently. Then I heard someone mention his name—I listened. "Have you seen Julius since the burning brick fell on his head?" Someone answered, "No, Willie took him to the medic's station." Another voice, "God, that Julius has the stamina of an ox—walking all that distance to the medic's with blood dripping down his face."

"Yea, his eyes looked real stary; he must have been in shock. It'll be a miracle if he comes out alive this time."

"Hey, here comes Willie." Everyone encircled Uncle Willie, plying him with questions. I tugged at Uncle Willie's jacket for attention, my shyness forgotten in a pursuit to find out how Papa was, but the men were too preoccupied with the seriousness of the situation to notice a little girl. I gathered the information I needed from listening to Uncle Willie give an account to the men: Papa was helping to extinguish a fire when a piece of burning debris fell on his head. "Oh, thank you, God." At least he was alive.

By evening things were somewhat under control. Miraculously, our little hut was undamaged so we were able to go home, taking with us quite a few people who no longer had a home. We were preparing to eat supper when Papa came up the path. His whole head was wrapped in thick white bandages with only his eyes, nose and mouth visible. I ran to him, he held my hand as we walked inside. No words needed to be spoken.

As the grownups talked about the fire, I heard Papa mention that it was Greta's house they tried to save. She had not made it to the shelter in time. The room started swimming around me. I heard voices telling me to wake up; someone slapped my face hard and asked if I could hear them. I asked, as I opened my eyes, if Greta's beautiful doll had burned up. No answer was given. Muttie was outraged to think that all I cared about was the doll; didn't I know that people were more important than dolls I was asked. I laid in the corner on my cot, listening to them talk again about my insensitivity and callousness. How I had no concern for anyone but myself. Was that really true? I tortured myself with the question. Then why did I have to live? It wasn't any fun to be alive anyway. I would just go to sleep and stay dead. In my mind I said good bye to Papa and everyone else and went peacefully to sleep, expecting never to wake up.

There was no air raid that night and I must have slept a long time for when I woke up, everyone was busy packing. The news was that the German army was retreating, out of Russia. There was one train available for the Germans who wanted to be evacuated from Russia. We'd have to be at the train station by noon—first come, first serve. No other trains were available. When this one was loaded, it would pull out with or without us.

My first thought was Peter. Where was Peter? He hadn't slept with me. I decided he probably couldn't find me with all the strange people in the house. I had to look for him. Our wagon was all loaded and we were on the way—no time to say good bye to some of our Russian neighbors and friends; no time for anything except to get to that train on time. We had to escape or die—now I remembered I was going to sleep last night to die, and here I was—still alive. I guessed nothing happened the way you wanted it to. Oh well, I had Papa and I had Peter, who had eventually found me, secretly tucked away.

When we arrived at the train station, people were shoving and pushing; scrambling into the box car provided for our escape. This was no time to be polite; everyone's life was at stake and if you had to crowd out someone else to save yourself, never mind about your conscience. The only thing that mattered was to get on that train. The soldiers were trying to make order out of chaos, unsuccessfully. Hurry, hurry, hurry—the gun-fire could be heard in the distance again. At first we settled into a car with all our belongings we brought like everyone else, but as the cars filled up and more and more people arrived, the belongings had to be discarded as we had to make room for people. In the end, there were forty-six people in the box car with our clothes and bedding on the floor for us to sit on and the food suspended in satchels from the ceiling. An officer made one last check and gave us instruction to close the shutter on the one little escape hatch in each car as soon as we were moving because we would travel through rebel country— partisan soldiers who raided trains for their own gain. Then he noticed—what was this, a cat? He cursed at my parents for allowing me to bring a pet when there wasn't even room enough for people. He grabbed Peter and threw him out, closed our door, and shortly the train started moving.

We all got our turn at looking out the "window" before the shutter was closed. There was my beloved Peter, running alongside the train, meowing. This time I cried. I didn't care about the scolding. I didn't care, period. I cried for poor little Peter. What would happen to him? I cried for the people on foot, still trying to catch up with our train, but it was too late for them too. The "window" was closed and the train gained speed. We would escape—escape from the Russians, escaping to where? and what? That was the topic of conversation by the adults. We children were expected to be quiet.

Once the window was shut, it was instantly dark just like in the shelters. The only light and fresh air we had was what came in through some of the cracks in the walls and roof. It was October 1943. The only nonperisable food we had in this box car was salted sheep meat, hard sausage, dark Russian bread and dried fruit. With no adequate ventilation and so many people confined in this small area, the perspiration odors mingled with the garlic-spiced sausage created a stench almost unbearable. It caused some of the smaller children to vomit, which added to the already putrid air. The stuffy atmosphere made everyone thirsty. The containers of water we had brought were preserved with vinegar to keep it from stagnating too fast. No one wanted to drink it at first, but slowly, out of desperation, we got used to it.

Before long we became aware of the fact that there were no provisions made for human body waste. We waited for the train to stop, but when the waiting became unbearable, buckets were used and the contents dumped out the window. During those times we were thankful for the darkness which provided some privacy.

On the blanket next to me was a small baby which somehow managed to snuggle up to me regularly before it would fall asleep. With the absence of diapers, I found myself lying on a wet bed every night. After a few nights, the smell became nauseating. I was sure I would choke to death any minute. I was unable to eat. I could not understand how anyone else could eat under these conditions. Muttie first encouraged me to eat, then begged. "Gatel, look at Gerhard; he smells the same air and he is eating." This was the beginning of years to come when I would hear those words: "Look at Gerhard, he's a good boy." Finally, she became angry and scolded. Once more I was labeled stubborn and selfish. I tried to force myself, but all I could tolerate was to slowly chew on some of the dried fruit.

By the third day, the train stopped. We had orders to stay in the cars until someone would open the doors from the outside, indicating that it was safe. We waited, and waited. All of a sudden we heard machine gun fire close by. We heard it hitting some of the cars. The train started up at full speed and slowly the shots faded in the distance. Now we knew the orders not to open the doors were for our protection and we gladly obeyed them. Every so often we heard more shooting or a bomb exploding, but the train kept moving. We just prayed that we would escape to Germany safely, never mind about all the discomfort.

The light coming through the cracks was bright, and on the few minutes a day when the window was opened to empty the bucket, it seemed unusually sunny and warm. The air inside was stifling. We had been confined for seven days when the train slowed down and came to a complete stop. Now what...no one talked. We held our breath as we waited. We heard voices outside. Our door was opened and the officer gave instructions. It was safe territory as far as they could tell. There was a small stream nearby. We would have a short stop for everyone to relieve himself behind some bush and to supply ourselves with fresh water for the rest of the trip.

The sun was shining warm, the singing birds were playing hide and seek in the brightly colored autumn leaves, and to breathe fresh air was absolutely heavenly. Everyone was out now. The first necessities had been taken care of and the adults were preparing to get fresh water when machine gun fire seemed to come from every-where. The train started up and everyone headed for a door to any car, never mind which one, just to be safe.

The tranquil sounds of nature we had enjoyed moments earlier were drowned out by the whistles of the shells piercing the air and the agonized cries, moans and screams of people injured and dying. There was no possibility of trying to rescue them. The train was moving; the men were literally throwing us children into the cars; the women were climbing in any way possible. The short ladders we had for this purpose had slid away from the cars. Finally the men had to climb in and close the doors. Miraculously, all the same people were in our car except one old man and Muttie. Where was Muttie, Papa asked. He said he thought he had seen her climb in. "Oh God, I have helped all these other people and my wife is lost," he cried. He could not console himself. For the first time I saw my Father cry like a baby. He was curled up like an infant, holding his stomach, sobbing uncontrollably. What would happen to us now? Muttie was gone and Papa, well, what about Papa. Would he ever be all right? There was Gerhard. I wanted him to come close so we could hold each other, comfort each other, but he didn't move from his spot. Was he waiting for me to come to him? No, Gerhard didn't need me. He didn't need anybody, he knew just what to do and do it right every time. People all around me were softly crying, wondering aloud to each other about which one of our friends and relatives had been left behind. Would we all perish like this—a few here and a few there?

The wheels of the train kept on clicking in rhythm. Somewhere along the way night had fallen and we were drifting in and out of sleep. Papa was moaning with pain in his still bandaged head when we heard a faint knocking on the outside of our "window." We listened. The knocking continued. The adults in the car discussed the pros and cons of opening the window to investigate. It was finally decided that it was safe to take a look. After all, an enemy would not attack by knocking at our window. The children were all lined up flat against the wall by the window to keep them out of the firing line in case there was any shooting. The men opened the window. Two arms were reaching down from the roof and Muttie's voice was saying, "Pull me in, quick." Muttie was inside with one swift pull, and the window shut again. Oh, what a reunion. She grabbed me first and just held me close, weeping softly. She told us she was able to climb up on one of the last cars after the doors were closed, and layed herself on the roof so as not to be seen so easily by the shooting Guerrilas. She had seen children laying dead on the ground as the train sped away and was sure I was one of the dead bodies. She had seen Gerhard climb into the car and knew he was safe. She kept thanking God over and over for giving me back to her. She loved me; she even said she wouldn't want to live without me. Oh, Muttie, I was so happy that she was back. Now Papa didn't need to cry any more and I would try to make her happy and make up for her suffering. I would be the best little girl any mother could ask for. I went to sleep in her arms, feeling loved and safe.

The train did not make any more stops. The sound of the clicking wheels and an occasional explosion were our twenty-four hour companions. We didn't complain any more about the stench or the indignities about using the bucket or the lack of privacy in general. In my new resolve to be the perfect daughter, I even ate whatever Muttie gave me even if I had to vomit—so what—it made her happy and when she was happy, she loved me. I needed that love more than anything else. I would do anything to be loved by Muttie.

Twelve days and nights we had spent in this cattle car when the train stopped. The doors were opened and we were instructed to leave all our filthy things behind and line up in front of each car in family groups. It was cold and a drizzly rain was falling as we stood there, shivering and waiting.

Chapter 2

We expected someone to show up shortly to say "Welcome to Germany, your homeland" and a hot meal to be offered. After what seemed to be forever, an officer with some assistants appeared, saluted with "Heil Hitler" and instructed us to salute with this greeting every time we addressed anyone. The penalty for neglecting this duty at any time would result in doing time at the concentration camp.

We were told to leave all our belongings in the train, to be returned to us at a later time, and start marching. His assistants would lead the way to a refugee camp where our "germanization" would begin. "germanization" indeed. What indignity after preserving our German heritage and language in a strange country for generations, we would now have to be taught to be Germans? The very thought hurt, but we had all learned to follow orders silently. The walk seemed endless. After twelve days of sitting in one little spot in the box cars, our bodies weren't used to this kind of exercise. Our lungs began to hurt from breathing the cold air and our clothes were wet to the skin by the time we arrived at Stargaart. It was supposed to be a refugee camp, but it looked more like a concentration camp with electric barb wire fencing all around and lookout towers with armed soldiers stationed at every gate. Word filtered through the lines to remember to salute when we got to the gate. The "Heil Hitler" coming from our lips sounded strange even though it had been used by the German soldiers in Russia. We had been reluctant to use this salutation, now we had no choice.

Once through the gate, we were issued our I.D. number with instructions never to be without it. We were divided into two groups: men with boys over eight years old in one, and women with girls and small boys in another. We were led into a very large hall (no heat but at least we were out of the rain). Orders were given by women attendants to strip down to the skin and leave all our clothes in a container in the corner. We were told our clothes would be returned to us after a disinfecting process. We were ordered to get in line, single file, completely naked and wait our turn to go through a small cubicle where some chemical was automatically sprayed all over each person to disinfect us, followed by a water rinse. Our women who had been instilled with extremely modest principles were traumatized by this kind of indignity. The boys and girls openly stared at each other and their mothers and grandmothers' bodies. Even in our primitive lifestyles in Russia, strict moral codes, including the right to privacy where our bodies were concerned, had been observed. Tears rolled down Oma's cheeks. Muttie offered to stand facing her, very close, to ensure some sort of coverage at least for the front of her body. Other women followed this example. The line moved slowly as we each came closer to the disinfectant booth. We were required to file by an attendant standing on a stool while she inspected our heads with a magnifying mirror for head lice. She was amazed that she found none.

When we stepped out of the booth on the other side, the task of sorting through our disinfected clothes began. It smelled of some chemical that made us nauseous. We gave up trying to find our own garments. If it fit in some kind of fashion, we put it on just to get this ordeal over with. Once dressed, we were reunited with the men who had undergone the same kind of treatment.

We were now ready to occupy our barracks. The rooms were of various sizes; some were big halls with many families occupying the space; some had room for only one or two families. Our numbers were called at the very end when only some type of storage closet was left and it was so small that there was room only for the five of us. We were very happy for this privacy even though the room had no window; at least we could be a family of sorts.

At the sound of the bell, we reported to the eating hall for our first meal which consisted of a semmel (German hard roll) with a little butter and a dab of jam and a cup of substitute coffee. Just to feel something warm in our stomach was comforting.

Fatigue was starting to take its toll. We were told to go to a certain room to claim our bedding which had been taken out of the train and also disinfected. Again nobody was concerned about getting their own; all we wanted to do was to lay down in a quiet spot and sleep without the threat of bombs nearby. The blankets and pillows smelled even stronger of disinfectant, but the need for sleep at this point took precedence over every other concern. In the privacy of our closet-room, we knelt to thank God for His protection over us on this trip.

* * *

The much-longed for sleep was of short duration. We all woke up during the night feeling a stinging sensation all over our bodies. From the sound of voices coming from the other rooms, apparently everyone had the same problem. It seemed those barracks were infested with some kind of bug called "Wanzen" in German. I've never heard of them in America, therefore don't know their name. They are tiny black mites that appear only at night. They burrow themslves under a person's skin and feed on the person's blood until they swell up to the size and color of a ladybug, at which time they crawl out again and disappear in the wooden walls of the barracks. At dawn you could see them crawling up and down the walls like strings of red beads. The spot they used on the skin would be tender and sting for days; and of course there was a new attack every night. Also, they seemed to have favorite people to attack or it was just felt more severely by some. Gerhard, Papa and Muttie did not suffer from them too severely, but Oma and I were becoming steadily weaker from the loss of blood and our bodies' reaction to them as time went on.

Everyone was awake on account of this nuisance when the bell rang, signifying our assembly at the center of the camp for the raising of the flag. We were instructed to follow a songleader to the accompaniment of a trumpet played by a soldier, in the singing of two songs that we were told had to be memorized and sung at the raising and lowering of the flag each day. "Die Fahne Hoch" ("raise the flag") and "Deutschland, Deutschland, uber alles", (Germany, Germany, land above all"). Some of the lyrics were "the Jewish heads are rolling" and "today we own Germany, tomorrow the whole world." We were offended by the lyrics, refusing to participate. When it was noticed that we were reluctant to sing, the command came that we would have to stand right there until we knew all the words and would be tested individually. Each person who had memorized the songs was to raise his hand and demonstrate by singing the songs solo; then he was allowed to leave for the next meal which consisted of very thin cooked oatmeal in the morning, with more coffee substitute—no milk or sugar or bread—and a very thin soup at noon usually made with fishheads as a base and the small "semmel" in the evening.

The topic of discussion by the adults this first day was the right or wrong of our singing these terrible words to the songs:

Muttie: "How can we call ourselves Christians if we voluntarily sing about the virtues of killing other human beings?"

Papa: "So what do you suggest that after all the hard-ships we've gone through to come to Germany, we wind up in a concentration camp for refusing to sing a song?"

Muttie: "Well, if we profess to live by principle, we need to be willing to go anywhere for Christ—what's wrong is wrong—you can't make it right to suit your circumstances."

Uncle: "I think you have to look at the whole picture here; are we actually harming anyone by singing these words. I mean do Jews die every time we sing this song?"

Aunt: "No, the Nazies are going to do whatever they want no matter what we say or do—and who would we help by us adults wasting away in the concentration camp while our children would be raised with Hitler's ideals. I say let's just sing the words solo to satisfy requirements, then just mumble when we have to sing with the whole group at flag-raising time."

Papa: "Yes, I agree. Let's just concentrate on staying alive. The war can't last forever."

Oma: "Children, children, where is your faith? Let's just leave this whole problem with our Heavenly Father. He has a thousand ways to save His children. Instead of strategy, we need to pray."

Our consciences had become dulled from continued psychological abuse and starvation, so we followed orders like meek sheep and made excuses when necessary. We hoped and prayed for a deliverance. How could a whole nation blindly follow one crazed man into doing these atrocious things, we wondered; but then, we knew how. We had experienced the same thing under Stalin. His threat was Siberia,— Hitler's was the concentration camp. Was the whole world insane? Would sanity ever return? Right now I just wanted not to be so hungry and so tired.

* * *

Slowly the camp life pattern emerged. Added to the nightly torture of the Wanzen, we discovered we were all infested with headlice. Where they came from no one knew. Some claimed we had acquired them during the disinfecting process. After all, we never had them before. Every morning and evening we had to go through a delousing ritual. A louse comb (a special comb with very narrow teeth set close together), was used by one person on another's head. Beneath the hair was spread something white, paper or cloth, so the lice could be seen as they were combed out and then crushed. But this procedure didn't get rid of the eggs, so it was a never ending process. All the women and girls had long hair; consequently, this was a painful ordeal to be performed twice a day.

To add to our Wanzen and louse misery, an epidemic of skin rash broke out in the camp. Either we all caught it at the same time from somewhere, or it was highly contagious because nobody seemed to be exempt from it. The itching was so intense that the only way to find relief was to scratch until we bled. The rash traveled all over our bodies and we were afflicted with this condition for the next few years. But more important things needed to be handled. We were to become naturalized Germans.

During Hitler's regime, it was a common practice to bring people from other countries that Hitler had conqured to Germany to be given German citizenship. This was done mainly to have more young men to serve in the army. These people were called "Volksdeutsche," translated "Common Germans." We objected to this naturalization process claiming to being German by heritage. We had documents dating back several generations, proving our German nationality but we soon learned that we were only to obey orders, not question them. So we shortly became Volksdeutsche; therefore we were considered by the native Germans to be nothing more than displaced Russians. At this time, being concerned with all our physical afflictions, we didn't care to press this matter. After all, we were now Germans entitled to what Germany had to offer.

November 15, 1943. My eighth birthday! I was now required by law to attend school. I was determined to comply with whatever rules necessary to make Muttie happy. Besides, all my various fears had left me, what could happen to me that hadn't happened already? Death was the only thing and I wasn't afraid of that. It would be a welcome end to all the misery. Only one thing mattered as long as I was alive—I had to be a good girl to keep home life peaceful. With this newfound freedom from fear came a certain contentment and school wasn't as scary as it had been in Russia. I decided to make things easy for the teacher. The first time I was called on to answer a question, I bravely stood up and told her in front of the whole class that I wouldn't know any answers because I was considered to be a simpleton, unable to learn anything, but that I would sit quietly and not cause her any problems. The teacher was a very kind old lady and for some reason took a liking to me. She visited with me during recess and discovered my talent for knitting and crocheting, and taught me the basics of adding and subtracting numbers by using my knitting stitches. With this confidence of learning numbers, I was also able to comprehend the alphabet. I was getting somewhat excited about showing off my knowledge at home, but nobody seemed interested. The only thing I was complimented on was the fact that I didn't cry because I had to attend school and that I was obedient. Okay! I had found the secret to happiness and I had my teacher's attention which proved to be a lifesaver later on when, because of severe enemia caused from the poor diet and loss of blood because of the Wanzen, I once more started fainting in class as well as at home until I was unable to leave my bed. I was too weak even to chew the semmel in the evening which was the only thing I was able to keep down. Muttie would sit by my bed and chew a little piece at a time and then put this mush in my mouth and force it down. For a long time I laid in bed in this semi-coma, too sick to live but too well to die. I would hear Muttie's voice in the distance saying: "Poor, poor Gatel. I should have let her die of the measles and save her from all this suffering; and who knows how much more is yet to come?" I wished she had too. She would sit up all night by my bed and with a darning needle pick the Wanzen out of my skin before they could deprive me of what little blood I seemed to have left. I was told later that I was so near death that Muttie even gave up feeding me the chewed semmel mush. The teacher came to see me, bringing a small apple from somewhere. Muttie's hopes were raised thinking that maybe this would give me some needed nourishment plus an appetite to eat the other food. For weeks the teacher stopped by every day with one apple, and Muttie patiently chewed it first, then fed it to me, and slowly I recovered.

* * *

Now that we were citizens of Germany, we had rights, privileges and responsibilities. Up to this time we were confined to camp and our only jobs consisted of a variety of duties to help run the camp; but now we were allowed to go to the nearest town once a week to familiarize ourselves with the area and the native people. It was early spring, 1944, and on the first day we had permission to leave we made it a family outing. The excitement was about equal to a senior prom. We made sure our clothes were washed and ironed; hair combed and braided just right. We were singing as we walked in the sunshine. It turned out to be a very long walk through a dense forest. Slowly houses appeared and before we knew it, we were in the middle of what seemed to me a big city. There were streetcars, stores and sidewalk cafes. People dressed up with hats and gloves. They were either rushing in and out of the stores, or leisurely strolling down the sidewalks. We were expecting to hear only German spoken—instead, most of what we heard was broken German or Polish. Of course we were in German-occupied Poland. People stared at us. Some laughed, others cursed at the sight of us refugees. No wonder—in contrast, we looked like beggars from another century. All the women we saw had curled, short hair; buns and braids were a thing of the past. We tried to sit down on one of the sidewalk benches, but the people already seated there jumped up and talked among themselves.

Polish being somewhat similar to Ukrainian, my parents had picked up enough of the language to understand some of their conversation. Muttie's eyes opened in amazement as she looked at Papa. "Julius, did you hear that? They are saying we have lice and the "Gnatse," (that's what our skinrach was commonly called), just like everybody who lives at the camp, and they're afraid they'll catch it. You know what that means? It's the camp that's infested. "Ja," Papa answered. "We need to find a way to get out of there, fast."

The walk back to the camp seemed even longer and Papa had to carry me on his shoulders most of the trip. We did not take any further advantage of our permission to leave the camp.

Shortly after our outing, we had a visitor—this was also a new privilege, receiving visitors from outside the camp. After a short "get acquainted" chit-chat with my parents, he revealed himself as a minister of our denomination. The visit turned into an unofficial church service, his sermon consisting of a warning: "Brothers and sisters, I've come to warn you of the, danger of observing the Sabbath in the Third Reich Germany. Be gentle as the dove, but wise as the serpent."

"Try to serve your country," he continued, "without violating your conscience. Worship in secret for now—the day of deliverance will come." After the minister's visit, we had renewed courage, knowing that we had a church family "out there" praying for us.

One of our rights, we were told, was to find jobs outside the camp. Papa did not lose any time taking advantage of this possibility, and within weeks he found a job in a nearby sawmill, with pay. We were now required to pay for our room and board at the camp, but still had a small amount of money left to buy some food supplements. Also, we were now being resettled into communities. The people who proved themselves ambitious enough to find self-supporting work would be the first ones to be re-located (mainstreamed into society). I had hope—and sure enough, every few weeks a new group was chosen to leave the camp. We were sad to be seperated from friends and relatives, but there is a price to pay for freedom after all. There was a postal service and we would keep in touch.

One of the responsibilities of being German citizens was the military duty of our men. Many of the young, single men had already been drafted. Two of my cousins, sixteen and eighteen years old had said "Goodby", wearing their new uniforms. These young men were later captured by the Russians and are still living in Siberia.

Muttie's second cousin who was in his twenties, was chosen for the S.S. which was quite an honor. The horror stories he told when re-united with his family in Canada many years later, are unbelievable.

Enemy planes attacked closer to our camp more frequently now, and much time was once more spent in shelters, though the shelters here were more civilized. Recruits for the army were now taken at an older age; married men as well as single. Every day a new list of names appeared on the board outside the eating hall. Papa left for work before breakfast every morning and was unaware of his name being on the list the day it appeared. Muttie and Oma prayed every chance they had alone in our room for God to intervene. Late afternoon Papa was brought home by a fellow worker. He had been badly injured on his right hand with one of the power tools he wasn't used to. The answer to our prayers. He was exempt from reporting for armed duty until his hand was healed. In the meantime, our names were chosen to be among the next group of refugees to be re-loacted—halleluja!

Once more it was time to pack our meager belongings, say goodby to friends, and head for the train station. We gladly sang "Deutschland, Deutschland, uber alles" that morning. We had survived nine months in Staargart.

* * *

We were on our way. This time we traveled on a train with seats and windows to look out at the lovely countryside. It was early summer and all the landscapes moving past the train windows were bursting with color. We longed to be settled in our new home somewhere where we could plant some flowers. Oma kept up a steady stream of stories about the good old times of the Czar. Maybe it would be like that again. Our hopeful conversations were frequently interrupted by air raids, bringing our train to an abrupt stop and our thoughts back to the present. We were supposed to be supplied once a day with food rations, but more often than not this was unavailable and hunger was our constant companion.

We spent several days on the train when once more we were instructed to debark with our possessions and start walking to another camp termed "durchgangslager," meaning "short term camp." It consisted of one very large hall with one lightbulb hanging in the middle of the ceiling, with three-tier wooden bunks, wall to wall. This time there weren't even make-shift mattress pads like in Staargart. We were told to fold up our clothes for padding to sleep on. Oh well, at least the weather was warm and pleasant and we were allowed to come and go at our leisure. There was no barbwire fence or soldiers at the gate. The food, also, was somewhat better here. We had left all our friends and relatives behind and now learned to form new friendships with the other refugees. Since this camp was occupied by every nationality of volks-deutsche, all languages were represented—Italian, French, Hungarian, Polish, Czechoslovakian, etc. At least some people from Stargaard spoke German. Even that feeling of kinmanship did not last long as different groups of refugees were chosen daily and ordered back to trains at various times and we lost touch with even those new friends. We were now alone in this unfamiliar country.

The next couple of months are a blur in my mind as we traveled from camp to camp. One thing they all had in common was the toilet facilities. They consisted of a long line of stools without doors for privacy, and always a long line of people waiting impatiently in line.

Once it was your turn, everyone in the line was yelling to hurry. I would immediately freeze up and be unable to perform my duty. Constipation as a result was constantly giving me stomach cramps.

Each time we boarded a train we were hopeful that this would be our last trip, that surely this time we were going home. HOME, oh what a sweet thought. Home, where we had our cow, our garden, where I could pick flowers for Muttie, and I could go to the outhouse and latch the door for privacy. Home, where every Friday afternoon Muttie would bring in the galvanized tub and we could splash in the bathwater—where there were no bugs and itchy, scaly skin.

It seemed Muttie never touched me any more. It seemed that I was always sitting on Papa's lap. He would point to the pretty things we saw out the train windows. He would save some of his portions of food for me. Muttie would sit with Gerhard and they were laughing sometimes during their conversation. Maybe that's how it was meant to be—Gerhard and Muttie, and I had Papa. That was fair, wasn't it? Why did I want more? Was I really as selfish as Muttie claimed I was? I fell asleep one night with these thoughts as I was leaning against Papa's strong chest, noticing how dirty and sweaty we all smelled, but I felt secure—Papa's arms were holding me tight.

* * *

The train stopped at last at Sosnowitz, German-occupied Poland. It was a very large city, in fact it was one of the largest train stations we had stopped at so far, and people were rushing about by the hundreds. Everyone seemed to be in such a hurry. We sat in our train seats for a very long time, looking out of the windows, watching officers walking back and forth with papers to exchange and discuss. Finally, orders came for everyone to line up in front of the train. This was one of the re-settlement stations and they had room for only so many. The people whose names were on the list were to get their possessions from the train and start marching to their new home. Oh, how we prayed and waited to hear our name. As we held our breath in anticipation, our name was finally called. Our sympathy was with those who had to re-board the train, but there was no time for tearful goodbys.

We marched what seemed like through the whole city but eventually we arrived at our destination after we had left behind us all the stores, streetcars, office buildings, schools and countless bombed-out buildings. We were led to a cluster of small buildings. Once more, surrounded by barbwire fencing but the gates were open with no guards. It seemed to be some kind of abandoned settlement. We were told this had been a Jewish Ghetto. What was a Ghetto we dared to ask. The answer—a place where the Jews were kept confined until there was room in the concentration camps. We were later told by the Polish neighbors that only the day before we arrived, the Jews had been marched out of the Ghetto, forbidden to wear their own clothes which were exchanged for the dreaded striped uniform. They had been escorted by armed soldiers who used their whips indiscrimanently. As we entered the rooms, we were horrified at all the elegant looking clothes left behind, most of them ripped and blood-stained. We were told to clean up the mess and make ourselves at home. Food ration coupons were dispensed and instructions given as to where to report for job assignments. As soon as the head of the family had secured a job, we would be able to find better living quarters we were told.

Exhausted, we fell asleep on beautiful satin comforters left behind by those poor people whose only crime was to be of a certain nationality. There was no time to think about things we could do nothing about, we had to start living. Papa, Muttie and Gerhard left early in the morning. Papa went to register for a job, Muttie to sign up for the N.S.V. (I have no idea what those letters stand for, but it was a "volunteer" women's organization to help the war effort), and Gerhard to join the H.J., abbreviation for Hitler Jugend, (Hitler Youth). Oma and I tried to make some sort of home out of our new surroundings. We felt very uncomfortable, profiting from the misfortune of our predecessors of this Ghetto; but to throw away the things they left behind would in no way help them now, and our need was so great.

Late afternoon our family returned very enthusiastic about the new life we were about to start. They brought some food provisions. Our time from then on picked up the hectic pace of city life. Muttie was busy every day going to N.S.V. meetings where they were busy with various occupations. Mostly it consisted of packaging food rations for shipment to soldiers on the front lines and mending soldiers' clothes. Since she was an excellent seamstress, she gained a speedy reputation of being a valuable member. She loved all the activities inasmuch as she had never enjoyed being a hermit housewife or Papa's company— now she had a good excuse to be on the go which made life at home a lot more peaceful, and Oma was available to provide the home comforts.

After the first H.J. meeting, Gerhard announced that he would now have to be called "Gerd," the German nick-name for Gerhard. He looked so handsome in his new H.J. uniform; everyone seemed to be happy. What was the matter with me, why did I feel so out of place? What did I want? I wanted to be home with Peter where flowers bloomed; acres and acres of daffodils and violets and lillies of the valley hidden here and there, where I could play with my cousins— where were they? I wanted to hear people speak our Holland-German (Plattdeutsch). This High German we now heard, (though we could all speak and understand it), belonged in school, not at home. Home—this wasn't home. Oh, I was so tired, it would be so nice to be home where everybody would love everybody, and no bombs would fall, and no one would have to die any more, and people wouldn't have to be taken to Siberia or concentration camps. My day dreaming was interrupted—

What was this—Papa was coming home with a uniformed official in a horse and wagon. "Hurry up and pack everything, I'll start loading," he ordered Muttie and Oma. He had been assigned a carpenter's job and with it a home to move into. We were now being mainstreamed—real Germans—"Heil Hitler." Even I got caught up in the excitement. Moving to a real home—maybe there would be flowers. We didn't even have to carry our possessions through the city with everyone staring at us—we were treated with respect. We pulled up to a red brick house and could hardly believe it when the driver stopped. "Welcome to your new home."

We soon learned that the Polish people who had not been naturalized to become "Volksdeutsche" either by choice or denial by the German regime, were being discriminated against in the same way we as Germans had been in Russia. They were denied all privileges such as riding the streetcars and most civil rights, one of them being ownership of real property. Because of this, the Polish natives despised the Germans who had moved in, seizing their houses and businesses; mostly they were army officers who were entitled to have their families with them. The house we were to occupy had belonged to the Polish widow with her seventeen-year old son who were assigned the two small bedrooms upstairs with the food preparation to be done on a small hot plate.

After the driver had helped us unload our few possessions and left, the widow came downstairs. She spat in my father's face. "You rotten Germans," she yelled in a mixture of Polish and German; "You call us Pole dogs, when in fact it is you who are acting worse than animals. My husband died building this house; my son got injured in the same accident, and now you come here and seize the house, the only thing I have left to remind me of better days. Go ahead and report me, I don't care any more." For once, my father took charge: "Mrs. _____ first of all, you don't need to worry about us reporting you. We are all brothers and sisters—united in our suffering. We are Volksdeutsche from the Ukraine and have endured the same treatment under Stalin that you are describing. We didn't ask for your house—you know we are all just following orders. Why don't you look at this for the blessing it truly is for all of us that we are assigned to your house instead of some officer's family. We can live together and help each other out if you will allow us to help you. You may rely on me taking care of the male chores for all of us." The widow fell at Papa's feet amidst loud sobs, telling us of her seventeen-year old son's untreated injury that had resulted in bone cancer. He lay dying while she was not entitled to any medical help. My parents told her of our background and how we sympathized with her, and that we were victims of Hitler's war the same as she was. They tearfully embraced and we shared her home in a happy co-existence, helping each other for several months.

The friendship between me, a little girl of eight years of age, and her son, Jacob, a young man of seventeen, was developed quickly. He was totally bedridden and in constant pain. His whole leg was one long open festering wound. No medication was available for civilians—Poles at that. The ulcerated wounds had a terrible odor and no one wanted to be around him except me.

Papa didn't like me spending so much time with a sick person, but Muttie said, "Let her be; she can't seem to make any normal friends because of her backwardness. At least she has something to do." That was it—we were two misfits who'd found each other; but that was okay with me. I felt so grown up, handling this responsibility. I was being useful and the widow complimented me constantly about my conscientiousness. I read to Jacob out of my schoolbook I had acquired in Staargart, and with his poor German, I seemed to be smarter than he and he didn't seem to mind. He liked me to sing to him and never told me how I couldn't carry a tune. He told me many times not to worry about being shy—I had enough beauty to make up for that, (that was a new one); and how some day some handsome man would marry me and I'd have a whole row of little girls who would be just as pretty as their mother, and what a lucky man that would be. Many times his pain would be so intense he would have to stop talking and just groaned. At those times I would hold his hand and let him squeeze mine to ease the pain. How I loved Jacob and how I hurt for him.

* * *

Papa was earning fair wages and we were now able to purchase some things I had only heard of in Oma's stories about the good days. One of the things Muttie bought for me regularly was colored yarn to knit and crochet things out of—that was marvelous. The only yarn I was familiar with was the coarse beige, black and brown wool from sheep raised by ourselves in Russia and handspun by Oma. Now I could create beautiful patterns in vivid colors. Friends and neighbors commented at my talent. Muttie told me to enjoy it while it lasted, that when school would start in September, I would not have time to "play" with yarn any more. I would be expected to learn my school work properly like other children.

Papa in his new-found confidence as breadwinner started to stand up to her more frequently. In his attempt to provide me with some other involvements than knitting and sitting with Jacob, he started to take me out on Sunday afternoons. At first we just rode, around on the streetcar and looked in shop windows; but then one time we came upon a Movie Theater that offered children's movies on Sunday afternoon. What a fantastic afternoon we spent together. We even stopped at a roadside café and had a soda pop. How strange it felt to feel the bubbles tickle my nose. I watched Papa having just as much fun providing me with the opportunity for some fun as I was having.

When we arrived home, Muttie demanded to know where we'd been so long. She became absolutely hysterical to find out that we had been to a theater—to sit where sinners sat. "How dare you take her to a place like that?" she lashed out at Papa. "Haven't I suffered enough almost giving up my life to give birth to her—then to risk being sent to Siberia for defying orders not to use my home remedy to save her from the measles. Isn't it enough that I have to live with the burden of her inability to learn in school; now you are teaching her the things that will surely start her on the road to degradation! Oh, I can't stand all this heartache any more. The theater of all things—the most sinful place on earth. Oh, dear, all is lost for sure. What will come next."

Through the widow upstairs, we learned about other members of our faith in the city and found out that they worshipped secretly in small groups by congregating in their homes, pretending to have workbees or parties. We were warmly welcomed into their circle; so on Saturdays I went to religious services with Oma, Gerd and Muttie, and on Sunday I went to the theater with Papa. Papa assured me, "Gatel, don't worry about going to the movies; these children's films we attend are not a sin."

"Then why does Muttie say they are, Papa?" "Oh, Muttie is just jealous that I'm taking my pretty little girl instead of her."

"Well, if she wants to go, why don't you take her, then we could all go together and I wouldn't have to lie about what we do on Sunday afternoon."

"Honey, some day when you get older, you'll understand," he tried to sooth me.

I felt guilty about committing this terrible sin and deceiving Muttie, but Papa's enthusiasm was infectious so I blocked out all the negative feelings and concentrated on the fun we were having together. September drew nearer, time to start school again. With Muttie having high expectations of me, would I be able to make her happy as I managed to make Papa happy? This whole game of making people happy sure was exhausting.

* * *

The bombings were more frequent and closer as the summer drew to an end, and with it the dreaded school season. The schools on our side of town were bombed out so Gerd and I had to attend school temporarily in the more affluent residential section. To get there, we had a long walk to the first streetcar stop, followed by a long ride through the busy city. Gerd had already been roaming through the city during the summer and acted as my guide to the school, feeling very authoritative. Muttie was visibly proud of him. It took only a minute for introductions and he was right at home in his classroom, studying came easy for him. He was used to being the smartest in his class and this school was no different. For me, it took a lot of discussing by Muttie and the principal. It seemed their wartime policy was that a child had to be placed in the grade he should be in, according to his age. Since all children had lost some school because of the bombings and relocations, no consideration was made based on each child's ability. So it was decided at my age of eight—almost nine years old—I would be placed in the third grade. I'd only had a few months of first grade so far.

When we walked into the classroom which was already in session, I knew immediately that I was in trouble. This was a large school. The teacher was a very young, fashionable lady, and the children much more sophisticated and uninhibited than I was used to. They openly laughed and made fun of my homemade, out-of-date clothes and hair. I wanted to turn around and run away, never to return; but instead, once more I stood frozen to the ground and speechless. Muttie, in an attempt to evoke the teacher's sympathy for my shyness, explained to her my past failures in school performance. The teacher's response was that she shouldn't have to put up with retarded kids, but if I would sit quietly and not be disruptive, she would ignore my disabilities as much as possible. Muttie whispered to me that here I would be called Agathe, not Gatel, and Gerd would wait for me at the school gate and escort me home on the streetcar. With that, she left.

I was hoping I could die, or at least faint so I wouldn't have to face the rest of this day; but neither happened. After the last bell signaled the end of the school day, I moved along with the crowd in a fog, wandering around the schoolgrounds for a long time, trying to find the gate; suddenly, there was Gerd. Gerd had strict orders from our parents to watch over me to and from school like a big brother should, which really cramped his style. The first day as we walked to the streetcar stop, I had a cold and no hankie on me, so again, I did nothing about my runny nose since everything I did seemed to be wrong. The safest course was to do nothing, I figured. Gerd noticed my dilemma and told me what an embarrassment I was to him, and that I was to walk far enough behind him so nobody would associate the two of us together and I was to tell no one at school that he was my brother. He didn't have to worry about that—I didn't open my mouth in school.

The days dragged on. I endured school only to live for the time I could spend with Jacob after I came home. He spent hours drilling me on the multiplication tables I was required to memorize before I had even learned to add and subtract. His attention span was getting shorter and shorter as his cancer advanced, and many times he lost control and just screamed with the intensity of the pain, especially during the night we could hear him. No one could help.

I managed to put Jacob out of my mind every morning when the fear of school demanded all my energy. But when the day's ordeal was behind me, he was what I looked forward to.

* * *

One thing that fascinated me at this school was the fact that paper, pencils and even colored pencils were available. I had always enjoyed drawing pictures, but only with a stick in the dust. It was much more fun drawing on paper and I excelled at this. In this department I was smarter than the other kids. Unfortunately, this was not a required subject or even worthy of mention. I could do it only for my own enjoyment.

One particular day when we studied about the various types of cheeses produced in Germany, the homework consisted of us having to draw a picture of each variety with the name of it underneath from memory. I was eager to return my paper as I knew it was good. I had done a creative job with the most important cheese wearing a crown and all the others bowing to him. "The King of Cheeses" as the teacher had read to us. That night I fell asleep, dreaming of the recognition I would receive this time and how proud my parents would be and I would be laughed at no more. When school was over the next day, the teacher handed me a sealed note to give to my parents. "The teacher wants to see Papa or me tomorrow, Gatel—what did you do at school?" Muttie asked. "Nothing," was my answer. "We'll see" she said. When we arrived at school the teacher opened my picture up and spread it before Muttie. My spirits soared—"My art work is so good the teacher wants to compliment me to Muttie." I thought. Instead, I heard Muttie respond to the teacher's "What do you have to say about this, Frau—?" With "I, I'm sorry, Freulein—I don't know what to say —I know Agathe is very backward but I've never known her to cheat or lie before. I promise you her father and I will straighten her out. This will never happen again." My thoughts were moving through a thick fog.

What was it they were accusing me of? That evening Muttie demanded I confess who had drawn the picture for me, adding, "I know you are not capable of doing that yourself." I was afraid I would be accused of lying if I insisted that I had done it myself, so once again I kept silent which was the one thing that always infuriated her. She flew into a rage—Papa tried to calm her, and they ended up arguing with each other, forgetting about me. Couldn't I ever win?

I couldn't wait to get home the next day to tell Jacob. He would understand. But Jacob couldn't understand. He was drifting in and out of consciousness between pain attacks. During the night I listened to his screams, then suddenly there was silence and I knew what had happened. Jacob left a big empty hole in the depth of my being. I was sure it would never be filled again.

* * *

A short time later an unusually heavy air attack took place during school hours. We were all in the school basement, except a group of boys, Gerd included, who were at another school in a different location for some kind of drill. It was an attack by the British. We could tell by the way the planes sounded—heavy and many at once, followed by another attack a half hour later—repeated again and again, not giving the ground crews time to re-coup inbetween. The bombs were falling fast and close when we heard our building being shelled. When the bombing stopped, we realized that we were buried under our school building. The teachers had us all singing to keep us from panicking and eventually we heard the equipment outside, clearing away the debris. Among the people outside calling to us, I heard my brother's voice speaking words I will never forget. "Let me get through, my little sister is in there." He acknowledged me as his sister in front of everybody. Wasn't that proof that he loved me? It was my fault that he was ashamed to be seen with me. I would just have to learn to act "normal" so he could love me openly because it felt so good to be loved. He took me by the hand as we walked together to the streetcar. Never mind about the devastation all around us; I had my brother to protect me. "Look, world, this handsome H.J. boy is my brother and he loves me," I was shouting silently in my heart.

* * *

Now that our school building was demolished, our classes were divided and we were relocated into various other buildings. My brother was assigned one place, and me another. I had no time to worry about new teachers or children, for all my energy was expended in fear of making the trip to and from school alone. The streetcars were always so crowded and everybody was pushing and shoving and cursing at us slow ones who didn't seem to know where we were going. Keeping track of my streetcar pass was reason for severe anxiety in itself. What if I lost it? It seemed worrying about that possibility made the very thing happen.

We were dismissed early from school because of a report of a major air attack to take place later. We were to go straight home to be with our parents for this possible disaster. I was being pushed by the crowd to the center of the streetcar where there was no ventilation which brought on my motion sickness to add to my embarrassment of looking like a refugee. The passengers cursed and tried to move away from me except one older woman. She pushed her way through the crowd and ordered everyone to have some compassion. She then produced a hankie and cleaned me up as much as possible. I was so grateful; now all I wanted was to get home to our warm kitchen where it was quiet. Then the air raid siren sounded. The streetcar stopped and we were all required to run for shelter in the nearest building that was marked with the special sign. The bombs were already exploding in the distance when a man grabbed me, hoisted me on his shoulder, and ran to the shelter where he deposited me in the nearest available spot. We all sat there—a crowd of strangers listening to the explosions outside, each with their own thoughts and fears. Finally there was silence and again I was pushed along by the crowd, hurrying to get home. It had turned to evening; there were fires everywhere, and everything looked strange in the dark. Where was I?. I had become totally disoriented in the shuffle, so I started walking, following the crowd and sure enough—I heard the sound of a streetcar. I hurried and was able to climb on, only to find I had lost my pass. I was told by the conductor gruffly to get off and make room for paying passengers. Again I did what came naturally when I panicked—nothing. I just stood there on the street corner and watched as the line of passengers became thinner, shivering in the night. A very well dressed lady stopped and asked me about my problem. I couldn't find a voice; finally, she questioned me in such a way that I could answer yes or no by nodding my head. She got me on the right streetcar, paid my way, and put a mark ($1.00) in my hand with a smile. When I got off the streetcar at my destination, there was Gerd. He hugged me and told me how worried they had all been about me. He rubbed my cold hands all the way home. Where were my mittens? Lost in the shuffle, I guessed. But that was all right—it was worth it to have my brother pamper me like this. When we arrived home, hot soup and warm hugs and kisses were waiting for me, and a present. A present? Of course, I had forgotten—today was my 9th birthday. Muttie had been able to secure a china doll for me paying for it by doing some custom sewing. How absolutely beautiful. What a mixture of emotions. I was unable to appreciate the gift fully. I needed time to recuperate from this scary day. I heard Muttie tell Papa after I pretended to be asleep, "I certainly expected a more joyful reaction to that expensive doll; the older she gets the more she withdraws from me and I try so hard to make her happy."

"Oh Anna, not again," Papa groaned.

* * *

We were told in school that the war would be over before long and Germany would rule the whole world, but in reality we saw a different picture. The bombings became more frequent and more severe. The stories we heard were that the air attacks were mostly by the Americans. They had the machinery and enough ammunition, and their troops weren't as fatigued from years of warfare as were the Russians. But the Russians were making aggressive advances by land. They had already reclaimed Romania and Hungary, and Poland was supposed to be next. Would we fall into the hands of the Communists again?

In the meantime, I was fighting my own battle. After the incident on my birthday, I was absolutely petrified of being caught in another air attack. It was one thing to be brave in a shelter, sitting on your father's lap; quite another when it happens in strange territory all alone. Oma told me to pray for protection. Instead, I prayed for no attacks. Needless to say, the air attacks kept happening—my proof that prayer didn't work. Was there any truth in anything the adults were telling us?

We got in the habit of sleeping with our clothes on because of the inevitable sound of the siren alerting us to take shelter. I found myself in a constant state of anxiety, not wanting to be away from home even for a minute.

In the midst of all this turmoil, the Christmas holidays were approaching along with a severe snowstorm. It seemed that suddenly the function of the city was practically paralized as waterpipes and electricity were destroyed, either by bombings or the storm. We now had to carry water home in containers to be used very sparingly. Mostly we used melted snow.

The streetcars weren't operating very often, making it necessary to walk long distances. Loss of fingers and toes due to frostbite were not unusual. Thanks to my parents insistence on wrapping our feet with cloths underneath our woolen stockings, we were protected from frostbite but certainly not from ridicule from the other children who had not learned to endure Siberian winters.

Gerd had long ago learned to dress the way Muttie insisted, only to remove unwanted items as soon as he was out of her sight. I could not allow myself this deception since I lived by my self-imposed rule of perfect obedience. One afternoon school was held in the same building the N.S.V. ladies had their meeting. Christmas was only days away and the ladies gave a Santa party for the children of the lower grades with a Christmas tree and a visit from Santa with presents. During this party the storm gained momentum and Muttie was afraid of how to get me home unharmed since there was no more streetcar transportation available. In her usual aggressive manner, she asked one of the high-ranking officer's wife if I could spend the night at their house with her little girl and she would come to get me the next day. I wanted to die when this lady with her daughter who had never even spoken to me, took me along in their chauffered car. This was the first time I had ever been inside a private car. The driver wore a uniform, the lady smelled like perfume, and the daughter looked like a china doll. I felt as though I was contaminating the whole car with my wet woolen stockings, smelling like a wet dog, and to think I would have to undress tonight and have them laugh at my home-made clothes. I would have gladly taken frostbite if I'd been given a choice. I fought back the tears as I watched Muttie fade in the distance.

When we arrived at my new home for the night, I was absolutely awed by the splendor of this house. A maid came immediately to help us off with our coats, she held mine with her fingertips, wrinkling her nose in disgust. The lady made some comments to the maid on where I would sleep and apologized for bringing me there. I felt so uncomfortable, I could hardly breathe. Fortunately, the girl showed me her playroom and seemed almost to enjoy my company. The playroom was an absolute fantasy world with china dolls ranging from the most beautiful fashion doll to the most delicate lifesize baby dolls. A doll house with scale size dolls, furniture, dishes and even running water in it's little kitchen. When I saw the huge Christmas tree in the parlor with the sparkling glass ornaments, I could hardly believe I was still in this same world of bombs and storms and pain and misery. We were served cookies and a hot drink by the maid who also assisted us with our bath. Right there inside the house was a bathroom with hot and cold running water. I'd never heard of such a thing—even in Oma's stories about the Czar days they didn't have a bathroom in the house.

When I had to peel off my various assortment of under clothes made by Muttie resembling nothing like these fashionable people were wearing, I was mortified with embarrassment. I was given the most beautiful satin nightgown, yellow with lace on the ruffled sleeves and collar and told I could keep it. I held my breath as the maid tucked me in. I was all alone in a room. I had never slept alone in a room in my life. I was so scared—what would happen if we had an air raid? Would someone come and get me? What if I needed to relieve myself during the night—no chamber pot in this room—of course not—they had a toilet right in the house but where was this bathroom? Everything was dark. As soon as I started thinking about this possible problem, I felt the urgency. Oh, how would I ever live through this night. I was still wide awake when I heard voices following the chimes of the doorbell and shortly the maid came into my room and helped me get dressed. My father was here to take me home, I was told. Who needed prayers—not me as long as I had Papa; with him loving me, everything would be all right. He wrapped me up in a blanket and carried me all the way home in this stormy night. Before I sank into the safety of sleep, I heard Muttie accusing him, "Julius, you are spoiling her rotten; and not only that, you ruined my chance of developing a friendly relationship with Frau _____. Who knows how far we could go being acquainted with influential people like her, an officer's wife." Poor Papa. Would he always have to pay for loving me?

The Russian front moved in closer and suddenly the day before Christmas, Papa received orders to be drafted. January 5, 1945 the sound of the bombings were once more intermingled with gunfire in the distance. I could not bear the thought of Papa fighting on the front lines. I remembered how few of the soldiers ever returned from the front lines. It was time to pray. I asked forgiveness for thinking I did not need God. Please don't make Papa pay for my sins and please, please don't make him go to fight on the front lines.

Luckily, it was Christmas vacation and I didn't have to worry about school. I could direct all my energy to praying for Papa's safety. Until the last day, I believed that somehow miraculously we would hear that a mistake had been made and he would not have to leave. But the dreaded day arrived. Muttie kept me home from school because of stomach cramps. Papa was to report to a designated station in the morning. He had to leave during the night for the long walk. None of us went to bed that evening. We just watched the clock. As the time came closer to the departure and he started to dress in that strange looking uniform, I knew I could not control myself any longer. I was laying down on a sort of day bed we had in the kitchen, and I turned my face to the wall. Maybe by refusing to say goodbye, I could prevent him from leaving. I pretended to be asleep. Everyone had hugged him goodbye when I heard Muttie say, maybe it would be best not to wake me.

Papa's reply was, "I love that little girl with all my heart and soul, I thought surely she loved me enough to at least stay awake to say goodbye." I wanted to scream, "Please, Papa, I love you; I'm not asleep, don't go," but again I did nothing but lay there, frozen to the spot. I heard the door open. I felt a rush of cold air enter the room; I heard the howling of the storm outside and listened to my father's footsteps in the snow as he walked out of my life—FOREVER.

One week after Papa was drafted, the political situation deteriorated rapidly. School sessions were interrupted by air raids so often we spent more time in shelters than in classrooms, until finally more and more parents kept their children home and the authorities didn't seem to care. Everyone was concerned about themselves and their families as we watched the trains full of "Fluchtlinge" (meaning fugitives, word translation "Flightlings), coming through. We inquired where they were from and discovered that people were already being evacuated from the next city. We knew our turn would be next and started to make preparations. The Polish citizens were now awaiting the Communists with joyful anticipation the way we had waited for the German troops to deliver us in the Ukraine. When we received orders to report to the train station by 3:00 p.m. that afternoon, the Poles were openly hostile to the Germans. They knew the time of their deliverance had come. Now it proved beneficial to our family that my parents had treated the Polish widow we shared the house with so kindly. She proved to be the friend we now needed. She brought her friends and relatives over to buy some of our possessions we had accumulated and would have to leave behind. This supplied us with some much needed money later on.

Our orders to evacuate came at noon which gave us about one hour to get ready for the long walk through the snow to meet our train. My precious china doll and satin nightgown were sold quickly, no time for discussion about it—or tears. One old suitcase that had made the trip from Russia was quickly packed. Muttie grabbed her satchel. It contained important papers proving our heritage, her Bible, and a small religious book and a packet of photographs. She was never separated from this satchel, using it as a pillow at night.

The widow produced two strong young men with a sturdy sled, informing us that we would need their protection. The Poles were now chasing the Germans down the streets with clubs and throwing rocks at them. One couldn't blame them, considering the oppression they had endured. Quickly we embraced, shedding some tears. The young men tucked Babushka (Oma) in with blankets on the sled with the suitcase behind her, and we were off in the snow. We would rather die than fall into the hands of the Communists. We were overwhelmed by the mob of people at the station. The station had been bombed heavily, trains were blown apart with parts of human bodies strewn about, creating a striking contrast between the red blood and the pure white snow. One train after another was loaded with the officers' wives, and other influential women with their children. The absence of men was very noticable. They had all been drafted in the "Volksturm," (Folk Army) like Papa from the youngest to the oldest. How were we so lucky to have Gerd. Oma said it was a miracle from God. Why then hadn't He worked a miracle to keep Papa home? We waited, standing outside in the snow most of the night, listening to the explosions at the other end of the city. The troops were advancing by land. At last it was our turn. Once more we thanked God as the train pulled out of the city and wearily we fell asleep.

Day after day we kept chugging along, leaving the Polish cities behind us, making short stops only to use the toilet faciities and receive some meager food rations. The scenery eventually consisted only of dense pine forests. We were gaining altitude. We knew we were in the mountains. The explosions now sounded far, far away. We were safe once more.

Late one evening we arrived at a very small train station. We had come to the Riesengebirge (Giant Mountains). This was a very exclusive winter resort with all kinds of entertainment facilities— skiing being the most popular. The hillsides were scattered with beautiful little chalets. All were built with several bedrooms and baths to accommodate rich vacationers. They were some-what like today's bed and breakfast Inns. The Burgermeister (Mayor) of the village met us with an "army" of volunteers with sleds to take us to our designated homes, and assured us that we would not have to stay here too long since the war would be over soon and Hitler would supply us all with new homes and a secure life. Did he really think anyone believed him?

Again Oma was loaded onto the sled, and this time they found room for me too. Poor Muttie and Gerd had to walk and walk and walk. It seemed there was no end to our hike up the mountains. There weren't any visible roads and since everything was covered under a white snow blanket, the only sound came from the squeak of foot-steps on the snow. It was late at night and we were exhausted and shivering when we pulled up in front of this pretty little chalet. We were met at the door by a very attractive elderly lady who showed us to our room and said in a pleasant voice: "It is very late. We're all tired, I'll show you to your room and we'll get acquainted in the morning." It was a small room with two narrow beds and one wider. Oma and Gerd took the narrow beds with Muttie and me sharing the larger one. We could hardly believe our good fortune as we slipped between the clean, starched sheets under a huge feather-comforter and found that hot bricks had even been placed at the foot end to warm us up. For a long time I listened to the quiet—the wonderful quiet—before I drifted off into a sound sleep.

I immediately liked this place. The snowy hillsides with the green pine trees sprinkled with little chalets reminded me of some scenes of the Sunday afternoon movies I had seen with Papa, and the people seemed to be very refined. They spoke quietly and treated each other politely. The Burgemeister in his welcoming speech had told us due to the fact that we would be staying there only a short time, it would not be necessary to enroll the children in the local school. Since I was relieved of this major source of anxiety, I was able to relax in the warmth of our friendly hosts. When the lady of the house discovered Oma's talent for knitting and crocheting, she produced baskets of colorful yarn, begging her not only to knit for them, but to teach them as well. So we formed a pleasant circle of activity and friendship.

Gerd was anxious to go off and explore the area. Before he was allowed to leave, Muttie had a string of instructions for him, ending by telling him to act at all times responsible since he was now the man of the family. Turning to me she informed me that Gerd now held father status as far as I was concerned. All the held-back tears and emotions about Papa being drafted now came to the surface like an avalanche. Through torrents of tears I screamed at her, "Don't tell me that Gerhard is going to take the place of Papa—Papa is going to come back to us when the war is over, you'll see. This is all your fault anyway; if you

hadn't been fighting with him all the time, he wouldn't have left us—
it's all your fault—everything is your fault. I hate you. I wish the army
had drafted you instead of Papa." I was completely out of control. I had
never in all nine years of life talked back to her, let alone scream at her.
She slapped me hard across the face.

"You little hypocrite—pretending to miss Papa so much when you
couldn't even stay awake long enough to say goodbye to him." That
stopped the scene I was making. I retreated quietly into a corner with
my knitting, resolving never, never to act this way again.

Gerd came back rosy-cheeked with cold and excitement. "Muttie,
Muttie, guess what I found—a new friend. He lent me his skiis and
taught me to skii. Boy, skiing was more fun than anything I've ever
experienced." It became his daily activity.

At home, the women tried to set up some house rules which
consisted particularly of everyone helping with the weekly
housecleaning on Saturday. Muttie offered to do all the cleaning by
herself if she were allowed to do it on any other day. The lady asked her
directly if she was an SDA, then continued: "There is a whole group of
SDA's in the village and don't worry about the cleaning." We couldn't
believe our ears. Weren't SDA's considered the same as Jews here?

The next day being Saturday, we looked up this group and sure
enough, they openly congregated in one of their homes, complete with
singing hymns. Somehow the terror of this war had passed this village
by to a large extent.

The days went by with more contentment and happiness than we had
known for a long time, but the nights held a special torment for me.
Since Muttie and I shared the bed, she bestowed on me all her affection
previously reserved for Papa. Depending on her mood, she would
either hug me for hours so tight I felt suffocated, or she would cry
herself to sleep bemoaning Papa's absence; or she would recite in
detail my shortcomings of the day, demanding apologies.

At our worhip service that first Sabbath, the discussion was mostly
about the miracles of answered prayer. I wondered if prayer would
work in bringing Papa back. How could God answer the prayers of

someone as disobedient as myself, and now I had to add "disrespectful" besides, after that tantrum I had thrown? I would start by asking God to forgive me, then maybe after I could prove my ability to live up to His expectations, I could ask for miracles.

Sabbath approached again and Gerd announced that he wanted to go skiing instead of worship service. A bitter argument between him and Muttie followed, with Gerd insisting that he could make his own decisions since he was the man of the family, and Muttie telling him that he would incur the wrath of God for sure by profaning the Sabbath. Gerd left to go skiing with his friend. Oma, Muttie and I left to go to worship. I was wondering what these soft speaking people were thinking about all our loud arguing. As we walked, Muttie kept up a steady stream of complaints about us disobedient children which eventually was directed only at me—how was it that I always wound up being the guilty one?

We were quietly sitting in our room that afternoon, reading, when Gerd's friend appeared with a sled. He said Gerd had fallen while they were skiing and couldn't walk. We were welcome to use his sled to go get him. After some quick directions, he was gone and Muttie and I left with the sled to pick up Gerd. All the way Muttie tried to make me understand the consequences of breaking the Sabbath. Slowly I began to see God through Muttie's distorted view.

When we arrived at the site, we immediately understood the seriousness of this accident when we saw Gerd's leg hanging in a twisted, unnatural way. He cried out in pain as we tried to load him on the sled. It was a hard process trying to pull the sled uphill—Muttie pulling and me pushing from behind. Time after time we would make some progress only to lose our footing and slide back. It was starting to get dusk and our efforts seemed futile. Muttie decided to stay with Gerd while I would go to the house we assembled at on Sabbath, and ask for help. I bravely took off at a brisk pace through the forest when suddenly a pack of dogs ran up and encircled me with their tails lowered and showing their teeth menacingly as they growled. I was petrified. I stood glued in one spot as they slowly advanced. I was all alone—no houses in sight. It would be useless to call for help. Oma's words rang in my ears: "Gatel, whenever you are alone and in trouble, pray. Jesus will send unseen angels to help you."

"Oh, Jesus," I prayed, "if you have forgiven me of all my sins as I asked you, will you please rescue me from these dogs." I opened my eyes and watched as the dogs slowly; and quietly slunk away in different directions. This meant I was forgiven. Jesus had answered my prayer. I had to thank him, so I knelt down right there on the spot that held such terror for me only minutes earlier and prayed. Another thought came to me as I started walking again; didn't this prove that God was able and willing to work miracles on our behalf? I knelt down again and asked Jesus to bring Papa home safely. Now everything would be alright, I had Jesus to help me through my trials.

I felt light as a feather as I walked the remaining distance and this time I even received credit I felt was due me for accomplishing my task in bringing help to get Gerd home. Gerd was in much pain all night. We knew that civilians couldn't expect medical care when all doctors and medicine was needed for the army, but the lady of the house whispered to Muttie that she knew a doctor who might do it for money. How fortunate we were to have been able to sell our possessions to the Poles in Sosnowitz.

Gerd's fractured leg was put in the cast the next day. It fell to me to entertain him while he was bed-ridden. I remember feeling closer to my brother during that time than at any other time in our lives. A few days after his accident, we received orders for Gerd to be drafted in the army. How thankful we were for his broken leg. A week later we received orders to report to the train station again for further transport. Oh, how we hated to leave this tranquil place, but orders were orders.

* * *

For the next couple of months we crisscrossed Germany on one train after another. Law and order was a thing of the past as more and more of the military officers were needed to fight the losing war—not shuttle around civilians. The trains and train stations were bombed out, while more people were being evacuated to ride on the short supply of trains. Many of the train tracks exploded with landmines. We would be heading in one direction, only to be stopped by a demolished train station or tracks. Our only choice being to abandon the train and walk until we could make a connection again.

We now had the added problem of Gerd having his leg in a cast. With no crutches, using Oma's cane, he needed Muttie to lean on. Oma or I were unable to carry the heavy wooden suitcase Papa had made for us, so that had to be abandoned. We layered all the clothing we had on our bodies which made us stiff and awkward to move. We would get hot and sweaty on the crowded train, then get cold outside with the inevitable result of colds and flu.

No officers were assigned to read off names from the endless lists anymore. It was every man for himself. Everyone knew from observation that Germany was losing the war. The only questions remained—how soon? And whose hands would we fall into. The British and the Americans were our enemies as well as the Russians, and we had heard plenty of horror stories about their treatment of their captives. We certainly were witnessing their power in weaponry and military forces by their air raids with the heavy planes. But we knew from experience what life would be like in Siberia if we were captured by the Russians, so our constant hope and prayer was to be caught in the American zone when the inevitable day would come.

Being pushed around by the crowd of panicking people with yelling and rudeness all around, I longed for the quiet, peaceful days at the Riesengebirge. I daydreamed about living in comfort and beauty the way they did. I prayed regularly every morning and evening for the Lord to send Papa back to us. He would create the kind of home I now knew from experience was possible. But how would he ever be able to find us, the way we were traveling all over the country with no one knowing our whereabouts? God would surely have to work a miracle, but wasn't that what God was for—to work miracles on our behalf? Didn't He save me from the dogs? And didn't He save Gerd from being drafted? All I needed was enough faith—that's what Oma said. So I would have faith.

We were encircled by enemy troops at the train station in Prague. There was no way out of the city and we knew it was Communists keeping us captive. Would falling into Russian hands be our lot after all? Several days we sat or laid on the cold floor of this station where most of the roof was missing and none of the toilets were functioning any more, getting weak from hunger. The water lines had been blown up and we had to use water sparingly from barrels provided for us.

The water became stagnant and dissentary developed. With no sanitary facilities, the stench was almost unbearable when suddenly machine gun fire broke out very close. The Germans had sent extra troops and broke through the enemy barrier. We moved out on the trains instantly with gun-fire all around us, but eventually it became less and less until we could only hear it in the background. The train was headed for Bavaria we were told and eventually we stopped at one small village after another where small groups of people were allowed to leave the train to stay with the farmers of each area. Finally our turn came. The Burgemeister showed each family in which direction to start walking. He even produced a cane for Gerd. Tears flowed with gratitude from Muttie's face to be treated humanely again—even if it was only for just a short time.

We followed the path we were told would lead to a farm at the end. Later we found out it was a 20-plus Kilometer distance. It was a long time before we arrived at the farm, due to frequent stops necessary because of our weakened condition and Gerd's leg.

Eventually we arrived at this farm—such poverty we had never seen before. We learned later how poor yielding the earth was in this region. Nothing but rocks. They were still plowing the land with oxen yoked to plowing tools so old as to be considered antiques. The farm house consisted of two rooms—one kitchen sitting room, and one bedroom, plus a type of loft meant for the children who were now grown and gone except for one daughter who had married an "outsider" meaning from a nearby city. Her husband, of course, was serving somewhere in the army, but before he'd left, he built a small shack near her parent's house for her and their small daughter to occupy until he returned.

We were shown to the loft. After we each received a large piece of wholesome black bread with fresh-churned butter. We fell into a long awaited sleep, free from the noise of train stations and bombs.

* * *

After breakfast, we asked where we could wash up and wash our filthy clothes. We were amazed constantly at how primitive and poor these farmers lived. We were shown a small basin on a stool outside the house next to a make-shift shelter for their cow. The ice cold water from a nearby well felt somehow refreshing on our skin sores that were still itching and oozing since this condition started at Staargart. We took turns holding up a blanket around the person washing for privacy. The farmers were amused by our display of modesty. They were totally illiterate except for their daughter, Resel, who had some schooling. She was curious about what was happening out in the world and couldn't spend enough time listening to Muttie. The two women became good friends quickly.

Our immediate problem was Gerd's leg. The cast should have been removed a long time ago. The leg was starting to shrivel up and an ominous odor was noticeable. We persuaded the farmer to remove it with his hammer and chisel. It was a painful procedure for Gerd to endure, but Muttie assured him again that it was a small price to pay to be kept out of the army. After a few days of exercising and massaging the leg, he was able to walk with the cane and he insisted to go to town to look up the H. J. Group Resel had told him about. The only available school program in this village was offered by the local priest and a few nuns. This area, as most of Bavaria, was almost exclusively Catholic. Since we were of a different religion, Gerd and I were not accepted as students, which was very welcome news for me. Gerd immediately took over leadership of the H.J. and generally enjoyed playing the big shot kid from the city. I was happy just to be left alone to play with Resel's little girl.

Resel had a radio and she and Muttie listened constantly to the news updates, speculating on how much longer the war would last. It was turning to spring with the farm work going into full swing. The natural tiredness at the end of the day's work felt good in comparison to the fatigue of sitting on trains day after day.

One day a wounded German soldier wandered onto the farm from the thick forest bordering the field. He was half starved and incoherent. The weather was warming up so we made him a makeshift bed under an apple tree behind the house, and once more I became a little nurse. I enjoyed feeding him what little amounts he could tolerate and slowly he started to recover. From the report he gave us, there was a frontline the army was fighting against the Amies (German slang word for Americans), and in his opinion it was only a matter of weeks before the German troops would have to surrender as they were running out of ammunition and soldiers with no replacements being sent any more. So, most likely, we would become American captives. New fears arose, what would they do with us? Slowly more wounded soldiers appeared. Before long we were operating a field hospital behind the house—feeding the extra mouths put a severe strain on all of us, but no one complained when our rations became smaller and smaller. The day we heard on the radio that Hitler, our Fuehrer, was dead, the war was over. We did not go out in the fields—what was the use? Probably we would all be sent to some war prison camps. Our biggest fear was that our family would become separated. We huddled close together around the radio when we noticed that Gerd was missing. One of our recovering soldiers told us he'd left a few hours earlier to drill with the H.J. We anxiously waited for his return, Muttie, resolving firmly not to let him out of her sight when he returned. That evening he was being returned to us by American soldiers in a jeep.

It appeared the H.J. group had marched against the American tanks as they pulled into the village, carrying the German flag and singing "Deutschland, Deutschland, uber alles," ready to die for the "Fatherland." The American G.I.'s amused, had dispensed packages of gum. We were happy that only the boys' pride was hurt. One of the G.I.'s spoke German and instructed us that we would be unhurt and allowed to go on living on the farm as we had till now if we would peacefully surrender. We were asked if we were hiding any guns or soldiers inside. The German soldiers in the back yard, hearing the questions, saved us from having to either lie or turn them in—they all came out with their arms up in surrender. With two American soldiers walking as guards, they led the Germans away with the Jeep following, leaving a trail of dust. Could this be for real? We couldn't believe our good fortune of being in the American Zone the day the war ended. What was to come next? Now we had no government—all we could do was to take care of each day's work and wait for the future to develop.

* * *

Muttie was getting restless, sitting day after day, waiting and wondering. One day she set out walking to the nearest town in an attempt to find out if there was a chance we could be relocated in a more civilized area—possibly be reunited with friends and relatives—and—find Papa. She returned a few days later, hopeful. "I found a Red Cross Station who will provide us with temporary shelter. Hurry up, let's pack our few things and be on our way. These farmers never wanted us here anyway; they don't even have enough provisions for themselves, let alone feed us."

We thanked our hosts; Muttie and Resel embraced tearfully, then we never turned around to look back as we began another new chapter in our chaotic lives.

* * *

The main function of the Red Cross was to reunite families and relatives who had become separated through all the evacuations. We all spent long hours pouring over the endless lists of people's names coming in daily. We couldn't believe our eyes when we spotted familiar names and discovered they were in a train station shelter not too far away, awaiting assignments (the Americans were continuing Hitler's practice of placing refugees with locals who were fortunate enough to remain in their own homes, mostly farmers). We were given train passes and found ourselves once more on the train tracks to unfamiliar places, but at least this time we had a certain destination and did not have to fear the gunfire and explosives anymore. We were still suspicious of the Amies' motives but at least at the present it looked promising.

After arriving at the designated station, we were absolutely shocked at the multitude of people and injured German soldiers trying to find their way back to their families. Some of them had arrived home only to find their homes bombed out—the families gone—now they were trying to follow their trails, asking everybody if they had seen this person or that one. Some had discovered that their homes and families were in the Russian zones, forbidden to enter or exit. American soldiers were stationed as guards everywhere. Frequently there would be gunshots from German snipers out of some window, who refused to give up. Refugees were laying around on piles of blankets everywhere, too tired even to try and fend for themslves, their disappointment in their "Fuhrer" so great it left them crushed. We could see immediately what a monumental task it would be to find our relatives. The strategy we would work out was to use every person in our family to search over certain areas with my assignment being to stand by our little pile of belongings and act not only as guard over the possessions, but also as informant to Muttie, Oma and Gerd when they each returned at various times with their report.

I was worried about Muttie as I watched her walk away, looking so tired and stoop-shouldered. She had been plagued with asthma attacks ever since we entered Bavaria; it was blamed on the climate. Would I lose her too? What would happen to all of us? I was learning to tune out these thoughts and fears by switching to mental pictures of the beautiful house and kind people at the Riesengebirge. Some day I would live like that. Papa would come back—wasn't the Lord working one miracle after another? And wasn't I praying consistently? And didn't I have the faith required? Yes, we would live in a nice house someday.

I was brought back to reality by a young American soldier standing in front of me, holding out a Hershey bar. I took it, not knowing what it was. He pulled another one from his pocket and showed me that it was safe to eat by taking a bite out of his. When Muttie, Gerd and Oma finally returned to settle down for the night, I showed Muttie my chocolate bar. She explained to me what it was and how heavenly it tasted. I hadn't seen this much enthusiasm in her eyes in a long time. She divided it equally among us—I took the tiniest little bite and gave the rest to her, a love offering. She insisted I take my share. I told her I didn't like it, thinking that would convince her of my love. But instead, I received her usual reaction of disappointment: "Oh, Gatel, how can you not like anything that tastes so good. You're just trying to get attention. Can't you see that I have enough on my mind without having to worry about you constantly fainting from hunger? Just eat the stupid chocolate and stop making trouble."

Why was I constantly causing her unhappiness, I wondered. I loved her and I needed her so much. I wanted her arms around me, thanking me for the chocolate; instead, I had incurred her wrath again.

We all went to sleep on the cold cement floor in a sullen mood. The next morning we accidentally bumped into one of my cousins who led us to the rest of the group from our homeland, minus the men. Another miracle. Shortly after that, we were given our assignment for relocation. No train was going into the Bavarian forest country, so we set out walking and hitch-hiking periodically, and arrived at a small scattering of farms with a very small central village, carrying our papers, requesting the farmers to supply us with shelter.

* * *

With the war lost and a non-existent government, people were not very eager to comply with regulations. The farmers insisted they didn't have enough room for fugitives, but benefitting from free labor appealed to them. Reluctantly they decided to give us lodging on a small theater stage divided from an equally small auditorium by draperies, on the upper level of the local tavern-guest house. One of the farmers produced an old wood stove which was installed in front of the only small window in this room. The stovepipe leading through the open window to the outside. It was going toward summer, so the fresh air was welcome except when the wind came in the wrong direction, then the room filled with smoke, making any kind of cooking impossible. We were given potato sacks filled with straw to use as mattresses.

After a good night's sleep, we reported to the farmers for work. My assignment was to be in charge of a 7-month old baby girl. I enjoyed looking after this live doll tremendously. As soon as the farm lady noticed my love for little Renate and my conscientiousness in taking care of her, she left me totally in charge. I was allowed to take her on walks in the baby carriage, dress her up like a doll, or do whatever I liked to keep her happy and occupied. The two of us very quickly became inseparable, but again, my good fortune didn't last too long for as the week ended, the problem of our refusal to work on the Sabbath presented itself. The locals never having been exposed to a religion other than their own were led by superstitious beliefs that if they assisted us in any way, they would be cursed.

Out of fear, the farmers told us we could stay on the stage since they were required by law to provide this, but no more work unless we were willing to work Saturdays. Without work there was no food either, but we did not worry too much. At this time of year we could find wild berries and after the berry season we existed on wild mushrooms which grew in this area with profusion. Slowly our physical condition weakened and our prayers took on a desperate plea for help in the way of food for survival, especially since Fall was approaching and with that, the end of the mushroom supply.

I went through the motions of prayer as I was expected to, but in my 10-year-old heart, I rebelled. Why did God expect us to be different from everybody else? Did he enjoy seeing us suffer. I could not see the need for asking God to provide a miracle if all we had to do was work as we were expected to, and thereby supply our own provisions. I hated not belonging to a regular church as other children did. As far as I was concerned this whole idea of convictions was something my mother had dreamed up. After all, Papa had seen the reality of surviving in whatever way was necessary. By the time I had just about convinced myself that there were no other people who believed like we did, the miracle happened.

We waited and waited as Summer turned to Fall with a new problem of school opening. Gerd and I were not allowed to register unless we attended on all six days. We were too weak to care anyway by now—would help ever come? One day we were all sitting under a shade tree behind the tavern, wishing we could be out in the fields with the farmers earning a hardy meal, when we heard a strange rumble far down the road. The noise came closer. Everyone came in from the fields to investigate. We could see a cloud of dust as we recognized the sound of a motor vehicle. The large beige van came to a stop and as the dust settled, we read on the side of the Van in big bold letters, "Conference of Seventh-day Adventists." So—there really was an organization as Muttie kept telling me. Immediately I felt remorse for doubting God and Muttie, although my confusion about life was increasing to the point of doubting my every thought.

We stepped up to the two young men emerging from the Van. After much embracing, they produced some fruit and yogurt (the only thing our stomachs would tolerate after this long period of near starvation). After that, it was time to unload: Big round barrels of staples like dehydrated potatoes and corn, oatmeal, flour, even sugar and big cans of vegetable shortening. We hadn't seen this much food at one time in a long time—we children, never.

Now came barrels of clothes—beautiful multi-colored jersey dresses with big shoulder pads, so much in style at the time in America. But that was not all. Last came what for us were luxury items—things I had never seen before in my life: Turkish towels, bars of soap, tooth-brushes and toothpaste, combs, mirrors, scissors and needles and thread, and colorful yarn with knitting needles and crochet hooks. By the time boxes were opened containing crayons and color books, the farmers' children could no longer hide their envy. The two young men asked the parents if it would be okay for them to include their children in the distribution of some of these things. That was an offer hard to resist. Before the day was over, all the farmers' children and the children of our small group were enjoying our new gifts together.

Before our benefactors left the next day, they informed us that our names would be added to the list of refugees qualifying for the

C.A.R.E. package program. We had a little worship service before the men left in their van, leaving a cloud of dust and a group of very thankful and hopeful women and children.

While the grownups were dividing the clothes, I took my yarn and knitting needles under my favorite shade tree and settled down to some pleasant needlework. While my needles were clicking, I heard the women talking about how God works in mysterious ways—it seemed that some of the German soldiers traveling all over Germany in search of their families had reported our plight to some S.D.A. people who had contacted our church headquarters, leading to the aid we received.

* * *

So many changes were taking place in Germany so quickly now that it is difficult to focus on any particular incident. But then, this will illustrate the turmoil our life was in most of the time.

The death of soldiers on the front lines and of civilians through bombing and gunfire was over, but the after effects of the war were sometimes worse to endure. Adding to that, the feelings of defeat, depression and failure individually and as a nation. After hearing some of the reports about the Russian occupation in parts of Germany by people who had escaped the Russian Zone, we could only consider ourselves fortunate to be under the control of the American government, even though our pride prevented us from showing the proper respect and gratitude. But when we witnessed the positive changes in leadership, we quickly became "Americanized." One of the very first things done that won everyone's approval was the release of the Jews from concentration camps and their reinstatement as proper citizens. The German people were not in favor of Hitler's treatment of the Jews, but out of fear for their own safety, it had been tolerated.

The next step was to re-establish the postal service and the school system. Being able to make inquiries of families and relatives' whereabouts by mail, eliminated much of the aimless traveling in search for loved ones. With the mail service functioning, we were now receiving C.A.R.E. packages with regularity.

These packages were originally packed for the military and contained items we had no use for; such as several packs of cigarettes, chocolate bars, and a package of unground coffee beans. Gerd heard these things could be sold on the black market. He wanted to hitchhike to town to exchange our merchandise for much needed cash. He met with strong opposition from Muttie which resulted in him going without her permission. He returned with money and excitement. There was a whole new world out there, he exclaimed. "Muttie, just a few more trips to the black market and we'll have enough money to get us into some decent living quarters—no—even better; we can go to America. Just think of that."

"Gerd," Muttie said sternly, "you are not going back to the black market. We lost Papa and I'm not going to lose you too."

"Please, Muttie—I promise to be careful. Look, I came back safely this time."

"No."

"Well, then I'll go without your permission. You told me I was the man in the family and I'm going to provide a better life for us than we can ever have here in defeated Germany."

"Stop talking such nonsense, Gerd. We aren't even allowed to move into a different apartment without special permission, let alone leave Germany. And besides, where could we go anyway that it would be better for us?"

"Just listen to me, Muttie," Gerd went on excitedly. "I ran into some boys who were Mennonites from home—from Chortitza, they told me of a place called M.C.C.-Mennonite Central Committee, or something like that. We had to break up quickly because the M.P.'s had an eye on us but if I could just go back and find them again, I'm sure I could find out more information. If I do nothing, we'll sit here and rot while the rest of the world goes on living—please, Muttie."

I knew that Muttie would soften as I watched Gerd turn on the charm, she always did. How did Gerd do that, and why was I unable to get the same results when I tried?

After a few more trips to the black market Gerd had been able to make contact with the M.C.C. and was informed that indeed they did assist Germans from Russia to immigrate to Canada. Gerd and Muttie plotted that maybe we could be accepted for this program by the fact that we were Mennonites by heritage, even though not by religious affiliation. During all this turmoil I was being mostly ignored by Muttie and Gerd who seemed to be full of hope for the future. I was content to be with Oma, knitting. Every once in a while I would try to enter the endless discussions about the possibility of a future in Canada, only to be dismissed with "Don't bother us."

The nights were a different story. Muttie continued the practice of having me sleep close to her which was started out of necessity in the Riesengebirge. She would cry about how hard it was to be without a husband and how she hoped I would never experience such loneliness. She expected my complete empathy and sympathy. On one evening I tried to open up to her and share my own feelings of missing Papa, only for her to dismiss my comments with angry replies of how I could only think of myself. I learned again and again that my feelings did not matter and the punishment for asking to be considered for my own self was withdrawal of her love and affection.

The one bright thing in my life was Renate. The farmer's attitude toward us had softened somewhat and I was now allowed to babysit "my" little girl again. I spent many wonderful hours singing her to sleep in her carriage under the big shade tree I had claimed as my own.

One day the American authorities came to investigate the school system and informed the teacher that Germany was now under a democratic government and they would not be allowed to discriminate against us for religious reasons. We would have to be enrolled in school. Shortly thereafter the school week was shortened to five days a week, eliminating the problem completely.

Gerd was past 14 years of age (beyond 8th grade, which was the required schooling at that time), but I reluctantly started school once more at a disadvantage since the local children had already attended school for several weeks. An American doctor and nurse came to school to examine all children for malnutrition with the promise of food supplements for those who needed it. The boys and girls were separated. We had to strip down to our panties and stand in line as the doctor examined each one. When the doctor discovered my ugly skin rash, he asked immediately if the rest of my family had the same affliction. He gave me a big jar of foul smelling salve with usage directions for all of us. For the first time in two years we were relieved of the awful itching and burning that had tortured us since our arrival in Germany. Within the next few days, we were given food and cod liver oil three times a day at school. Feeling more energetic, I became somewhat more enthusiastic about studying, especially the reading became more enjoyable with more interesting reading material provided by the U.S. Government. I anxiously awaited Muttie's joyful response when I received my first report card with grades that totally surprised me. I held my breath in anticipation as she read the B's and C's on my report card with an A in Art. Also, my teacher had added a favorable comment about my behaviour. Surely this report would make her proud of me—she hugged me to her as she said sadly, "Poor, poor Gatel; you will never do good in school like your brother, but I want you to know that I will always be there for you." I pulled away from her and started to run to my shade tree retreat. I was called back sternly, only to be admonished once more for my rudeness. Of what use would it be to try and defend myself—I wanted to tell her that I didn't want sympathy, that I wanted recognition for my hard work; but I knew it would fall on deaf ears, so—silence was the answer once more.

* * *

Under my shade tree alone, I could retreat into my fantasy world. Yes, Papa would be back with us soon. How I missed Papa. How I needed him. I resolved to continue to do my best to surprise him when he returned. As a result, school did not hold the terror for me as it had in the past; in fact, I developed a real love for reading. Our teacher was also a good musician who brought his violin to class often. I was beginning to look forward to school activities. Christmas was once more near and we practiced for the first Christmas program I'd ever been involved in. I loved the endless practicing of singing carols. I was to be an angel in the choir—the first Christmas I was experiencing without bombs. We spent hours during school sessions making tree ornaments of foil gum wrappers given to us by American G.I.'s and our excitement grew as the holidays drew nearer.

Muttie had not had time to listen attentively to my reports of the Christmas program due to her involvement with the M.C.C., trying to gain permission to immigrate to Canada. I spent all my time before and after school taking care of Renate. About the only time I was home was during the night when I had to submit to Muttie's possessive love. Now I had double reason for wanting Papa to come home. I longed for my own bed so I could fall asleep with my own dreams and thoughts.

I was invited to spend Christmas Eve at the farmer's —mostly for Renate's benefit. Muttie insisted that I show my love for the family by spending Christmas Eve at home. Oma, who was normally quietly submissive to Muttie, spoke up in my behalf with such authority that it left Muttie temporarily speechless. Oma ushered me out the door and I enjoyed the most beautiful evening I had ever experienced so far. A big Christmas tree had appeared in the parlor (a room normally reserved for adults). Delicious food was served and presents distributed. After reciving my gifts, a very, very tiny doll with moving arms and legs, a piece of silky material for a dress, and some embroidery floss—all items unavailable in any store during wartime. I was so overcome with joy that I actually took the initiative to give Mr. and Mrs. Farmer a hug—an act that surprised even me. Now the lady gave me half a goose to take home to my family.

I rushed home with excitement—this was truly a magical night. I looked forward to being transformed into an angel for the midnight mass. Muttie was quite impressed when she saw my gifts and her anger at me for preferring the farmer's company to my families' softened somewhat at the sight of the goose she would be able to prepare on Christmas day.

We bundled up in our American coats and warm long-johns and set out for the village for the Christmas program. I couldn't believe I would actually be the star in our family—even Gerd would sit in the spectator's seat, watching me sing, wearing an angel's halo. In our conversation Muttie finally caught on as to where this program would be held—in a Catholic Church. She stopped short with all the previous anger in her voice again. "Why didn't you tell me this Christmas program would be in the Catholic Church. I was under the impression it would be at the school—isn't that where you've been doing the practicing with the teacher?" She demanded again, "Why didn't you tell me; you know you can't participate in a Catholic Mass."

"I did tell you more than once, but you didn't listen. You and Gerd are so busy trying to take us to Canada that you haven't even noticed me." For emphasis to my hurt feelings I added, "You just want for us to go far away across the ocean so Papa will never find us again—you never did like Papa and you just don't want him to come back to us." I guess I expected Oma to come to my defense again, or maybe I had gained courage from all the attention I'd received this evening; whatever motivated me, I spoke up. After being ordered not to talk back to her, we all turned around and walked back to what was suposed to be a home. I listened to the church bells chime in the distance, competing with the sound of crunching snow under our footsteps. In response to the tears that night, she tried to soothe me by telling me she had actually saved me from embarrassment by not allowing me to sing in the choir since I had no singing voice anyway. I fell asleep wishing there was no God at all, since all He ever did was take away what little pleasure I could find and making unrealistic demands. In my ten-year-old mind, things were getting more confusing than ever—didn't I have to hold on to the belief in God if I ever wanted to see Papa again?

Shortly after Christmas vacation two investigators from the M.C.C. appeared to question us and verify our existence in conncection with the Canada immigration we had requested. They left us very hopeful—all except me. I was convinced that Papa would never find us in Canada. So while Oma, Muttie and Gerd were exuberant, I was withdrawn and depressed, creating problems for Muttie and me since I was aware that to be a good daughter, my mood was supposed to match hers. Most of the other refugees who had initially lived with us on the stage, had gradually found other living arrangements. We had seen no reason to apply for this convenience since we felt confident that any day we would receive orders to report to M.C.C. Headquarters for departure to Canada—the promised land.

* * *

Our lives took on a sort of routine while we awaited permission to go to Canada. Gerd had found a man, who was in the radio building and repair business who allowed Gerd to be an apprentice of sorts—without pay. But Gerd was on cloud nine to be learning something he enjoyed. Oma did most of the housekeeping while Muttie hired out as a seamstress to the farmers who had sewing machines. Much of her time was taken up filling out forms and staying in communication with the M.C.C. about our Canada immigration with long waiting periods between completion of each step. During these times she was always anxious and depressed and I was happy to have my job at the farm to have an excuse to be away from the "firing line" since most of her outburts were directed at me. But, unfortunately, she had me as her captive audience during the night. The war was over, but for me the bombs still interrupted my sleep—only now they were verbal and cloaked in a mantel of love.

One day, Josh, my father's cousin who had been drafted about the same time as Papa, returned to what he thought was his family, only to find us instead (he later was reunited with his family and immigrated to Canada where they lived a prosperous life into an old age). He told us that he and Papa along with a few other soldiers had been ordered to blow up a certain bridge after the last German troops had crossed it to prevent the Russian troops to seize the city. It was so close to the ending of the war that Josh and some of the others had decided to hide until the end of the war and cross into the American Zone. Papa, with some of the remaining solders had been loyal and stayed to carry out the orders and had been either killed in the process or captured by the Russians in which case he would be in Siberia by now. I couldn't believe what I heard. How could God do this to me? I probably hadn't had enough faith—well, never mind about trusting God if He demanded that kind of love. It was the same kind of love Muttie wanted. I had to be absolutely perfect in order to be loved. Well, they could both keep their love—the price was too high. If Papa couldn't be returned to us, I'd make it on my own. We would go to this strange land called Canada, and I would find me a farmer who would love me the way Papa had loved me—for myself. He wouldn't care about my unattractiveness, only sophisticated city men needed pretty wives.

At last the long awaited letter requesting us to come to the city to be processed for departure to Canada was in the mailbox. We couldn't pack fast enough, and following some happy goodbyes, we were on the train once more. Upon arrival at the processing center, we were assigned some bunks in a large room with the news that we would depart for Bremerhaven to board the boat for Canada the next day. Oma, Gerd and I settled down in our room while Muttie had to go sign the last papers. We expected her to be gone only a short time, but when it turned dark and everyone was in bed and she hadn't returned, we went to look for her. As we came closer to the main office building, we heard loud voices engaged in what sounded like a heated argument with Muttie's voice rising above all the rest. We sat down on a bench in the hall and listened to the angry discussion. It turned out that one of the M.C.C. officers was from our home town and recognized Muttie as being one of the Mennonites who had converted to the S.D.A. denomination and therefore ineligible to take advantage of their immigration program.

We sat there listening to them argue fiercely about religious doctrine until 4:00 a.m. at which time the man in power terminated the discussion and told us to leave the premises immediately. I was glad I had made my secret stand against God. The Mennonite God wasn't any better than the Catholic or the S.D.A. God. Here we were now in a strange city, in the middle of the night with no place to go, and no money. We had used what little money we had for our supposedly last train ride through Germany.

Now where to turn? To the Red Cross Station once more. We were waiting at their door as they opened up in the morning. After a few days of being sheltered in another train station, we were assigned new living quarters in Flossenburg—a very small town in Bavaria with a fairly large concentration camp that had been converted to apartments for refugees. Not a word was spoken as we watched the scenery go by our train windows on our journey to our new home. We each had our own hopes, dreams and fears; and where was Papa? I hoped that he was dead and didn't have to suffer the horrible fate Siberia represented. Now that I was convinced I'd never see Papa again, the grief set in. I didn't think I could endure even one more day without him. I could hold the tears back no longer. I needed his arms around me to tell me that everything would be okay again; but my tears were misinterpreted by Muttie. She assumed I was crying because we were not allowed to go to Canada and assured me we would try again somehow through another agency. Would she ever understand me?

* * *

Germany's government was stabilized to some extent by the American occupation. The winds of change were blowing freely, raising hopes for the future in the hearts of many. The German reichsmark (the current money) was practically worthless in terms as to the purchase power. Rumors abounded that a total change in currency would take place soon, maybe overnight. Those who had any money at all protected themselves against this possibility by investing their money in things like gold and diamonds from the illegal black market. The rumors proved true when one day it was announced that by midnight that day, our money would cease to be recognized as legal tender. Everyone had to report to their local office established for this purpose the next morning, to receive their "starter money" in the new currency. All adults received 30.00 deutsche mark—the common joke of the day was that now everyone had the same amount of wealth for one day.

Immediately stores in the cities were opened up, full of merchandise. Also, some small industries started to appear. We had settled in our two-room apartment with a shared bathroom for the whole building that had served as a cell block during the concentration camp era, watching all the activity around us. The Americans were restoring parts of the concentration camp (the cremation furnace, the gallows, etc) for tourist attraction along with building a small chapel for tourists who came to pay their respects to the thousands who had died innocently. Weekends were lively with the traffic of tourist buses. As I watched these American, English and French ladies in their beautiful silky dresses, hats, high heels, and nylons, a deep longing for a better life started to germinate. Would I ever be able to live in a nice home with pretty clothes? In an attempt to reach for this dream, I lost some of my painful shyness and started to socialize a little more with the other children at school and some neighbors.

In one of the apartments lived an old lady with an invalid daughter. They were unable to completely care for themselves and after some visiting with them, it was decided that the old lady would teach me the almost lost art of bobbin lace making she was an expert in, for the exchange of my helping with laundry and housecleaning. I was totally caught up in the pleasure of creating these beautiful pieces of lace from the very thin thread the old lady supplied. The finished product was to belong to her to sell as payment for the lessons. Muttie claimed I was being taken advantage of and insisted I stop taking lessons and concentrate on my school work. I couldn't understand her attitude since my grades were steadily improving. Why was everything I enjoyed doing a source of contention to her? Gerd was unable to find any work in this small town, but had no trouble finding companionship. At 16 he was an extremely handsome young man with the charms to match his good looks. He found the local dance hall more attractive than worship at home on Sabbath with Oma, Muttie and me. The arguments between Muttie and Gerd seemed to be constant. The two of them would break into a heated tug of war everytime he was ready to go out, with Muttie breaking into tears after he left; then she would continue to complain about his behavior and eventually I was always to blame for her misery, especially late at night when he didn't return and I was still sharing her bed even though there was room for two beds. When I requested my own bed, I was accused of not loving her. When Gerd finally returned, usually with a hangover, the argument would continue until somehow they always ended up hugging and laughing.

When another neighbor heard of my ability of lace-making, she offered to buy the thread for me in exchange for the finished product. I jumped at the chance to get more practice. This time I decided to fight for what I knew was a fair request, convinced that Muttie's denial was unjustified. I got my way but it left me terribly depressed when Muttie withdrew her affection for a long time, especially having to sleep with her when she refused to talk to me until I finally apologized, although I didn't feel I had done anything to deserve this silent treatment. Why was it that Gerd could fight with her and have her laughing the next minute, and I was being punished endlessly. At least I was able to work on my lace unhindered after that. When word spread about my talent, people started placing orders and paid me, enabling me to buy my own thread. The days went by rapidly with enough lace work to keep me busy.

* * *

One day we received a letter from the U.S.A. It had been forwarded to so many places it had taken forever for us to receive it. The sender's name on the envelope read 'Daniel Isaac'. "Daniel Isaac," Oma gasped, "Could this be the Isaacs?" she looked at Muttie questioningly.

"Mama, I don't think so—that would be a miracle, impossible to believe," she said.

Gerd grabbed the letter and said while ripping open the envelope, "So, don't keep us kids in suspense you two—who are the Isaacs?"

"They were a young missionary couple who came to the Ukraine in 1901—he was the man who baptized your grandfather and me along with five other families just before they were ordered to leave Russia because of the Bolshivic Revolution. Gerd laughed heartily in his lighthearted manner.

"You're right, Muttie, that is impossible—even if you believe in miracles."

Muttie said, "Well, you're holding the letter, read it already—now who is causing the suspense?"

When Gerd finished the letter, written in poor German, we all stared silently at each other in disbelief. It was indeed from Daniel Isaac, asking if Oma was the same person who had provided shelter for him and his young wife almost fifty years ago. They had gotten hold of our name and address through one of the many thank you letters we had written to the various addresses pinned to some of the garments that we had received in that first distribution of clothes and food from the church conference. The letter ended with, "What can we do to help you come to America?"

The Isaacs wasted no time in answering our letter with an offer to sponsor us to come to America on the D.P (Displaced Persons) program. The necessary forms were completed and we were told that a little house, complete with furniture, dishes and groceries in the cupboard, was waiting for us—donated by their local church. America would welcome us with open arms. America! The land of dreams and opportunities. California at that—we heard it was sunny year around and oranges and grapes could be grown in your own back yard. Our excitement knew no end. Again the wheels of government red tape moved slow. While Muttie was busy answering questions on paper and making trips to Weiden (the nearest town with government offices) Oma was keeping house. Gerd continued on his pleasure trips to the local dance halls where American jazz music played and the dance in fashion was the 'Samba' and 'Rumba', and where there were always enough girls—also with nothing to do but have a good time. Muttie worried about this situation constantly. America seemed to be the only answer—where jobs were available to keep young people out of trouble.

I pursued my pleasure with my bobbin lace. I was completely addicted to this fine art and a little pleased with my own ability. Muttie was so preoccupied with the pursuit of our America immigration and worrying about Gerd, that I could go about my activities pretty much unnoticed. A representative from the newly-formed Y.M.C.A. and Y.W.C.A. (Young Men's, Women's Christian Association) was sent to our school to tell us about the after-school activities they were providing. It consisted mostly of various art and craft work, plus some outdoor trips. In Muttie's absence, Oma gave me permission to join. I was absolutely euphoric when I saw all the art supplies made available to us. We were individually interviewed about the interests we had, etc. I was asked to bring some of my lace work since that was unknown to the director.

Immediately, I was supplied with thread, enabling me to sell my finished products at a profit. Consequently, I gained the respect of some of my schoolmates which led to forming some friendships. I was living my own life without too much concern about this move to America. I had my America right here. The Y.W.C.A. was conducting an art contest with prizes—the director encouraged me to enter a tablecloth I had just finished. I complied. Muttie was furious when she found out, once more calling me dumb for not realizing that it was just a way for them to get the tablecloth without paying for it. Again I summoned the courage to tell her that even if that was the case, I owed them that much for all the thread they'd supplied me. It turned into an argument with me losing control again, just like in the Riesengebirge— only this time I didn't feel ashamed. I knew I was right and it felt real good getting rid of some of the anger I'd stored up over the years. But the withdrawal of her love for days afterward was painful, and so I apologized again, just to gain her affection.

Months later, when Muttie was called to the city for an interview about America immigration, we received a phone call from the Y.W.C.A.office in Weiden. Since no civilians had phones yet in Germany at that time, the Post Office would accept them and forward them along with the mail. The mailman said the connection had been real bad, making it hard for him to understand everything but he knew for certain that I had won a prize in an art contest and I was to report to an address in Weiden he had written down—the next day.

Now what to do—Muttie was gone, Gerd was who knew where; so Oma had to make the decision. I couldn't believe what I was doing when I found myself on the train, headed for the city—alone. I didn't have enough money for the streetcar, so I started walking, asking directions as I went along. Me—talking to strangers. This couldn't be real, but it was because my feet started hurting.

Luckily the building I was looking for wasn't too far away. When I arrived, a group of prize winners from other localities were waiting for me and we were all ushered into a small van type vehicle and from what I over-heard from my fellow travelers, we were heading toward Nuernberg. Now fear gripped me like a vice. How long would it take us to get there? How would I manage in the big city by myself? Would I need any money? And now I was starting to get carsick—my usual problem. Where was Muttie? I needed Papa. Oh God, how could I get out of this dilemna?

The young lady sitting next to me must have noticed my distress. She asked if I was sick. The driver stopped just in time for me to go outside to empty my stomach. I was so embarrassed: But everyone took a sympathetic attitude; maybe because at age 12 I was the youngest one in the crowd. We had to make several more emergency stops which mortified me, but I survived, gaining confidence in myself.

When we arrived at a huge building in Nuernberg, we were welcomed royally. The U.S. Marine Band gave a concert in our honor. We got a sightseeing tour of Nuernberg, and a banquet after we returned, followed by the prize winning ceremony with the presentation of prizes. I received a green leather purse with a $50 gift certificate from one of the new American stores for coming in second in my category. I was also recognized as the youngest prize winner for the whole region.

I moved through this experience as in a dream, silently, having no words in my vocabulary to meet this situation. Flash bulbs went off and later I was given a newspaper by someone with my name among the winners in an article about the Y.W.C.A.

One of the young men in our group had a supply sour balls he had purchased in Nuernberg for our trip back hoping it would take care of my motion sickness problem. It did, making it possible for me to arrive in Weiden with some dignity. The walk back to the train station was a pleasure with all the memories of the previous few days replaying in my mind, but when darkness set in, I quickened my steps to get away from the scary city streets.

When I went to the train station window to purchase my ticket, I was told the next train wouldn't leave until noon the next day and that I didn't have enough money for the ticket. I bravely asked if I would be allowed to sit in the station until morning when I would try to walk home. "To Flossenburg?" the clerk asked amazed. When I answered yes, he said there was a supply train going in that direction at 3:00 a.m.—he would ask the engineer if I could ride along in the engineer's cabin with him for free. Since it was against the law to loiter in train stations, he offered me his cot to rest on in the back room.

It was a long way home from the last stop the supply train made, but I arrived at noon the next day, feeling very proud of myself. I had really accomplished something on my own.

As I walked in the door, Muttie turned the anger—from Oma who had born the brunt of her outbursts on me. Poor gentle Oma. Now that Papa was gone, she had to suffer on my account. I tried to tell Muttie that I had only done what I was told to do, but she couldn't listen to what I had to say. Her only demand was how could I have left her to worry like this. Now that I was home safe, I could understand the seriousness of my offense and I tried to apologize. Eventually she calmed down, but nothing more was said about the prize or my ability to fend for myself. A big fuss was made the next day in school and I became somewhat of a local celebrity. The tablecloth was returned to me. I handed it silently to Muttie to be sold, and the whole incident was left in the past.

* * *

The long-awaited letter telling us to come to Weiden for our physicals finally arrived. The next step was Munich to await our departure for America. Whatever little amount of money we were able to earn, seemed to go for trainfare about this immigration business. Why couldn't we just forget about it and buy some furnishings and house-hold items like other people did? But then, I wasn't consulted about my preferences, it was my duty to be happy about the decisions made by Muttie and Gerd. So, with all the joy of dreams soon to be fulfilled, we sat in the doctor's waiting room. In a matter of hours, our business was complete and we were told once more to wait for the important letter that would decide our future. Waiting was always the hardest thing for Muttie to endure, causing her moods to fluctuate between euphoria and deep depression. Oma and I had long ago learned to cater to her moodswings. Our ability to do so was highly tested during these next months. When the news finally did arrive, it was not according to our expectations. It seemed there was a spot on Oma's lung that showed up on the X-ray which needed to be cleared up before we could be considered eligible for immigration.

While we saved every penny for Oma's treatment, the quota for the D.P. Program had reached its limit and our request was denied totally. Muttie was absolutely crushed and it became my self-appointed duty to try and cheer her up, especially at night before going to sleep. I would rub her back and talk to her of all the opportunities we had right here in Germany. Secretly, I was happy about not going to America. I liked it here in Flossenburg where I had made friends in school. The closeness I shared with Muttie created by her need of affection was a pleasant new experience for me. If I could get the affection and love I needed from nurturing instead of being nurtured, it was better than no love at all. Eventually, she rose up out of her depression and decided to take an active part in making a life with a future for us here in Germany. Her first concern was to get Gerd a job and out of the dance halls. We had acquired a small radio and heard on the news about all the progress being offered in the bigger cities in the job markets. Telefunken—a radio manufacturer, was opening up in Nuernberg, hiring employees. Muttie gave Gerd what little money we had for trainfare and told him he had experience building radios, to get on the next train to Nuernberg, get a job at Telefunken (even if it was a floor sweeper) and send us his first paycheck for moving to Nuernberg.

Two weeks after he left, we received a letter from him with money for the move. Besides a job, he had even found a small unfinished cottage to rent from one of the young men he was working with, and just like that—my comfortable little world crumbled again as we sold what few possesions we had accumulated and headed for strange territory. Once again I was filled with fear since I remembered from my own trip to Nuernberg how intimidating the city appeared. What would the new school be like? Would I be able to keep up?

Gerd was waiting for us at the train station to escort us to our new "home" which turned out to be located in a smaller town about 35 kilometers outside of Nuernberg. That news eased my anxiety somewhat and Muttie's happy spirit was contagious, even I became cheerful as we walked through the gate, past a fair-sized house to the little cottage in the back garden. The owners who lived in the front house had prepared a dinner for us and welcomed us warmly. During our "get acquainted" visit, we discovered that the lady of the house was also of the S.D.A. faith and that there was a small congregation right there in Zirndorf, but also a very large church in Nuernberg. We had truly found "home" and even I was thankful to God that night for all the blessings—it had been a long time since Muttie and Gerd were in such total agreement about everything. Maybe now the endless fights would stop.

* * *

The little unfinished cottage had only one usable room, but we did have our own private outhouse and beautiful garden surroundings. And most important—Gerd had a steady job. We started purchasing some things like regular mattresses with the intention of settling in this place permanently. This was going to be "home." The school atmosphere was more advanced and sophisticated here, again with the girls my age wearing short curly hair—the American way instead of the customary braids. I spent almost all my free time doing homework, just to keep up. Life took on a pleasant routine with school work and church involvement. I felt very comfortable with the tiny congregation as we met in one of the member's homes.

Gerd had formed a friendship with a young S.D.A. man who had a motorcycle. Together they attended church in Nuernberg. Muttie was very anxious to have the opportunity to see an S.D.A. church with hundreds of members, a large choir, and hear a real preacher give a sermon. Her opportunity came at my expense.

I was going on 14, but with the late start I got and so much school time missed due to war activities, I was only in the sixth grade. The school system in an attempt to place all students in their proper grade according to their age, conducted tests to move us up into the grade compatable to our age. Suddenly, I was told that I would graduate from grade school in a few weeks. This was good news to me, to be all through with the pressure school presented. As the custom was at that time, the public school issued a graduation certificate in a very small ceremony, but the churches offered quite a big service, usually with a banquet following, depending on what religion one was affiliated with. Muttie found out about this type of ceremony being held at Nuernberg and decided to spend the money necessary for the whole family to take the bus to the city for this occasion. "Gatel, this will be a real honor for you to show in public that you passed the necessary tests to graduate two years early. I will be so proud of you standing up front for all to see."

I froze. "Muttie, what do you mean, standing up front? What am I going to have to do up front? I don't know anybody there. I don't want to go up front in church or anywhere else. I'll die of embarrasment with these little girl braids; no other girls wear them any more. Everybody has permed hair—we'll be the laughing stock—." I choked down the rest of the words I wanted to spit at her as I watched in panic how her expression took on a determination I recognized all too well.

We rode the bus in silence. I was so scared of the upcoming ordeal I was hoping the bus would somehow meet with an accident—but nothing dramatic happened except for my car-sickness. Because of this problem I was glad when we finally arrived in Nuernberg and had to walk quite a distance to the church, the fresh air providing what I needed to recover from the car-sickness.

The service was already in progress as Muttie dragged me all over trying to find the right person to talk to about getting me into the program. Dying of embarrassment, I was taken to the platform to be joined with the other graduates already there. The officiating minister was handed a paper with my name and info, causing a disruption. It turned out that part of the ceremony consisted of the students having to answer some questions. When my turn came, of course, I found no words and once more, although I was able to graduate from school two years early by passing the test, I wound up being the "dummy" in front of this huge church congregation. All the way home on the bus I was told about the embarrassment I caused the family. It didn't matter any more—some day I would grow up and be able to retreat into my little home on the farm somewhere and raise children with a husband who would love me and not expect things of me I wasn't able to give. I had become quite good at retreating into my fantasy world when the real world was too hostile.

Muttie quickly found an apprenticeship position for me with a local dressmaker where I excelled and it was a wonderful relief not to have to worry about school. One Sabbath a church representative appeared from Stuttgart, making the rounds of all the churches with the information about a boarding school of higher education being opened by our conference with the opportunity for students to finance most of their own tuition by working at the school, supplied jobs in various areas. Muttie decided that would be the perfect place for me to learn how to socialize and immediately signed the necessary papers without asking me even one question about my desires. I knew from her enthusiasm that it was useless to argue with her.

A few weeks later, after giving up the work I loved, I was on the train for the unknown—and I was supposed to function as an adult, all alone when so far I hadn't been allowed to make my own decisions even as to what to wear. Somehow I found my way to the school and was assigned a room with two other girls who seemed to know everything; so I just followed what they were doing and somehow managed not to get in any trouble. The time was so filled with classes and work schedules, that the days just flew by with Sabbath being the highlight of every week with worship service in the morning and long group walks and sing-a-longs after a festive dinner. If I had been able to stay there, growing emotionally and spiritually, I might have relaxed enough to enjoy high school life in boarding school. But after only two months I received a letter from Muttie, explaining how sick she was and how much money it took for medical bills and what a hardship it was for her to pay part of my tuition and how she was unable to sleep without me in bed—and why did I ever leave her? After showing the letter to the dean, arrangements were made for me to be excused and I was home before Christmas.

Shortly afterwards I received my grades in the mail and I was surprised how good they were—maybe I wasn't as dumb as I had believed.

* * *

My apprenticeship position was filled by someone else and it was difficult to find another one in such a small town. Meanwhile, an American toy factory had been built on the outskirts of town where people were being hired to work on the assembly line. I was eager to apply and contribute to our support financially, hoping to move to a regular house or apartment and start to fulfill my dream of living a more refined life. The response from Muttie was that it would have to be discussed with Gerd. During supper when I opened the subject again, Muttie and Gerd decided that a young girl from a "proper" family couldn't work in a common factory. The only people working in factories were riff-raff. I mentioned the names of several girls who were working there that Gerd had been dating which he said was only proof of what he was saying—they were girls that would do anything (whatever "anything" meant), not the kind any self-resepcting man would want to marry. Muttie attacked this subject immediately— "Why do you go out with them if that's the kind of girls they are?" The discussion about my wanting to work turned into a heated argument about Gerd's social life. I didn't know what I was expected to do so I just sat at the table and continued eating, afraid to say anything more or to get up. Then Gerd jumped up from the table yelling at Muttie that he was an adult and it was none of her business where he went or with whom, especially considering the fact that he was supporting all of us. Turning to me he shouted, "And you, Gatel, aren't happy unless you can cause trouble." With that he stormed out the door, leaving Muttie in tears complaining to me all evening about the hardship of raising children alone. Here was Gerd, living the life of sin and I was ready to go work in a factory with the lowest class of people on the earth and neither one of us cared about her ill health, and about how badly she needed Papa—she could only hope and pray that I would never be faced in life to be husbandless. There was no greater hardship than that. This continued until late into the night when once more the topic turned into worry about Gerd's where-abouts. I longed to get some sleep, so I resorted to my proven method of relaxing Muttie enough to put her to sleep by apologizing for causing her so much heartache and promising to consider her needs more. The subject of my working was never mentioned again.

With no apprenticeship positions available, I turned again to my lace making which for some reason infuriated Muttie. Again and again she would attack me with statements like "Why do you have to sit here playing with the bobbins? How are you ever going to find a husband, sitting here. Look how popular Gerd is, he's acting like a normal young person. You'll turn into an old maid and let me tell you from experience, it isn't easy going through life without a husband."

I learned to read her moods so well that I was able to tell just by the way she'd look at me that I was annoying her by my very presence, so I developed a habit of going out for long walks in the nearby woods, making her believe that I went to get acquainted with other young people. My silence to her eager questions as to who I had met, she interpreted as secretly seeing some boy; now her concern was over who and what we were doing; she assumed the worst and accused me of things I had no idea what she was talking about. I had never formed close enough friendships to talk about what boys and girls were doing together except to hold hands and kiss. The most important thing going on in my life, now that I didn't have to worry about school anymore, was how to stabilize things at home to keep everyone happy. Many days I succeeded and reaped the rewards of being loved which I craved so much. The message was clear—when I did everything right, the atmosphere was happy and loving; when discord arose within the family, it was something I caused or at least could have prevented. It was my job to identify the problem and find a solution in any case, because after all, I was the one who wanted Muttie's love. Many days

I succeeded, resulting in some very warm and loving times together, like the time I sold a lace collar for $20.00 and Muttie, feeling especially generous with me, told me to keep it as a 15th birthday present a month or so ahead. I was told I could spend it on myself. In an attempt to keep this warm wind blowing, I decided to spend it on a set of matching dishes I knew she longed for. I prepared a surprise party for what would have been Muttie's and Papa's 25th anniversary. She was very touched by this gesture and showed her appreciation in many ways for a long time afterwards. This was the kind of family life I was striving for. Some day I would have someone to love and build a wonderful family with. That "some day" of my dreams was coming closer as we had moved to a small place in another small town which also had a small S.D.A. Church with quite a few young people. One of the young men, named Adolf, took it upon himself to walk me home from church youth meetings, saying I needed protection. He was as shy as I was and we usually walked all the way to my place with the only words spoken being "Good Bye" at the door. But one day he reached over to hold my hand and from then on, I just lived for the walks home from church with my hand in Adolf's.

My daydreams about the perfect home with Adolf came to a halt suddenly when we were told in church that the D.P. Program for America Immigration was once more in progress and if we were interested, there were Adventist volunteers in America ready to sponsor us. The whole procedure of filling out forms and waiting, followed by medical exams, etc., took place again. One week before my 16th birthday, Adolf and I embraced for a last tearful "Auf Wiedersehen," for the next day we were scheduled to board the train for Munich to await our departure for America.

For over three months we lived again in a refugee camp, reading the "board" anxiously every morning, searching for our names. The last day in February, 1952, it was our turn. We were allowed only one trunk in which to take whatever possessions were most important to us and whatever we could carry on board in one hand. Since we were not allowed to enter the U.S.A. with any money, we went to town in Munich to spend our last deutsche Marks. Muttie divided it equally among us—15 D.M. each. I didn't have to think, I knew immediately what I would buy as I headed for the doll section at the huge new Woolworth in Munich. I finally had in my possession the biggest "store bought" doll I could find, but I had to carry it on board the ship in Bremer Haven without the benefit of a suitcase which caused quite a few chuckles. The last papers we had to sign were to renounce German citizenship; we were now termed "Staatenlos" (without a country). The emotions ran deep on everyone's face as the ship blew its deep-sounding horn, and we started moving.

* * *

By the time we passed England, we were suffering from motion sickness so severe we didn't care if we would ever see America. All we wanted was to get away from the ocean which was particularly stormy this time of year. The old army transport boat "General Muir" was in disrepair with the showers not functioning by the third day at sea. Muttie and I were too sick even to bother to get undressed to sleep at night. As long as there was plenty of cold air blowing, we could keep the vomiting down to a minimum, but during the night we were sick continuously. At dusk every evening the announcements came about the time changes and other information given in several languages besides German and English, ending with orders to clear the deck so the doors could be locked for the night. Muttie and I were laying in a corner on deck only semi-conscious when the announcement was made one night, not hearing it or responding to it. Gerd was sleeping in another area with the men, and Oma was in a cabin because of her age, so nobody missed us when we didn't report to our bunks. We spent the whole night on deck, unconscious with the waves sweeping over us. I guess the cold temperature revived us by early morning. The salt water had dried on our clothes, skin, and hair, and one can imagine what we looked like by the time we arrived in New York Harbor on the 9th day. The motion sickness had stopped for us the previous day, and after spending the whole last day cleaning the ship from top to bottom as required, we were exhausted and thankful to be able to sleep undisturbed by seasickness attacks. By 4:00 a.m., the person on the loud-speaker announced that we were getting close to port. The Statue of Liberty was visible. The doors would be opened early for anyone wanting to watch as we entered the U.S.A., the promised land. Not one person stayed in their bunk. As we stood on deck, watching the early sun rays reflect on the copper of "The Lady," creating a mysterious glow, there wasn't a dry eye anywhere. We were here—we had arrived after seven years of trying—we were entering the land that held a future for us. Would we be accepted? Would all our dreams come true? What were the dreams in all these people's heart, I wondered. I was sure of mine—it was the same since we had stayed in the Riesengoburge—all I wanted was a husband to love me, provide us with a small house and the necessities of everyday life. I would give him beautiful babies, keep the house spotless, and give him all my love and loyalty in return. Would my dream come true?

Enough of the daydreaming—there were orders to be followed. We were ushered through many gates and tunnels, it seemed like, until we stood in line at different gates, each one showing the letter of the alphabet, corresponding with the first letter of our last names. This was Ellis Island where countless foreign immigrants have been processed to one day become American citizens. Our line was long and moved very slowly. The Red Cross people were there handing out hot chocolate and sandwiches—and smiles. I couldn't understand why nice looking, well dressed ladies like that would want to spend time in a dirty old place like this, smiling at people who looked like us—not to mention what we must have smelled like.

At the gate the customs officials couldn't believe that a young lady of sixteen would actually be carrying a naked doll (I didn't have enough money for one with clothes), so they assumed we must be bringing into the country some kind of contraband. The doll was dismembered and inspected carefully, then handed back to me—all its parts in a paper bag. I was so concerned over my terrible appearance, that the pain of this loss of the only doll I had ever owned, didn't set in until much later.

We were now advancing to the next gate. Now everything was announced only in English. The Red Cross people were interpreting for us, but it was very frightening to have to depend on someone to speak for you. How would we ever make it to the train without being able to speak the language. As we came closer to the last gate, we noticed a man, woman and a young lady—assumably they were a family, talking to the gate keeper. We heard our name mentioned—fear gripped us. Would we be turned back for any reason? We could not go back to Germany. We had voluntarily renounced German citizenship. What would happen to us?

The gate keeper spoke to the family in English, again saying our names and ushering us through the gate. The American family pulled us aside with a smile. The lady spoke German, saying: "We are your brother and sisters in Christ. We attend one of the S.D.A. churches here in New York. We have been sent here from the Conference to assist you with whatever you need and to help you board the train. Welcome to America." Then this beautiful lady wearing a coat with a fur collar, and high heels actually embraced us as, dirty as we were. Remembering this Christian act helped me many times in years to come when I would be disappointed in my fellow believers, and was an inspiration to me on my own road to christian maturity.

We had to take a trip on the bus with the ferry to get to the main city—the train depot. As we were ready to board the train, I felt even more conspicuous in my salt covered coat. The daughter of this family removed her own beautiful fur collared coat and handed it to me with her parents nodding in agreement. After discarding my old one and I could feel the smooth satin lining touch my arms, I felt transported. My gratitude once more left me speechless, but the tears escaping from my lids made words unnecessary. Now I felt American. I had confidence; my dream would come true. I would believe.

We were handed a box of sandwiches and other goodies to enjoy on the train as we waved a farewell to these dear Americans, whose names we didn't even know. Now we were on our own—no more interpreters, no more loudspeakers giving information that we could understand—just us in this new and hopefully wonderful country that was to become our home forever.

Chapter 3

After experiencing this kind of Christian love, I was all set to see a saint every time I got acquainted with an S.D.A. christian—or was it only Americans who showed such benevolence? It was a rude awakening when we finally arrived at our destination. It turned out that our sponsors were opportunists who took advantage of the D.P.'s by sponsoring refugees only to obtain free labor for their nursing home business. It took us four months of maneuvering to escape this cloister—our term for the nursing home set in the country all by itself, isolating us from the rest of the world due to lack of transportation. After establishing ourselves in Cleveland, I found it ironic to be expected to work in a sewing factory when in Germany I was considered a tramp just for thinking about it. My way of retaliating was to dress and behave contrary to Muttie's wishes. "Rebellious teenager" was the label I earned later. Muttie, at a loss as to how to handle this new person I was becoming, resorted to being a martyr."I brought you here to America to give you the opportunity of a lifetime," she lamented. "left all my friends behind. I didn't do it for me; I'm too old to benefit from this. All of it, I did for you—all the sacrifices I've made for you and this is the thanks I get."

I screamed at her since that was the only way I knew how to communicate with her. "Yes, yes, I know about all the sacrifices, starting with saving me from the measles; why didn't you just let me die then, if I've been nothing but trouble to you. And I never asked you to take me to America. I was perfectly happy in Germany. I would have married Adolf and you wouldn't have to worry about my make-up and fingernail polish now." This statement took her by surprise since she was completely unaware of my hand-holding romance with Adolf. She retorted with "Oh, my poor little Gatel, you are in for a big disappointment if you set your sights on good-looking guys like Adolf. They go for the pretty girls, you better get more realistic in your expectations." Gerd and Muttie both laughed at the absurdity of what I'd said. I was mortified with embarrassment at my presumption—all I could say to close this discussion was, "My name isn't Gatel anymore; the American term is Aggie and that's the only name I will answer to. You want me to be happy to be American. I will be so American, you'll be sorry."

"Yes, Muttie," Gerd interrupted, "my American name is Gary."

Trying to live up to my promised threat about Americanizing, I delighted to do anything that would cause Muttie concern. I had gotten acquainted with some other D.P. girls who talked some broken German at the factory, who were only too happy to modernize me. By early July when I boldly announced to her that I was going to the movies with my two factory friends, Muttie felt it necessary to consult with the minister about my rebelliousness. It was decided that I needed to go to the church's annual ten-day camp meeting coming up the middle of July. They would have special prayer for me. The statewide camp meeting was located in Mount Vernon, about two hours drive from Cleveland. I would be riding with the minister.

At camp meeting I felt more alone than ever—everybody there seemed to know everyone else—except me. I was unable to gain any spiritual blessing because of the language barrier—from the tent meetings, so I spent most of the time taking long walks by the lake, contemplating my future—missing Papa.

The last Sabbath there the minister introduced me to Mary. "You will be riding home with her," I was informed. Mary had been raised in a Swiss-German family and remembering a little German, she was able to make me understand that her son was to come pick us up—she was anxious, having expected him the day before. When he finally arrived, visibly hung-over, we knew the reason for his delay. She introduced me to him: "Martin, I want you to meet Aggie. She is a German girl and doesn't talk English. I promised her a ride home."

"Hi, Aggie. I would be happy to teach you English," he said with a twinkle in his electric blue eyes as he took my hand. All the same feelings enveloped me that I had felt when Adolf held my hand. I was too self-conscious to say a word. He had to be at least seven feet tall, I thought, with beautiful blond wavy hair and with an air of mystery surrounding him. He quickly loaded our things in the trunk and asked his mother to sit in the back.

During the long trip home I picked up enough of their conversation to learn that Martin was engaged to a girl named Phyllis. Knowing this, I was totally surprised when he made it a point to drop off Mary first—then asked if he could call on me. "You know what I mean," he winked at me and was gone. I leaned against the door, giving my heart time to stop thumping loud enough for Muttie to hear—for she still insisted on sharing a bed with me. Knowing this possible romance would lead nowhere since Martin was engaged gave me the courage to pursue it since it would be proof for Muttie that even campmeeting couldn't straighten me out.

* * *

Gary answered the door the morning after I had returned from camp meeting while I was dressing for work. Muttie came to the bedroom to summon me to the living room. In wide-eyed astonishment she announced, "Aggie, there is an American young man at the door asking for you; a handsome man. How does he know your name?"

I walked into the living room very confident. I was flattered that Martin had showed up so soon—this was just the kind of ammunition I needed to show Muttie that I was able to handle my own life. I introduced them and explained to Muttie how I had met him, sure that she would be furious at how her camp meeting plan for me had backfired. I'd heard her preach to Gary not to get involved with American girls, so I was sure she would forbid Martin to take me out, and I would be able to remind her forever of ruining my wonderful future with a handsome American after becoming an old maid according to her predictions.

Gary, who had picked up English faster than the rest of us, interpreted between Martin and me. It turned out Martin had come in a car (we assumed his) to take me to work. Muttie said absolutely nothing as I walked out the door with Martin holding my hand and opening the car door for me, with neighbors peeking through the curtains.

Martin was waiting for me when I got off work in "his" shiny car. I wondered if he didn't work, but with the language barrier between us, I was unable to ask such questions subtly. We arrived at my apartment with Muttie having prepared a festive dinner. Martin was invited to eat with us. Gary had unlimited questions for Martin; on how and where to buy a car, mostly. After all, Martin was an American; he knew everything. When he finally left, Muttie was exuberant. "He looks just like Paul, the Paul of my youth. He will break your heart just like Paul did to me, but of course I know it's impossible for you to resist a man like this. Just be prepared for the day when he leaves you for a prettier girl. I really can't understand why he picked you to begin with. Just enjoy it while it lasts. I'll be here for you when you need me."

I wasn't prepared for this kind of reaction from Muttie. But then, I still didn't need to worry too much since I knew that Martin was supposed to marry this Phyllis. That night before going to sleep, I asked Muttie, "Tell me about this Paul I've been hearing about all my life, Muttie."

"Oh Aggie, it's a long story. When I was about your age, one summer a family from Moscow was visiting in our village. They had a very handsome son, Paul. He was as irrestiably charming, just like Martin—and the same blue eyes. He had me believing that I was the only girl in the world for him. By the end of the summer when I was making wedding plans, he suddenly was gone without even saying goodbye. That's when I married your father, because he was ready to save me from becoming an old maid—a jilted one at that. You can imagine the disappointment; you know how short of a man Papa was.

I never did love him. Still, not a day goes by that I don't think about Paul. Martin is just like him—handsome men enjoy hurting women, you'll find out.

* * *

I wondered about this Phyllis as time went on since Martin was there at the factory, waiting for me every day and we rode the street car home. "His" car turned out to be his sister's. He never left me until 10:00 p.m.—my curfew. Usually we just took walks to the corner drug store for a Pepsi and then he visited with us—mostly with Muttie and Gary. Muttie was totally enamoured by his charm. Sometimes it seemed to me he came to see them more than me.

By the time the temperatures and the humidity reached the high 90's early August, the job under the glass roof of the factory with all the steam presses along the sides of the room became almost unbearable. I, along with other operators would faint from the heat and exhaustion repeatedly.

Muttie found work as a "domestic," working in the prestigeous Shaker Heights district. Muttie and Gary were discussing my plight at the factory one evening, favoring the idea of sending me to school. After all, in America, kids attended school until they were 18 years old, and since I seemed to be unable to pick up English fast enough to help me get a better job, this was apparently the most logical answer to our problem. They were talking about me and my future as if I wasn't even there. I knew the procedure. If I were to say anything, it would only turn into an argument, especially considering my rebellious behaviour lately. Things sure weren't turning out the way I had planned. Now I would be sent back to school—the one fear I thought was in the past. How did I get into this predicament? I was being punished, I was sure, for my rebellion against my mother. I would ask God to forgive me and be obedient again; then, maybe I could convince them not to send me back to school.

That evening while we were sipping our Pepsi, Martin wanted to know the reason for my apparent tension. The fountain clerk could understand some German, so with his help I told Martin about Muttie's plan for me and my fear of school. He told me not to worry, he would take care of everything.

The next day he asked Muttie for my hand in marriage. He had never mentioned his intentions to me—indeed, he had never even kissed me. I could not believe what was happening here—nobody even noticed my presence. They were all busy making plans. Surely this was just a bad dream.

I could not imagine being married. I had never even cooked a meal. I felt very tense and uncomfortable around Martin. I could not put my finger on the reason for this; maybe it was just the fact that we couldn't communicate. I would make a special effort at speaking English. I would just be good and wait and the whole thing would go away—just like the bombs had always stopped falling sooner or later. The bombs—that's what I felt like now—the bombs were falling but this time I was the only one who heard them, or who felt the fear, and nobody to protect me. Oh, Papa, where are you. I need you so badly. God, Papa isn't here, You need to come to my rescue. You promised. I need You now. The voices of my family seemed to be coming from far away, the room started spinning, and I drifted into oblivion—safe at last. The cold water in my face revived me enough to hear that an engagement party was scheduled for November 15—my 17th birthday, with the wedding following in December.

* * *

Slowly I got caught up in the excitement of wedding preparations. I had never seen Muttie so happy and enthusiastic before; and most important, pleased with me. We spent a lot of time together, shopping for material and sewing my white satin wedding gown and pink honeymoon suit.

Muttie talked in awe about her little girl having grown up so fast. Couldn't she see that I wasn't grown up at all—that I was scared to death? But I allowed myself to enjoy all the attention I was getting. Martin was a charmer around people, treating me affectionately and showering me with flowers, candy and thoughtful little gifts. However, he seemed different when we were alone, cold and at times even hostile. I blamed it on frustration caused by my inability to communicate in English.

It was decided I should take advantage of a night school course in English, offered three times a week for foreign-speaking adults. It was wonderful to be in a whole room full of people who were just as inadequate at speaking English as I was. In this setting, I gained confidence and discovered that I had actually picked up quite a bit of language skills already. I only needed the courage to practice it on people I came in contact with. With this new-found confidence, I mingled in social conversation with a small group of Germans after class. It turned out that two young men lived near my apartment and we started walking together in the same direction, talking and laughing about some of the humorous experiences in our new country. When our paths parted and I continued my walk alone, Martin jumped out from behind one of the bushes, livid with anger. He grabbed me by the arm, literally dragging me along, shouting obscenities, calling me names, and threatened to "take care of things." This is how we arrived at the apartment. He pushed me down in front of Muttie, yelling at her about my promiscuous behavior and ordering her to straighten me out. Her response to my explanation was that I must have done something more than just walk with these fellow students to cause Martin to behave so irrational. I swore to her that I had done nothing wrong and that I had noticed Martin's temper before—like when I had carried the tub of popcorn the "wrong way" at the movies recently. At once the discussion turned to my sinful behavior of attending the movie houses, with me screaming at her for never seeing the good in me, ending the fight with me telling her that I didn't want to get married. Her answer to our problem again was to call the minister in hopes that he would straighten me out, which brought on another fight—why didn't she ever call the minister to straighten out Gary? Her answer was, "Why do you hate your brother so? It seems that you are just full of hate—I don't know why Martin even wants to marry you."

When the minister came over, the session progressed differently than I had expected. He said he knew Martin's family well, and this episode didn't surprise him at all. He was just glad that Martin had shown his "dark" side before it was too late. He told us that Martin had a "medical" discharge from the army for attempting suicide and that he had been barred from attending S.D.A. boarding school for belligerent behaviour. His closing statement was that he would rather officiate at my funeral than the wedding.

After the minister left, Muttie and I were able to talk calmly and we decided to cancel the wedding. She soothed me by stroking my hair, saying "Poor little Aggie, I told you he would break your heart but you are lucky you have a Mother who loves you no matter what you do." What had I done? But never mind about that. At least this ordeal was over. If I couldn't have her love, I would settle for sympathy. I fell asleep in her arms that night feeling like a protected little girl.

When I came home from work the next day, I had mixed feelings about not having Martin's attention any more and at the same time feeling relieved that the upcoming wedding plans were canceled. Mostly, I felt a severe loneliness. I needed Papa. I needed to feel the way I felt in his presence—accepted. To be able to just be myself—isn't that what love was supposed to be? Muttie said that was selfishness; maybe it was. After all, if I didn't want to marry Martin, why did I feel a longing for him now. Oh well, I just wouldn't think about it any more, it was over.

Muttie came into the bedroom where I was changing clothes, happy to be alone with my thoughts. "Sit down, Aggie, we have to talk." I knew by the tone of her voice that it was going to be unpleasant. "Martin was here earlier, he has lost his job because he was unable to work due to worrying about what he'd done. He is really sorry, he says he loves you so much that just seeing you talking to those fellows made him jealous. He says it will never happen again. Aggie, he was down on his knees in front of me, swearing his love for you. He said he would kill himself if you didn't marry him. You know, Aggie, you won't ever find anyone so crazy in love with you again. You know what a stubborn, rebellious character you have. I have been able to overlook that because as a mother I love unconditionally, but you won't be able to expect that of a man. Any man who marries you will expect a loving, obedient wife and here is a man who loves you enough to want to marry you in spite of all your faults. Besides, just think of what it would look like to all our friends for you to break off the engagement. Everyone would say that you couldn't even hold on to a man for a few months. I told Martin not to come over until tomorrow to give you time to get over the hurt. Then you better ask his forgiveness and stay away from that night school. You'll be able to learn English like the rest of us if you just set your mind to it."

I had no more energy left to fight; was she right? Was I really that hard to get along with? I certainly hadn't been very nice to Muttie lately. I took a long walk, filling myself with remorse for not treating Muttie with the love she deserved; and, well, maybe engaged girls shouldn't talk to other boys. What did I know anyway. I fell into bed exhausted, then sort of sleepwalked through all the wedding preparations, doing what I was told, smiling when I was expected to smile, feeling relief when Christmas was over and December 27, my wedding day drew near—relief that soon all this activity would be over with and I wouldn't be pulled in every direction.

We had rented a furnished one-room apartment with a shared bathroom. All my clothes and personal belongings were merged there with Martin's—too late to turn back now. Why would I want to? Martin had been the absolute perfect suitor since that one incident. Muttie was probably right—I was just an ungrateful, selfish person. I would sure have to change if I wanted Martin to love me.

Chapter 4

I was the model of obedience all through the wedding preparations, questioning nothing. Martin gave instructions on how it was done in America, and Muttie enthusiastically carried them out. As I stood in the church foyer, alone, waiting to walk down the aisle, I wondered how my family had come to the decision for Gary to be Martin's best man, making it necessary for me to walk down that long aisle alone, when Martin had three brothers.

Had Gary preferred it that way? Wasn't he supposed to be my father substitute? Yet, here I was, standing all by myself, surrounded in white satin and tulle. I looked down the church aisle, watching my maid of honor walking in step to the music toward the men standing at the end in their black tuxedos, looking so handsome. No wonder all the girls were falling all over themselves to get a date with Gary—his very presence commanded attention, standing there next to Martin— Martin, the tall handsome man I was to belong to in a few minutes. Why couldn't I feel thrilled at the thought of being a wife to Martin, this stranger? That's why, I thought, because he is a stranger. And all these people—I noticed just about every seat was filled—who were all these people? Strangers. Suddenly everybody and everything looked strange. I noticed the white orchid in my trembling hand. My body was shivering in the cold hallway, but I felt a hot cloud envelope my head. In my mind I heard a little girl crying hysterically, was that my voice? I felt a hand on my shoulder and a voice saying, "Aggie, it's time for you to walk down the aisle, the organ has been playing 'Here Comes the Bride' several times." I was firmly anchored to the spot but I watched my body start to move, walking in perfect step, slowly, to the front of the church as I was watching, feeling an extreme sadness. The girl stood calmly, the flowers steady in her hand as the ring was placed on her finger, she repeated the vows clearly and was introduced as Mr. and Mrs. after the wedding kiss. That was a good performance, Aggie, I said silently to the girl as we merged again.

The reception followed at our apartment. Two older ladies had decided to decorate the living room with streamers and bells during the ceremony. One of them had used a rented folding chair as a stepladder and had fallen, injuring herself. An ambulance was at the house tending to the patient as we, along with all the guests, arrived. We all had to wait outside in the snow until the ambulance sped off with the lady having suffered a broken hip. It was hard after that to get everybody in a celebratory mood which was okay with me since I felt more like having attended a funeral anyway—my funeral.

It wasn't long before Martin escorted me into the car we had borrowed from Gary, (to my embarrassment), amid the showers of rice to depart to Erie, Pennsylvania for our one day honeymoon. Martin had to stop driving several times to take some pills to help him stay awake for "what lays ahead" he said. I felt absolutely terrified, wondering what this thing that was supposed to happen at honeymoons was all about. I was sleepy, I wanted to be at home in my own bed, even sharing the bed with Muttie was better than what I was evidently heading for. Martin couldn't even wait for us to unpack the suit-cases. He took time only to lock the door and brutally attacked me. What had I done to deserve this, I wondered; wasn't I supposed to be loved on this special night? It was over in minutes when he jumped up and yelled at me: "Your performance was disgusting—don't they teach you anything in the old country? How do you expect a husband to desire you when you lay there like a cold fish." He ended the tirade by throwing some magazines at me, telling me to look at the pictures—that's what he expected me to do; and with that he dressed and slammed out the door. I was absolutely horrified at what I looked at when I saw the magazines.

As I gained knowledge about these things in later years, I realized it was hard core pornography but at the time I was gripped with raw fear of Martin's return and his expectations of me. I was in this dingy hotel room without a phone, in a strange city, and it was in the middle of the night and I was totally alone except for a maniac who was about to come back—only I wasn't sure that he was a maniac—maybe that was just my interpretation of him. Maybe this is what married people did.

I was still sorting out my confusion over what my obligations were when he returned. He was all smiles as he said, "Now, show me what you've learned, my little Fraulein?" I ran into the bathroom and locked the door—it took him only a few minutes to pick the lock open. He grabbed me by the arm and dragged me to the bed, telling me that I was his wife—he owned me, and I better cooperate if I knew what was good for me. I buried myself under the pillow so no one would hear my screams as the whole procedure was repeated. I must have fainted because I regained consciousness at dawn with Martin next to me, sound asleep. We spent the trip home talking amiacably as if it was just an ordinary day, arriving home all smiles and eager to start housekeeping.

* * *

I soon discovered being married to an American didn't ensure one of an affluent lifestyle. The "apartment" we had rented based on our income consisted of one very tiny bedroom with an alcove providing a sink and a stove. We were to share a common refrigerator in the main kitchen and a bathroom with five other tenents. I also learned about Martin's extreme and sudden mood swings and his apparent dual personality. But most of all, I spent my time learning from Martin how to be a proper wife. I was to do what I was told unquestioningly. I was to turn over my paychecks to him for management, and cook elaborate meals on the food budget he had determined.

When I found the courage occasionally to question his wisdom such as why I was expected to clean the bathtub before he would take a bath (since it was always left dirty by the neighboring tenants), considering he was out of work most of the time and had more free time than I did, his answer was always the same, "That's how it's done in America."

I found myself under an enormous amount of stress. The work at the factory was physically demanding. The motion sickness I experienced on the streetcars depleted me of energy. Learning how to cook, especially being unable to read any receipes in English and in general being unfamilier with the American dishes he demanded, when I hadn't even learned how to cook European dishes, and considering the limited amount of grocery money available to me, left me mentally fatigued. Carrying the bags of groceries home on the streetcar tired me and adding to all that, the fact that I was unable to sleep for fear of being attacked (for that is a correct description in our case of what should be called love making), left me in physical pain most of the time and emotionally exhausted.

I walked a constant tightrope to ward off his temperamental outbursts, but failed miserably most of the time—like the day he came home very late and I had to tell him that I had lost one of the tiny diamond chips out of my wedding ring. He twisted my wrist so hard I couldn't help but cry out in pain as he looked at the ring.

"You b—, I should have known better than to buy you a diamond ring. You don't know how to take care of nice things, having lived like some animal in camps all your life. Now you get down on your hands and knees and look for that diamond—and while you're on the floor, get a bucket and rag to clean the house. I'm sick and tired of living in a pigsty," he said as he pushed me to the floor, adding in disgust, "I should have known better than to marry a d—D.P. shikse."

Of course it was useless to look for anything that small and expect to find it. I explained to Martin that there were no other places to look, when he ordered me to scrub everything down again and not to quit until I could produce that diamond. He towered over me like a giant, insisting I scrub harder and harder, yelling threats about how he would take care of me if I didn't comply. I had not known him long enough to know whether he would make good the threats or not, so I kept scrubbing when suddenly he said, "I'm tired and need to get some sleep if you expect me to perform as a husband later on. You're making too much noise splashing that wet rag around, you probably lost the diamond outside anyway." He handed me my coat and told me to go out and look for it. It was in the middle of the night—in winter. I heard him lock the door behind me. I wandered around in the dark and cold until I was shivering in front of my door again—afraid to go into my own apartment. He opened the door and scolded me for being outside in the dead of winter and in the middle of the night, as if it had been my idea. I couldn't believe this kind of craziness. After he'd used me for his pleasure, I listened to his deep breathing, knowing I was safe for a while. I relaxed enough to give some thought to my future.

The one thing that concerned me was that I did not want any children with this man. I knew by now that ours was not a normal marriage. I did not know what was normal but I sure was learning the hard way what was abnormal. One of the older ladies at the factory had taken me under her wing somewhat and at our lunch break I confided in her a little bit. She told me to get some protection against pregnancy immediately. That night Martin seemed in an exceptionally good mood and I approached him with my suggestion for birth control, for economic reasons, I told him. His reaction surprised me as he laughed sheepishly saying he should have told me before that he'd had an operation following an accident on the ballfield when he was 16 years old, which left him sterile. He consoled me very tenderly about the fact that we would never have any children, not realizing my tremendous relief.

Somehow this nightmare would end just the way the war ended and all the hardships connected with it, and at least I didn't have to worry about any children inheriting his character traits or possibly being subjected to the kind of abuse I was. All I had to do once more was to endure what life handed me and eventually I would be saved —never mind how.

* * *

A few days after the "diamond" incident, we had dinner at Muttie's. During our visit there I was shocked to hear Martin describing our night of the lost diamond. "Muttie, you have some daughter," he said. "She was so sad to lose that little diamond, she insisted on looking for it all night—and cleaned the house as well while she was looking. I'm sure glad I married a little German who knows how to keep a clean house—no American girl would do that—what a lucky guy I am. I had to hold her and comfort her the rest of the night." He ended the narration with "isn't that right, 'Shorty' (one of his nicknames for me in public; in private it was "dumkopf"). I was so stunned at this blatant lie that it took me a few seconds to organize my thoughts. Just as I was about to tell the true story, Muttie said, "Aggie, the least you can do is show the proper gratitude to Martin for being so considerate of your feelings." I knew then it was too late to reply with anything but a humble, "I am." Martin was right there in the kitchen helping with the dishes and flattering Muttie and showing open affection toward me. I could feel a real bond forming between Muttie and Martin. It made me feel uneasy as though I now had two people confessing to love me, but showing different in their actions. I immediately chided myself for being jealous. How could I be so selfish, wanting to deprive my Mother of her son-in-law's affection? I should consider myself lucky to have a husband who loved my Mother—considering all the "mother-in-law" stories one heard.

While Martin was engaged in conversation with Gary in the living room, I had a few minutes alone in the kitchen with Muttie. She wanted to know how married life was, so; gathering all my courage I tried to confide in her about how painful our "lovemaking" was for me. Her reply was simply that it was only temporary and in time I would come to enjoy it. Obviously she refused to listen to what I was trying to say and I decided it was useless to try. She was determined to see me as a happy wife and daughter, and I better play the part.

Before we left, Martin complimented her again about the delicious dinner and added, "Maybe you could teach your daughter how to cook like that; a man can't live on love forever, you know." They both laughed, they criticized me for being so serious; didn't I have any sense of humor at all? All the way home Martin put me down for being the sourpuss of the evening and that I better learn some social skills if I expected him to take me anywhere but Muttie's.

When I served the same dinner we'd had at Mutties a few weeks later after I'd gotten directions from Muttie on how to prepare it, he threw the food at me and the dishes on the floor, yelling in disgust, "Only a foreigner would serve her husband garbage like this." I learned quickly that I was married to two men—the private one and the public one. I would just have to learn to be more at ease around other people so we would socialize as much as possible and keep our private time to a minimum.

In the meantime, I was laid off at the factory, giving me more time to devote to cooking and housekeeping skills. But at the same time, Martin was feeling the pressure of only one paycheck which made him even more temperamental. Soon Muttie was able to get me hired at the city hospital laundry where she had been working for a while. With the added income we were able to rent a regular furnished one-bedroom apartment with our own kitchen and bathroom. I had proven myself in American food preparation by asking questions of my co-workers and learning to read receipes. Martin and I were developing some friendships with other couples we met at our church and I made sure we didn't spend too much time alone. I put on a happy face during the day, privately dreading the nights.

One day the nursing supervisor at the city hospital approached me to offer me the ward clerk's position that needed to be filled. I came to the conclusion that my English must be better than I thought if I was able to perform in a clerical capacity. At first it took all my concentration, but I fell into the groove soon enough and even received some compliments about my work.

One of the nurses hinted a few times that it wouldn't hurt for me to have some updated clothes for the job. I was surprised when Martin was ready to go shopping at my suggestion. I think this was the most unsettling aspect of Martin's personality—that he always seemed to react opposite from what I expected, keeping me totally off balance at all times. Shortly after our shopping trip, he had come to the hospital to pick me up. He was convinced that I had wanted the new clothes to attract the attentions of some man at the hospital. When my shift was up I was surprised to see him standing by the elevator. I could see by the dark look on his face that it would be a long night. "I saw you flirting with the guys on your floor—is that why you needed the new clothes? Some b—— you are—asking your husband to pay for new clothes in order to attract other men so you can cheat. I'll just have to show you tonight how cheating girls are treated." The tirade lasted not only through the night but continued after I returned from work the next day when he told me that he had been fired again because of missing too much work. I now suspected that he spent most of his time spying on me. I felt I was under constant surveillance.

Jobs were easy to come by in the 50's. Muttie could only heap praises on him for finding a new job so quickly—once more I was criticized for not appreciating the best husband in the world when I showed some concern over so many job changes. I tried to point out how I liked the stability Gary showed in keeping the same position. I was sternly admonished by Muttie not to compare Martin to my brother. I was always to consider my husband the best over any man in order to be considered a good wife. The most important thing for me to be concerned about was to make myself into the kind of wife Martin wanted and never to point out his faults. One thing was sure—Martin and Muttie liked each other—it was more obvious each time we visited, and I was grateful for that.

* * *

The confidence I was gaining on my job led the way to more confidence in my housekeeping skills and I learned to focus all my interest and energy in these areas and block out the fear of the nights as much as possible, telling myself that if I had been able to endure the hardships of the war, I would be able to survive this. I reminded myself frequently of all my blessings, but I continued to be confused by Martin's inconsistent behavior toward me. He would praise my various abilities to people, but ridicule me in private. He continued to shower me with gifts—to my friends' envy, but verbally abused me for things like spending 15 cents on a dime store hankie when I'd forgotten to bring one from home. I was living on a constant emotional roller coaster, trying to establish some type of routine, only to fight a new problem continuously.

It was late July-August when my motion sickness on the streetcar to and from work increased to the point where I was vomiting almost continuously, making it difficult for me to perform my duties at the hospital or at home. I blamed it on the heat and high humidity. Martin's hostility toward me grew worse as my illness became more intense. Cooking, especially, became a burden as the smell of food sent me rushing to the bathroom. Martin attacked this vulnerability immediately by telling me in the morning not to bother with any cooking in the evening, that he would bring home hamburgers. Then, when he'd arrive home without any food, he would accuse me of being lazy, again and again referring to the mistake he'd made by marrying a D.P. On other nights he'd come home when I had dinner half prepared and announce happily that he was taking me out to eat—to turn off the stove; then again his mood would change abruptly to disgust when I had to run for the restroom at the restaurant. He was consistent in one thing though, when we were in Muttie's presence, he always showed concern for me and treated me affectionately, convincing Muttie that her daughter was well taken care of.

My illness progressed to the point of fainting after getting off the streetca on one occassion, I don't know how long I was unconscious. I believed that my problem was probably dehydration caused by so much vomiting. I found myself waking up in a strange house on the living room couch with an older couple hovering over me. After giving them my address, they drove me home. Martin had arrived from work early because of another job loss, therefore he was more concerned over his unemployment problem than my health, He promised these people that he would have me checked out by a doctor the next day, at their insistence.

Muttie wasn't too concerned about my condition since she was convinced that all that was wrong with me was that I was pregnant and the sickness would only last a short while. No amount of telling her about Martin's sterility would sway her prediction. The next day Martin took me to his family doctor who was partially retired. He looked like he should have retired twenty years earlier and his office along with him. I felt creepy the whole time he examined me in this dingy hole in the wall. Giving me a bottle of pills for my nausea, he sent me out to the waiting room and called Martin in. I could hear him tell Martin to be more gentle during lovemaking or my injuries could get him in trouble if I ever went to see another doctor. I prayed silently that Martin would heed the doctor's advice; he did—he didn't touch me at all for weeks which gave me some time to concentrate on getting well. I had no confidence in this old doctor who claimed there was nothing wrong with me, so I only pretended to take the pills he gave me which may have proved a blessing. The vomiting and the fainting spells became more frequent, causing me to lose my job.

With both of us out of work, we accepted Muttie's invitation to come live with her and Oma, occupying Gary's room left vacant when he was recently drafted into the U.S. Army. In my physical weakness, I welcomed the thought of not having to cook or work until I would get over whatever was wrong with me. Before long, Martin found another job and with Muttie at work, I spent many contented days alone with Oma, taking up my old hobby of knitting and other needle work.

A few blocks away was a large high school. I found myself drawn there when I felt up to taking slow walks. The girls were my age. They seemed so happy and carefree, skipping down the steps in their poodle-skirts, laughing and talking to each other and flirting with the boys. I wished I was one of them. School didn't seem so frightening anymore. I felt old and tired in comparison.

I somehow made it through my 18th birthday, but was hardly able to stay up for Thanksgiving dinner. Muttie still claimed I was pregnant but began to show concern that my condition wasn't improving and insisted I go back to the doctor. After my second examination, the doctor claimed that he could feel a growth on my uterus that was probably a tumor and should be surgically removed. Since he did not do any surgery anymore, he referred me to a specialist at the city hospital. The doctor there took a complete medical history followed by an examination. After giving me time to dress, he returned to the examining room all smiles. "Congratulations," he said. "You're going to be a little mother in the spring." I told him that was impossible since my husband was sterile. His reply was that he didn't know who had fathered the baby, but that I was definitely five months pregnant, he could hear a heartbeat.

He referred me to another doctor since this was not his specialty and left the room. I looked up the new doctor's office immediately and insisted on seeing him right away. I must have seemed pretty desperate, for in a short time I was once more on the examining table. This doctor was german, which made it possible to communicate with him freely. He was a very caring, fatherly type of man, and sympathized with my situation but confirmed the other doctor's diagnosis. He said his first concern was my constant vomiting, depleting me and the baby of the nourishment we needed. He explained that there was a new "miracle" drug on the market to treat nausea. It was manufactured in Germany but hadn't been approved by the U.S. Drug Administration. He knew another german doctor who kept some in stock, wrote down the name of the drug and this doctor's address, and made a return appointment for me. I trusted this gentle older man right away and once more it made me wish for Papa being home.

When Martin came home, he had a fit about me throwing money away on two different doctors and how dare I want to spend even more on pills. The very fact that their diagnosis showed pregnancy proved what "sheisters" they were. He would prove them wrong. Muttie was thrilled that her diagnosis was correct. I was in the bathroom, vomiting, listening to them fighting—wishing I was dead. The reality of my condition started slowly to descend on me like a dark, heavy cloud. I cursed God as I went to sleep. How could He let this happen to me? I had been obedient, I had tried to do my best, waiting for Him to deliver me from this unbearable life with Martin. Instead, He added to my burden by giving me a child when I was still a child myself. After giving me the false security of Martin's sterility, this was supposed to be a God of love?

* * *

Amidst the Christmas holiday preparations, Martin decided that he wasn't the father of my baby and he moved out. He also felt no obligation toward my support. I was too sick to work and too depressed to care. December 27, our first anniversary, Martin came to see me with a proposition, "I've been thinking," he started—"I would like to come back and for us to be together again. Maybe there is a chance the baby is mine. Doctors don't know everything. But you will have to take some blood tests to prove that I'm the father if you want me back."

"You must be crazy to think I want you back, Martin; and how dare you insult me by demanding a blood test. If you don't know me enough to know that I would not be unfaithful, then I certainly don't mean very much to you. And what about trust? Aren't married people supposed to trust each other?" I was working myself into a frenzy when Muttie stepped in.

"Aggie, calm down; this isn't good for the baby."

"That's right, Muttie, just think about the baby—I don't matter at all here—not to any of you." Heavy sobs were convulsing my body as Oma came to my rescue.

"Here, here, Gatel—you matter to me." She held me close as Muttie apologized to Martin.

"You've got to remember, Martin, she's pregnant. Women in the family way are oversensitive sometimes."

I interrupted—"Why are you making excuses for me to this american play boy—it's Martin who should apologize to us." I ended the whole scene by locking myself in my bedroom. I fell asleep listening to Muttie and Martin discussing my future as if I was totally incompetent to make any decisions myself. Judging from my behavior, I couldn't blame them. Martin was evidently back to stay, I decided,when I saw him asleep on the living room sofa the next morning. Muttie and Oma took care of me as if I was a baby from then on, shielding me from Martin's temperamental outbursts by reminding him of my "condition."

I took advantage of this excuse by allowing myself to wallow in self-pity and sinking deeper into my depression, seeking escape mostly in sleep. Many days I never even got dressed. My morning sickness lasted all day, right to the end of my pregnancy. The results of my routine blood tests showed an R.H. factor. More complications.

Muttie had a T.V. delivered one day to keep me company during my long, lonely days. It was 1954—the year the first soap opera was tried. I learned correct English by the lines of "As The World Turns." This type of melodrama was exactly what I needed to match my mood. Martin and Muttie were enjoying each other's company—I was glad they left me alone and that nothing was expected of me.

Somehow, this baby I was expecting wasn't real—somehow, sooner or later, it would all go away, like the war, like Papa, like Germany itself; just get lost in the past. Yes, that's what would happen to this baby.

Muttie started to buy some baby things in an attempt to cheer me up. Martin told her that wasn't necessary. He explained to her the american custom of baby showers. He must have mentioned it to his sister because one day Jane came over and apologized for not having given me a shower yet. It was because the baby would most likely be born dead because of my R.H. blood type, she said; and it would be a shame to waste all those baby things. Again I became hysterical and told her to leave. My newfound rebellion against God gave me energy. It felt good to release the anger I had stored up for so long. I didn't know how to assert myself, so I became aggressive.

I emptied the alcove in our bedroom we had used as a closet, and started to paint it and fix it up for a baby's room. I would show them that my baby would live. How dare they speculate about me not being capable of delivering a live baby.

Muttie showed a tremendous amount of love and patience during this time, calming Martin whenever I pushed him too far, often subjecting herself to the verbal abuse meant for me. Her biggest concern was for him not to abondon me and the baby. I took advantage of this new self assurance I'd developed by refusing to submit myself to any sexual abuse as well, threatening to scream if I had to and let

Martin deal with Muttie—by now I noticed this strange power play between them over me.

One evening in spring, we were waiting for Gary to come home on leave after basic training and some special courses, preparing him for the signal corp in the army to serve overseas, in Germany of all places. We were all happy that he wasn't being sent to Korea. We watched him jump out of the taxi, looking so sharp in his uniform. Everybody ran out to meet him—I stayed in the background. I felt ugly in my ballooning body. I don't know what motivated Gary, but he ran past everyone to hug me first; it felt so good to feel his arms around me in genuine affection that I could feel all the hardness I had built in my heart for protection—melt; making it impossible to hold back the tears. But I quickly regained my composure. Through the whole visit I kept looking at Gary, thinking how much I loved my brother, wishing we could show our feelings to each other; maybe he loved me as I loved him; it sure felt like it when he hugged me. It was hard to say good bye as he left to board the boat for Germany. I was convinced I would never see him again, —but this time I was prepared to control the tears. We were now counting off the days to my due date—would the baby be born on Mother's Day?

* * *

After being in heavy labour for 38 hours, the doctor decided to have some X-rays taken. He informed me that the X-rays showed an old fractured pelvis. I remembered an accident on the farm in Germany. This explained the severe pain I was experiencing that time. It was decided that I would need to have a C-section. I had to sign consent forms. I was confused, tired from heavy contractions—I didn't know what to expect even from normal childbirth; now I was to make these serious decisions and here I was all alone, (Muttie and Martin were both at work), nobody to ask for advice. I was overcome with total panic as I was being transferred to the operating table with the blinding light above. I remember watching people standing over me, holding their gloved hands in the air, ready to attack me. I heard the screams coming from my throat, but they sounded far away as I faded into oblivion from the ether.

I heard a voice asking me to wake up, over and over. Finally more voices were ordering me to open my eyes and speak to them. I thought I was answering—couldn't they hear me? I drifted off farther. I wanted to stay in this warm, comfortable world I was floating in, but the voices were more insistent. Why couldn't they leave me alone? All I wanted to do was sleep. It felt like I had been asleep for a very long time when I was awakened by Muttie's voice: "Gatel, you have to wake up—I sacrificed my whole life trying to save you, first from the measles and later from starvation. I didn't do all that just to lose you now. You have to try—you can't just give up. Come on: Open your eyes." She was crying. I just had to make an effort to wake up. As soon as I opened my eyes, there was a flurry of activity by the nurses, the doctor was summoned and injections given. What was all the fuss about? Where was I anyway? To my questions, Muttie answered by telling me that I had had a very hard time delivering a baby girl, that I had been prepared for a C-section, but before they were able to operate, I had given birth naturally. Now I had been unconscious for almost three days. What was she talking about? I was just a little girl myself, how could I have had a baby? They left me alone to rest for a while and I was trying to fit the pieces together of what Muttie was trying to tell me; but nothing made any sense. I didn't know what I was doing in this hospital except that I was hurting every time I tried to move.

By evening Martin showed up, which brought everything into focus. At the sight of him I became nauseated and the vomiting started all over again. After several days of this, the nurses were saying how they'd never seen anyone react so violently to the ether. No one suspected, least of all me, that the cause was my husband—not the ether.

The baby had to have blood transfusions and other special care because of my R. H. blood factor, and had to be kept in the incubator. Everybody felt sorry for me not being able to hold my baby—little did they know how glad I was that I didn't have to. I wanted nothing to do with this baby that was part of Martin and had been forced on me.

Martin picked me up in a borrowed car the day I was discharged. He yelled at me all the way home about the trouble I was causing him; couldn't I do anything right? Wasn't it enough that this whole hospital stay was going to cost a bundle, but who knew how long the baby would have to stay in the hospital. Did I think he was made of money? "You foreigners have only one thing in mind, come here to our country and bleed us Americans of every dollar we have," were his closing words.

Strangely, none of this phased me. All I wanted was my own bed and to be left alone. At home Oma had prepared a nice lunch for me, made up my bed with clean sheets, and placed a vase of flowers on the nightstand—the first and only flowers I received. Martin had to leave immediately to return the car to it's owner and grumbled about having to take the streetcar back home, saying "At the rate you're spending my money, I'll never be able to buy my own car."

"So what was your excuse for not having your own car before you met me?" I shot back. We glared at each other—then he was gone.

Oma soothed me by telling me that new fathers acted that way sometimes, not to mind him. For a moment I wanted to pour my heart out to her about the way I felt about this baby, but the moment of intimacy was broken by the telephone ringing, so I kept my dark secret buried inside.

I continued in my depression day after day, when finally after two weeks our baby was released from the hospital. I dreaded the thought of actually holding this strange baby, but there was no way out—the nurse handed her to me—I was on my own. My whole body trembled as I held this little bundle of responsibility I was not ready for.

Again Oma had prepared a nice welcome for us and I was thankful that Oma and I were alone on this occasion. Once I unwrapped the baby and looked at her tiny fingers and toes and looked into her wide open eyes, I felt a wave of pity for this tiny human being; what was in store for her? Would her life hold as many fears as mine had? She started to cry; instinctively I picked her up and as I held her tight to my body, she stopped crying immediately. Slowly I felt my bitterness that I had built up against Martin melt as I looked into Martin's eyes reflected in this miniature face, a replica of my husband's. The love I wanted to give to

Martin that he seemed to reject, I now started to feel for this innocent child, my child. I would see to it that her life was happier than mine had been. I would give her the love that I knew she would need to grow up healthy. The love I so desperately needed, I would now give instead. From that moment, I could hardly put her down. She was my little Charmaine and I would shield her from all of life's hurts, no matter what I would have to do—so, this was love.

* * *

Very soon, Charmaine's resemblance to Martin was very evident, leaving no doubt whose daughter she was. With the new parental responsibilities, I was hoping that Martin would manage our finances better, enabling us to establish our own apartment. Instead, he seemed to spend money even more foolishly than before. He treated himself to massive amounts of ice cream and pop as he sat in front of the T.V. every evening while I tended to Charmaine. She was a very demanding, nervous baby who needed to be held almost constantly. I spent most nights in the rocking chair, trying to keep her quiet so Martin would not be disturbed.

My biggest fear was that Martin would lose his job again, putting my dream of our own apartment farther off into the distant future. During this time I discovered Martin's obsessive tendencies, beside his apparent irresponsibility. I was pushing for savings to establish a proper home for our daughter while he seemed intent on pursuing whatever pleasure he was addicted to at the moment. From the evidence, I found in unexpected places, he indulged his interest in pornography and with his decrease in sexual interest in me and the constant lack of money, I had no choice but to believe him when he made joking remarks about being able to buy better sex than what he could get at home.

One day he announced that I was spending too much time with the baby and started taking me to the movies—every night. This went on for weeks. I started to resist. I was tired of sitting in the dark theaters night after night, wondering about my baby at home. Muttie was only too glad to have Charmaine to herself and urged me to continue to go with Martin saying, "You know how that goes, Aggie; if you don't go with him, he'll take someone else." I felt increasingly anxious about spending the money and leaving my baby every night and devised a plan to change our lifestyle. I found a make-shift apartment, consisting of a very small room, doubling for both living room and kitchen. With steep stairs leading up to a small bedroom, with a toilet under the stairs, no bathtub. The cost was only $25 a month. I reasoned that we spent more than that on the movies, hoping that without the convenience of a built-in babysitter, this apartment would serve two purposes. Martin agreed to it reluctantly, but became very sullen and eventually started going out by himself just as Muttie had predicted.

When month after month we were late with the rent and I never seemed to have enough grocery money to prepare nutritious meals; with a heavy heart I placed Charmaine in Oma's care during the day while I went to work in a factory. The hard assembly line work combined with the hardship carrying Charmaine with diaper bag, etc the 8 blocks from the streetcar to Oma's, then back again, and the car sickness on the way to and from the factory, the long hours and the sleepless nights spent with Charmaine's teething, left me totally exhausted and irritable. Muttie was unhappy that I had insisted on moving out and took advantage of the situation by reminding me frequently of how I had brought this on myself and that I would lose a good husband for sure if I didn't do something about my attitude.

The savings I had pictured that would accummulate from both our paychecks did not materialize either—in fact, we seemed to have even less money than before I worked. Martin borrowed money from Muttie which she would ask for when I got paid, repeatedly requiring my whole paycheck, while he would continue to borrow more.

I got acquainted with one of my neighbors who was working for the phone company. She told me that they were looking for overseas operators who could speak both English and german; the company would train me. Before I knew what was happening, I was hired at a fantastic pay scale in comparison to factory work. And I was able to ride in my friend's car to work. I was ecstatic. Martin was furious.

"What are you trying to do—ruin me entirely by letting everyone see that you can earn more money than me?" he shouted. "Well, I'll show you," he stormed out of the house. His "showing me" consisted of him working overtime, night after night. I was happy to see him taking some responsibility for our support—even if the motive was wrong. I expected his anger to subside when he would find out what the extra money could provide for us, but this was only a fantasy on my part.

During this time Gary was being discharged after serving his tour of duty in the army. While stationed in Germany he married a german girl and they returned with a baby named Heidi. With the companionship of my sister-in-law, Erika, who was an only child and just as happy to gain a friend and sister as I was. I was preplexed, however, to see them rent a beautiful apartment and buy new furniture. She was able to buy fashionable clothes and never seemed to be short of money. I was told that Gary was earning less than Martin and Erika was not working at all. How was that possible? I decided if they could afford to live in a dignified manner, then so should we be able too. Why, even Muttie, on her little income was able to live more affluent than we were, and she had Oma to support.

I took matters into my own hands and used my next paycheck to rent a decent apartment for $50 a month. It was in the basement of a large apartment complex and had plumbing pipes running across the ceiling. We were unable to open the windows because of the dust created by the cars since the small windows were at street level; but it did have a nice bathroom and two bedrooms; and it was right next to a streetcar stop.

When I told Martin about it, a bitter argument followed with him storming out—this time he didn't return during the night like usual. I was too embarrassed to ask Gary to help me move the next day, so I made arrangements with my co-worker friend's husband to help me move in exchange for some sewing I would do for her. Then I painted the whole apartment and placed our few pieces of furniture as attractively as possible. Martin's mother knocked at the door unexpectedly. She said that Martin had called her from Minneapolis to wire him enough money to take the bus back home. "And you better straighten up and not put so much pressure on the poor boy—you know a man can only take so much. Who do you think you are anyway, demanding all these things. If it wasn't for us Americans, you'd still be rotting in some refugee camp and here you are, acting like you are a lady. If you want to keep a good husband, you better start treating him right. I don't know why he wants you anyway." With that she threw her head back and left—never even wanting to see her granddaughter who was toddling around the spacious new apartment, unaware of the strife going on around her.

Exhausted from the moving and anxious about Martin's disappearance, I sat down on the floor, holding my precious baby close to me, permitting the tears to flow that I'd held in check for so long. Charmaine kept wiping at my eyes with her tiny little hands, saying "Mommy cry?" What was I doing wrong—I wasn't asking for anything out of the ordinary and I was willing to work to contribute my share. Why was it that Erika deserved to be treated with so much love and consideration while I was constantly being accused of not being a good wife. I resolved once more that I would have to change, but to what? What was it that men expected, really? Erika seemed to have the anwer—I would learn from her I decided.

The next day Martin was back, all contrite for leaving, but at the same time insisting that I was to blame.

The only way that we could make it, he said, was for me to quit my high falutin' job so he could get his self confidence back and for me to behave like a grateful wife. I felt that I had no choice but to obey his wishes, and also, the prospect of staying home, taking care of my baby was very tempting. He promised to handle the money with more care and pay the rent on time if I would just show confidence in his ability to take care of us by quitting my job. I was full of hope as I finished my two week notice. Martin had never reasoned with me before, only given orders. Maybe he had learned from this experience. I would have to do the same. After all, this was what I wanted too—for me to be home taking care of my baby and husband. I would show him how frugal I would be and show the proper appreciation for his effort. Finally, we would start our life together properly.

* * *

For a few weeks my dream of a more or less normal home life seemed to be coming true. I took pleasure in keeping the house as attractive as possible, sewing slip covers for the second hand furniture we acquired, experimented with new receipes and I took Charmaine to meet with Erika and Heidi at the park in the afternoons. As we watched our toddlers playing, we spent many pleasant hours exchanging ideas and information. Without appearing too obvious, I asked many questions about Erika and Gary's intimate life in an attempt to learn what I was expected to do in order to become a better wife. I worked daily at improving myself, but the harder I tried to be loving and pleasant, the more it seemed that Martin was getting restless with staying home in the evenings and he found different excuses for being gone. I was not satisfied any more with just being left alone. Where in the past I was grateful for not being hurt physically when he wouldn't touch me or even notice me, I now longed to experience some of the love and affection described by Erika in her marriage. Slowly, Martin was sliding back into his old spending habits again and when we got an eviction notice because of failure to pay the rent, I found myself once more looking for work.

Oma had fallen down the steps and was slowly recuperating from a broken hip and therefore unable to babysit as she had done in the past. Also, now that Charmaine was learning to talk, I didn't want her to spend all her time around someone who was unable to speak english. The answer, it seemed, was to an evening shift job so Martin could take care of her after work and she could stay in her own environment and it would also take care of Martin's roaming in the evening where I suspected all his money was going on who knew what.

I was hired at a bakery, operating the bread slicer after business hours. This time I insisted on paying the rent and for the groceries before I turned over to Martin what was left. This created arguments every pay day and I waivered back and forth, giving in to his demands one week only to go back to my original plan when I ran out of food repeatedly. There was constant friction at home but we continued to show a loving united front whenever we were with people, especially my family. Many times Erika held Martin up as an example to Gary, pointing out the flowers and little gifts he was constantly showering me with and flaunting at everyone.

Once I pointed out that I would rather not get the flowers and be allowed to stay home to keep house and be a proper Mother. I yelled "Oh sure, when Erika criticizes her husband, everybody agrees with her; but when I do the same thing, I'm the bitch." The whole thing turned into an argument with everybody leaving upset and I was being blamed. After they left, Martin stormed out as well.

I swung between moods of depression and an enthusiasm for life. I was dreaming of heaven while I felt like I was living in hell. I still had my fantasy about a more refined life style as I remembered from the Riesengeburge and, more and more, as I came in contact with other americans, I detected the same courtesies between family members as I was dreaming about. How could I bring this kind of atmosphere about in my home, I wondered. Charmaine was growing fast. I wanted to give her the kind of secure, loving homelife she deserved, but I couldn't do it alone. I tried to talk to Martin about my dreams and wishes, only to be told all would be well if only I would learn to be satisfied with the way things were.

I hated to go to work in the evenings. Charmaine started a habit of crying and clinging to me when I left. Was he mistreating her in any way? I felt more uneasy every time I left her, but I had no choice but to continue on, with no solid evidence of anything being wrong. I hated the job; the place seemed somewhat eery at night with only the bakers being in the backroom and everything dark around me. One night I saw something shadowy run across the floor in front of me—I knew immediately that it was a rat. I ran in the back and told the baker. He said that was impossible—they kept a clean place here and nobody else had seen one before. Oh well, maybe my imagination was getting the better of me. I went back to my machine when only minutes later, this rat ran right over my foot. I ran out of the bakery, intending to never go back. On the way home I was shaking all over and imagined people jumping out of the bushes at me. I became scared on the street car which was usually uncomfortable at this time of night anyway. It seemed that the only people riding it were derelicts. Going through the long, dark tunnels I felt I was suffocating. I was gasping for breath when I finally arrived at my stop. I ran all the way home, wanting to be in familiar surroundings. I found Charmaine asleep with no one else there. So this was what was going on when I wasn't around. About a half hour before my usual arrival time, Martin walked in—surprised to see me there. The stress of the evening had robbed me of all self control, and I lit into him without any restraint. "You rotten, no-good S.O.B.— I'm out working myself to death, trying to keep a roof over our head, expecting Charmy to be well cared for by her father, when all along you've been out every night doing who knows what, leaving our baby alone. No wonder she's been crying when I leave every night. You're even worse scum than I thought. Right now I hate you so much I could kill you." My voice rose to a high pitch as I continued screaming, "I hate you; I just hate you."

He stopped my tirade by using his fist to punch me in the stomach. As I sagged to the floor in pain, I hissed at him, "Get out and don't ever come back." He did. Leaving me there on the floor, bewildered and hurting.

I heard Charmaine crying. Of course we had awakened her. How long had my poor baby been crying out of fear of her own parents. I rushed to pick her up, trying to calm her down, feeling like the lowest worm on the face of the earth. I was still rocking her long after she was asleep, wanting to keep her from all harm; to protect her from this strange, hysterical woman I had become.

Slowly, what I had done, began to sink in. I had abandoned my job, sent away my husband, and terrorized my innocent child. I loathed myself and fear began to set in—how would I survive? Would he come back? Even a bad husband was better than to have the parenting responsibility all alone. Even a sporatic paycheck was better than none; and what would Muttie and Gary say if I had to face them with the fact that Martin was gone for good? I held Charmaine in my arms in total terror until morning—somehow God would have to take care of this problem; it was too big for me. God,—oh that's right—I. had rejected

God, I could no longer count on His help. I would do nothing. Everything would work out by itself. Martin was probably at work right now and would come home in the evening, pretending that nothing had happened the same way he did when he had a temper tantrum. I moved through the next day, doing my usual things, preparing an especially nice dinner and waited for Martin to come home. I watched the door until the dinner was cold and soggy, but nobody walked through the door.

As the days went by with no word from Martin, the realizesation dawned on me that not only was I alone with a two-year old, but I had no job, the rent was due, and worst of all, there was Muttie to be reckoned with. In my mind, I could already hear all the "I told you so's." How could I possibly face her with yet another failure.

Muttie surprised me with her reaction to my news. She was comforting and sympathized with me on my dilemma. It occurred to me how understanding and supportive she was every time I failed at something. Did she want me to fail? She took over completely, telling me not to worry about a thing; Charmaine and I would move back with her, adding: "You should have never moved out in the first place, but I knew there was no use in trying to change your mind, stubborn as you are."

I wanted to lash out at her with words like, "Why do you consider me stubborn to want to establish my own family home, when that is considered the proper thing to do for everyone else?" But I held my tongue; I needed her to help me, just like she had predicted. I suggested we sell some of my furniture to prevent her apartment from being so over-crowded when she responded with "Well, sooner or later, you know Martin is going to come back; he loves you in spite of your willful nature just like I do; just give him some time."

I took a deep breath as I was about to make a decision that would affect my whole life and I knew Muttie's reaction when I disagreed with her. "Muttie, I don't want Martin to come back; your opinion of him is based on a part he plays for you. When we are alone, he's different. I don't want to live like that anymore."

Muttie said, "Aggie, you see, there you go again, showing your ingratitude and selfishness. Of course, he hasn't been treating you as good as you'd like, but you're making it awfully hard for him to do better with all the financial demands he's told me that you make on him. If it isn't one thing, its another that you want and denying him his rights as a husband at night—how long do you expect him to put up with such childish behavior. Oh yes, he's told me all about it, the poor boy needs somebody to confide in; you sure haven't made it easy for him. I know, because I've been your Mother now for almost 22 years and it hasn't been easy loving a child as willful and selfish as you have been. But its time to grow up now and count your blessings like the fact that you have a loving Mother, willing to take care of you until Martin comes back."

At the small belt and buckle company where Muttie was presently working, they needed desperately an experienced sewing machine operator, where I found myself at work the very next day, leaving Charmaine in Oma's care once more. Every day I hoped I wouldn't hear from Martin. I just knew I would be able to survive better on my own—just being able to sleep soundly every night had a reviving effect on me.

Charmaine started asking for her daddy which tore at the very depth of my soul, but Muttie kept reassuring her that he would be back soon. The more time went by without a word from him, the more hopeful I became at the possibility of his absence becoming permanent. Then one day there was a letter in the mail from Martin. He was in California, staying with one of his brothers who had moved there a year earlier. He enclosed a phone number, asking me to call him collect. The phone call was kept short. He had a good paying job. It was absolutely beautiful in Hollywood. If I wanted to join him there, he would rent an apartment for us. Muttie was urging me to convince Martin to come back instead, when just about then Gary and Erika came in with their news: Gary had some months earlier applied for a job in the electronics field at one of the big aircraft companies in California. They had accepted his resume and were even paying to move him with his family to the Los Angeles area in California. Muttie was jubilant. "How the Lord answers prayers in mysterious ways," she sang as she made all the plans.

Within two weeks, all my possessions were sold. The proceeds were used to buy an airline ticket to California. With my last paycheck, I treated myself to a complete new outfit, for Charmaine as well. We were not going to land at the L.A. airport, the land of beautiful people, looking like street urchins.

Martin waited for us at the airport, looking sharp in the new clothes he'd bought on credit. He led us to a nice looking used car he had purchased on credit also, explaining to me that he was earning enough here in California to support us in style. We carried our sleeping baby into a beautiful new furnished apartment in Hollywood. The only time I'd seen anything as fancy as this apartment was in the movies. For the first time since we were married, he tried making love without using force or inflicting pain—unsuccessfully—blaming me for his failure. I promised to learn and do better. I was willing to do absolutely anything to have a happier life with Martin than we had had so far.

After he left for work in the morning, I began to feel very uneasy about this costly apartment, a closet full of new clothes, a car—how could he be earning this kind of money? I was anxious for Muttie, Oma and Gary with his family to arrive to relieve this panicky feeling of isolation from my family I was experiencing—chiding myself silently for being disloyal to my husband, even if it was only in my mind. Wasn't I supposed to feel secure with him? Why was I feeling so discontented and unsettled?

* * *

Martin's addictive personality became evident also in the handling of credit. Once he was accepted for credit by financing the car, it became a challenge for him to apply for every credit card available—and he used them with total abandon. If I raised any objections, his response was "I'm spending it all on things for you and Charmaine; you aren't happy one way or the other. In Cleveland you were constantly hounding me to get us better housing, better furniture, better this and better that; now that I'm giving you the best, you're complaining." As the months wore on, his whole paycheck was going on time payments with nothing left over for food and we were sliding behind in the rent again. I knew I had to do something but I was afraid of rocking the boat since Martin was treating me better and seemed happy most of the time.

Muttie and Oma had found a very nice apartment in a suburb of Los Angeles with Gary and his family living not far from them. I asked Erica to secretly look around for a nice reasonably priced place we could rent in their area. When we had located a very neglected but darling old house that was surrounded by a new housing development, I used the excuse that I would be happier living closer to my family to convince Martin to move. Since he was unable to pay the rent at our new highrise anyway, it didn't take much to persuade him.

I was so engrossed in my domesticity that it took some time for me to notice Martin's strange behavior. Many evenings he claimed to be working overtime, but there didn't seem to be any more money coming. When I questioned him about it, his answers didn't ring true. The pornographic magazines I still found scattered occasionally seemed to be concentrating on his new fascination with homosexuality. His favorite recreation on Saturday evenings was to leave Charmaine with Muttie and take me to Hollywood, to walk on Hollywood Boulevard to pick out the "queers." When I felt ill at ease and preferred to get together with friends and family, he went by himself, returning home later and later.

While browsing through a bookstore, I'd come across a sex manual. I decided it was time to learn from experts what I was expected to do as a good wife; maybe then I would be able to keep my husband at home. I was so happy with our living conditions now that I was anxious to please Martin in every way. The book said a wife was to take an active part in lovemaking and at times even initiate it.

On one of Charmaine's frequent weekend visits to Muttie's, I planned a romantic evening. With a candle-lit dinner waiting, I met Martin at the door, wearing a revealing negligee. I was surprised to see Martin walking up the driveway. To my question, "What happened to the car?", he stormed at me: "The car was repossessed, that's what happened to it; and what's all this? Candles, a new outfit, expensive food: No wonder there is never enough money the way you insist on wasting it." Somehow I managed to get him in a better mood after dinner, and I hesitatingly followed the book's advice. There was a short period of time when he showed some tenderness and I started silently to congratulate myself for having found the secret to a better married life, when suddenly he pushed me away. "You slut, I knew it all along—you're nothing but a german Schickse—this kind of sex I can get in Hollywood—they get paid for it so I expect them to throw themselves at me; but you—you're supposed to be a good girl—married girls aren't supposed to know how to do these things. It's your job to be available when your husband wants you, that's all. Where did you learn about this stuff anyway? What are you doing while I'm out slaving my fingers to the bone to pay for fancy night-gowns. Married women don't wear that kind of stuff—women—I hate you all anyway—now a guy knows what to do—you just disgust me." He grabbed a blanket and went to sleep on the couch.

I lay awake the rest of the night, thinking about some of the things he'd said. Was he homosexual? Was he having an affair with someone? Man or woman? The thought nauseated me. Toward morning I had finally cried myself to sleep when he woke me up, telling me to hurry with breakfast or we would be late for church since we would have to take the bus. In church he had responsibilities up front while I sat in a daze, wondering how he could pray in front of God and people so sincerely after last night. Was he crazy, or was I crazy? All these people sitting around me—did they live the same way we did in private? Was Muttie and Martin right about me—did I expect too much? Would everything be better if I just learned to accept things the way they were? I found myself asking God for help silently, then reminding myself that I no longer believed in all this "fairy tale" religion. But then, who would I turn to? Was I doomed to feel so alone and rejected the rest of my life?

* * *

It was 1957, the time when it seemed like everybody was relocating to California, including Martin's sister, Jane, her husband Jerry, their two children, Erving and Louise, and Martin's mother. On their motor trip through Texas, Jerry was hospitalized with a heart attack, so Jane stayed with her husband and sent the children with Mom to us by plane. Not only did that put a tremendous burden on our too-small grocery budget and make our little "two-bedroom, one bath" house terribly crowded, but I was promptly replaced as the "lady of the house" by my Mother-in-law. First she scrubbed down the whole house and instructed me to keep it that way "now that you have learned how it's done." Next was the laundry—according to her the only way to wash clothes was with her brand of detergent, and whoever heard of washing whites without the use of bluing. Again, after my initial instruction, I was expected to follow orders. There was no end to the sympathy Martin received for having to live with a foreigner.

I quietly did what I was told to do, reminding myself that this situation would end as soon as Jerry would be able to travel, which shouldn't be much longer since he was improving rapidly. When they arrived, I waited daily for them to make some plans to find a place of their own, only to discover that they seemed to think our arrangement could continue indefinitely, with me acting as maid, cook and baby-sitter. Their favorite pastime seemed to be ridiculing my housekeeping, cooking and foreign accent. Since there wasn't a private corner anywhere, and we had no car to go off in by ourselves, it seemed impossible to talk to Martin about my unhappiness. When my little three-year old started to make "put down" remarks about me, I knew something had to be done.

Gary was in the process of buying a new car. I swallowed my pride and asked him to sell us his old one without a down payment and low monthly installments. After throwing a tantrum about how he didn't need his in-law's castoffs, Martin accepted the proposal, mostly out of necessity.

The following Sunday I arranged a picnic just for the three of us with the intention of resolving our strange living arrangement. I had all the good intentions of talking about our problem like two civilized adults, but of course it ended up with another screaming match—Martin accusing me of not trying hard enough to become americanized so his family would like me better, and me retaliating by yelling, "If you would learn to handle our finances properly so we could live like Americans, maybe it would be easier for me to fit the role." Nothing was accomplished and we drove "home" in bitter silence.

The next day I started making plans to establish myself in another apartment with or without Martin, announcing to him that I refused to live in a flophouse. He didn't take me seriously, commenting amongst laughter, "so now you're picking up slang when you can't even talk english." I knew that I would have to tell Muttie of my intentions since she would find out anyway in case Martin refused to move with me. Muttie was in full agreement, saying, "Yes, Aggie, you and Charmaine can't go on living like this; this is worse than the camps." She helped me rent a very small, inexpensive apartment near a shopping center where I found work as a sales clerk in a yardage store. I took only the pieces of furniture I absolutely needed and set about making a pleasant, peaceful home for me and my daughter; it turned out Martin stayed in the house with his family. Muttie and Oma were babysitting Charmaine and Muttie helped out financially when I ran short. During the lonely hours when Charmaine was asleep, I reflected on my life so far. I was only 22 years old and living alone with a child—what was I? A widow—no, I was not even a divorcee. The thought of divorce had never even crossed my mind. All I wanted was to live peacefully and I had that—or did I—was that really all I wanted? No, I wanted a loving husband by my side. I wanted to build a life for our future like Gary and Erika were doing. They were in the process of buying a new house on the G.I.Bill and happily expecting their second baby. Gary was attending college two evenings a week to be promoted to a higher-paying position to support his growing family—that was the life I yearned for; but happiness came to me in another form —totally unexpected.

* * *

Muttie persuaded Gary, Erica, me and the children to come in for some "Kaffee and Kuchen" after a Sunday afternoon excursion to

Gary's new house that was nearing completion. I hid my feelings of envy toward my brother and his family for all the apparent success they were enjoying, and joined in the happy family atmosphere as we walked toward Muttie's apartment, when Oma met us on the front porch waving "Die Mennonietische Rundschau," (a monthly German publication she had been subscribing to ever since we settled in the U.S.A.). She was breathless as she tried to point out a little marked ad in the classified section. We knew it had to be something important for Oma to get that excited. Eagerly we all crowded around the little newspaper as Muttie read out loud: "Julius is looking for his family, wife Anna, children Gerhard and Agathe, possibly Anna's Mother Agathe. Anyone knowing of their whereabouts, contact (name at a Canadian address). In shocked silence we all sat down on the front porch steps, unable to speak. Slowly the news started to sink in as the tears of joy flowed. We embraced each other. Gary was the first one to regain his composure. What are we doing here, standing on the front porch crying. Papa is in Canada, looking for us. Let's not lose another minute. Gary obtained the people's phone number from the assistance operator, and with trembling hands, dialed the number that might well produce the voice of our father, the most important person in our family whom we had believed to be dead. For thirteen years we had wondered and worried about him and here was the evidence that he had done the same about us.

After a short discussion, Gary slowly put the receiver back in its cradle. "These people in Canada have a relative in Siberia who knows Papa—we can write letters to Canada and they will forward them for us since no mail from the U.S.A. is allowed into Russia yet." As Gary spoke these disappointing words, hope welled up in our hearts that we would not leave one stone unturned to help Papa enter the U.S.A. The first step was to write that initial contact letter. It would take seven months for us to receive a reply; seven months of hoping and praying; yes praying. I immediately felt deeply ashamed for not showing more faith in the Lord's leadings; clearly He was answering my prayers from long ago, only in His own time. Slowly as I relied on God's care more, and with the hope of Papa's return in my heart, the depression about my own situation lifted somewhat, making daily life more bearable.

Martin started to come and visit Charmaine more frequently. It turned out that once more he'd lost his job. He wanted to come back to us. By making me feel responsible and guilty for his job loss, he opened the door. After all, he couldn't be expected to be able to concentrate on his work with his wife and daughter separated from him. I had little desire to reconcile since my life with Charmaine was more rewarding the last few months than it had been before. His next step was to convince Muttie of his good intentions. Like always, it didn't take much persuasion with her. I tried to hold my position when Muttie once more brought out the heavy artillary by reminding me how much financial aid she was providing me with and that I couldn't expect that forever. Besides, we all needed to save every penny to try to help Papa come home.

I now relied on the Lord and prayed fervently for a raise so I could support myself and my child without any help; but the answer once more came in a different form. Would my life ever settle down to a predictable routine. I felt like I couldn't stand another day on this emotional roller coaster ride.

* * *

It was Thanksgiving day, 1958. The plan was to have dinner at Gary and Erica's new home. We felt that we had much to be thankful for. Very early in the morning Erica went into labor and had to be taken to the hospital. On the way they dropped off little Heidi and the Thanksgiving turkey at Mutties. Just as we sat down to our Thanksgiving feast after taking an abundance of photos which Muttie insisted on at every family gathering,Gary burst in the door shouting, "It's a boy, its a boy; look at these big footprints." Everybody hugged and congratulated Gary. The family joy was complete with a boy to carry on the name.

After dinner, Gary wanted us all to go see the baby at the hospital, but I declined with some poor excuse for needing to go home early. Muttie detected my mood change and demanded an explanation.

"What's the matter with you, Aggie? Hanging a long face when this is such a happy occasion for us all?"

"Nothing's the matter, Muttie, I'm not hanging a long face."

"Don't call me a liar—it's obvious something's bothering you. Gary, isn't she hanging a long face?—out with it, Aggie, what's your problem?"

Gary wanted to keep the occasion argument-free: "Leave her alone, Muttie, after all, a person can't be happy all the time."

"Well sure, not all the time, but at least on special occasions like this."

I started making preparations for leaving when Muttie held me by the arm demanding "You're not leaving till you tell me what's wrong. You'll have me worried all night."

"All right, all right," I yelled; "It's impossible to have any privacy in this family. What kind of mood do you expect me to be in, watching my brother live in the lap of luxury, having a son after a daughter—perfect family, perfect life, and I'm having a hard time making it from one day to the next."

Gary and Muttie both started talking at once, their voices mingling with criticism. "Aggie, how do you expect to live any different. You don't know what you want. Martin is anxious to come back to you but you refuse. Then you're unhappy because you don't have anybody to take care of you. You can't have it all, you know."

"That's right," I shot back, "I'm selfish, stubborn, stupid and demanding; and it would be so nice for you if you just wouldn't have to claim me as daughter or sister," I added sarcastically. "Well, you won't have to worry about that any more—I'll see to it that you won't have to be bothered with me from now on."

Knowing this was totally irrational but enjoying the feeling of power I held temporarily, watching the fear of what I might do form on Mutties face. I started for the door. Oma handed me a bag of food with a warm hug and told me she would pray for me and not to worry; "Jesus loves you just the way you are, honey."

Charmaine and I slowly turned the corner to our shabby little duplex at the end of our twenty-minute walk home to find Martin sitting in the car, waiting for us. How much more was I to endure this Thanksgiving Day. I chose my words carefully as we started talking. I couldn't handle making one more person angry at me. It was all I could do to handle my own self pity at the moment. Slowly and tenderly Martin wrapped his arms around me, murmuring softly, "Yes, honey, it was a painful Thanksgiving Day for me too. Let's not go an like this. Please. I have some good news. If only you'll listen to me, we can make a great new start. I found a new job at almost double the pay and as much overtime as I want. I found out that even though I have "psychiatric problems" discharge from the army, I still qualify for a G.I. Loan to buy a house. There is a new tract in LaPuente (a L.A.suburb) that requires only $100 down for a G.I. You can quit your job here and fix up a brand new house just the way you like it. Nobody else's dirt to clean up first like you've always had to do previously. I promise I'm a different man. This separation has taught me a lot and I've really grown up. If you'll just give me another chance, I'll prove it to you, please."

Charmaine was jumping up and down, begging, "Please, Mommy, say yes—I want to live in a nice house with Daddy. Please say Yes." My head was spinning. I had "a heart of stone" Muttie had said once, maybe it was true; maybe I was just creating my own unhappiness. I deserved better myself and this kind of life wasn't fair to Martin either.

He looked so sad and at the same time so hopeful at me. All our happiness, it seemed, depended on me. Suddenly a flash of insight hit me—maybe this was an answer to my prayer for a raise—different than I'd expected, but doesn't God answer prayers in mysterious ways? And didn't I end my prayer with "Thy will be done?" As if Martin could read my mind, he continued his pleas with, "We'll be able to go to church together again like a real family—you won't be sorry, I swear."

I could hold back the tears no longer—tears of sadness for the past mingled with tears of hope and gladness for the future. As I fell asleep next to my husband that night, I had proof for myself and Muttie that I was capable of forgiving.

* * *

Friday morning I woke up late with the bright California sunshine forcing it's way into my bedroom window. The house was quiet— where was Martin? Charmy should be up making noise. After the long hours of laying awake, thinking about everything that had happened the day before, I must have fallen asleep toward morning. Now I would be late for work.

As I walked through the apartment looking for my family or clues to their whereabouts, a cold fear gripped me—could this all have been a sham? Had he kidnapped my daughter? I heard the motor of Martin's car stop in front of our door. He came dancing into the house carrying Charmaine on his shoulders, giving me a big bear hug along with orders to get all dressed up. "I'm taking my queen and princess out for breakfast, he said, and then we'll go pick out our new home."

I objected, "But Martin, I have to go to work; in fact, if I don't hurry, I'll be late."

"Everything is taken care of, my love," he sang. "I called the store and told them the only job you would ever have in the future would be to take care of your family. From now on I will make the decisions and be the kind of husband you deserve. Now, go get ready, I'm starving."

I floated on air the rest of the day as we toured some low-priced model homes which looked like mansions to me. After we picked out "our" house, we drove to Muttie's to tell her all our good news. I expected her to be overjoyed after the way she had lately criticized me for not wanting to reconcile with Martin, but instead, her only response was directed at me: "So, after all the help you have accepted from me, you couldn't even ask me first?" And to Martin: "You really want me to believe that this time you're going to live up to your word?"

I started to spout off to Muttie about how she left me totally confused, that I had thought my decision would please her, but Martin broke in and humored her out of her mood and we left—me being so proud of my husband for handling what could have been another family fight, and euphoric about our new home and the apparent change in Martin.

Since the holidays were approaching, the days of anticipation for our February move-in date just flew by. Everyone in our family seemed to be blessed in so many ways. My brother with his family were enjoying their new home along with their darling little son, Ritchie. All of us had received our first letter from Papa, with a photograph to prove his identity. We were sad to hear about his hardships in the Siberian war prison, but so hopeful that soon we would be able to bring him home. But on top of the happiness list was my name. Not only had I been given another chance at my marriage, but a new home besides. Martin continued to treat me with love and affection; not only to me, but he seemed to genuinly enjoy our little daughter, bragging to everyone who would listen about her accomplishments. Our home was filled with laughter and merriment. Once the Christmas holidays were behind us, we could focus all our attention on our almost-finished home, when one morning I woke up with a queezy feeling in my stomach. When this pattern continued, I was anxiously watching the calendar and then finally went to see a doctor to confirm or deny my suspicions. Since Martin and I had reconciled, everything was going along so harmoniously that I didn't have the heart to bring up the subject of birth control—so the possibility existed even though the doctor had reassured us at Charmaine's birth that she would in all probability be our only child. With a sigh of relief, I received the test results— negative—a few days before our move-in date. This was not the time to rock the boat with another baby. Martin was treating me just the way I had always imagined it should be and I wanted to keep it that way.

I was living in paradise; planting flowers, fixing the house into a home, getting acquainted with some of my new neighbors, enjoying being a homemaker. Martin complimented me frequently on all my efforts and worked overtime to provide us with some of the "extras" to make life enjoyable. My "morning sickness" continued to create some anxiety for me but I always reminded myself of the negative test results.

One weekend Muttie was visiting, staying overnight. Martin was taking Charmaine on some kind of church outing while the plan was for Muttie and me to enjoy a day of experimenting with my new sewing machine. Muttie observed my flu symptoms Sunday morning, and in her forthright manner said, "Aggie, you're pregnant; how far along are you?" I confided my suspicions plus the negative test results to her. Tests were not to be trusted, she stated firmly. There was no doubt as to my condition. The question was, what was I going to do about it? That question had not even occurred to me if indeed I was pregnant— what could I possibly do about it.

When we drove her home that evening, she took me into her bedroom and produced some pills. "Here, Aggie, these are quinine pills. They are strong and will produce a miscarriage if you do it early enough. I know, because it happened all the time in Russia when we had malaria attacks." I couldn't believe what I was hearing, objecting hysterically to her suggestion when she shook me firmly by my shoulders, saying, "Look, Aggie, you've finally figured out how to treat Martin to produce some responsible behavior from him, don't ruin it all by having another baby. You know by now that he's immature to some extent and can't possibly handle the responsibility, not to mention what the poor child might inherit. You were lucky with Charmaine, don't push your luck."

I pushed her away from me, crying: "Besides, I'm not pregnant anyway, what do you know about modern tests; you always think you know everything—you can't even talk english properly but you know better than a doctor with a medical degree."

She put the pills in my purse and with a sad look told me, "You will see that I'm right and if you're smart, you'll take the pills; it will just bring on your period. If you're so sure that you're not pregnant, then what are you so worried about? When will you ever learn to trust me?"

I stormed out of her house.

Martin didn't pay any attention to our quarrel coming from the bedroom since he was getting used to seeing me leave Muttie's place in tears. All the way home I was painfully aware of the fluttery feeling in my stomach, and the fact that I had missed my second period, not counting the little spotting episode during our move. Muttie's words about having nothing to worry about if I was so sure of the accuracy of the test rang in my ears. All night I wrestled with my problem until I decided to go back to the doctor who administered the test again to make sure, then I would decide.

After the examination, the doctor said there was no need for a test. He confirmed the pregnancy. I had no choice but to tell Martin. It occurred to me that maybe Martin would be happy about my news, after all—he seemed to love having Charmaine—that was it—I pictured the whole scene like out of a movie: He would throw me up in the air with shouts of delight, telling me how much he loved me, showering me with kisses.

After dinner, when the bedtime story was read to Charmaine and the last kisses dispensed, I walked into the living room where Martin was watching T.V. and reading the newspaper simultaneously. With a prayer in my heart I approached him. "Honey, I've got some wonderful news to share with you." He looked up from the paper. "I went to the doctor today," I continued.

"Are you sick?" was his question.

"No," I answered. "We're going to have another baby."

He looked at me with an icey stare. "That's impossible, you know what the doctor said; besides, we've been using birth control."

Fear gripped me. This was not according to the script. I tried again, "Honey, we didn't for a while before we moved. The doctor said it's for sure." Tears were starting to flow. "Please, honey, be happy about it. We are going to have another baby."

"No," he spoke through clenched teeth. "Maybe your going to have another baby, it certainly isn't mine. So that's what you were doing while we were separated. I was knocking myself out trying to convince you of my love while you were out getting yourself knocked up. I should have known. You're nothing but a german schikse." With that he slammed out of the house, returning a short while later as if nothing had happened, saying "You're not getting rid of me that easy this time."

When I tried to open the subject again a few days later wanting his advice on how to pay for the doctor, etc., his answer was: "the subject is closed. If you want to have that baby, it's your problem." From that I gathered he had talked to Muttie and knew about the pills. I held the pills in my hand, it would be so easy to take them. How could God hold me responsible for it. He hadn't done His job very well to protect me from this dilemna. I had to make a decision soon. Slowly I flushed the pills down the toilet, one at a time. Sadly I thought about what lay ahead. Maybe Martin just needed more time to absorb this new, after all he'd come around after we had Charmaine. That's probably what would happen again. Once he'd see this new baby, his attitude would change; but I would once more have to face seven more months of pregnancy without his love and support when I was just coming to the point of expecting to be treated affectionately. Why did it need to end when I needed it the most?

* * *

Martin continued to treat my pregnancy as if he had nothing to do with it, answering to my suggestion that we find a doctor to deliver our baby for a fee we could afford, that it was my problem and not to bother him with it.

Muttie had just recently accepted a job as nurse aid in the out-patient clinic at a large teaching hospital in Los Angeles and moved into a small apartment in walking distance. Through her I learned that one could obtain medical care at the clinic at a very reasonable rate. I dreaded having to sit the better part of the day in a large waiting room, then to be examined by a whole group of student doctors with the chief doctor making explanations and giving instructions. I considered the whole process very degrading, but since we didn't have maternity coverage on our health insurance, I had no other choice. It became clear to me that this would indeed be my baby—even Muttie refused to get enthusiastic about it.

I started to take in sewing to pay for the clinic visits and to have some of the remnants to make maternity clothes for myself.

For some reason, maybe because of the very fact that everyone seemed to think I had committed a crime by choosing life for this baby instead of abortion, my love for this tiny living human being grew deeper than any emotion I had ever experienced and I vowed to be a good mother to both my children. I would raise them properly, give them a good education with good earning potential so they would never have to sit in a clinic like beggars.

When my delivery date drew near, I pleaded with Martin to buy a washing machine, explaining that the money we spent at the laundromat would easily make the payments, ending by saying, "and with all the diapers and baby clothes I will soon have to wash, we won't be able to save all the laundry for Sunday—the only day you are home with the car to take us."

His cold reply was, "You wanted the kid, you figure out what to do with the damn diapers." He slammed the door behind him as he stormed out and didn't return until after work the next day, leaving me to think all night about our marriage—our whole lifestyle. Surely this wasn't normal.

The next day, after my clinic appointment, I took the bus to Sears, picked out the lowest price washer and signed the contract for payments I knew I could make out of the laundromat money, explaining to Martin that "After all, you said for me to figure out what to do, and I did." The washer had been delivered so there was nothing more said about it; besides, it was the day before school started, a busy day getting Charmaine all prepared and early to bed, only to get her up a couple of hours later to drop her off at Muttie's on our way to the hospital.

The doctors had prepared me for possible complications during the delivery since I had developed toxemia during the month before, but everything went smooth and my second daughter fulfilled my hopes for another little girl. She was perfect in every way and absolutely beautiful. Her big sister never forgave her for ruining her first day of school, but Dorothy Ann was too little to be aware of her crime.

I couldn't wait to take her home. I wanted to hold her every minute of her life, protect her from all harm at all times. I was so totally wrapped up in motherhood this time, I refused to see the changes taking place in Martin. The fact that he didn't come to see me at the hospital or even be available to pick us up on my discharge day, didn't worry me too much. I was sure once I was home with the baby he would fall in love with her as much as I had. I called a neighbor and arranged for her to give me transportation home in exchange for some sewing she wanted me to do. By not looking at the ominous signs around me, I had convinced myself that my world was perfect: as I laid my new baby in a second-hand bassinet that I had lined with pink ruffles—with my five-year-old eagerly asking to hold her new sister. When the baby wrapped her tiny fingers around Charmaine's hand, Charmy laughed with delight, "What a little corker" she said. The name stuck and Dorothy was known as little Corky from that moment on. The three of us spent the rest of the day enjoying the event. Martin returned home from work late, took one look at me holding our precious baby and said, "This is the last night of overtime work. If you think I'm gonna bust my butt working to support a lazy wife and her kid, you're crazy."

* * *

Not only did Martin stop working overtime, but he frequently missed regular work due to staying out to watch what I presumed were "adult" movies till 2 or 3 a.m. and then calling in to work sick. I had gotten acquainted with some of the young nurses who worked with Muttie who kept me sewing steady for them, but that little income was like a drop in the bucket when I applied it to the past-due utility and house payments.

I began seriously thinking about looking for a job once more, only to run into a dead end every time. The new housing development we had bought into, had no bus connection and no industry nearby. The nagging thought I had periodically that I should learn how to drive kept getting more insistent. I remembered my one attempt at driving when we still lived in Cleveland and all the verbal abuse inflicted by Martin.

Just before our discovery about our second baby, Martin had bought a different car with an automatic transmission. I had observed him when he was driving and convinced myself that driving might be something I could learn if I didn't have the clutch to contend with. Before I could gather enough courage to approach Martin about the possibility, something happened to force me into it.

One afternoon Martin's foreman called to inform me that he had found Martin unconscious in the men's room with his wrists cut. I was so shocked I didn't even think to ask him what hospital he'd been taken to. Here I was with two small children, a husband hospitalized, a car in the garage, and I had to beg neighbors for a ride to anywhere. I knew I had to make some decisions before I would be completely buried in bills.

After spending the night sobbing in my pillow at the thought of leaving my precious babies with strangers while I would go out to work, I set out on my mission the next morning. With Charmy in Kindergarten, as soon as Corky was asleep for her morning nap, I took the car keys with trembling hands and opened the garage door. I sat behind the steering wheel of our car, and without thinking about what I was doing, I found myself praying "Dear God, I don't know if I even have the right to talk to you; in fact, I don't even know if I believe in You, but I have no one else to turn to. I can't allow myself to be killed on the road, my children need me. I have to do this. There is no other way for me to support us except to learn to drive. Please keep me safe."

I felt a strange calm come over me as I inserted the key. The motor started. I could feel the power I held in my hands. A flood of tears I could not control forced their way out from under my eyelids. My whole body started to shake. Raw fear, like what I had experienced during the war, gripped me. "I can't do this," I shouted. "Please, God, don't make me do this, You have other ways—work a miracle—find me a job close by, but don't make me go out on the street with this powerful machine, please, please, please." Slowly my body stopped shaking and I realized that no miracle was about to happen. The car motor was running and I better start my first driving lesson while Corky was still sleeping. I backed in and out of the driveway the first couple of days, then ventured out into the culdesac after which time I asked a neighbor to take me for my driving test. I had no time to lose. I'd heard from Muttie that the hospital laundry was hiring and I needed that job—for that I had to be able to drive.

I flunked the driving test the first time, but after knowing what to expect, I passed it two weeks later. My next door neighbor was eager to take care of my girls since that provided her with a little spending money and with a heavy heart I left my three-month old baby that I had made such lofty promises to at her birth, in Elaine's care as I drove out of my drivway, scared to death, knowing I would have to drive in L.A. traffic when my only driving experience so far was three weeks of driving in my low traffic neighborhood sidestreets.

When I finally arrived at Muttie's station, the nurse quckly produced the smelling salts to keep me from fainting. Someone gave me some grape juice and slowly I stopped trembling. At the laundry the supervisor told me that the position I was applying for was filled, but then she added: "You're too smart a girl to be working in the laundry anyway, you go up to the medical records and ask for Mrs. Gibson. I will call and tell her you're coming." Obediently I did as I was told. Mrs. Gibson subjected me to two hours of testing, then told me she could put me to work in the chart room, but it would have to be the 3 p.m. to 1 a.m. shift, would that fit in with what I had in mind? I was suddenly on a cloud—would that fit in? It would be perfect, especially after Martin would be home from the hospital; at least the children would be able to go to sleep in their own beds and I could be home in the morning to see Charmy off to school. "Thank you, Lord," I prayed silently, and "Thank you, Mrs. Gibson, I'm very grateful." I shook her hand, reported back to Muttie, and faced my driving ordeal on the return trip. For a six weeks training period I was to work regular daytime hours. My hopes that Martin would be released by then were realized when the psychiatrist called me to his office to discuss Martin's discharge plans.

* * *

I was sitting in the doctor's office. listening to a long list of do's and don'ts I was to follow in cooperating with the treatment prescribed for Martin. He handed me a prescription and an appointment slip. Martin was to see him once a week as an outpatient.

On the way home the doctor's words echoed in my mind. "This man cannot handle any pressure, being so deep in debt on top of his problems with homosexual tendencies—was too much for him and insisting on having another baby just pushed him over the edge." Evidently the information the doctor received from Martin was that tha baby was planned—and who put us in debt anyway—all of a sudden I saw myself the way the doctor's discription was of me—as a selfish, hard-driving woman, making too many demands on her poor husband. As if Martin could read my thoughts, he started to explain that we would have to sell the house and the washing machine so he wouldn't have the pressure of time payments because we would now have the added expense of the hospital bill which wasn't covered by our health insurance plus the weekly visits to the psychiatrist. To my questions as to how he planned we would live rent-free and where the money for the laundromat would come from, he had no answers. I added, "What about the car payments ?" Then added very softly "I guess if we're going to move back to L.A., you can take the bus to work."

"No, I need the car." It was a firm and final statement I recognized as not to be argued with. I didn't know where his pay was going—it seemed that all the bills were left for me to pay out of my earnings. I assumed that most of it was going to pay off the hospital and psychiatrist. Martin was not doing as well as expected, I was told, and had to increase his appointments to three times a week. We were so far behind in house payments that fore-closure was inevitable and with the stress of one car for two jobs, I was looking for an apartment close by the hospital. Feeling relief to be free of the obligation of the house. And I hoped to take advantage of Oma's babysitting service once more.

In an attempt to shield Martin from the stress of house hunting, etc., I took off one day to seriously find us shelter. By doing it during my normal working hours, I reasoned, I would not have to bother Martin about it until I had found something suitable. I got lucky. The first place on my list was only a twenty-minute walk from the hospital, and although it was only a very, very small one-bedroom, it was a single house. I hated the thought of being confined in an apartment after experiencing the freedom of our own back yard. This place had a fenced in back yard and most important, the rent was very reasonable.

After obtaining Muttie's approval in order to borrow the deposit, I was anxious to surprise Martin with the news and my early return home. As I turned the corner of our street, I noticed several cars parked in front of our house and in the driveway, blocking the garage door I parked on the street and walked into the kitchen door. To my horror the house was dark and filled with cigarette smoke. I heard sounds coming from the living room. I stood there unnoticed by Martin and his "guests" for some time, unable to take in the reality of what I saw. Martin was showing pornographic films. The reality of where he'd been spending all his evenings before I had started working began to sink in—now that he was housebound he'd just moved the whole scene to our home. I couldn't believe it. How sick: The whole business nauseated me. I turned the lights on and through clenched teeth told everybody they had three minutes to clear out—including Martin. I took the children to Oma's the next day and tearfully told Muttie what had happened. She agreed that it was impossible to leave the children in his care, so they would just have to sleep at her house and we would enroll Charmy in school near her since we'd be moving the following week anyway.

That evening a humble Martin was at the door, begging me to go see his psychiatrist before I made any decisions to shut him out of my life. I didn't see any harm in fulfilling his request. In the doctor's office, I was once more convinced of my guilt in this whole matter. I was told that this was part of his illness and by making him feel dirty about his sexual activities, his recovery would only take that much longer. He was working hard at his problem and needed the freedom to recover in his own time. "After all," the doctor finished, "he didn't leave you when you were trying to work through your problem on this second baby—that's what marriage is all about, to support one another through the hard times."

I walked out of his office with mixed emotions—sympathy for Martin, loathing myself for driving him to such misery, but also anger. What exactly was Martin telling this doctor. My problem about my baby, indeed: So, I reasoned, what would I accomplish by being stubborn. I would just have to make sure that he kept his sick behavior away from home and the children. Besides, I didn't have enough energy to fight it any more. Corkey seemed to be getting one ear infection after another. I wasn't getting enough sleep, and the sewing I was still taking in on top of my regular job was all taking it's toll on my health. All this talk about poor Martin not being able to handle all the pressure—well, what about me; nobody seemed to care about the stress I was under. I was beginning to suffer from severe mood swings. One minute I would be angry and determined to improve my situation against all odds, only to wind up feeling guilty (about what, I didn't know myself), ending up depressed, not caring what happened. I knew I couldn't go on like that but I had no idea as to how to make a change. So, in a fog, we moved out of our lovely home into this old dilapidated shack, so small one could hardly turn around without bumping into something. I kept my job but the house was just too small to continue sewing for others. I was thankful to have Muttie and Oma so close for the children's sake, hoping that my depression would not cause them too much damage.

* * *

With Muttie and Oma living so nearby, dropping in frequently and unexpectedly, I felt it was safe enough to leave the children in Martin's care in the evenings until I could get a day shift. I spent my mornings at Mutties, in her large sewing room, able to continue my custom sewing for extra income. While Corky napped afternoons, I did all my house work, then left for my hospital job. I was drifting deeper into my depression, feeling exhausted all the time, and I suffered from mountains of guilt. When I was sewing at Muttie's, I felt guilty about leaving my housework undone; when I was at work, I worried about the girls' welfare. Muttie recited in detail every day Corky's bratty behavior, showing favoritism to Charmaine, while Martin ignored Corky most of the time while interacting happily with Charmaine. To compensate, I overprotected Corky. I could see what was happening but felt helpless to do anything to change the situation. I forced myself to be cheerful around the girls, but was short tempered with Muttie who never missed a chance to point out my short-comings but who was also there for me to help any time I needed her.

I was completely at a loss as to what to do about Martin. At times he seemed to be trying to contribute to our happiness, but just about the time I would start to enjoy the atmosphere, he'd go into one of his dark moods and we'd be back to square one with me wondering what I had done to upset him.

Slowly I developed a friendship with one of my co-workers with whom I was able to make a shift change and also able to rent the house she was vacating in Maywood when their new house was completed. Financially, things seemed to be improving since Martin for some unknown reason was allowing me to do all the budgeting and turning most of his paychecks over to me. I was a little puzzled at this new change, especially since he seemed to always have money anyway. I had learned not to ask questions that might upset him for fear of him doing something crazy again and winding up in the hospital, leaving me with little income and added expenses. Consequently, where the money came from, remained a mystery to me.

We moved into this spacious old house with a beautiful big sun porch that I was able to convert to a lovely sewing room with a private entrance for my clients. A retired couple lived next door who were only too eager to take care of Corky while I worked. The only problem was the long bus ride to work but at least I was able to entertain our families and friends again, not having to be embarrassed about our living conditions.

Charmaine did excellent in her new school and Martin seemed happy enough; in fact, one day he announced that he was cured and would not have to continue seeing the psychiatrist any more. It seemed a little strange that he should be cured so suddenly but it far was it from me to question it as long as he seemed to be so much better. I wasn't going to rock the boat, especially since Corky's infections didn't get any better. The doctor said she had been on such high doses of antibiotics for so long for treatment of her constant ear infections, that she had built up some sort of immunity to them. She had to be hospitalized with pneumonia. Martin and I decided together that since we didn't have the psychiatrist to pay for any more and he was getting some overtime again, I could probably earn enough with my sewing to quit my hospital job in order to stay home with Corky since the doctor was reluctant to release her without the proper home care. I felt quite confident as I walked into my supervisor's office to give my notice. This time things would work out—I just knew it. I had endured everything I needed to and now I felt I would reap my rewards. At last we would have the kind of life I'd dreamed about and wanted to offer my children.

* * *

The summer of 1961 was wonderful. My sewing business was thriving while at the same time I was home with my girls. Corky wasn't recuperating as fast as I had expected but I was confident that under my consistent care she would soon regain her health. Charmaine had completed first grade amidst praises from the teacher of being her star pupil. Tests were administered proving her high I.Q. and the principal suggested we move her up one grade since she had been doing third grade level work.

The girls and I enjoyed our time together in the lovely house we were living in with the pleasant shady yard surrounded by roses and bouginvillias. We sang songs and I listened to Charmy reading stories to Corky to the tune of the whirr of my sewing machine. Even the children's squabbles were a pleasure since I considered it a privilege to be there to settle them instead of relying on a baby sitter.

Martin wasn't home much since he had taken on a second job in the evenings because he wanted to learn about some new machinery, he explained. I was thrilled to see him finally take on some responsibility and never questioned him about the late hours. When he was home, he was full of good humor, often showering us with gifts and surprises of trips to a nearby ice cream parlor. I was a little curious about the extra money he always seemed to have, but was afraid that by mentioning my concerns, I would spoil the happy atmosphere. Besides, Muttie, Gary and I had been pretty much pre-occupied with our free time the past few years, working on various steps to bring Papa home from Siberia. It was a slow and costly process. Each form we returned as requested, translated in Russian, backed up with documents and containing the right amount of money, was responded to with demands of more paper work, and always more money. Finally the whole procedure had advanced enough that we were instructed to send the required air fare. We were jubilent: When the plane arrived, we were prepared to show Papa a life in this great country he couldn't even have dreamed about. We searched every face debarking the plane but no one resembling Papa was on the plan nor was he on the airline schedule. "We should have known better than to trust the Communists," Oma said. Yet we knew of several people who had returned from Siberia to be re-united with their families in Canada—including two of my cousins.

We wrote letters to Papa and to the Russian government demanding an explanation. We received a letter from Papa's cousin who was living near him, via some friends in Canada, pleading with us to drop the matter, for we were only hurting him by our attempt to stay in contact with him. After having my hopes raised so high, I mourned his loss even more this time than when we were first separated because in my heart I knew I would never see him again. But even more than that, I grieved for him the loss of his family, plus the terrible life he must be subjected to in Siberia. Every day I wondered if he was cold or hungry; every night I wondered if he had a bed to sleep in. And every night I missed him.

After two years of wondering about him and hurting for him, we received another letter from his cousin. This time with a photo. It showed my father in a casket, only a few words accompanied the picture. "Julius died of forced starvation, you will see him again when Jesus comes," it read. I had a hard time to believe in a Jesus at all, let alone in a second coming of this King Jesus. What had my father ever done to deserve this kind of life, along with millions of others. How could a God of love who had the power to put a stop to it, let this kind of cruelty of man to man continue? That night, after the girls were asleep, I took the picture out of my purse and looked at it a long time—finally, the long held-in tears could not be con-trolled any longer. I had to admit—I was glad Papa was finally resting forever; and now that I knew with a certainy that he was not suffering any more, I was able to let go of my own suffering. There was a strange peace in knowing that there was no more future to fear for Papa or hope of being re-united with him. I had a strange longing to join him, but that was not my fate; I still had my life to live and my children to raise. I had mourned for my father long enough—he was gone forever.

* * *

If Martin seemed pre-occupied, I didn't have the time or energy to let it concern me for Corky's health was deteriorating. She was hospitalized on several occasions. This unexplained infection was spreading; she was now having serious kidney problems. Martin was receiving strange phone calls with his response being, "I can't talk now," and similar answers when I came within hearing distance. Who was he talking to? When I questioned him he told me I had enough to worry about Corky, he didn't want to bother me with little annoyances and besides, he would have it straightened out soon. What needed to be straightened out, I wondered; but he was right about the worry over Corky's health being enough for me. Yet, when I tried to seek comfort from him, he made it clear that Corky was my worry not to concern him with it.

I spent most of my time at the hospital or doctor's offices, coming home exhausted. Usually Martin was still at work. I had lost track of his schedule long ago. Sometimes he would be home unexpectedly early, often he was on the phone, only to slam down the receiver when I entered the room. Many times when I would answer the phone, the caller would hang up. For a while I suspected that Martin was having an affair, mostly because he was making no sexual demands on me. But then, I heard bits and pieces of phone conversations about "paying up or else," so I knew money was involved. Was he gambling? Did I have a new problem to worry about? Was he earning all this extra money or where was it coming from?

I had just brought Corky home from the hospital again, they had managed to get her temperature down to a managable degree. I looked down at my sleeping cherub—she was so tiny; at almost two years old, she weighted only 16 pounds. Her fair skin was almost transparent with blond curls framing her little face, long lashed eyelids covering the most beautiful dark blue eyes—the one thing Martin had endowed both girls with.

I must have been standing there for a long time because I felt Charmy pressing against me—looking up at me with questioning eyes, "Mommy, do you love Corky so much because she is sick all the time?" came the hesitant question. I realized I had neglected Charmaine—I offered to have her sleep with me "until Daddy comes home from work" to show her how special she was in her own way. After reading a while, we both drifted off to sleep together. I heard the phone ringing for a long time before I wakened enough to answer it. "Mrs.____, this is Sergeant ____ I am calling to tell you that we have your husband in custody here at precinct station # __. He is being held on seven counts of ___." I hung up, went back to bed and immediately went back to sleep. Slowly I re-awakened—what had I heard on the phone? Was I dreaming? Charmaine was still sleeping next to me, what time was it anyway? I looked at the clock—4:00 a.m. I was wide awake now, something was dreadfully wrong. I decided to call the police station to verify the phone call I thought I had received earlier, but while I was struggling into my robe, I heard Corky stirring. I knew I would have to make her needs a priority. When I was finally able to reach the police station, I was given the same information as before. I had not had a nightmare: I sat on the couch in the living room in a daze as the phone started ringing. It seemed Martin had been arrested along with two of his brothers and one brother-in-law for extortion, operating a prostitution house and impersonating a police officer. They had been arrested under gunfire in a parking lot—now his family expected me to go down town with them to secure a loan from the bail bondsman to free them on bail. I could not believe our phone conversations—they were talking about things I had never even heard about, now I was personally involved in these things. This didn't happen to real people like me—my head was spinning. I had a hard time distinguishing between the real and imaginary. I had to talk to someone I could trust.

Somehow Martin's sister seemed to be concerned only about how fast we could get the "boys" out of jail—not about the seriousness of their crime. She was still talking, urging me to hurry and make arrangements for a babysitter so she could pick me up—I stopped her in mid-sentence with a few words: "Jane, you go get them out if you want to, I couldn't care less if he rots in jail. I don't ever want to see Martin or any of you again." I hung up and dialed my brother's number, knowing he and his family had just returned from a two-week vacation and he still had a few days before returning to work. Before I could approach him with my problem, he enthusiastically told me that they had already received their slides from their vacation and would like to come over that evening to show them to us at our house. He ended by saying he would pick Muttie up on the way. Erica came on the line and we calmly discussed the food we would serve like any two housewives living normal lives. I hung up and started to make preparations for the coming party, thinking how crazy this whole thing was. I drifted in and out of reality as I went through the day, taking care of my duties. Why hadn't I told Gary? Muttie called during the day, why didn't I say anything to her? Was I just as crazy as Martin? I would talk to them tonight I resolved; then, as I rehearsed my speech, I realized how bizzarre this all sounded. Again I decided I was just making this all up in my head. I was just over-tired from all the waking nights with Corky and long hours of sewing. That was it—I was hallucinating.

I called Martin's place of employment. I would hear his voice and know that everything was o.k. I dialed the number and identified myself to the supervisor. His voice startled me. "Aggie, where have you been? Don't you know what happened last night? Didn't you read the papers?" Oh my God, I thought—I'm not crazy, this is real. The papers—how terrible! I would not be able to cover up for him this time.

In the afternoon Gary and Muttie came in. "Aggie, why didn't you tell us when you called? What is the matter with you? How long have you known about this? How could you let something like this happen to blacken the family's name? For a while I humbly listened to them as if I had been the one committing the crime until something inside me snapped and I started screaming at them, especially at Muttie, accusing her of pushing me into this crazy marriage in the first place. I became completely hysterical and out of control, leaving Muttie in tears as well.

Gary finally saw the futility of the situation and took control, saying: "O.K., whatever the reason, it is done; now let's see what the first thing is that we have to do." Together we made plans for the next few days until Gary could go and talk to Martin to make some sense out of all of this. I was glad when they finally left. Then I had to face the silence that followed. I now had the task of explaining not only Martin's actions, but my behavior to Charmaine. How do you explain to a seven-year old that her father is in jail and her mother is losing control. My heart was breaking as I looked into her innocent but very troubled blue eyes, shining with unshed tears. How could I re-assure her that everything would be alright when I had difficulty believing it myself.

When the night was turning into dawn without any sleep to relieve me of all the thoughts circling in my mind, I suddenly thought of Germany. How different my life would have been. In Germany crazy people were locked up. I would not have fallen into this kind of trap. I longed for the security of a solid home life. Papa was dead. I could not retreat into my fantasy of him coming home to rescue me any more. I thought of Adolf. I could feel his warm embrace the evening we parted for the last time. I thought about my dream of a happy home for the future. With this new development, that dream was also dead. How could a family with a criminal at the head of it ever re-gain respectability? I thought of my two innocent children. How could Charmaine escape this past and ever have a secure future; of Corky, so sick—maybe it would be a blessing for her not to live to face whatever lay ahead. My life had never been this black before. I decided if it wasn't for the girls, I didn't want to live; but I had a responsibility to them. I was 26 years old and felt like a shriveled up old woman. How could I will myself to live?

* * *

When Charmaine's teacher called to tell me that Charmaine was being taunted by some of her classmates who'd heard their parents discuss the arrest of her daddy, I was glad for my decision a month earlier not to enroll her in the third grade as was suggested. She would have enough to handle emotionally. I knew then that I would have to start making preparations to move far enough away where the children's father's reputation would be unknown. I also had to think seriously about finding a job with medical insurance. Who knew how long Martin would be in jail. And after that—that was too long into the future to even think about. I had to provide myself with means for survival now.

It had been a long day at the hospital. Corky's condition worsened. I was told she needed an operation which would be serious since the operation was to be done in spite of the present infection and high temp; but to wait any long would mean almost certain death.

I had signed the consent papers, then made arrangements for Charmaine and me to stay at Muttie's a few days until Corky would hopefully be out of danger. Charmaine needed a break from school anyway to learn to cope with everything that was happening. After a few anxiety-filled days of waiting for Corky's fever to go down after the kidney operation, we all breathed a sigh of relief when she woke up asking for a drink. The infection was subsiding. The surgery a success. Now, all we needed to do was to nurse her back to health and get her to gain some weight. She was too weak even to hold a toy. Charmaine and I returned home exhausted. Charmy was eager to get back to school. She was a real little trooper. I was so proud of her. With her determination she would be able to face anything, I reasoned, praying she would not have to. Somehow I decided I had suffered enough already for the three of us, maybe my girls would be spared.

As soon as we walked into the back door, I could feel someone's presence. I switched on the light—there sat Martin in the dark, waiting for me. He ordered Charmaine to go to bed because he needed to talk to me. After tucking her in, she asked me with a trembling voice, "Are you going to be all right, Mommie?" My heart ached for my little girl who was expected to behave like an adult in the midst of all the chaos. How could I reassure her—a warm hug would just have to do. Silently I vowed, "I'll make it up to you."

Now I faced Martin. "What are you doing here, and how did you get out of jail? The nerve you have, coming back here…"

He cut me of. "I just want to explain—just hear me out this once, then you can throw me out if you want to."

"O.K." I snapped at him. "You have a half hour to explain if that will make you feel better; but then I never want to see you again." As he talked, I couldn't help but feel sorry for him, too. All his previous bravado was gone; he was totally deflated. What was driving this man to self-destruction, I wondered. I was too tired to follow everything; my mind was on Corky and Charmy. What right did Martin have to destroy our lives as well as his. He was droning on and on about how he'd become addicted to prostitute sex. To begin with, he got involved only for the money. "You know," he continued, "how you always wanted nice things. Well, that was one way to get fast money. After a while, it wasn't just the money, I was hooked."

Here was the answer. Again it was my fault! I had driven him to it. I had a hard time accepting this, but I was too tired to fight it out at the moment. He ended his confession with "If you'll please let me stay here, I'll sleep on the couch. It will sure look better for me at the trial if I'm still with my family—even if its just co-habitation. My boss didn't fire me, I'll continue to turn over my whole check and you can at least stay home with Corky till she recovers. Please, for all our sakes; especially the kids, consider what I'm asking; let me sleep on the couch tonight while you think about it."

We stood up—I felt whoozy; I knew I would have to get some sleep soon or I would get sick too. He started to reach for me. "Don't touch me," I hissed between clenched teeth. "We'll talk more in the morning." I went to the bedroom and blocked the door.

* * *

My dread of finding Martin in the living room, probably waiting for breakfast, turned to relief when I spotted a note on the table in the empty room. It read: "My dearest Aggie, Thank you for your kindness in allowing me to stay. Have gone to work. Will meet you at Muttie's this evening and we'll talk over our problems, asking for her help in trying to solve them. We both know what a sincere Christian she is, and how much she loves us—Forever yours, Martin."

I don't know how long I sat there sobbing into the crumpled note when I felt Charmy shake me. "Mommy, are you crying because Daddy is gone again? Maybe if you talk to him real nice, he'll come back," she pleaded. "No, darling, Daddy is at work. We'll have dinner with him at Muttie's house tonight. Please don't worry, everything will be all right," I reassured her as I looked at the clock to see how soon she would leave for school. I felt the need for privacy—to be alone with my grief, my anger, my hurt—mostly my self pity. I knew I would have to make some heavy decisions for all our sakes. My mind raced in circles all day, condemning myself one minute, justifying myself the next; hating Martin and pitying him at the same time.

I was finally able to draw some comfort from the knowledge that Corky was making steady progress after holding her at the hospital in the afternoon. She would make it but what kind of life would I be able to offer both my girls? That question haunted me continuously.

Gary answered the door at Muttie's, explaining "Muttie called and asked us to come over to help you decide what to do." Muttie finished with "You know, Aggie, your brother should be the one making the final decision since he will be the one to have to help support you if you wind up alone, not to mention the $400 loan he co-signed for when Martin needed money the last time." The lump in my throat slid down into my stomach and formed a big rock—this was going to be a long evening, I could tell.

Martin arrived and Muttie announced cheerfully, "First we will have a nice meal during which time our problem won't be mentioned. Then we will have our discussion." When Muttie gave instructions, nobody argued with her.

After dinner Oma offered to do the dishes while the children went off to play outside. Here it comes, I thought, the same old subject. "What to do with poor, incompetent Aggie." All the pros and cons were being considered with Martin doing a good selling job in a very humble way. I knew how it was going to turn out. I also knew that no matter what I might say, it would not carry any weight. Somebody was saying, "What's the matter with you, Aggie. Why don't you say something. Don't you care what happens to you or the girls?"

"What difference does it make how I feel," I said sarcastically. "I could tell you all that I hate Martin and what he's done to us, and you would still want me to stay with him just because you're afraid that I couldn't support myself and the girls and poor Gary would have to act like a brother for a change and help me. Oh, we can't have that! By all means, let's sell Aggie down the river, but even that's not enough—I have to tell you that I'm happy about it! Yes, and not only that, but in the end I'm to blame for Martin's behavior."

Muttie gasped, "Aggie, stop it. We all know that you're over-tired from Corky's hospital ordeal, but if you weren't so preoccupied with that one member of your family, you might see your neglect to the others; how can you be so unforgiving?"

"Yes, Mommy, we learned in Sabbath School that you have to forgive if you want to go to heaven," I heard from the doorway—my poor little Charmaine—how long had she been standing there? How much had she heard? "Yes, darling, I forgive Daddy so we can all go to heaven," I answered as I picked up my purse, ending the evening with "Don't worry, I won't be a burden to anybody, let's go home, Martin!"

Martin scooped up Charmaine and winked at Muttie as we left. When we closed the door of Charmaine's bedroom, I told Martin, "There is one thing you didn't confess to my family—that is about your sexual involvement with the prostitutes. I saved you the embarrassment and kept quiet about it, but if you think you're going to sleep in my bed, I've got news for you—we can live under the same roof if that's what you want so bad, but I'll never be your wife again. You can make me feel guilty about expecting you to support us, but you'll never convince me that you had the prostitutes for any other reason than pleasure. You make me sick."

The next day when I returned from the hospital, a beautifully wrapped gift box lay on my bed—the card read: "I know how much I hurt you by telling you of my unfaithfulness, but I also know that you are a good Christian and can forgive. I will give you the time you need to get over your hurt. When you are ready to put the past behind us, please wear this and I will know that we can start over once more as a real husband and wife—white stands for purity." Inside the box I found a beautiful white lace nightgown. I thought about the absurdity—when he was the one who had repeatedly broken his marriage vows, but I was supposed to wear the white for purity—well, he would have to wait till a cold day in hell for me to wear this.

* * *

Thanksgiving was approaching but time progressed slowly since it was difficult to get into the holiday spirit with this cloud of Martin's arrest hanging over us. No matter how hard I tried to pretend it never happened, I was reminded of it constantly. He had to go to appear in court frequently—first for the arraignment, then for the trial with other hearings inbetween. Before and after each hearing he'd sit for hours on the phone discussing what happened and what his and his brother's chances were of getting out of a prison sentence. My main concern was to shield Charmaine from all of this as much as possible. Much of my time was spent taking the children out or at least into their bedroom to read stories to prevent them from hearing about their father's crime. I did have one bright spot in my life. Corky was recovering satisfactorily and her good health reflected in her sunny personality; at least she was too little to know about the revolting things going on around her.

Charmaine seemed to be handling it well, but oh, how it pained me to have her subjected to this kind of experience involving her father. It was obvious also how my brother and his family felt about this blot on the family, for, where in previous years we always assembled together for Thanksgiving dinner, we were not asked this year. We spent the Thanksgiving holiday alone.

By this time I was getting very concerned about Christmas as well. With the high payments to the bail bondsman, we had little left of Martin's paycheck. I had not had a single customer for dressmaking since the story about Martin's arrest appeared in the paper. How could I deprive my girls of Christmas presents on top of our unstable daily life. This was of little concern to Martin since he was more worried about his trial date approaching fast.

The second week in December he went to trial, insisting for me to be there because it would look better for him. I don't know where I got the courage from, but I firmly refused, saying I did not want to be in any way connected with him. I busied myself all day with Christmas activities in order to forget about the reality of the day. I didn't need to ask about the outcome of the trial when Martin arrived home—it was written on his face—he had been found guilty of three counts of the seven charges. "What happens next?" was all I asked. Martin replied that the sentencing date was set for the first week in January. "So let's enjoy the holidays together, it may be the last one we have together for a long time," he continued. Somehow we made it through Christmas, but once I had accomplished the task of creating a holiday atmosphere for the girls, I could hold back the depression no longer. New Year's Eve, as I listened to guns going off in the distance at midnight, I contemplated what 1962 held for us. Martin was still sleeping on the couch. Well, I thought, that's the way I wanted it, wasn't it? No, my mind answered. What I want is to lay here in my husband's arms, making tender love, talking about a promising future, not about a possible prison term. And what about me and the girls—what will happen to us if he really does go to prison? Could I possibly support the three of us indefinitely? The sound of guns reminded me of the war. Would my war ever end?

Thankfully I sent Charmaine off to school a couple of days later; at least I would have some privacy to talk to Muttie on the phone or have a good cry if I needed to. I was looking forward to the sentencing day— at least the decision would be made, however the judge and jury ruled; and I would be able to go on with my life. Somehow, once I came to this conclusion, I was able to calmly drift off to sleep. I was awakened by Martin entering my bedroom. "Night after night I've asked you to wear the white nightgown to show me that you were ready to make a new start, but you had no intention of wearing it. I should have never allowed you to shut me out of our bedroom; you only think of yourself, you bitch."

"By telling me to come to you when I was ready and then pressuring me every day to do my duty, you're only showing your true motives and that is to get what you want regardless of my feelings; you told me that you would be satisfied just to live here—even if it meant sleeping on the couch forever. Well, it might just turn out that way. There is a limit to my patience. I don't think I will ever be able to forgive you for what you've done, not only to me, but to our children. And I never promised to wear that white nightgown—that was your fantasy not mine. I haven't done anything to be ashamed of to have to wear white to show my "new purity." I've kept myself pure all along except for what's rubbed off from you. Now get out of my bedroom," I hissed.

"I'll get out all right," he snapped. "After I prove to you that I'm still your husband." There was no time to escape his attack—I scratched, kicked and bit, but I was no match for his masculine strength. After hours of me crying quietly while he slept, a repeat performance took place at dawn, "to last you for a long time in case I go to jail today," he whispered. "In case you get any ideas while I'm gone, you just remember this night—that you will be my wife for the rest of your life."

All day those words echoed in my mind. "The rest of your life, the rest of your life." Was I really doomed to live like this the rest of my life? Then I didn't want to live any longer, my mind answered. I watched Corky playing on the floor beside me. "I have to live for her." Slowly a new thought formed—it wasn't me that shouldn't live—it was Martin. He should be dead. I fantasized about all the different ways he could die, followed by all the different ways I would like to kill him. In my mind's eye, I took pleasure in watching him die in different ways, begging me to save him, to rescue him, with me laughing at him. I felt a rage inside that was frightening.

The ringing of the phone summoned me back to reality. It was Jane. "Martin got five years—you should be proud of yourself—not even being there on the worst day of his life. But then, come to think of it, the worst day of his life was probably when he met you. Well, I hope you're happy now—you've finally ruined him completely."

179

* * *

I was watching the men load the discarded Christmas trees into the garbage truck in the California downpour of rain, feeling totally overwhelmed with what lay ahead of me. With Martin in prison, how would I be able to manage with two small children? Slowly the realization sank in that I did not have to worry any more about Martin walking in the door, making demands or bringing unsettling news. I would not have to worry about any more tortures like the night before; I should have divorced him a long time ago, I thought to myself. The very word sent shivers down my spine. Divorce was for riff-raff, not respectable people. Respectable, ha. Who was I kidding? With a husband in jail. Well, the law had done for me what I had not been able to do for myself. I was now truly alone. I would be able to sleep peacefully if nothing else—sleep. I remembered again the night before and suddenly a new fear struck me—what if I were to find out that last night's attack resulted in pregnancy. I could not let that happen. I made a firm and immediate resolution not even to find out. I went straight to the phone and dialed the clinic's number and requested to be scheduled for the D.& C. (dilation and curettage) the doctor had been urging me to have to correct some female problems I'd been having since Corky's birth. Muttie could not understand why I chose this particular time to add more complications to my already unstable situation, but was cooperative in watching the children for me, agreeing with me that I would need my health to be able to handle a new job along with the total responsibility for my family.

While I was in the hospital, Mrs. Gibson, my old supervisor, came to see me, asking what my plans were for the future. My indecisive response motivated her to give me some motherly advice. "Aggie," she said, "you can't consider taking Martin back when he is released. You are a very refined lady if you'd give yourself half a chance. If you stay with this man, he will drag you down so far you will never be able to live with yourself. And what will happen to the girls when they get older? You can't expose them to the kind of life Martin has to offer them. Honey, you are a very loving and trusting girl. The problem is, you've put your trust in the wrong person, now is your chance to divorce Martin while he is in jail. He can't frighten you out of it. Then you can make a fresh start. You deserve better than this."

I had a lot of confidence in Mrs. Gibson, not only was she a good supervisor, but she seemed to be a genuine Christian. I felt I could trust her advice. She left, urging me to come see her when I was ready to go to work. Now I felt I had an anchor—somewhere to start.

After a few days of recuperating, I sat in Mrs. Gibson's office, hoping to get my old job back. After some discussion, she again offered some sound advice: "Aggie, you need to get away from here where everybody is aware of what Martin did; if not for your sake, then for the girls. They shouldn't have to live with this stigma. Make a new start in a place where you will have the benefit of being accepted on your own merit." To my question as to where I would go, she seemed to have a solution also. She was well acquainted with the staff at a large hospital in a small community located approximately 200 miles from L.A. She would call ahead to the Medical Records Department and recommend me highly if that's what I decided to do. Hope surged through my veins, even as she spoke. A fresh start as she suggested was exactly what I needed. A small town would be perfect for the children to grow up in, far enough from Muttie so I could function without her constant criticism, yet close enough to stay in touch and rely on her if I needed her.

"Please call your friend, Mrs. Gibson," I pleaded. I'll be there tomorrow to apply for a job and thank you for your advice." We shook hands as I prepared to leave. Then she gave me a warm embrace with a "Good Luck, Aggie."

* * *

My knees were shaking, my knuckles white from holding onto the steering wheel, showing the anxiety I felt inside. My kind retired neighbors had offered to watch my girls at my home to save them from further trauma while I set out for the two hundred mile trip to hopefully my new life.

I purposely didn't want Muttie to know about my plans for fear that she would either talk me out of it, or that I would look foolish if I failed to secure a job. I felt euphoria alternated with terror at what I was about to do. This was the first time in my entire life that I'd attempted something significant without my mother's counsel, or following Martin's orders. I did not have to worry about Martin—he would not be able to interfere with whatever I was doing for five years. By that time I hoped I would have divorced him and have him out of my life forever.

As these thoughts floated through my mind while I was driving, I realized that my mind was made up about divorcing Martin. How long had this decision been in my subconscious? A great sadness swept over me for my precious little girls. They would have to grow up without a father but then, how much of a father would they have in a man with a prison record; indeed, how much fathering had they received so far. Yes, I was making the right moves. I felt confident as I drove into the hospital parking lot. But my insecurity surfaced again when the office supervisor told me she had absolutely nothing open at the moment. She must have noticed my dissappointment for she added, "If you're willing to do anything to start with, I could find out if a position is available in Housekeeping or the Nursing Service." I held my breath as she dialed—then informed me that the Nursing Supervisor would like to see me. I was hired to be trained as Nurses Aide. I was so eager to be on my own in this peaceful-looking community nestled at the San Bernardino foothills, that I happily accepted the offer and asked only when she wanted me to report for work. I would worry about how to make ends meet later; at least I had a start.

It wasn't until I started the car that all this was sinking in. I was to start working next Monday—today was Wednesday. In a few days time I was going to have to find a babysitter for Corky. Well, I took a deep breath and decided to start by setting my priorities—first things first. I had to find a place to live, That, I found out was not very easy since there were few rentals available due to the high demands by so many medical students. I spent the rest of the afternoon exhausting every possibility without any results. Would I have to turn down this job opportunity for the lack of housing? I had to find something in walking distance to the hospital since I knew I would not be able to keep the car.

In desperation I looked up the phone number of the local minister only to be told that he was in church for prayer meeting. An old familiar but long suppressed feeling stirred in my heart. Did I really want to continue to be angry at God? I struggled with my desire to give in to relying on God's guidance the way I had been taught and the fear of being disappointed again.

I walked into prayer meeting late. We formed little prayer circles—I was determined not to release the tears that were collecting under my eyelids as the silence was surrounding us after everyone had prayed and was waiting for me to end the prayer session. Finally, the words slipped out in a whisper, "Lord, if you want me to settle down in this town, help me find an apartment tomorrow."

As we all rose from our knees, a lady came over to me and said, "I have a small house that is locked up, for personal reasons I've decided not to rent it out any more, but if you'd like to look at it, I feel I was led to prayer meeting tonight for this purpose since I normally don't attend; in fact, I'm not even a church member."

On the way to the little house, I told her about my job and children. "It's not a big place—you decide," she said as she unlocked the door and we looked through the rooms with a flashlight. "I'm afraid I can't afford a two-bedroom place for what the going rate is in this area," was all I could tell her. "Would $35 a month be too much?" she asked. I couldn't count out the money fast enough amidst a string of thank you's.

"Don't thank me, I don't know why I'm doing this—thank God." She handed me the keys and we exchanged the necessary information.

The next morning I felt stiff and cold from sleeping in the car. I decided to use the bathroom in my new house to get ready for another busy day. By noon I had the utilities connected and secured an elderly woman next door for babysitting Corky and enrolled Charmaine in school. It was time to go back to make moving arrangements and face Muttie. I bravely faced Muttie with all my news, even before I went home. To everyone of her objections I had a well thought out answer. I could not believe my own ears when she finally backed down and closed her end of the discussion with "Well, if you don't care how much you hurt me by moving so far away, then I guess I can't stop you. But how will you move?" My timid reply: "I thought maybe Gary could rent a trailer to hook up to my car, then drive the car back to L.A. to return it to the dealer since I won't be able to make the payments."

Muttie answered: "So—when you need us you know who your family is. Aggie, Aggie God will have to lead you through more hardships to break you of your selfishness."

I interrupted: "Never mind—I'll find someone else."

Her triumphant reply was: "I guess you'll have to since Gary is in Bermuda for six weeks. You're so preoccupied with your own problems you think of no one else—remember he had to go with his company on some testing project?"

I lost my temper and yelled at her about what kind of a mother she was anyway that she would only take pleasure in pointing out my faults. My last words as I fled out of the door were "I'll do just fine on my own—I was hoping to get your support, but I should have known better."

I sold the piano and T.V. set the next day and with the proceeds hired a man to move my furniture to our new location Sunday. After buying a white uniform required for my new job, I had $20 left for groceries. I felt rich. My two daughters were asleep in the next room and I had a new job to go to the next day. Somewhere from the storehouse of my mind, I recalled some words I had heard or read some-where, "This is the first day of the rest of my life." How true.

* * *

The peaceful routine I had envisioned did not materialize and now that I didn't have Martin to blame for my problems anymore, I heaped guilt on myself mercilessly. When the load got too heavy, I blamed God. After the prayer meeting incident, I wanted so desperately to cling to the trust in God as my Heavenly Father as I'd experienced it that evening, but how could I when He allowed all these unbearable things to happen; not only to me, but to my innocent children. My earthly father certainly would have done a better job of protecting us from harm. I felt so alone and helpless in my decision to rely only on myself.

The first day on the job I fainted. I was still bleeding after the D & C surgery and with all the lifting I'd done while moving, it had turned into hemorrhaging. I was hospitalized until the next evening with blood transfusions, followed up with some injections. Needless to say, the girls were terrified when I didn't return from work as promised. After that, Corky clung to my neck every morning, screaming uncontrollably. It reminded me of my daycare experience in Russia when I was about Corky's age. I felt the pain for the both of us. To my amazement, she kept calling for and asking about the whereabouts of her daddy. I was totally confused as much as he had ignored her, why would she be missing him so much. I was too young and inexperienced to know that children's behaviour does not always follow a logical path.

Contrary to my expectations, Charmaine never even mentioned her father. In fact, she was absolutely the most well behaved model child any mother could expect, shouldering responsibilities way beyond her seven and one-half years of age. Since I had to report for work at 6 a.m., Charmaine had to rise the same time Corky and I did in order to have a hot breakfast and have her long hair braided. After I left to drop Corky off at the babysitter and continue on to the hospital, Charmy was expected to stay in the house alone until it was time for her to leave for school. She stopped off at the hospital on her way to spend ten minutes with me in the lobby during my morning break. On the way home, she waited for me in the lobby to the end of my shift, then we walked home together. We came to look forward to our time together.

The car had been repossessed, so part of Charmaine's job was to help me carry the groceries home. She was a real trooper—never complained and never disobeyed—until we got home with Corky—she tormented Corky endlessly. I was confused by her behaviour; never interpreting her bullying her little sister as a cry for help; the pain she must have endured in keeping all her fears and hurts inside.

My health slowly improved but the children took turns being sick. The year 1962 felt like the coldest winter I had ever experienced in California and it seemed to rain constantly; at times the rain being mixed with snow. Our little house had cement floors with no carpeting. It was hard to keep Corky at three years old off the cold floor. She caught a cold the first week we had relocated and with her lungs still being weak, she came down again with pneumonia. Now leaving her with the babysitter was doubly painful, but almost worse was the fact that Charmaine had the flu and I had to leave her alone to tend to herself all day. To round out my measure of misery, I absolutely hated my job. I hated to touch people in private parts of their bodies; I hated the bedpan routine, the vomiting, and most of all the smell of all the sickness mingled with the smell of ether and other medicines; and it was hard physically. A backache became my constant companion.

Since we had no T.V. or telephone, we were completely isolated from the world beyond our little home and the hospital. Since I had told everybody that I was divorced, I couldn't seem to make friends with young mothers—divorce being quite a stigma in the sixties. The single women had their group of friends among the student nurses. I cried myself to sleep every night. I began to remember only the good times I'd had with Martin—this really scared me. I began to pressure myelf to file for divorce, reasoning that being divorced would make the separation permanent.

I started to take in sewing again to pay for a lawyer. The lawyer suggested I go to the legal aid, explaining the process involved. I spent the money I'd saved for a baby-sitter and bus fare to go to Los Angeles to the Legal Aid. I was told it was against their policy to sue someone who was incarcerated for divorce; I would have to see a private lawyer. I returned home feeling guilty for having spent money that should have gone for necessities on this wild goose chase.

During this time, Gary had returned from Bermuda. He with his family and Muttie came to see us, bringing dinner with them, all set to have a good family visit. Somehow I managed to ruin the day—what was the matter with me—I lamented to myself after they left. Couldn't I keep the love or friendship of anyone. The argument started with

Muttie: "All of you are sick—it's obvious that before long you'll collapse from exhaustion, and now you're talking about a divorce. How are you going to raise two children by yourself—judging by their unhappy faces you're not doing a very good job of it right now."

"Muttie, I'm doing the best I can."

"Yes," she interrupted, "and you could do a lot better if you'd just get your prioities straight—take good care of your poor little children instead of chasing around the country looking for lawyers."

"That's right, and if my wonderful big brother could see it in his heart to lend me the $300 for a private lawyer, I wouldn't have to chase around the countryside looking for charity."

It was Gary's turn to get into the argument. "Aggie, you call it a loan, but what you're actually asking for is a gift. You will never be able to pay me back because it will take you a lifetime just to learn to stand on your own two feet—never mind about the past debts, and may I remind you of the $400 loan I made to Martin. It will sure be a lot easier to collect that from him if he comes back to you at the end of his prison term, than if you divorce him."

* * *

I learned that "aloneness" and "loneliness" are two different things. I felt lonely most the time while being married to Martin. I had gotten accustomed to the feeling of longing for intimacy, for sharing my feelings with someone; that longing was so strong that at times it was physically painful; but it was nothing in comparison to the panic I was experiencing now in the knowledge that I was permanently alone— alone, not only with my feelings but with the reality of living with the total responsibility of the children. I began to worry about my health. What if something were to happen to me, what would become of my girls. The slightest cough or fatigue would cause an anxiety attack with a cold sweat enveloping me, my hands trembling and my heart beating so rapidly, the pounding hurt my ears. Then it would subside suddenly, only to leave me worried about the attacks themselves.

I tried to present an upbeat attitude around the girls and hide my fears on the job, waiting every day for night to come so I could allow the depression I really felt to sweep over me.

With time, the California spring returned with all our health restored as well. We were able to take walks in the evenings and the girls played outside some of the time, giving me some freedom to be alone. I was confused by the need for solitude, only to be antsy when I had some.

Muttie sent us Greyhound tickets to visit with her over the Easter holidays. I was determined to make this a happy visit—unlike the one before; and for once I succeeded. On the bus trip home, I realized how much I missed my family. Actually, I discovered in my mind that what I missed most was some adult companionship. I felt saturated by being needed. Taking care of patients' needs all day, followed by catering to the kids all evening, with not even a T.V. to hear a normal adult voice, I would just have to make another genuine attempt at forming some friendships.

My fellow employees were all friendly and nice to work with, but when I heard them talking about parties, showers, and get-togethers, I was never invited. A divorcee was just too much of a threat.

The conditions were just right for making acquaintance with strangers. Once, eating lunch in the hospital cafeteria, a tall man with a heavy southern accent asked me if he could sit at my table. This was nothing unusual since the cafeteria was always overcrowded at mealtime and sharing tables was the norm. What was unusual was that this stranger insisted on engagining in conversation even though I was trying to read—a habit I'd gotten into to cover up my embarrassment of not having any friends. Before I realized it, my lunch break was over. I hated to leave my table partner and all the rest of my shift I could think of nothing else except how good it felt to have a little male attention. I dreaded going home to the only human companionship being that of two small children, feeling guilty for even thinking such thoughts. What kind of mother was I anyway? Shouldn't my children be sufficient for my happiness?

It was summer by now. School was out and I dreaded coming home to a long list of complaints from the baby sitter about Charmaine's behavior. I could not understand this since she was an angel around me, except for her treatment of Corky. I was trying to think up a solution to this problem as I descended the front steps of the main hospital building, when a man's voice demanded my attention. I looked up and recognized my lunch companion. "I couldn't get you out of my mind all afternoon, may I drive you home?" he asked. I don't remember accepting his offer, but shortly we drove up to my house. He took us all out to dinner that evening. When he returned us home, he did not have to ask for an invitation to come again. The girls were begging him to come back tomorrow. Very politely, his answer was "That's up to your Mommy." Three pair of eyes were pleading with me. After the date was set and the door closed behind him, I noticed how different the girls' behaviour was from the usual—so, they were just as tired of being surrounded only by their mother as I was with them. I convinced myself that the only reason I had consented to a second date (was it a date?) was to please the children, but deep down I knew that I was just counting the hours.

We talked about Jim all evening and the next morning. Just being taken for a ride in the car was such a treat. For a whole week he was our constant companion. Then, just as he had appeared out of nowhere— he was gone. It occured to me what a chance I'd taken. I had no idea where he was from, where he worked, or what he was doing here in this small town. When I subtly inquired about him, I discovered that nobody had ever seen him. The loss I felt, and the disappointment— was nothing in comparison to the hurt the girls experienced. For the first time since we moved away from my family, did Charmaine show any emotion. "You made Jim leave just the way you made Daddy go away, you're just a mean and nasty witch," she sobbed, pushing me away as I was trying to comfort her.

Complete emptiness and misery filled me as I waited for days to see Jim appearing somewhere, but it did not happen, and slowly I came to understand that I, as well as the girls, were finally allowing ourselves to grieve for the loss of Martin. We had transferred our feeling from Martin to Jim. I did not have much time to spend in self pity, however, since the need for taking care of the daily demands had to take precedence.

Charmaine had been exposed to chicken pox just before school let out, and it was now evident that she would have to allow this childhood illness to take its course. Of course Corky came down with it, followed by both of them catching measles. During the hottest time of the year, they were in bed with high fevers, necessitating the need for a baby sitter to come to the house since the kids were too sick to be taken out. Martin had been writing letters regularly which I had never opened. Now, one day I came home from work with Charmaine handing me a letter from her father. She said, "He wants to come home in September, but of course, I know you won't let him." I was trying to sympathize with her while the words registered in my mind—September? "Let me see that letter." I sat there stunned. This was just too much. What happened to the five year sentence?

* * *

During this time of chickenpox and measles, Muttie had an operation requiring six weeks recuperation. She offered to come stay with us to babysit with my sick girls during the last four weeks of her time off from work. She arrived a couple of days after we received the letter from Martin. Still feeling outraged over the injustice of it all, I showed her the letter, saying: "Now you see why I should have gotten the divorce over with when he was first imprisoned."

"Are you sure you want a divorce, Aggie?" she asked calmly. "I've been receiving letters from Martin all along and he really doesn't strike me as a criminal. In fact, I really feel sorry for him. He was under so much pressure and was only trying to please you by providing the extra money you seemed to crave; granted, he was going about it in the wrong way, but I think his motives were good anyway."

"What about the involvement with the prostitutes?" I railed. "I suppose that was for my good as well?"

She looked at me seriously, finally saying, "A man will go elsewhere if he's not satisfied at home; I think you know what I mean," she ended by suggesting I go see Martin at the "Honor Farm" where he was serving his sentence.

After giving this advice some thought, I decided to do just that. With Muttie looking after the girls, this would be the perfect opportunity for me to face Martin with all my complaints—if nothing else would be accomplished, I was sure I would feel better for telling him what a low-down scum of the earth he was.

When I arrived, I couldn't believe this "Prison." It was located in a beautiful part of the California dessert. The buildings were sunny and looked fairly new. Men were out on the tennis court. It had the appearance of a resort I thought. We did have to go through some minor security procedures and after that, the visitors were able to see the inmates in private rooms.

Martin entered, looking tan and healthy, wearing his regular clothes, telling me about the nice job he had working in the dispensary, the good food they were being served, and some of the movies they had been shown on Saturday evenings. When I recognized some of the titles as new releases, I could not stand to hear another word. I said, "This is a real outrage. Your innocent children have to suffer for your crime while you're living here in the lap of luxury—some prison. This is a real joke."

He answered, "If you'd only read the letters I sent you, I explained to you where to go for financial help. There is government assistance for families like mine. I tried to look out for you and the girls, but obviously you never read my letters." He looked at me with sympathetic eyes and continued, "You know I did all this only for you, can't you see how much I love you? What man would go to the lengths I did to provide the luxuries for his wife that were demanded of him?"

I could not believe what I was hearing. This man had actually convinced himself of his innocence and was obviously succeeding in convincing Muttie of the same. He continued, "Even so, I still love you more than ever and I want nothing more than to come home to you and prove it to you."

"Never," I growled at him. "You will never cross over my doorstep again."

"Now, Honey," he continued, "I hate to give you an ultimatum, but if you leave me no choice, I have to warn you that I'll take the girls away from you by having you declared an unfit mother. Now I'm sure you don't want that, so I suggest you think this over carefully before you try anything. I'll be released in a couple of months and I've already told the authorities that my loving wife and children are waiting for me, so don't make me out to be a liar."

I rode the bus back, feeling outraged, scared and totally confused. I knew Martin—he didn't make too many idle threats; but I was also sure that it would be impossible for him to prove me an unfit mother. He had to be bluffing. I would just have to wait till he got released then go back to the Legal Aid. This is what I told Muttie I had decided when I arrived home. She was still trying to convince me of his love for me. "What about his brothers," I stormed at her. "They have such an undying love for their wives too? And what about their pressures? How is it that everybody else is able to handle everyday pressure in a normal way, like Gary for instance; but Martin has to be excused for his wrongdoing because of his great love for me? Am I that hard to love; that it requires a person to lie and steal?"

Quietly she answered, "Maybe that's some thing you need to answer yourself, but you can always count on my love for you, dear, no matter what."

I went to sleep that night, like so many other nights, overcome with guilt. Was I really that bad? Well, wasn't I taking advantage of Muttie babysitting when she should be resting at home. Maybe I did drive people to desperation. I finally settled the matter in my mind that even if I was acting selfish, my life was better without Martin and no way was I going to allow him to come back to us—ever.

* * *

It was Muttie's last week with us when the doorbell rang—and there stood Jim. I was so stunned I didn't even have the presence of mind to push him away when he hugged and kissed me as if that was nothing unusual. The girls were dancing all around him, wanting him to come in and stay. He told them to leave us grownups alone for a while to talk—then he'd visit with them. They obediently went to their bedroom. "Now, Honey, aren't you even going to introduce me to your Mama?" he drawled, oozing southern charm. I slowly regained my composure and asked him why he had left before and why he was here now. "Well, Honey, you see, since Martin is my good friend and wants his little wife back, I figured we better not carry on any longer; and see, that's why I'm here now. I really don't want to talk about our little affair, but if that's what it takes for Martin to get you back, I'd just have to tell the judge, now wouldn't I?"

In total disbelief I said, "Jim, what are you talking about, we had a few visits together, with the kids present at all times—you call that an affair?"

"Well," he said, "not the visits with the little darlings around, but what we did after they went to bed. Well, you see I would just have to tell the truth about that—for Martin—you understand. I'd have to describe your scar from your gall bladder operation and everything; but I'm sure you'll think better of it and not make me do that." He turned to Muttie and said, "I'm right sorry, M'am, that you had to find out about it; this sure is a sweet little girl you have here. If Martin didn't want her back so badly, I'd kinda like to keep her myself." He tipped his cowboy hat and said, "I'll see myself out, honey."

Muttie and I sat there staring at each other. Martin is blackmailing me, I thought to myself. To Muttie I said, "Now you see what Martin is capable of doing to get what he wants. He needs a home to come to in order to be released early."

Big tears started rolling down Muttie's cheeks as she whispered, "Aggie, do you have any idea how it makes a Mother feel to hear about her daughter what I just heard about you?"

"Muttie, you don't believe this garbage about me, do you?" I shouted. But even as I spoke I could tell that there was no doubt in her mind. I was crushed. What was the use of trying. Quietly I said, "Believe whatever you want—I don't care anymore."

"That's right," Muttie continued, "that's your problem all along— you don't care about anybody but yourself. Just think of what you'd be putting your children through by stubbornly insisting to file for divorce."

I left the house. I had to walk away from her words. I could not absorb any more. I walked until I was sure they were asleep, then crept in to get a few hours of sleep myself, only to stare at the ceiling till it was time to leave for work, thankful that nobody else was up before I left.

The following week end Gary came to pick up Muttie. He'd arrived while I was at work and I could tell immediately when I entered the house that Muttie had given him her version of Jim's story. Gary tried hard to make some small talk with no cooperation from the rest of us. Muttie and I had spoken to each other only when absolutely necessary since Jim's visit, and the tension between us was very noticeable. Eventually Gary approached the subject. He tried to be kind, but the verdict was against me just the same. "I understand that you're lonely, Aggie, but if you're going to take up with every guy that knocks at your door, you'll be better off staying with Martin, at least he's the father of your children. I can only imagine the mess you'd be in if you wound up pregnant; then Martin could really take the girls and where would they be then, being raised by a man like Martin. At least, if you stay together Muttie, you and I will have some influence over him. Maybe if you could learn to accept him the way he is instead of demanding a lifestyle he's uncomfortable with, he'd relax and things would be better."

Gary got up to leave. Muttie gave me a hug and said, "Good by my little Gatel. I'm so sorry that you've made such a mess of your life. Just remember, I love you and will always be there for you."

They left. I sat down at the kitchen table prepared to have a good cry, but the tears didn't come. I was all dried up—feeling empty, with no future. There was no escape from this. I couldn't possibly take a chance on Martin pressing charges for custody of the girls. They were my whole life. I went about doing my chores like a robot. In order to block out the pain, I was also blocking out whatever pleasure life had to offer—a body without a soul is what I was.

* * *

After a short visit from Martin's probation officer instructing me on how I was to treat Martin after his release to make entry into free society easier for him, I was told that he would be coming home September 18, 1962, my Mother's birthday. I prepared the children for their daddy's home-coming by trying to make it a happy event. He was supposed to arrive at 2:30 p.m. We waited dinner for him as our anxiety grew. By 6 p.m. I went to use my neighbor's phone to call Muttie for possible information. Muttie's voice sounded musical as she answered "Hello-o."

"Well, you sound happy," I said in the telephone.

"Why shouldn't I be, I just had the nicest birthday surprise. Martin made it a point to stop here first—before he saw anyone else. He brought me a big bouquet of roses. You know, Aggie, he is truly sorry for causing so much trouble and I sure hope you can make him happy enough to keep him on the straight and narrow this time because you'll never find another who loves you as much as Martin. Can you imagine the thoughtfulness of my son-in-law to remember my birthday in the midst of what all he's been through."

Yea, I thought, as I walked back to the house—and what about all that he's put us through.

I didn't have too much time to indulge in self pity though since Martin drove up minutes later. I wondered how he acquired a car while in jail, but it was too much effort to ask. The girls were happy to see their daddy, but just as much to have a car again for they begged immediately to go for a ride.

We drove to a nearby city for an ice cream cone and before long, family relations were restored again to its pre-prison conditions. Martin seemed surprised that I didn't try to make him sleep on the couch again. I quietly said, "No, I'm yours, you've made it plain that you own me; I will not fight you anymore." (To myself I added, I'll just quietly wait for you to die.)

"Well, that's good," he replied, "because things will be different from now on. I've smartened up in jail. I know how to make money now and how to handle it. From now on I will make all the decisions. I will be the man of the house—the priest of the family."

"Yes Sir," I saluted.

And things were different indeed. He managed to get a job in a print shop fifteen miles from where we lived within a week and told me to find a decent house to live in and to quit my job. It was embarrassing for a man to have his wife working to help support the family. Since I hated the job anyway and didn't care much about anything any more, it was easy to follow orders. We were lucky to find a newer 3-bedroom house that needed a lot of refurbishing in a nearby housing development. Charmaine went back to school separating the girls long enough each day to stop the constant quarreling. I spent hours fixing up the house from painting to sewing curtains and bedspreads.

Every day I was confused by my emotions; on the one hand that I felt no interest in the domestic activities that normally made me happy—and on the other hand that I was so convincing in covering my depression with surface enthusiasm. We invited my family for dinner after the house was completed. Everybody was having a good time and Gary and Muttie both approached me at different times asking, wasn't I happy now that I had re-united with Martin. Just look at how nice a life I had and here nobody knew about his past, etc, etc.Oh yes, I was happy I reassured them, impressed .with my acting ability.

Muttie's health was failing. She had to have major surgery for the fourth time. This time to have a hysterectomy for uterine cancer. While she was in the hospital, Oma had a stroke and had to be taken to the hospital as well. Martin was great about driving us back and forth to L.A. to look after both of them since Gary was stationed on a U-boat somewhere in the Pacific Ocean for six weeks on some test project. Oma was partially paralyzed but able to talk. "Aggie," she told me, "I am going to die. I need you to do two things for me. They told me that in this hospital there are no children allowed. I want you to persuade the doctor to transfer me to a nursing home so I can say goodby to the little ones properly. And then I want you to make me a special dress to be buried in—not black. As a proper Christian girl and then a woman, I never wore anything but dark blue and gray with a lace collar to add for going to church. I want to go out of this world in a light blue satin gown with lace and ruffles." I fought back the tears as I re-assured her that she still had a long life ahead, but I would see to it that her wishes were granted.

I was proud of Martin the way he negotiated with the doctors to have Oma moved to a nursing home. At home I worked all week on Oma's burial dress. All her life she yearned for some colorful clothes while we had all assumed she liked dressing gray and navy—what other secrets would be buried with her. All of a sudden I could see how we had all taken her for granted all her life, and she had never demanded any attention except for these last two wishes. Something similar to sadness stirred inside my otherwise lifeless body. I was trying to put the pieces together. Martin was finally treating me the way I had wanted him all these years, and now it didn't matter any more. I was well on my way to feeling guilty again when I reminded myself that there seemed to be plenty of things going on with Martin that did not fit in with his otherwise "establishment" behaviour. I had the feeling it was just a matter of time for it all to blow up again.

Muttie was out of the hospital and doing well the following week end when we picked her up on our way to the nursing home. Oma asked to see each of us separately. She hugged the children to her for what she obviously felt to be the last time. My turn was last. "Did you bring me the dress?" she whispered. I opened the box, revealing layers of lace-edged ruffles in light blue synthetic that to her was silk. We both cried as her gnarled fingers lovingly caressed the smooth fabric. I hugged her as I said, "Good bye, we'll see you next Sabbath." She shook her head, "No, Aggie, I won't be here next Sabbath. The next time we'll see each other will be in the new earth." Once I had allowed a few tears to escape, I was unable to stop the flood I'd held back for so long. Nobody questioned me about it on the long trip home since it was well known by my family that there was a special bond between Oma and me.

When we arrived home, there was a note on our door left by a neighbor—we were to call Muttie. As I dialed the number, I knew what I would hear. Oma had closed her eyes after we left and peacefully gone to sleep forever. She had died quietly just as she had lived 86 years.

* * *

Muttie's arthritis made working almost impossible for her and finally after she was injured in a car accident, she was able to retire early on a disability. Now that she did not have to live near the hospital anymore, she moved to be near us as soon as she found a nice small apartment. With her so nearby and the girls getting older, I accepted a sales clerk position with a local yardage store, a twenty-minute walk from home because I felt too insecure with the inconsistency of the grocery allowance I received from Martin. This job turned out to be good therapy for my depression. I was able to indulge my creative instincts by sewing for the girls, Muttie and myself from remnant material I received free.

I also formed some wholesome friendships I greatly needed with the other six women my age at the store. For a while it seemed that we were falling into a comfortable lifestyle except for this uneasy feeling I had about Martin. I was learning to live with the suspicion of homosexual activities based on his friendship with a male nurse he'd met at the honor farm. Jerry came to visit with Martin, (not his family) regularly. They would always take off together somewhere that involved staying overnight. But it was more than that—the inconsistency of Martin's income for instance—. Then there were periodic secret phone conversations—usually followed by a migraine head-ache that required an injection by the doctor; but he would go to a different doctor each time.

To keep my equalibrium, I immersed myself in my own activities until another unexpected problem demanded my attention for the next year. In a backyard accident, Corky had injured her right hand. She was hospitalized for some time and finally had to have surgery with many months of physical therapy treatments with the final prognosis being that she had lost the use of her hand permanently, but she miraculously recovered. Through all of this, I was able to hold onto my fabric store job, working many evenings and Sundays to make up for time lost on those trips for therapy. The owner rewarded me with a good raise for my loyalty to the store. Little did he know how much I needed this job for my mental health.

In my joy over Corky's recovery, I expected things to settle down to a comfortable routine, when Muttie had some sort of an attack during church services. She was rushed to the hospital by ambulance. The diagnosis was angina. We were told that these attacks would probably repeat themselves and a heart attack might be in the future.

Sunday morning I was eager to go to the hospital to check on her condition. Knowing the hospital did not allow children, I took a chance on leaving the girls home alone for a short period. Martin was supposedly at the car races with Jerry. This decision turned out to be a life saver for my children for as I pulled out of our driveway, a speeding semi-truck hit me broadside on the driver's side, causing the passenger door to swing open. I was thrown twenty feet into the orange grove across the street. Some attendant had left the irrigation on too long, creating a deep mud hole. As a result, I was pulled out of the mud with only a whiplash and no other injuries. The car was totaled, the investigating officer called it a miracle that I was alive, adding that if the kids had been in the car, they would not have survived most likely.

We had been looking to buy a house on a "rent to own" basis because the house we had redecorated so carefully, had been sold; now with the small insurance settlement we were able to make a modest down payment on a house in the same development.

The day after we moved, Martin came home with the news that he'd been fired. It seemed his old pattern was repeating itself. He found another job before long, but with much lower pay. I wondered if the reason for that was that he would lose the little side business I suspected him of having—namely, printing pornography on his own time, and if he'd been fired when the owner possibly found out about it. I knew that his interests along this line hadn't changed because I saw Jerry's car parked in front of an adult movie house one evening during their "visits." My uneasiness grew, but I would not allow the possibility of another attempt at separation enter my mind.

Chapter 5

The owner of the yardage store was making a little speech at the retirement party given at a local restaurant for our store manager, paying tribute to her many years of loyal service to the store. My mind was drifting as we waited for our dessert when suddenly something he said caught my attention. He was naming me the manager of the store—the other six women applauded. I was told to think about it and meet him the next day to discuss the details. The party lasted long enough for me to digest this offer.

Even though it was late when I came home, I was exuberant enough about my promotion to tell Martin the minute I walked into the house. "Sh sh," was his reply. "I'm in the middle of a movie." I bathed and puttered around the house till the end of the movie—I was too excited to sit still in front of the T.V. When Martin finally turned off the set, I blurted out again: "Isn't it wonderful—with my new salary we'll have enough income again to decorate the house the way we planned before you changed jobs."

"You're not seriously considering taking this position, are you? You know you can't handle it. I don't know why your boss even offered it to you. The rest of the girls there must be real doe-doe's if he couldn't do any better than a foreigner with no education at all. If you take it, you'll fall on your face in a month, but I guess you don't care about embarrassing yourself. Well, I won't let you embarrass me too; therefore I forbid you to try anything so foolish."

I lay there a long time, listening to the rythmic breathing meaning Martin was sound asleep. By morning I had convinced myself that Martin was right. I told my boss that I was flattered but I didn't think I would be able to do a good enough job for him, reminding him of my lack of formal education. He assured me that what motivated him to offer me the job was my integrity and honesty—everything else could be learned. He would give me time and the old manager would be available part time to train me. We parted, shaking hands in agreement that I would train for my new position, starting the next day. One of my first responsibilities was to hire a replacement for me. I felt ten feet tall, walking out of the store that evening.

When I told Martin about my decision, he blew up, over-turning furniture, throwing whatever object was in his way, shouting at me, "You bitch, your only reason for taking this job is to show me up. We agreed that I would be the boss in the family with you submitting to my decisions the way the Bible tells you to do."

"The Bible also tells you as a husband to love your wife the same way that Christ loved the church," I dared to answer.

"You see—this is what a job does to a woman—it makes her think that just because she earns some money, she can talk back to her husband; well, I'll be dammed if I let you earn more money than me. I order you to quit that job right now."

"Nobody is going to order me to do anything—you don't scare me any more with your temper tantrums."

"O.K.—you want to be a smart aleck—take this: either you quit the job or I'll quit mine and just let you support me. As long as you want to wear the pants in the family so badly."

I went over to Muttie's, looking for approval. Her response was very similar to Martin's, only her demeaner was different. "Poor little Aggie," she started again. "I'm afrad you're biting off more than you can chew; remember what a hard time you had at school and what if you can't do it, then you'll have no job at all. Why can't you ever be satisfied with what you have? You're always reaching for what you can't have. I guess it's still that old childish competition with your brother. When will you ever accept the fact that you won't ever be a match for him. We're all born with different talents and different amounts of intelligence. I don't blame Martin for wanting to protect you from failure. That's how we act towards the people we love, but of course you wouldn't understand that since you use up all your energy in pursuing the things that are out of reach for you."

I walked miles that evening trying to sort things out. I had finally accomplished something to be proud of, and instead of a celebration, it was causing only friction. What was I doing wrong?

Doubts crept in my mind again about not being able to do the job just like Martin and Muttie predicted. I came to the conclusion that the only way I would be able to prove myself was to try it—I owed myself that much. Here it was again—my selfishness as Muttie repeatedly pointed out to me. Time for the usual guilt trip.

I was surprised at my efficiency the next day after all the turmoil at home and the lack of sleep. I was confident after the first couple of days that I would have no problems handling this job, but I was to learn again the consequences for crossing Martin's orders.

The next Monday when I came home early, Martin was home. "What are you doing home; Martin, are you sick?" I asked.

"No," came the reply. "I told you only one of us is going to wear the pants in the family; you want to be the boss so badly, you run the whole show, just make sure you pay all the bills like I've been doing all these years."

I could not believe my ears. "You mean you quit your job over this?" I gasped.

"Sure," he said. "After all, it was just a little menial job. In your family, one has to be in management to count."

I had to sit down. I felt like I had lead weights hanging from my shoulders. What was going to become of us, I asked myself silently. There was no use in trying to talk to Martin when he was in this kind of mood. My short term euphoria over my accomplishment had ended in disaster at home. I felt so tired, I just wanted to crawl in the corner somewhere and sleep forever.

* * *

For a few weeks Martin sat around, didn't bother to get dressed most of the time, and seemed to take delight in messing up the house and making the kids miserable by changing channels in the middle of their T.V. programs, eating things they were not allowed to have between meals, and just causing friction in general. I was just starting to wonder how long the girls would have to pay the price for my small success, when he suddenly changed his behaviour drastically from lethargy to frantic activity. Every day he would get all dressed up and be on the go somewhere putting many miles on the car by the evidence of the speedometer. Often he would have long phone conversations of a business nature, and once more I was puzzled and anxious about our future.

One day he stopped by at the yardage store and told me to take off early, "Why?" I asked.

"Because we're going shopping—you need a decent looking outfit for our interview, not one of your homemade rags."

"What interview?"

"Never mind about that."

"Martin, I can't just walk off the job in the middle of my shift," I said.

"Of course you can," he sneered. "You're the boss—you can do anything you want to do. Besides, if this deal I'm shooting for works out, you won't need this stupid job anyway." Knowing he would create a scene, I had no choice but to go with him quietly.

The next day when Muttie arrived to stay with the girls she said with a twinkle in her eyes, "Boy, Aggie, will you be lucky if this works out for Martin."

After some time of silent driving on the freeway, Martin started to explain that he was in the process of going into business for himself. He was negotiating with someone to go into partnership on a bindery and advertising business. Today he was meeting his financial backer to sign the papers. The backer was bringing his wife and had requested for

Martin to bring me. Before we entered the prestigious restaurant, Martin whispered for me to keep a low profile so as not to give away my foreign background. He really wanted to impress this man. I did as I was told, copying the other lady by eating only small portions of my dinner and skipping dessert. We took a tour through the bindery. The contracts were signed. We parted, shaking hands, got in the car and rushed to meet a real estate agent, pre-arranged by Martin, who drove us around all afternoon, showing us houses near the bindery. We took a break for supper with an agreement to meet later in the evening with our decision.

When we finally sat at the restaurant table alone, I didn't know where to start asking questions, but Martin was riding high now. He didn't have to be prodded. His first words were, "Well, you thought you were the only one who could get promoted into management. I managed to get my own business. The bindery is employing seventeen people. After a year, I'll have that up to thirty. Our days of nickel and diming it are over, baby. You want a husband you can be proud of. Well, you just wait and see."

We returned very late at night, putting all our plans into action. Three months later we had sold our house. I had given up my job and we had moved into our new large three-bedroom house on a nice cul-d-sack in an L.A. suburb, just before school started. Martin through himself into the business full time while I fixed up the house and got acquainted with my new neighbors which was not hard since they all had children close to the ages of ours and we had the only house on the street with a pool.

* * *

I was thrown into a different lifestyle so abruptly that I didn't have time to analize my feelings about it until school started, giving me some private moments to reflect on everything that was happening. Martin was making the most of his "local businessman's status, joining the Chamber of Commerce, a men's service club; holding office at the church; managing a little league, and in general, living in the fast lane.

All the neighbors accepted us enthusiastically. I was kept busy preparing for one pool party after another.

Since Erika was an excellent swimmer, she and Gary with their family were frequent weekend visitors, usually bringing Muttie along.

One day as I was serving cold drinks by the pool, I was overcome by a melancholy feeling—was this what I wanted? This frantic running from one meeting to another? This competition of trying to impress the neighbors? This flamboyant use of our income?

The girls were thriving in the California sun. Charmaine was an excellent student, giving us plenty of reason to be proud of her; and Corky's health was improving rapidly. Gary was getting regular promotions—he had sold his original house to move into a more prestigious area, into an impressive custom built two-story house. It was fun to watch them decorate it with quality furnishings.

We were all living the plastic life of the sixties. Barbie dolls and G.I. Joes were under all the Christmas trees. We were busy attending Christmas programs at school and at church. The only blot on the pleasant landscape of our lives was another serious operation for Muttie. She had to have three-fourths of her stomach removed. After the operation she stayed in my home for six weeks, during which time we were able to work through some of our differences. For the first time in my life, she was complimenting me. How well I was nursing her back to health and what a fine mother I had turned out to be.

It was Muttie who validated some of my suspicions that Martin was involved in some secret activities again. I allowed her to point out some of his strange behaviour that I had been aware of for some time myself. I decided later that I had done the right thing in making her believe that she had been the one to discover that he was printing pornography in the evenings when the rest of the workers had left for the day. Much later, when I needed her support, I was able to count on her simply because she felt important, having discovered Martin's involvement in pornography.

We were approaching the second summer in our new location when things were noticeably deteriorating. Martin was never at home; or he was locked in a dark bedroom for days with one of his headaches. The pills he was supposedly taking for his headaches, he was making use of indiscrimanently. During the times he was home, the kids were not allowed to have fun in the pool since he couldn't stand the noise. The business was suffering. The income sporadic. Many days now I had to help out in the bindery when he couldn't meet the payroll. Often, when I was in the middle of a job that neared its deadline, he would send me home abruptly when he'd receive one of his mysterious phone calls.

Our checks were being returned N.S.F. Then the company checks he would write to cover our personal checks would bounce till our account was closed. Money was unavailable now for necessities like pool chemicals. Our house payments were falling behind and we were getting shutoff notices for our utilities. Communications of any type between us had stopped a long time ago when I gave up making attempts at making a marriage out of our co-habitation with no success. The only work being done at the bindery was now accomplished by ourselves plus help hired by the day as the jobs required it.

For weeks we had been processing some large orders with no visible income. When I questioned Martin about it, he told me that they were credit customers and next month the money would be rolling in again.

School had started with the children walking to and from school with a shopping center between the route. One day Charmaine came running home trembling. She had seen Martin talking to a man behind a building at the shopping center. She thought she had seen the man hold a gun to Martin, demanding payment. After calming Charmaine, I was the one trembling. I tried to convince myself that Charmaine's twelve-year-old mind was running away with her, mixing fantasy with reality, but deep down I knew what she had seen was probably true and that I would have to keep a protective eye on the girls.

When the first week of October rolled around, the week we were supposed to collect for all those orders I had worked so hard to put out on time, Martin told me to take the day off, that I had earned it. I was glad for the time to catch up on my work at home. When he didn't show up for supper, I became somewhat suspicious and went to the shop to find out the reason. It was evident immediately when I walked in that no one had been there all day. My heart was beating in my throat as I drove into our garage. I knew instinctively that something was drastically wrong—but what?

* * *

After a tense night of waiting for Martin, I was eager to go to the shop in hopes of finding him there, only to find the shop locked—the phone ringing. When I answered, the caller hung up. I was scared; my hands trembling as I dialed some numbers in search of Martin, with no results. By afternoon I felt I owed the girls some explanation. When I tried to re-assure them that their daddy would probably be back late that evening, that he'd just forgotten to tell me of some trip he had to take, Charmaine surprised me with a wisdom way beyond her twelve years, "Mom," she said, "use your head; if he'd just taken a trip wouldn't he have taken the suitcase with some clothes? His toothbrush and razor, at least? No, he took off to hide somewhere from the mob that he's involved with, just like the coward that he always is; he talks big till he gets himself in a jam and then he either takes off or gets sick with his stupid headaches and leaves you to clean up his messes. I'm sick of the way he looks at me and touches me,—I hope he stays away for good, since that's the only way we can get rid of him, you not believing in divorce and all that. I hate him, I just hate him."

This outburst led me to give some serious thought to our situation. Charmaine's strong, bitter feelings had to originate deeper than just his irresponsible and sometimes embarrassing behaviour—the way he had touched her, she had said. I had noticed myself how physical Martin had become in his affection for Charmy. When he'd given her some transparent sexy looking nighties for her last birthday, I had dismissed my suspicions as female jealousy.

Now I was beginning to feel panic—just how far had Martin carried his perverse desires? I could not think about the possibilities, but I made a firm on the spot decision. I would divorce Martin if for no other reason than to protect my girls, and no one was going to stop me this time.

I could not wait for him to come back so I could tell him once and for all what a low life he was, and if he would try to stop me, I'd kill him with my bare hands. I spent the night thinking of all the ways I could end his life—vengeance was sweet, even if it was just in theory.

By the next morning I had to take control of the situation. Martin had obviously left with no intention to return. The nightmare began. First, I needed to come up with some cash for groceries. I started calling all the outstanding accounts, only to be told the same thing by each one: that Martin had picked up the payments the day he had given me the day off—then he'd left after he'd collected from all our accounts.

After giving an account of what was happening to Muttie and Gary, we decided that there was nothing else to do but apply for help with the welfare department until we got this problem unraveled. I drove clear across town to use my new foodstamps to save the embarrassment at the local market where I was known.

After the necessary papers were signed for our backer to dispose of the bindery, it was discovered that Martin had not been paying the business taxes for some time, and a warrent was issued for his arrest for tax evasion.

Our utilities were disconnected—neighbors lent us an ice chest to keep sandwich makings and milk cold. Our credit card bills started arriving with huge balances due—long sheets of recorded purchases by Martin. Now when I consulted with Gary about my new problem, he agreed that the only thing I could and should do was to divorce him since I could be held responsible for all his debts. I sold my set of china which had been a Christmas present the previous year to a neighbor to pay for a lawyer. The lawyer's advice was to file for bankruptcy first of all to absolve myself of all these debts; but to go ahead with the divorce. Martin would have to be served with papers—how could that be accomplished with no knowledge of his whereabouts.

As if in answer to my problem, I received a bouquet of roses on my birthday with a note attached from Martin. He was sorry for everything and would like to make things right with me. He would call me the next day to receive my answer. I promptly called the police who were able to track him down. He was jailed once again, awaiting his arraignment.

While the lawyer was preparing the divorce papers to serve him, he'd been arraigned and released on bail. I received a letter from the local state mental facility that Martin had entered their security ward after attempting suicide by driving his V.W. off a 30-foot cliff. He was being treated for physical injuries as well as his mental condition. He was asking to see me. The letter ended with the psychiatrist stating that a visit from me would be very helpful in reassuring him of the necessity to stay there; that he was able to check himself out after 30 days voluntarily. I wrote a letter back saying I hoped he would rot in the crazy house.

While all of this was taking place, Halloween and Thanksgiving had gone by with me farming the girls out to Mutti's and Gary's as much as possible to be exposed to some holiday activities. Now Christmas was approaching. The girls wanted to have a real Christmas at home. I tried to explain that I had no money at all for a tree, let alone for a holiday dinner, and how would I cook it without gas? Corky had $1. she wanted to buy a Christmas tree with. I could not deny her this small joy. When we arrived at the tree lot, I showed her in which section to look for some very small, maybe somewhat imperfect trees, but she insisted to look at the big, beautiful trees with me reading off the prices. I tried to negotiate with one of the salesmen on one twig of a tree, explaining that $1.00 was all I had when Corky ran over to me breathless with excitement. "Come, look, Mommie. I found the perfect tree over there in the corner." Tears were filling my eyes as I tried to tell her it was a very expensive flocked tree. A young man who'd heard the whole transaction took Corky by the hand and said, "Show me this perfect tree and I'll tell you if you can afford it." He slowly took the price tag off the tree and looked at Corky saying in a slow drawl, "Why, look at this, little lady; it costs exactly $1.00." I decided that if there was a heaven, a very special place would have to be reserved for this young man.

While we were decorating the tree, a knock on the door brought more Christmas excitement. A church club for juniors called THE PATHFINDERS had been discussing Charmaine's plight and decided to play Santa Claus. The Pathfinder leader brought over the gifts, including $30 for extra holiday expenses. We celebrated Christmas in our own house, knowing it would be the last time since foreclosure proceedings were already in progress. The lawyer sent a paid messenger out to the mental hospital to serve Martin with the divorce papers as he came out, since he was not allowed to serve papers to an inpatient on the day he was to be released, only to find he'd been released the previous day.

We were back to square one on this divorce attempt and my time was running out. The house was to be repossessed shortly and I had to be a resident of that county for the divorce hearing in January. If we could only get Martin served with these blasted papers. I resorted to lowering myself to Martin's standards and start lying. I called Martin's sister and pretended to have had a change of heart, telling her I had papers for Martin to sign from his backers; they were willing to pay the back taxes, absolving Martin of the tax evasion charge if he was willing to sign the bindery over to them, saving them the expense to fight him in court. I must have been convincing, adding that Gary would have to bring out the papers since I was scared to drive on the freeway. Jane agreed to have Gary come out to their house, she would see if she could get Martin to meet him there. Gary was reluctant at first, but finally agreed to be part of this scheme. I spent my last $5 to have papers typed up that looked official at first glance. Then I waited for Gary to come pick me and the girls up to take us to his house just in case Martin would get violent when he found out that he'd been duped.

It was very late when Gary arrived with a "cloak and dagger" story about how one of Martin's brothers had taken Gary out on a long drive after satisfying themselves that the papers were legitimate. Gary was then blindfolded and taken to some park where he gave the papers to Martin for his signature. To Gary's relief, the brother was eager to return before anyone might have followed them. The girls and I spent a few days at Gary's, then returned to our house for the appointed day when all our belongings were being confiscated, arroding to bankruptcy law, by the Loan Company who had all our household goods as collateral.

After the truck pulled out of the driveway, we followed with a carload full of personal effects which we were allowed to keep along with our old car since it was considered worth less than $200.

Somehow I felt the same panicky insecurity I remembered feeling when our train pulled out of Russia—only now I wasn't a little girl any more, depending on Muttie and Papa to make things all right. Now I had two sets of eyes brimming with tears fastened on me, depending on me for their security. We were heading to Gary's, knowing we could stay with them only a short time. What was ahead for us? Tomorrow evening we would celebrate the entrance of 1967—a new year—would it bring us luck?

* * *

"Congratulations," the lawyer said. "You are a free woman."

"Well, ladies," Gary addressed Muttie and me, "since this is supposed to be a victory, I'll take you out to lunch before we separate." In the restaurant, the silence was awkward for a while when I tried to show my gratitude for their help with a choked "Thank you, both."

Gary was embarrassed by my tears and tried to hush me up by saying, "What are families for."

Muttie retorted, "I don't know what you're crying about, Aggie; after all, this is what you've been wanting for the last 13 years. Now you're trying to get our sympathy? You better be happy with your choice since this is only the beginning of hardship. I know; I've been without a husband now for a long time and it isn't easy, let me tell you..." Her voice faded into the background.

Fear, mixed with anger and loneliness got the better of me and I turned on Muttie with a verbal outburst showing anything but gratitude, until Gary gave strict orders for both of us to stop immediately. I was sorry for some of the awful things I had said and resolved to never let this happen again, only to repeat this behaviour whenever I found myself unable to cope in the years to come.

Now, besides my many other failures, I had a new reason to loathe myself. Muttie's prediction proved only too true. It was a tough road I had to travel. Not only did I have to fight the reality of a divorcee and single parenthood, but I had to fight the demons inside who were convicting me daily of my shortcomings with Muttie by my side, faithfully pointing out my every failure and ever ready to forgive and help where needed.

Since I was now receiving welfare assistance, I was sent to a college for extensive testing to determine my ability to support the girls and myself. This turned out to be a morale booster as I learned that my aptitude test showed me superior in many areas. The counselor encouraged me to take a G.E.D. test in which I scored 92. I was euphoric to be able to have a high school equivalency education to enter in job applications; but sank to the bottom of dispare when this did not land me a better job immediately. A pattern of behaviour developed where I was either riding on cloud nine with some apparent success, only to become terribly depressed when things didn't work out.

We were staying at Gary's house which created added pressure. I had to find a job before I could rent an apartment since I would have to find something in walking distance, knowing my old car would run it's last mile very shortly. Besides that, I knew we were imposing on my brother's family and my children needed to be enrolled in school. Most of all, we needed the privacy to deal with our emotions in regard to the divorce and all the turmoil it had caused in our lives. We desperately needed to be a family again. The girls needed the security of their own space. After two weeks at Gary's during one sleepless night, I stopped waiting for something to happen and acted totally on instinct.

I woke up Corky to take her with me so I wouldn't be accused of using Erica as a baby sitter, and we left while everyone else was still asleep. I used 50 cents of my 75 cents I had, to put gas in the car, and spent the last 25 cents on a newspaper. All the reasonably priced rentals seemed to be in Anaheim which was only about 15 miles away from Gary's. I located the local hospital, being pretty sure I could get a Nurse's Aide position considering my prior experience. Then we started walking, widening the radius around the hospital checking out one apartment after another. They were either too expensive or they didn't accept children. We were getting awfully tired; it was nearing noon and Corky was getting stomach cramps, which seemed to be happening quite frequently lately. Food seemed to help. I feared she was developing an ulcer. Making a mental note that I would have to get her checked by a doctor as soon as I would receive our medicare card. A welfare benefit I would later be very grateful for.

We passed a fast foods restaurant. I explained patiently to Corky why we would have to wait till we got to Erika's for lunch. In her 7 year old voice she answered, "but the french fries smell so good." In the background I heard Corky's voice, "Mommy, let's pray to Jesus that He'll send us some hamburgers and french fries, please."

I remembered my disappointment at the very same age-when I put my childish faith in God to return Papa to me. "No, Honey," I answered. "Jesus doesn't answer those kind of requests."

I was still talking when she squealed, "Look, Mommy, Jesus answered our prayer without us even saying the words; look!" She uncrumpled a $1.00 bill laying by the curb." Now we have to thank Jesus, you know," was her solemn advice.

My earlier murderous thoughts about Martin echoed in my mind—how could anyone as sinful as I talk to God? "Please, Mommy, we have to thank Him right now."

"We will when we get home," I soothed her.

"No, no, right now," and she knelt down on the sidewalk, pulling me down with her. Her "little girl" voice thanking Jesus for this miracle so sincerely almost melted the rebellion in my heart, but I regained my "in charge" attitude quickly.

Joyously we retraced our steps to the restaurant for lunch, noticing a "For Rent" sign I had missed earlier. We chatted happily while we ate—Corky was confident that this $1.00 bill had not only bought us lunch, but was a good luck omen besides. I hoped she was right and indeed after some food, things did look a little brighter. We approached the building with the vacancy sign. Corky tried to encourage me by saying she would pray that it was cheap enough and they'd take kids while I was doing the negotiating.

As we entered the manager's apartment, I noticed toys along the hall—an encouraging sign. It was a nice one-bedroom apartment upstairs for only $90. a month; but she could not rent to welfare recipients. I begged her to hold the apartment until the next day when

I would have a job and the first month's rent. She was reluctant, but finally agreed, adding, "I don't know why I'm doing this."

I spent the afternoon getting hired by the hospital for the swingshift. Now, all I needed was a loan from Gary for the rent and all would be well.

Chapter 6

Gary's reaction to my request for $100 was negative. I hadn't expected him to be enthusiastic about it, but I certainly did expect him to see the logic of it. "After all, Gary," I said, "Monday I'll start my new job and I'll pay you back with the first welfare check I should receive any day now." Gary found more obstacles to my plan than I could ever imagine.

"What about furniture, Aggie, who will babysit while you work; what about transportation when your old car breaks down; Anaheim doesn't have the bus system L.A. does you know." He went on and on about all the things that could go wrong.

"Gary, I don't know what you and Muttie want me to do; it's obvious I can't stay at your house indefinitely, but you discourage me from trying to be independent. What exactly would be right in your opinion?"

"I want you to grow up and show some good sense for a change."

"That's what I'm trying to do," my voice sounded shrill. I knew we'd be in a no-win argument if we continued—already he had me totally convinced of my stupidity and incompetence once more.

In tears I drove to Muttie's, wondering all the way, why was I such a glutten for punishment? Muttie and Gary always agreed on what was supposed to be good for me. To my surprise again, Muttie poured on the sympathy. It was on this night that I started to understand some of Muttie's motives, but I didn't learn until many years later that she was a prisoner to her own emotions, not realizing at the time what effect her actions had on me. I began to see that in order to get Muttie's cooperation, I had to be totally dependent on her. She had to be in control. For many years I followed a pattern of running to her when I needed help and sympathy, only to turn against her when I felt more in control of my life and hated my own weakness in times of trouble.

We formed an intense love-hate relationship. Her answer to my present problem was that she would rent a small apartment to be nearby to babysit the girls after school which would solve my major problem. She lent me the $100 eagerly, agreeing that the furniture problem would take care of itself since a stove and refrigerator was furnished.

I returned to Gary victorious, not realizing that I had exchanged one person over the other to have control of my life. Gary did lend us some sleeping bags till I was able to buy some used furniture. We found a rental for Muttie only four blocks away which was a big help since I was hired for the swing shift and would not feel safe leaving the girls alone all afternoon and evening.

I hated the nurse's aid job as much as before, but it was a paycheck. I slowly adjusted to being single—my moods fluctuated drastically which was scary. I felt as though I had a stranger living in my body at war with my normal self. I succeeded in putting forth a calm exterior with the girls—then blew it the minute Muttie would cross me. This always ended in a bitter quarrel with both of us parting in tears. Then I would spend hours condemning myself for my lack of control, worry about the effect this would have on the girls, and feel guilty enough to take a peace offering to Muttie with an apology, whether I felt I had been at fault or not, reminding myself how I needed to be grateful to her—she always graciously and long sufferingly accepted my apology, adding how it was easy for her to forgive me because of her great love for me, never admitting to her own guilt. What little self-esteem I had, went down to nonexistent. I hated Muttie for always having the solutions to my problems and her eagerness in pointing out my weaknesses. I hated Gary for his affluence and apparent happy family life. I hated Martin for robbing me of what should have been the best years of my life, now gone forever, and for leaving me to fend for myself in raising our children. But most of all I hated myself for being too insecure to stand up for my rights. On the other hand, I now had the freedom to run my household without the constant fear of Martin's secret life infringing on our real life and causing disaster.

Many days, especially on my days off, the girls, Muttie and I would go to the beach or Disneyland with my free passes provided to me as a hospital employee. Martin had been arrested again, giving us a few months of no interference from him.

In the Fall of 1967 he was released and immediately our safety was threatened. I was proud of myself for arranging with both girls' schools not to allow him to pick the girls up at school since that's what he threatened to do. He called me repeatedly at night. I changed to an unlisted number, then the calls came at work, jeopordizing my job.

One night Charmaine called me at the hospital in a panic, saying Martin was parked in front of the apartment. I called the police, enforcing my restraining order on him. It took hours to calm the girls down enough to go to sleep. I stayed up all night, watching him cruise the streets around the apartment. He was arrested again, then repeated the whole terrorizing procedure when he was released a few months later.

* * *

Before we knew it, Christmas was approaching again. I couldn't stand the thought of me working on Thanksgiving and Christmas as scheduled, leaving the girls with no family of their own. I felt it would be hard enough on them, watching their cousins open non-stop presents as was their custom. I knew that without a father, they at least needed a mother during this special time of the year.

I applied for assemblyline work at a processing plant preparing books for libraries. It was a long trip to Tustin every day, but the higher pay would make payments on a newer car which I needed anyway. I felt I had made a wise decision, reporting excitedly to Muttie and Gary. Gary sighed heavily, "Oh, Aggie, will you ever learn? Why didn't you talk to me about your plans first. You made another big mistake."

"Yes, Aggie," Muttie cut in, "you know that Gary carries the financial responsibility for you and the girls if you lose your job. The least you can do is ask for his advice before you make such weighty decisions."

I started crying. "Why did I make such a terrible mistake in your opinion? I'll be earning more money and with a more reliable car, I would think that you would be relieved not to have to worry about the old one breaking down constantly—and can't you see that its tearing me apart to be leaving the girls alone every night?"

"Aggie, you can't afford to reach for such luxuries as a newer car, can't you understand that?" Gary tried to soothe me while Muttie added "You should have thought about the girls' plight before you insisted on a divorce so hastily."

That did it—she had pushed my vulnerable button again. I screamed at both of them, "Will you please explain to me what's wrong with taking a job with better pay—that's what people do all the time to get ahead—including you, my high and mighty brother."

Now Gary's voice rose, "At the hospital you have job security—on this job you won't know from day to day—I will have to worry every day about the possibility of you sitting at my doorstep for shelter again. A person with half an ounce of intelligence would figure that out herself."

The whole scene ended again with Muttie sympathizing with me for being out of control. While my hysterical crying subsided into a cowardly whimper, I heard Muttie say to Gary, ignoring me as if I wasn't even there: "She doesn't know how lucky she is to have a brother like you."

Their prediction turned out to be accurate again. By the end of February, the plant moved to Ann Arbor, Michigan—any employees who wanted to relocate would retain their positions. For a short moment I considered this option, reasoning that without Muttie by my side constantly, I would be forced to make my own decisions. With more time alone at home due to my being unemployed and the girls in school all day, I was able to gain some control over my rollercoaster emotions; on the other hand, the fear of not being able to provide for my family and the constant phone calls and threats from Martin who was out of jail, created a very unsettled feeling of doom that seemed to hover around me frequently.

On Easter Sunday we were having dinner at Muttie's. The conversation revolved around the good news Erika and Gary shared about expecting another baby. Envy opened my heart to dispair and loneliness. Their laughter and cheerful conversation sounded far away as my gloomy feeling turned to anger in the old familiar way. "Careful, Aggie," I told myself, "Stay in control." Ericka must have noticed my unusual silence; she tried to include me in the conversation—her kindness drew tears instead.

"Here we go again," Gary moaned. "She has to ruin a happy occasion every time." I responded with a torrent of pentup emotions — all directed at Muttie and Gary. As I heard the words of accusations tumble from my mouth, I knew I was out of line and something deep down in my being wanted to apologize—and be loved by my family, but at the same time I was convinced that if I showed my true feelings, I would lose control and thereby be "lost." As I tried to sort out my feelings, driving aimlessly after I'd stormed out of the party, I was unable to clarify in my mind what exactly "lost" was, but somehow the feeling was overwhelmingly scary—as if I would just dissolve into nothingness.

I drove for a long time as I slowly calmed down—then realized that I had left my children with the people who no doubt spent the rest of the afternoon criticizing their Mother's behavior. Guilt flooded my soul; how could I be so selfish. I would have to make it up to them—again. Would they continue to be able to forgive me, or would I alienate them too?

Gary's car was parked in front of my apartment as I turned the car into the carport. Oh God, now there would have to be another confrontation, with the girls present. I was right—Gary opened the door with a stern "fatherly" expression, "Aggie, these tantrums of yours have to stop. Can't you see what you're doing to Muttie? I had to take her to the hospital again. When she is ready to leave, she will live with us to be protected from your angry outbursts. You know she's not supposed to have stress."

"Stress! You tell me. Stress and I suppose I'm the only one who gives her stress. What about you and Erika? Muttie can't even spend the weekend at your house without calling me to come and get her, but of course you can't see that."

Gary cut me off, "I'm not staying another minute to listen to your tirade, Aggie. I know it's not easy for you but you know it's not my fault you married a bastard—and on top of that, it's obvious with your personality you'll never find another man to marry you. And what kind of stress do you suppose that puts on me, huh?"

"On you," I screamed. "On you—what in the world does that have to do with you?"

"Well, it makes you and the kids my responsibility, doesn't it? Think about that," he said as he slammed the door behind him.

* * *

After comforting and reassuring the girls most of the night, then sending them off to school with promises that our lives would change for the better, I spent hours contemplating our future, trying to make plans to live up to my promises. I read the Bible and other religious literature. I prayed. I meditated. Nothing worked. First I felt empty, then scared, then angry. Oh, that was comforting—a familiar feeling. How dare Gary accuse me of having a personality so terrible that I couldn't attract another man who would make himself responsible for us" I'll show him," was my last thought as I grabbed my purse and I flew out the door, turning the key in the car with confidence. At the shopping mall I justified spending the month's grocery money on a new outfit and hairdo by telling myself that "nothing ventured—nothing gained" would be my motto from now on. The next day I was determined to find a job—after all, no man would want a woman living on welfare.

By evening I was able to tell my family the good news that I had been hired as a counter girl in a drycleaning store. I was to start the next day. Muttie was concerned about my plans of leaving the girls at home alone after school and during vacation (which was only a month off) but

Charmaine felt very grown up to be trusted with watching out for Corky and assuming some of the home responsibilities.

I enjoyed the slow pace of my job after all the hard work as nurses aid and factory assembly line pressures, not to mention the pleasant encounters with some of the customers. And I looked forward to the little visits with the driver from the plant who came twice a day for pick-up and delivery of the garments—often it was the manager himself. I was proud of myself when he complimented me on how clean I kept the store and the cash always matching the amount on the register tape.

One day a new man, named Bill, made the run. We talked a few minutes. He told me he had his own dry cleaning business and used the same plant as the chain I was working for. The plant was short a driver and he had offered to help out this particular day. "And isn't it lucky for me," he added. "I'll pick you up after work and take you out to dinner." I looked at him surprised, being inexperienced in how to respond to propositions. "I mean, it's o.k., isn't it? You're not married or anything, are you? You're not wearing a ring," he commented.

"W-w-ell, y-yes," I stuttered, blushing a deep red.

"That's nice," he said, touching my cheek.

* * *

A chain of circumstances carried me like a piece of floating driftwood, caught in a waterfall. Bill demanded all my free time which made me feel needed and wanted. Also leaving me too tired to analize our relationship. He encouraged the girls to call him Daddy shortly after we met, bringing them little gifts and often taking them along on our dates making them family outings instead.

He was moody and his long periods of sullen silences made me anxious but instead of looking at the situation objectively, I compared his quiet personality with the blustery bragging of Martin and blamed myself for causing Bill to go into his moods with something I'd said or done. Still—during one of his "periods" as Charmy called it, I decided to confront Bill. The encounter left me drained from trying to get some verbal response from him to help us work through our difficulty, only to wind up in tears of frustration at his silence. He left, looking hurt and rejected, and once more I was overcome with guilt, but nevertheless, I did decide to end the seven month relationship.

I had my "Dear John" speech all prepared to be used when Bill would call me—only he didn't call. My life seemed empty without Bill. The girls kept asking about him. I didn't have any answers—then events took place to force me into decisions I lived to regret many times.

Charmy injured her knee, requiring surgery for a dislocated kneecap, leaving her entire leg in a cast for six weeks. I had to take a leave of absence from my job to look after her. Corky had recurrent stomach cramps, needing medical attention; and while I was feeling very needy myself, Gary came home with, for me, the worst news possible. He had been promoted to general manager of the European division of the aircraft company he was with. Since Muttie was still living with them, she was considered part of his family and would go with them to live in Bonn, Germany.

To conceal my embarrassment at losing Bill and also expecting Bill to come back to me and forgive me, I had not mentioned to Muttie or Gary what had taken place, and Charmy and Corky had followed my lead. Now Muttie was bubbling over with excitement. "Aggie, can you imagine this good luck? I'll be able to visit all the places we used to live at in Germany—see how they've changed—what an opportunity. And aren't you proud of your brother?" Gary cut in: "I won't be leaving for a couple of months yet, we have to put the house up for sale and do some preliminary traveling connected with this promotion. Let's have one nice family party—no arguments this time. We all have things to celebrate. We have a new baby boy, a new job with prestige and good pay, and Aggie—well it looks like Bill is pretty serious—she will probably make a new future for her family too. Yes, we will have a family celebration. Aggie, I know Bill doesn't like to socialize but surely you can get him to come. Maybe our leaving will build a little fire under him to propose—what do you think?"

I wished now I had confided in them. No, what I really wished was for Bill to do just what Gary had suggested. Wouldn't it be nice to be making plans for the future, and a baby—no, I wasn't too old at 31 I dreamed as I was cuddling Gary's little Allen. I remembered only Bill's virtues. The morose silences had faded from my memory.

The phone was ringing as I unlocked our apartment door. Bill, it has to be Bill, I wished. I answered breathless with anticipation. "Where have you been all this time," Martin's voice came over the line, "I've been watching you. What happened to your boyfriend?" he continued. "Did he dump you when the going got too rough with Charmy's leg in the cast? Or did you drive him away with bitchiness, the way you did me?"

Trembling, I put the receiver down. "No, no," a voice screamed in my head. "I didn't drive him away—no, no. I'm not the bitch Martin claims I am."

My next thought was, "I'll show him—I'll show them all." I dialed Bill's number and apologized tearfully. "I'll be right over," was all Bill said. He never mentioned our one-sided fight or his long absence when he arrived. He folded his arms around me protectively and stayed the night. We talked most of the night, ending with him saying, "You know I'm an Irish Catholic; I expect to have lots of kids and being still single at 36, I don't have any time to lose. Are you willing to give Charmy and Corky some brothers?"

We were married shortly before Gary with his family left for Germany amidst a whirlwind of activities.

Chapter 7

My stormy marriage to Martin should have prepared me for the unpredictability of life with Bill, but my fantasy of marriage had influenced my expectations for so long that it left me unprepared to deal with the reality of life. I saw things only in black and white terms— good or bad—your fault or my fault. After the divorce from Martin, I had convinced myself that everything was Martin's fault. He was to blame for every pain I had experienced, the same way Muttie had blamed the war for all our misery. Instead of accepting responsibility for my part in a problem which would have enabled me to do something about it, I looked for someone or something to be the cause. Now— when things didn't go right with Bill, I immediately assumed it was my fault—reasoning that after all, if this situation kept repeating itself, it must be my fault. I made an honest effort now to reform myself.

I went to see a marriage counselor but had to terminate the visits for lack of money—Bill controlled our finances completely. During our last session, the counselor suggested I read the newly released "I'm O.K. you're O.K." book. My eyes were opened to the reasons of some of my personal turmoil, and I hungered for more answers. Pop psychology being popular in the 60's, I found a never ending supply of paper backs on the bookshelves. I felt guilty depriving us of what little grocery money I had at my disposal to buy books but that didn't stop me—I was insatiable. I was finding in these books some tools to use in an effort to make our marriage work.

The harder I tried, the more Bill resisted, and the more our situation frustrated me. It seemed as though Bill was trying to make it impossible for me to love him while at the same time he demanded proof of my love continuously.

Shortly after our marriage, he sold the dry cleaning business to go into real estate. He expected to get his license in six weeks. Every day he would sleep until noon, then lay in the recliner to study the material for the exam, only to fall asleep in a few minutes. By evening he would demand an elaborate dinner in spite of my spartan food budget. Then he'd sit up until all hours of the night to watch late movies—insisting I accompany him—when I mentioned that I had to get up mornings to see the girls off to school he told me they were old enough to get themselves ready and I better prove my love and loyalty to him by complying. He failed his first real estate test but made no effort to find other employment; instead, he enrolled in the second exam schedule in another six weeks.

Before the scheduled test date, he purchased a new car without so much as mentioning his intentions to me—a brand new Cadillac—the luxury model, no less. To my concerned look, he responded with, "I wanted to prove to you that I have confidence in passing the test the next time. I used what was left from the sale of the dry cleaning business as a down payment—the monthly payments are almost $1,000 a month—that will motivate me to sell houses like pancakes— you'll see."

Meekly, I said, "Bill, I was proud of you when you had a successful dry cleaning business—you don't need to prove anything to me."

Then, this normally quiet man, flew into a rage. "See, there you go again—always stifling my efforts. Every time I try to do something great, you want to punch me down again. You don't want me to succeed—you want me to stay in this rotten hole of poverty we're in, just like my old man; you can't fool me, mom—you hate him and you hate all the rest of us the same way. Well, the rest of the bastards you produced may not ever amount to anything but this one will, no matter how you try to stop me, you bitch." He slumped down on the edge of the bed, cupped his hands over his face, and released sobs that shook his whole body. Instinctively, I put my arms around him the way I comforted my babies when they were in pain. His sobbing turned into soft whining as his limp body molded itself into my arms. In a little boy voice he cried, "I'm sorry." He slid down on the bed and in a moment he was sound asleep.

I walked into the kitchen to get my bearings. In a daze I went through the steps of fixing me a cup of tea. I was feeling queezy to my stomach. I recognized the symptoms and was not surprised—we were married almost three months and did not use any precautions.

Now as I was sipping my tea, the enormity of our problems began to make an impression. He had confused me with his mother, evidently. What would I learn about him next. It occurred to me that Bill was a virtual stranger. He had told me that his family still lived in Ohio, where he was raised except for one brother who had also moved to California, that his brother was an alcoholic, spending most of his time in the taverns. Out of seven brothers, Bill was only the third one to be married, and the other two had married late in life like Bill. "Why?" I questioned myself now, and why did he feel such hatred toward his mother? What kind of future was I facing with Bill—the handsome, affectionate Irishman with kind, blue eyes that spoke volumes when he looked at me. His thick reddish brown hair formed neat rows of tight waves, inviting me to run my hands through it when he was in a playful mood—mood—that was the key word about Bill. His moods could change in an instant from being fun and playful to instant rage, followed by long silent spells as I was to find out on this occasion. He stayed on the bed, sleeping so long I began to worry, but I didn't dare wake him up, not knowing what I would en-counter.

In a very short time the girls and I learned to read Bill's moods and adjusted our behavior accordingly, catering to his every whim. The one thing that seemed to make him euphoric was the prospect of having our own baby —so everything came to revolve around this expected event. Although I felt a lot of inner tension, I managed to create a fairly happy atmosphere in our home.

Bill seemed to be irritated by everything the girls did. Charmy, who at 14 liked to play the radio during every waking moment, was chastised frequently for playing it too loud; and Corky, a giggly nine-year-old, couldn't do anything to please Bill no matter how she tried, and try she did, making herself a pest to him only to aggravate the situation. She had gotten it into her head that the only way she could really be his little girl was for Bill to adopt her—his answer was, "When you can behave perfectly so I can be proud to have you for a daughter, I'll give you my name." This became a cruel game—Corky would dance to Bill's whistle like a trained circus animal only to fall short of his expectations. I didn't believe that Bill was sincere about adopting them at all and decided to confront him about the unfairness of his charade. "Bill," I said, "I'm really concerned about Corky and Charmy trying so hard to become your daughters in name as well as in reality, children should be accepted for themselves, not for how perfectly they behave. I remember my own painful attempt at pleasing Muttie when I was growing up."

I tried to illustrate what happened to me by making a comparison. "Don't bring my mother into this, woman, I'm warning you," and his eyes turned to cold ice cubes.

"Bill, I was talking about my mother, not yours," I said slowly, hoping the words would sink in but it was too late. The all familiar change in personality took place as in previous times. I learned that mothers were a forbidden subject with Bill, along with a whole list of other subjects not to be discussed—narrowing down the area of conversation to current events and the weather.

While Bill was wallowing in morose silence since he'd failed his second real estate exam, I had miscarried, leaving me very vulnerable. Physically, I was not in the best of condition and emotionally I was turning into a nervous wreck, walking the constant tightrope of trying to keep the kids out of Bill's firing line. And Bill was home at all times without giving me any breathing room; eventually I would blow up at everybody when I had the least reason to.

On one occasion, I tried to make up for it by sending the girls to the movies to give Bill and me time to talk things through in privacy. He interpeted my attempt at communication to be an invitation for love making and took full advantage of our time for this purpose, leaving me feeling empty and resentful—and pregnant. In a desperate attempt to receive some nurturing, I confided to Muttie some of my feelings of loneliness on my next visit. She had returned from Germany, because "it wasn't home any more". My melancholy matched her feelings of hopelessness, resulting in a mutual decision that what she needed was a vacation. Suddenly we were packing and by evening I was waving at her boarding the plane for Canada to visit her cousins. On my trip home, I began to tremble in dread of the consequences I would have to pay for my late arrival. To my relief, everyone was asleep but somehow the quiet unnerved me—especially when it continued day after day after day, not even a "pass the salt" at the table. After a couple of weeks of the silent treatment I made an appointment with a marriage counselor. I was desperate to make this marriage work and realized I needed help, or was it Bill that needed help? To my surprise, Bill agreed to see the counselor with me. My hope soared, especially when the results seemed to be favorable. We were able to discuss some issues and, I thought, resolve them. Bill even showed some empathy when I miscarried the second time. He made an ominous statement, though, when he announced, "Well, to show you that my heart is in the right place, I'll even adopt the girls; then, maybe you'll see fit to give me my own child—hopefully a son."

I stuttered, "Bill, do you think I'm miscarrying purposely? I don't have any control over that." I wanted to continue clearing up this accusation but my words faded in the background as the girls clamored for Bill's affection, peppering him with questions, "When, Daddy?" and "How long before we can use our new name?" Bill enjoyed the attention while I was left alone with my apprehensions.

* * *

I dreaded having to contact Martin regarding consent for the girls' adoption by Bill. Again, I was taken by surprise when Martin couldn't get down to my lawyer fast enough to sign the necessary papers— would I ever learn to understand men?

This was my question to the marriage counselor on my last visit. Bill was no longer accompanying me to the sessions, claiming it was a waste of his time. After the adoption he informed me that I would have to terminate my visits as well, since our funds were now limited due to the fact that he was assuming full financial responsibility for the girls. The counselor was reluctant to stop the therapy. "I know, Aggie, that you are hopeful about your future with Bill, but you need to understand what you are facing, living with Bill's passive-aggressive personality. What differentiates passive-aggressive behavior from a simple case of "the sulks" or even an occasional grudge is that passive-aggression is a pathological reaction to authority. The clinical description is that of a person who channels aggression—energy fueled by anger into passive behavior that slows down, or "stonewalls" the efforts of another. Due to Bill's obvious sick relationship with his mother, he considered all women authority figures and therefore resisted all my attempts at building an adult relationship of two equal partners, leaving me totally frustrated." Realizing that Bill had full control of our finances, the therapist suggested I see a psychiatrist who would be able to continue therapy, paid by my health insurance. He recommended a female doctor to eliminate any possibility of Bill's jealousy rising to surface in connection with my weekly visits to the doctor.

The doctor put me at ease on my first visit, inviting me to call her Carol and focusing on my behavior instead of Bill's—that made sense of course, since she had never met Bill. I learned that you can't change someone else—only yourself—and that only by changing my own reaction to Bill's moods, would I be able to tolerate our situation. No one had ever paid as much attention to me as Carol, and I began enjoying the experience of reaching into my inner self to learn the various aspects of my personality. Things might have progressed with better results had I been able to concentrate on my therapy. Instead, circumstances required me to look for employment again when Bill failed the real estate exam for the third time, which didn't surprise me considering the fact that he never studied—he was too busy monitoring my activity. I had to terminate my new position as manager of a small yardage store in Laguna Beach after only a few weeks of employment when Bill finally accepted the reality that he was not going to make it in real estate and started working for the city maintenance department since the proceeds from the sale of the dry cleaning business were depleted. His working hours were too irregular to maintain a schedule of sharing the same car, there was no bus system, and of course his need superceded mine.

My plans of locating work nearby were interrupted when Muttie called from Canada. "Aggie, you will never guess what I'm calling about."

"No, Muttie, I can't guess, but tell me before I explode from curiousity." It felt so good to hear her voice, I had missed her terribly—to my own surprise.

"During one of my visits with various friends of my cousins from home, Aggie, a relative of your father's—can you imagine—his wife died recently in Siberia, just like Papa. We want to get married, Aggie, and I want you to come to the wedding."

"When?"

"In two weeks."

I just about fell off my chair. "Muttie, don't you think that's a little fast?" I added. "Shouldn't you ask Gary first?"

"What do I need to ask Gary for. I've made my own decisions all my life; I'm not about to start asking for advice on how to run my life now," she continued. "I will pay for the plane fare for you to fly to the Vancouver Airport and meet you there—then we will have to take the bus to cross the ocean to Vancouver Island on the ferry—that's where Henry has a house on five acres. Aggie wait 'til you see the island, it's breath takingly beautiful."

"What about your apartment with all your furniture in L.A.?"

"Oh, I've got that all taken care of—you can dispose of all my things and give notice to the landlord. No use in me coming back to do that. First of all you will come to the wedding. Oh, and buy yourself a beautiful dress for the occasion (of course I will pay for it). I want to show you off to all my new friends here. Then I'll give you a list of what I want to keep and you can have it shipped. Aggie, can you believe it—I will be a property owner in my old age—ha, ha."

I had never heard her so excited—breathless. "Of course I'll come to the wedding," I managed to stammer.

* * *

Traveling through Oregon and Washington State on the Greyhound on my return trip to California, I had time to reflect on my life as I soaked up the beautiful lush green countryside—so different from the brown, dry hills of California.

My life—a life that I seemed to have no control over—I heard Carol's voice in my mind—many things I learned about myself disturbed me deeply. I would have to make some changes—stop floating through this journey called life, like driftwood, controlled by events, largely caused by others. Never mind about relying on God to provide the answers to my problems—I would have to grow up and take charge. The book, "I'm O.K, you're O.K." the first councelor had suggested I read, had been a real eye opener to me and led to an insatiable hunger for more—I read every pop psychology book I could lay my hands on, learning how to live a mature, independent life by trial and error. Bill felt threatened by my new assertiveness and sabotaged my every effort at self improvement. The games we played were very destructive to each other—to ourselves—to our family life and the children. When I experienced another miscarriage while I was busy liquidating Muttie's belongings, he accused me of purposely killing our babies—the problem was his methods of showing me his fears and anger—we had practically no verbal communication. The pattern was for him to respond to anything I did or said by doing something destructive to our relationship without saying a word of accusation. I would drive myself crazy trying to figure out what I had done each time to incur his wrath until I would lose all control. Then, after weeks of total silence between us we would have a big confrontation resulting in Bill laying down the law and me meekly promising to follow his dictates, then building up deep resentment and rage.

One incident of this type occurred when he had the door leading to our bedroom walled up and a separate outside entrance built. I found my clothes dumped on the living room couch—he never said a word of explanation, just continued to live a bachelor's life in the bedroom, leaving me wondering why I was being punished.

Through all this, the girls were excellent students at school and stayed very close to me, but continued their arguing and bickering between each other—they both seemed to accept Bill's craziness in stride, referring to his moods jokingly as "his period." Charmaine excelled academically to the point of graduating one year early—with honors, at that. I was extremely proud of her. She found a job as a receptionist in a doctor's office while she attended a para-medical school at night and became a medical assistant in a short time, leading to a good position in the local hospital. She was making friends with fellow employees and, suddenly I found myself helping my seventeen-year-old daughter, move into her own apartment she was to share with a nurse—where had the time gone?

* * *

When Bill decided to replace the door to the bedroom again, I was so happy to have things return to "normal" that I didn't question his crazy behavior, even when his orders for me to move back into our bedroom again was worded in such a way as to suggest it had been my doing in the first place. After all—I had been conditioned all my life to accept the blame for anything that went wrong. I learned later—in therapy—that, unfortunately, while passive-aggressive behavior patterns stand out in hind-sight, they're not all that easy to identify at the time. You really don't see it at the beginning—even later on, you tell yourself you're just going through a temporary period when things aren't going well. It takes time to realize there is a deliberate strategy involved. Passive-aggressive people love to produce anxiety attacks in their partners, they feel rewarded by them. One way this is accomplished is by routine procrastinations—by agreeing to do something a certain way—or even suggesting to do it that way—then not follow through—acting helpless when confronted. Then retaliating again when you try to correct the mess—accusing you of being bossy.

When I tried to play the game by his rules and almost lost my life in the process, I knew I had to get out of this sick pattern to protect myself and Corky.

The first night we shared our bedroom again, he swept me off my feet with his charm, blaming all his immature behavior on the fact that we seemed to be unable to have any children. "Darlin, if you could just love me enough to make having my baby a priority, I would be a different person altogether," he cried.

"Bill, what do you mean,' making it a priority,'" I questioned.

"Well, like moving all your mother's things around, the doctor said for you to take it easy."

We talked long into the night, Bill impressed me with his willingness to do whatever was necessary to make ours a successful marriage.

"Honey, you were telling me how beautiful Oregon is; what would you say we sell the house and use the money to move to Oregon and establish ourselves in one of those nice little towns you mentioned seeing off the freeway on your way back from Muttie's wedding. After all, a piddly little job like I have here, I can find anywhere, and I hear living is a lot cheaper in Oregon." I was ecstatic—this was wonderful to make plans for the future; and besides, I was eager to remove Corky from the California coast. Living in the Newport Beach area, the girls practically lived in bathing suits and I had noticed the whistles directed at Corky whenever it was my turn to drop her and her friends off at the beach; it would be healthy for her to be raised in a little country town.

The doctor recommended hormone shots when he pronounced me pregnant again, to prevent another miscarriage—and to rest, keeping my feet elevated most of the time. Giving up the clerical job in a nearby department store I had during my exile from our bedroom, was easy— after all, we were now a united family again, making plans to move away from this area. As soon as the school year was over, Corky would start Junior High in Oregon.

Staying in bed most of the time for five months created a strain in itself as Bill expected Corky to keep house perfectly, critizising her for the smallest short-comings, such as hanging the wrong color towels in the bathroom or finding an occasional cup with coffee stains in the cupboard. When Corky received an invitation from Muttie to spend the upcoming summer vacation on Vancouver Island with her and Grandpa and Corky's favorite cousin, Ritchie, who was coming from Germany to spend the summer with them also, Corky did not have to think it over twice. I felt relieved of the tension created by Bill's criticism and looked forward to having the privacy Bill and I would need to bond with our new baby.

Unfortunately, once more our plans did not materialize. Bill's mood became more morose and distant as time went on and I began to regret my agreement to have another baby and felt a faint hope for another miscarriage—when I started spotting I was overcome with guilt, feeling I was making it happen simply by wishing for it. May was approaching—the month we had scheduled to sell the house and prepare for our move to Oregon. Instead—on Charmaine's 18th birthday dinner, Bill announced that the house was already sold, and he planned to use the proceeds to invest in a van to start another drycleaning route. "What?" I blurted out—"A dry cleaning route! We are living in the age of polyester—this is 1972—haven't you heard? People wash their clothes. Even men's leisure suits are washable. People have automatic washers. Just because we live in the dark ages doesn't mean everybody else does—or have you been so preoccupied with the prospect of this baby that you can't think clearly at all any more. Come to think of it, you should be doing a lot of thinking considering the fact that you live in total silence most of the time." My sarcastic remarks were meant to sting—I was so up tight from all the tension in our home for so long; and now to find out he'd made all these important decisions without including me—I felt so much hurt and anger I finally dissolved in tears. Apologizing to Charmy for ruining her birthday dinner, we left the restaurant. As I hugged Charmy she said quietly, "Now I know why I was so anxious to move out of your house. I feel sorry for Corky."

In the car on the way home, I opened the subject again. "Bill, how do you expect to make a living running a delivery route in a small town in

Oregon. People there don't live a high roller life like here in California. They pick up their own dry cleaning."

He answered in such a low tone, I had to ask him to repeat it. "We're not going to Oregon."

I became almost hysterical as I continued my questioning. The discussion ended with, "The subject is closed."

I recognized the tell tale signs of the all familiar cramps as we drove Corky to the airport to board the plane —destination Canada. By the time we had returned home, I was hemorrhaging, the pain unbearable. Unlike the previous pregnancies, this one had progressed into the sixth month and miscarriage did not happen spontanious I had to be hospitalized. When I was asked to sign surgical consent papers to remove the already dead fetus, I first recognized Bill for the sick man he really was—he refused to allow the surgery, claiming that his Catholic religion forbade him to take part in an abortion. The whole hospital scene was turned into a circus with the priest having to be called to make the decision. I was unable to think clearly due to the intense pain and in the midst of all the confusion, the baby was delivered without surgery in the emergency room by the nurse. The priest had arrived and I watched him baptize our son. The doctor was finally allowed to give me something for the pain and I drifted into oblivion to the sound of muffled voices. I regained consciousness in the stillness of the night, feeling pain in my heart far greater than in my body. I had seen my baby—it was really not a miscarriage but a real baby. I longed to hold him. In my mind I knew it was a blessing for the baby and for me, but in my soul I only felt the loss.

I was too numb even to ask for more pain medication. Somehow, the physical pain seemed a welcome companion as I allowed the tears to wash away the pain of the last few months and open up the way for what lay ahead.

Bill came the next day, only to leave me money for cab fare home— no explanation why he would not pick me up in the car—no condolences or sharing of the loss we had experienced. I knew I had to get away from Bill to survive.

Mechanically, I loaded Corky's and my personal posessions into our old car while Bill was out in his new van, establishing his dry cleaning route, and waited in front of Charmaine's door when she returned from work.

"Charmy," I began, "I'm leaving for Oregon—by myself."

"Are you divorcing Daddy, Mom?"

"I don't know, all I know is that I have to get away from him right now to save my sanity; and I have to do it while Corky is out of the way to save her the trauma of what I may encounter in Oregon. I love you, honey, and I hate to leave you on your own as young as you are. I will let you know an address as soon as I have one and I want you to know my door will always be open for you."

"I love you," we repeated simultaneously as our tears mingled while we embraced.

I watched all the familiar sights disappear in my rear view mirror as I slowly headed out of the L.A. area. When the last rays of the sun finally disappeared on the horizon, I pulled off the road and fell into an exhausted sleep seeking escape from my emotional as well as physical torment.

The golden rays of the setting sun sparkled on the dome of the capital building of Salem, Oregon as I wearily entered the city in pursuit of a home.

With the aid of a local map hanging on the motel wall, I chose a small town fifteen miles out of town. After supper and a good night's sleep, I would explore my future home—mine and Corky's. I mused about this in the car the next morning—how the people in my life were slowly leaving me—first Papa, then Gary with his family, followed by Muttie—and now I'd left Charmy behind—and Martin, and Bill who I determined to put out of mind as soon as they entered—only Corky was left. It would be me and her against the world.

Luck was with me. Within a week I had secured a sales-clerk position with the small department store in town and was able to stay in one of the twelve rooms of the local motel in exchange for maid services. This was not too difficult since only four to five rooms were occupied every night.

I was down to $8.00 on my first payday as I searched for an apartment. School was to begin in another week and I started to panic slightly when it slowly dawned on me that rentals were almost impossible to find—one of the not so pleasant discoveries of small town life—along with only one newspaper being published every Thursday—the classified consisting of one-fourth page.

Somewhat discouraged, I voiced my concern to the other salesclerk at the store. "Maybe I can help you," she said. "My uncle has a very small house a few blocks from here."

"Everything is only a few blocks from here, Ida," I laughed. She agreed, finding that remark not as humorous as I intended. "Anyway," she continued, "my uncle used to rent it out to a single woman with two little girls. Due to her negligence, there was a fire and my uncle had to completely refurbish it and now he wants to sell it. He is afraid to rent it out again—but he might change his mind if I recommend you."

The tiny, old house was almost completely hidden by two gigantic black walnut trees, giving it a very secluded, homey atmosphere. As soon as the owner unlocked the door and held it open for me, I knew I was home—surrounded by shrubs and flowers that needed tending. The interior of new paint, wall-paper and carpet was a surprise; but then I remembered the fire my collegue had mentioned—that explained the "newness." I pleaded and finally begged to rent the house, suggesting I make a cleaning deposit.

"No, little lady, the folks around here go by handsakes—I believe you that you'd take right good care of the place, but I'm too old to be bothered anymore." Then he added, "but I'd sell it to you on a contract—and with low interest."

My heart sank. "No, I can't afford to buy a house," and then questioned "how much would you want down anyway?"

"Oh, about $1,000 down, $100 a month should have it paid for in about 12 years—you're still young enough to get it paid off."

I'm not exactly the best mathematician in the world, but even I was able to make some simple computations. "Well, how much are you asking for it total?" I held my breath.

"$10,500," he announced proudly.

This sure isn't California, I thought to myself. This is where I wanted to raise Corky. I already pictured her in my mind being married to some nice, stable farm boy. "Will you promise not to show the house to anyone til tomorrow?" I asked. "I need to call my mother before I can make a decision."

"Oh, don't worry about that; the last person inquiring about it was about two weeks ago."

Muttie agreed to lend me the $1,000 down payment on the condition I put her on the deed, saying "That's the only way I can make sure that Bill won't sell it and squander the money as soon as he finds you."

"Oh, Muttie, why do you always have to expect the worst? Bill is not going to come after me—and even if he did, what makes you think I'd take him back?" I could feel the conversation getting out of hand and quickly reminded myself silently that I needed Muttie's help—as usual. I changed the mood to congenial and Muttie was eager to take care of my need—as usual.

* * *

Corky arrived in Salem by Greyhound, eager to see her new home. I was struck by how beautiful and grown-up she looked, descending the steps of the bus. Her thick, long hair framed a delicately made-up face. "When did that start?" I pointed to her lips.

"Oh," she answered, "same place as that"—she pointed to the never ending suitcases being unloaded with her name on the tags. I was momentarily distracted by the attentiveness of the young man unloading the luggage—and the way Corky responded to the attention. When had she grown up? In one summer? Without me even noticing? What else had I not noticed about my precious little girl while I was pre-occuped with myself. Well, that would change—I would now have plenty of time and attention to devote to Corky.

Comfortably settled in the car, Corky explained about all the clothes she said were in the suitcases. Gary had made a short visit at Mutties to pick up Ritchie and noticed that Corky was about the same size as his Heidi—when he returned to Germany, Erika had mailed all of Heidi's discards to Corky—some items still new with Paris, France tags on them. "You look like a movie star," I told her as she modeled all the beautiful clothes that evening—in our new home. We slept, wrapped up in blankets on the floor, feeling like queens—the furniture would come, we promised ourselves.

It did—every pay day we came across just what we needed—with a little touch of paint here and there and the use of some fabrics and an old sewing machine given to me by a new acquaintance, we had all the necessities in no time. Corky liked Junior High but had to try hard at making friends. Californians were not accepted too readily in Oregon at the time, with cars displaying slogans such a "Californians go home," or "Come to visit but not to stay." Corky's designer clothes didn't help her either in this little country town where overalls were the uniform for most of her school mates.

One Sabbath morning, feeling lonely, we watched people enter the little church visible from our front room window—ironically it happened to be an SDA Church. "Remember when we used to attend church regularly, Mom?" No answer seemed to be necessary. We walked into our separate bedrooms and moments later, dressed appropriately, we walked up the steps, into a congregation of about 45 members.

It was comforting to participate in singing the old familiar hymns and kneel in prayer. How long had it been since I last talked to God? After the usual fellowship dinner, during which we were welcomed warmly, Corky slipped her soft slender hand into mine, reminiscent of an earlier time when she was a clinging toddler. "Mom, can we do this regularly again?" she almost whispered.

I nodded, too overcome with emotion for words. For a few weeks we enjoyed the peacefulness of our family life—our family of two. Then— one Sabbath, as we returned from church, Corky's grip on my hand tightened as we both noticed a figure pacing in front of our house— Bill. He embraced us, took the keys out of my hand, unlocked the door, and held it open for Corky and me, surveyed the house while chatting amiacably about the money from the sale of the house that had finally come through—how he had enjoyed a nice visit with his family back east, and how sorry he was that it had taken so long to join us. I listened open-mouthed to the non-stop chatter as he unloaded his things, hanging his clothes in the closet, as if this was all according to plan.

Somehow it seemed unnatural to object to be taken to nearby Portland for dinner at a fancy restaurant to celebrate our being together again. Just like in the past, I obediently accepted his decisions without discussion, feeling totally incompetent. When he surprised me at Thanksgiving by inviting Charmy to visit us, paying for the expense— and I observed my whole family together again, I convinced myself that my decision to reconcile was the right one—or had I ever consciously made that decision, a little voice questioned. I pushed away the thought. It would be good this time—why, look at us, even the girls weren't quarreling any more; and Bill really was a different man, standing at the head of the table, carving the turkey.

The Christmas holidays were approaching—with a heavy snowfall—the first snow Corky had ever experienced. I watched as she frolicked with Bill, shoveling the sidewalk and putting up Christmas lights.

"Please, Lord," I prayed, "Let it continue to be good."

My prayer went unanswered. Bill's mood changed abruptly when during the holiday rush I passed out at the store and I was taken to the hospital for surgery—a hysterectomy was necessary due to complications from the miscarriages. I was relieved to know that I would regain my health after the operation for I had become severely anemic from all the bleeding.

Bill came to the hospital the night before the surgery was to take place to confront me about my decision to have the operation. "You know, of course, that by having this operation, you are deliberately closing the door forever to any possibility of us having children?"

"Bill, I don't have a choice; my life depends on it," I pleaded.

"So, you're mind is made up?"

"Of course it is."

He turned to leave. "Then there is no future left for us, my things are packed in the car and I've rented an apartment. I expected your answer to be this—you've confirmed it—you're proving that you never did love me—we're through." He was out the door.

As I was drifting off into unconsciousness, my last thoughts were concern for Corky being left alone. "Please God," I prayed, "Take care of her."

I had made arrangements for some church member to pick me up at the hospital on the day of my discharge, only to be puzzled and embarrassed when Bill walked in, ordering, "She doesn't need charity; she's my wife and I'm taking her home."

My new friend saved the day with a quick response, "Oh, that's great—I knew you were picking her up—I'm just here as a back-up. I didn't know if you could get up this hill without snowtires, not being used to icey roads, considering you just came from California. I'm glad you made it," turning to me she said, "I'll be stopping in to see you soon, Aggie, get well quick."

From that day on, Bill kept me upset and off balance all of the time and added to his disruptive behavior was my new hormone imbalance. I accepted the blame for the disharmony in our home. Things were happening at a whirlwind speed. First of all I noticed a visible change in Corky's attitude toward Bill, where before she had been vying for Bill's attention, she now shunned him. I tortured myself with questions, wondering what had happened while I was in the hospital since it seemed to have started at that time. I remembered Corky's answer to my comment that I was glad Bill hadn't left her alone after all, while I was hospitalized. "Yea, I wish he'd stayed in Salem." When I questioned her, "Why, honey, what happened?" She just brushed me off with "Never mind."

Then followed Bill's obsession with how to use the $16,000 we had made on the house sale in California. Coming home one day he announced "I'm not going to continue to live in my mother-in-law's house." When I tried to reason with him, he said "It's too late to change my mind, I already bought another house; we're moving next week."

Shortly after we moved into "his" house, he found a seven-acre Christmas tree farm for sale. "This will make us big money," he boasted as we evicted the renters from my little house and moved back in because the big house had to be sold to buy the Christmas tree farm. All this time, while he was too busy investing his money, we lived on my meager sales clerk wages. In the meantime Charmaine had fallen in love and was planning her wedding. I was determined to give her the kind of wedding I felt she deserved, saving expenses by sewing all the bridesmaid dresses and changing jobs to a higher paid position with the state offices in nearby Salem to pay for the rest of the expenses, since Bill refused to see the necessity for a wedding at all.

Somehow Corky, Muttie and I survived the trip to California for the celebration, but Muttie refused to go back with us. "Aggie," she said, "I don't know why you put up with this crazy man. If you had tried half as hard to make your first marriage succeed, you could have had a good life. I can't stand to watch you let him kill you; and believe me, that's what he is going to do eventually. He's already changed you into a different person."

Muttie had aroused my anger again. "Well, then you should be real happy, Muttie, since you never did like my former self," I shot back as she boarded the Greyhound for Canada, tears trickling down both our cheeks, belieing the harsh words just spoken.

When the Christmas trees were only two years away from harvesting, Bill decided he couldn't wait that long for his big fortune to materialize. He sold the farm to use the money as a down payment on a franchise of a fast food restaurant. While Bill was in Fresno, California training for the position of owner-manager, Corky and I were trying to deal with the prospect of having to move to New Jersy since we were told that's where the restaurant Bill was assigned to was located. While we did not want to move that far away from Charmy, Muttie and the new friends we had made in Oregon, I knew there was no way out and I would have to sell my little house. Muttie refused to sign the necessary papers. "Aggie, the only reason I insisted on having my name on the deed when I lent you the down payment, was so that you would have a roof over your head when your so-called marriage would collapse. I'm not going to let you sell the house and turn that profit over to that b—you're married to. As sure as I live, I tell you he's going to flop at this too and you'll be happy to have a house to come home to. The way the real estate prices are going up, you'll never be able to buy another. You can rent it out in the meantime."

I was too tired to argue with her and I worried about how to tell Bill—needlessly, for in a couple of weeks he was back home, announcing he'd backed out of the restaurant contract "All they want is free labour; they had me washing dishes most of the time. I'm not their lackie." I was exhausted from all this emotional upheaval.

Wearily I asked, "Bill, what are you going to do about a job now? The money is running out you know."

"Yes, I know the money is running out—I don't need to be told by a woman what to do. You just can't let one opportunity go by without rubbing my nose into my failures, can you. Well, I'll show you, I'll show..."

"No, Bill, you don't have to show me anything. I have faith in you. I'm sorry I said that," I begged, afraid of what he would do next to "show me."

During all this time he'd retained that apartment in Salem, and every time we had an argument, he'd move out, only to come back in a few days.

This time he returned triumphant in a big Peterbuilt freightliner truck. I just about fainted when he told me the payments were $1,000 a month, quickly explaining that he already had a contract to haul cargo to Montana. He would be leaving in a few days.

It was once again Christmas season and Muttie with her husband, Henry, had come to visit. I was at a loss as to explain Bill's irrational and impulsive behavior, but became even more embarrassed when he called on New Year's Eve from the Salem Greyhound station, asking me to pick him up. To our questions, "What happened?"

He said, "I don't owe you an explanation."

Muttie told him in a few choice words what she thought of him, ending the evening in an argument with me driving Muttie and Henry to the Greyhound station. The amused attendant at the ticket window questioned, "Are you trying to keep us in business, lady?"

243

Later, Bill just said about the truck venture, "It was too dangersous, driving the semi on those icey roads. I sold the rig to another trucker I met at a coffee stop." It came back to haunt him when the trucker defaulted on the payments after putting enough miles on the truck to make it almost impossible to sell the vehicle—with Bill being liable for the monthly payments. After that venture, the money gone—Bill decided once more to become a real estate tycoon. This time he passed the test on his second try and signed up with an agency in Salem. His success in that field was short lived when he'd made a shady deal and the new owners promptly sued him and his liscense was revoked.

I had to leave for Canada because Muttie had suffered a massive heart attack. For a while her condition was so grave, I concentrated all my energy on dealing with her recovery, not worrying too much about the home situation. Bill was driving a bus now and Corky, at 15, should be able to run the house efficiently enough till I would return I reasoned. Muttie recovered but never regained her health completely. I was angry with Corky for staying at her girlfriend's the last few days of my absence; scolding her only for shirking her home duties, instead of asking for a reason. I was too tired to think, much less care about anything. For me, life had become merely a survival test, and I was slowly losing the battle. Bill continued to jump from job to job with long periods of unemployment in between, creating the perfect situation at home for what happened during the summer of 1974.

Corky was waitressing at the local fast foods to provide herself with clothes for her first year of high school, working evenings—sleeping in mornings and using the midday hours for bathing, etc. I was walking quietly through the living room barefooted when what I saw made me stop short. Bill was crouching down by the bathroom door, using the old fashioned key hole as his personal peeping device while Corky was occupied inside the bathroom. Bill must have felt my presence for he jumped up and spun around, guilt written on his face. The picture became clear to me—how could I have been so unsuspecting. Ever since my surgery Corky had found reasons not to be left home alone with Bill. I was too shocked to open my mouth. Standing there, glued to the ground, Bill brushed passed me, whispering between clenched teeth, "Well you really haven't been much fun in that department lately, you know." I collapsed, sliding down the wall I was trying to lean against as he rounded the corner of the hall and out the back door.

Corky emerged from the bathroom, her hair wrapped in a towel and smelling of talcum, reminding me of her baby days only a short time ago. "Mom, what are you doing on the floor? Oh, you're white as a sheet, what happened? Did you see a ghost?" She helped me up and made me lie down, clucking over me like a mother hen. I heard her go through her dressing routine—she turned off her stereo, planted a kiss on my forehead and rushed out to work. Only then was I able to release the gut wrenching sobs as the reality of the situation began to sink in. I was overcome with panic. I needed help. Corky needed help—we all needed help. Where to turn? I reached for the phone, unaware of who I was calling until my minister's voice answered on the other end of the line. "Can you and your wife come to see me—right now—I need help desperately," I choked between sobs. "We'll be right over," was the answer. I was still clutching the receiver as the doorbell rang— moments later I collapsed in the wife's arms.

I was all done explaining the problem to my visitors listening to the minister's advice, when Corky came in the back door, unnoticed, to retrieve her waitress uniform she had forgotten in her haste earlier, overhearing just enough of the conversation to misunderstand. "Aggie," the minister was saying, "your church family has offered before to pay for parochial school for Corky. I know how you feel about charity, but I think you need to seriously consider accepting our offer. The very first thing you need to think about is to protect Corky, while you try to work out the problem with Bill, and boarding school would remove Corky from the present situation."

It sounded like the perfect solution. We prayed together before the man and his wife left. I felt calmer with a plan of action. I waited for Corky to come home, and waited and waited—neither Corky nor Bill returned home that whole night. I assumed Bill was staying in his apartment again, which suited me fine; but where was Corky? I called her boss who answered my questions with surprise. "I thought she was home, she left in the middle of her shift last night, said she was sick."

Just as I was reaching for the phone again, Corky walked in, her face puffy, obviously from a night of crying. The talk with her that I had planned so carefully, turned into an angry confrontation. I was not prepared for the accusations hurled at me not knowing that Corky had overheard what she interpreted as the first thing to have to do, Aggie, is to get rid of Corky.

Her last words as she stormed out of the door again were: "If you want to stay married to that f— b— so bad that you'd rather throw me out, your own daughter, I'll oblige, but don't expect me to go to some church school like a nun just to accommodate you. I'll be out of here tomorrow. You won't have to worry about me any more."

I reached for her, both of us crying hysterically. "Oh, honey, you've got it all wrong."

She didn't let me finish. "Oh, no, Mom, you've got it all wrong; and I'm not sticking around for you to ruin my life the way you're ruining yours." She was gone—I was shaking.

For the next few months things were happening with lightning speed. I felt like a piece of driftwood being tossed around by angry waves, bumping into a new problem every time I tried to avoid an existing one.

Thinking Corky was staying with her girl friend, Debbie, I decided that probably wasn't such a bad idea for right now, and I should call Debbie's mother, Darlene, to explain the situation. "No, Aggie," Darlene said on the other end of the line, "she's not here-ah, uh—I don't want to add to your worries, but I do know where she is—I'm surprised you haven't suspected."

"Suspected what?" my voice started shaking again. "Darlene, please tell me everything I should know. I'm afraid I've neglected Corky lately and lost touch with her activities. She's been working such long shifts lately and—"

Darlene interrupted, "Aggie, haven't you wondered how Corky has had the energy to work those long hours and cope with first year of high school and a boyfriend, and—"

"Wait a minute, Darlene, what are you talking about? A boy friend—I haven't heard anything about a boy friend—and yes, I have been wondering where Corky is getting all her energy from."

"Speed, Aggie, speed is the source of her energy. Jason got her started on that, and on booze."

"Stop, Darlene, back up, you're going too fast and half of what you are saying I don't understand. What is speed, and if she's drinking why haven't I smelled anything, and—"

"And I suppose you don't know who Jason is either?" Darlene finished the conversation with, "we haven't allowed Debbi to associate with Corky for a while. If you want Corky to have any decent friends, you'd better straighten her out."

I received a crash course in the next few days about the various capsules and pills I'd seen occasionally in Corky's pockets, the fact that Vodka doesn't smell on your breath, and Jason—the 22 year-old high school dropout who was supplying Corky with all of these things—and now with shelter as well—and the price Corky was paying. I didn't need to ask anyone about that. I shuddered. "How could things have gone so bad, so fast?"

I searched Corky's room for any evidence that would convince me I was over-reacting—and found only answers to the contrary. "How could I have been so blind, so wrapped up in my own problems to not pick up on some of the clues? I talked to her teachers, her boss—everybody knew all about Jason—everybody but me. I looked up this man, planning to reason with him—maybe he didn't even know that Corky was only 16. He—and Corky—I'd heard lived in a sleazy trailer park outside of town. I was met by two giant German shepphards, racing toward my car as I drove up the driveway. It was obvious they were trained to protect their property, needless for me to get out of the car. I saw shadows behind the frayed drapes—I sounded my horn to gain someone's attention. My eyes surveyed the littered, weedy yard as I waited. Broken down old cars were parked everywhere. I couldn't imagine my baby living in this filth. "Do something," a voice demanded inside of me. It was obvious I was being ignored on purpose.

I went home to retrieve the little bag of marijuana I had found in Corky's room. Armed with my "evidence" I walked into our local police station. I would report my own daughter to the authorities. I had to get her back home fast.

The police station experience was a real eye-opener. They knew all about Corky's situation. She had filed a "youth emancipation act." I was told as long as she attended school, supported herself and didn't get into any trouble with the law, the police would do nothing. The bag of maiyana? "Oh," they laughed, "the grass isn't enough to be worried about. It's less than an ounce, all the kids are smoking the stuff."

My mind was in a whirl-my body was going through the motions of everyday responsibilities. Bill was coming and going—sometimes staying in Salem and sometimes claiming his place at home. I had started sleeping in Corky's bed for two reasons—I couldn't stand the thought of Bill sleeping next to me, and I wanted to be aware of Corky's return the minute she walked into her room, I made arrangements with the school principal to assist me in allowing Corky to skip a class now and then for me to pick her up at random times at the school in order to keep in touch with her and hopefully convince her to come back home. I would take Corky to the restaurant during our special visits and have my speech all prepared—only I was never able to deliver it—Corky made it clear that our conversation would be limited to fashions and the weather if I wanted our dates to continue—she was in control. But her eyes were brimming with unshed tears every time she said, "Goodby, Mom," keeping my little flame of hope burning.

When, during one of our visits I noticed evidence of physical abuse, I was sure we were only one step away from Corky accepting my invitation to return home. Corky instead denied the abuse, blaming the bruises on some accident. Although she was trembling while trying to convince me of her story, she was not ready to admit her mistake. I had raised her to be prepared to pay the consequences for her actions and she was going to prove to me that she was an adult. She stormed out of the little cafe, running back to school, her long blond hair matted around her flushed face—the beautiful hair she used to shampoo and style twice a day—my precious baby, being abused by someone because she felt she had no home———. This was all my fault. By making the wrong choices in my own life, I had ruined my daughter's life as well, while all along I had convinced myself it was for her sake

I was keeping some kind of family life—or had it been for my sake. Muttie was right; I was a totally selfish person. I didn't deserve to live.

I wasn't aware of getting into the car or driving home instead of back to work. I didn't notice Bill's car in the driveway—I just needed the safety of some privacy. My mind was racing as I threw down my purse and keys, heading for the living room, and there sat Bill—comfortably on the couch, feet on the coffee table, drinking coffee and watching T.V.

"You," I hissed between clenched teeth. "It's you that's causing all this misery for all of us."

He smiled, "What are you whispering for—I can't hear you."

"You want to hear me"—my voice shrill I continud, "You will hear me. I've put up with your tormenting me with your silent treatments long enough," I was yelling now.

"Would you rather I scream at you the way you're doing to me right now?" he asked slowly, calmly. His unconcern unnerved me completely.

"If you think that screaming at you is unpleasant, you haven't seen nothing yet, buddy."

I lunged at him with both fists, knocking the coffee cup out of his hands. It went flying across the room, crashing into the T.V. The sound of breaking glass fed the flames of fury inside me. I picked up a heavy glass candy dish and hurled it into the front window—glass was flying everywhere. The fear on Bill's face gave me courage to continue. "You bastard, I should have thrown you out a long time ago. I thought we could make it work, but you didn't even try, all this time lusting after my daughter, a child. What kind of slime are you anyway,—to think I thought I loved you. I despise you, scum of the earth is what you are. I want you out of here right now—get out of my sight. If you stay, I'm going to wind up killing you, and you're not worth going to jail for. Get out of here, Bill, or I'll kill you." I was still throwing things as Bill made his escape out the front door to the sound of my voice echoing in my ears—"I'll kill you, I'll kill you."

Bill was gone—no one left to vent my rage on but myself, "I'll kill you, I'll kill you" I kept repeating as I walked into the bathroom and reached for the various bottles of pills Bill had used for "muscle relaxants" over the years. "I'll kill you, I'll kill you," the voice said as I methodically swallowed the pills till the last one was gone. I kept searching the medicine chest—pain pills left from my surgery—anti-histomines for sinus problems—libriums for Bill's nerves—sleeping pills for my insomnia—the last one, finally. I would crawl into my nice comfortable bed—oh good, I'd left the electric blanket on, it was warm—rest—that's what I needed—as I drifted off. Oh, it felt so good—no more problems. I would sleep forever.

Chapter 8

The one good thing that came out of my suicide attempt was that I was forced to seek psychiatric treatment. I was also fortunate that the doctor assigned to my case happened to be of the same religious faith that I was raised in and was now having a difficult time practicing due to some of my stilted view-points learned from Muttie who saw God as a demanding task-master, not a loving Father.

I was able to place my confidence in Dr. Howard since his basic values matched mine. Together we worked through some of the obstacles in my mind that had caused me to make decisions out of fear or rebellion instead of based on sound judgment. Rather than analize my behavior, he helped me to understand my motives and raised my self esteem. I longed to start attending church regularly again, but was too embarrassed to face my friends since I was finally gaining the courage to file for a second divorce. After all, wouldn't they say in agreement with Muttie, "Well, one divorce may be a mistake—but having a second one only shows that you're not willing to work hard enough to make a marriage last, always taking the easy way out." So, instead, I withdrew my membership in the church so as not to bring reproach to the church by not living up to its standards. Periodically, I would attend services on a Sabbath in one of the big congregations in Salem, slipping in and out of church unnoticed.

The divorce was painful and nasty. Bill insisted that the little house he'd previously refused to live in, now was rightfully half his property.

I realized Muttie had made the right (again) decision when she'd insisted to put her name on the deed. Bill lost, but only after a long drawn out court battle. At long last on a beautiful spring day, I stood on the courthouse steps in Salem, a single woman again. This time there was no Muttie and Gary to shake my hand, give comfort—or even be available for an argument.

Walking into the empty house, the realization that I was now truly alone was overwhelming. When in my life had I ever been totally alone? Never. Always I had longed for some peaceful privacy, but always I had been surrounded by people and demands—now my time had come. I slowly sank into the softness of my comfortable chair—the quiet around me was unnerving—I looked around the room; here and there I noticed empty spaces where Bill's face had smiled in the wood-framed photo taken during a happy moment—now an empty spot on the bookshelf.

The coffee table looked bare without the crystal candy dish—I relived the moment of rage when I had hurled it through the window. Mostly, I noticed the absence of clutter created by a teenager who was missing. Would Corky ever come back? I waited for the tears to come to cleanse me from all this pain. I willed them to come, but my burning eyes stayed dry and my body refused to leave the chair. My hands began to tremble, my skin became clammy, yet I felt a flush wash over my whole being—a panic I had never experienced before enveloped me. I spent the night glued to the chair, watching the night shadows slink around the room until daylight brought the courage to go through the morning routine of preparing for the day.

Strangely enough, through all this turmoil, I was excelling at my job to have been promoted to clerical specialist, handling problems and customer complaints. During my lunchbreak, I found myself describing the previous night to Dr. Howard. "Your experience is not unusual," Dr. Howard reassured me. "They're called panic attacks; you will probably have reoccurances of the episodes for some time until you feel confident to handle life on your own."

Dr. Howard's prediction was correct. For the next two years I came to live in fear of another attack until the fear of the incidents was almost worse than the attacks themselves. But I was also living with fears based on reality. Bill's persistence of demanding a reconciliation amazed me.

"If only he had put half as much effort into making our marriage work as he was now, investing in getting me back, the divorce would not have taken place," I reasoned. But each time he did some especially thoughtful thing to gain my attention; he would prove his selfish motives by some vicious revenge the minute I did not respond favorably to his advances. There was hardly a day that he was not in my life somehow—waiting for me in the lobby of my office building, parking his car outside my bedroom window, playing sad love songs on a tape recorder; even ringing the doorbell of a new friend I had recently been introduced to when he spotted my car outside her house. I came to expect his presence everywhere, leaving me with a feeling of annoyance at all times. Then, when several days would go by without a sign of Bill, I would become anxious, wondering what he was up to.

I knew I would have to take his persistence seriously and protect myself when one Sunday afternoon as I was having coffee with my friend, we heard a strange sound like the chattering of glass, and discovered that her car window had been shot out. Monday after work, I discovered two small holes in my bedroom window—the policeman who investigated, confirmed that they were caused by rifle bullets—not bee bee guns as I had suspected.

After counseling with Dr. Howard and a lot of wavering back and forth, I came to the decision that a move was in order.

Corky had married Jason the day she turned 18, not needing parental consent any more, and from all appearances she would never return home again, eliminating the need to keep the house. I would sell the house and rent an efficiency apartment in a security building near the State Office—it would be convenient and safe—only one problem— Muttie's name was still on the deed.

While I was agonizing over how to present my plans to Muttie in order to gain her cooperation, Muttie herself solved my dilemma. During her routine phone call the following Friday,—"Gatel," she said hesitantly (she still used my original name during times when we were very close—"Gatal," she continued, "I need you." She broke into tears, speaking haltingly, "Gatel—I—need you." Sobs now came across the wire.

"Muttie, what happened, what's wrong?" Somehow, I pieced together the words interrupted by weeping. Muttie had a large malignant tumor and was scheduled for a radical mastectomy the following Monday. The time had come to leave fear behind me and drive my car up to Vancouver Island. The Greyhound would not be able to accommodate me this time. By Sunday evening my car safely parked in Muttie and Henry's driveway. Muttie and I for the first time in our lives shared our true feelings for each other as we sipped herb tea and reminisced late into the night.

When the discussion turned to my decision to sell the house, she was in full agreement stating, "Aggie, you have really grown up. I trust you to be able to take care of yourself now, especially since you have freed yourself from Bill finally. It's been so painful for me to watch you torture yourself, trying to be loving to a man whose only desire obviously was to destroy you. If only you had tried half as hard with—"

I cut her off, "Muttie, we are finally establishing a closeness we have both longed for all our life, please don't spoil this moment for both of us by bringing up Martin again."

"You're right, Aggie; let's leave the past behind us and look to the future. You are finding your way back to Jesus and He will help you to be happy again and He will restore my health if it is His will. We will have confidence based on that promise by our Heavenly Father—now, give me your housepapers I need to sign."

* * *

God's will for Muttie turned out to be different than expected. She survived the surgery but did not regain her health. She deteriorated rapidly, needing to be placed in a nursing home after nine months of struggling to care for herself, Henry and the house with me driving up to Canada every three months to lend assistance with whatever the need was at the moment. The day finally arrived when Muttie herself made the decision to be placed in a nursing home. Gary flew in from Germany providing me with a nice, long private visit with my brother whom I adored more than ever in his motel room the night before we moved Muttie and Henry to a German/Mennonite nursing home in Abbotsford, B.C. Gary and I both knew that Muttie's days were numbered and we would have to make her a priority in our lives. We came to the agreement that I would make all the trips necessary to meet her needs, with Gary making himself responsible for the cost.

After settling Muttie and Henry in their rooms and watching Gary's plane fade behind the clouds, carrying him out of my life again, most likely forever—I was again overcome by panic attacks on the trip home. I would have to pull the car over to the side of the road, totally overcome with fear and trembling. My mind kept repeating, "You need somebody, Aggie; you're truly all alone now. God does not expect that of you; you need somebody to love you—need—need—need."

"Stop it," I screamed silently, closing my ears with my hands, "Stop it! Stop it!"

Slowly I drove on again. I was so-o-o tired. I needed my bed, my home; no, what I needed was strong, masculine arms around me. I calmed down at the thought. I could still feel the rough tweed of Gary's jacket when he hugged me at the airport. His aftershave still lingered on my cheek. A still small voice stirred me to tears. "It's a complete trust in Jesus you need; not a man." I pushed the voice out of my heart—"No, no, no," I answered. "Jesus only produces tears, just like now—tears. I don't want any more tears. I want to laugh; I want to dance; I want to love; I want to live."

Calmly the thought came, "What's stopping you?" I welcomed the feeling of calmness. This must be the answer—it feels right. I'm not crying. I'm in control. I'm going to live.

Chapter 9

I pursued the pleasures of single life with my usual determination to follow through on my decisions, only to discover I was becoming more miserable than ever. I accepted every invitation I received and was completely surprised to find that men considered me attractive. I made good use of my talent in fashion designing to dress elegantly, yet provocatively—it worked. I never lacked for a date or invitations to parties and celebrations. I made sure never to return to my apartment until I was physically and mentally exhausted, so I would have having no periods of solitude fearing more panic attacks.

During this time I also became a grandmother at the age of 42. Corky presented me with a tiny little granddaughter in August, and Charmy followed by having a handsome strong looking boy the following February. Although I could admire Casey only on pictures since Charmy was still living in California, I was able to cuddle and hold my little Tiffany as often as I chose. Most of all, I loved sewing darling little dresses and taking her to the local mall where she always received much attention from the shoppers. She had her father's huge black eyes and black hair, but repeatedly people would exclaim, "She looks just like her grandmother."

One day I reminisced over my old photographs Muttie had been able to protect through the whole war, to discover that yes, indeed, the resemblance was evident. Why had I been labeled the ugly duckling of the family I wondered as I saw the pretty, little girl on the pictures, smiling at me. The more time I spent with little Tiffany, the hollower my social life seemed to me and it was difficult to suppress the feelings of a longing for a tranquil home life.

As if these conflicting emotions weren't enough to deal with, I had the added concern for Muttie, making several trips to the nursing home in Abbottsford every month. I watched her deteriorate, bringing the reality of her life slipping away to force my thoughts to the time I would have to let her go—this brought total panic to my entire being. Once more my energy level was at the lowest when Ray, a man I had dated several times, proposed marriage—very unexpected. Since I no longer believed in love, I was able to make my decision based on logic, forgetting about my feelings of insecurity and how my emotions were still overriding my decision making abilities. I should have been alerted by Ray's statement, "The first thing we need to do is look for a nice (putting emphasis on "nice") house. I figure that with my monthly income from rental properties, we could easily make substantial payments if we could use proceeds from the sale of your house as downpayment." The fact that I had never mentioned the money from my house sale indicated that he must have done some research totally escaped my notice. Instead, I allowed my mind to focus on the big, beautiful house he was describing we would live in. Before I had time to think things through, I received a call from the nursing home— Muttie was scheduled for more surgery the next day. "Her chances of survival are very slim," the voice on the wire informed me, "but she insists that she would rather die on the operating table than linger on in a slow, agonizing death." Muttie's problem was her stomach and she would have to be tube-fed without the surgery.

I arrived at St. Paul's Hospital in Vancouver, Canada at 4 a.m. Muttie and I had two hours before she would receive her pre-op. I scooped her up in my arms as I leaned over her bed, noticing with shock how light she was. I rocked her as I had done my children and as she had rocked and comforted me during all the terrified nights of bombings, our tears mingling as our cheeks touched. Finally the words came, "Aggie, I will not see you again after today. We both know that. And I have some things to say to you that should have been said a very long time ago. I haven't always done right by you and I need your forgiveness. I know God has forgiven me because He knows my motives, and even though some of my actions have hurt you, it was always done out of total love for you. The mistakes I have made were due to my own problems…"

I hugged her tighter, "Sh-sh, Muttie; of course I forgive you, just as I know you have already forgiven me for all the heartache I've caused you. I love you and I can't let you go like this. We deserve to have some pleasant times together yet."

The nurse came in with the hypodermic needle poised. We knew the time had come to let go. "I'll see you in heaven, Aggie," she said as they wheeled her through the double doors.

I was unable to reach Gary until late afternoon, when I was able to report to him that yes, indeed, she had survived the operation. Gary in his usual businesslike manner replied in a crisp voice, "Well, thank you Aggie, for being there for both of us—and be sure to send me the bill for your expenses." His comments kept repeating in my ears all the way home, making me feel completely rejected as a sister—was I just another business problem for him to deal with? Couldn't he tell that I needed some reassurance on a personal level? Or didn't he care? Was I still just his baby sister interfering in his important life.

Ray did a good job of picking up the pieces on my arrival at home, He moved at such a fast pace I had no time for objections. We were married and moved into our beautiful split-level house in Portland the day after Thanksgiving. What had finally persuaded me to think this was a good arrangement is difficult to determine. He gave me emotional support when I had no one else to turn to. Muttie was no longer able to, depending instead on me to supply all the strength for both of us. Gary was too busy to be bothered with my problems. Charmy never was one to be sentimental—she was busy living her own life in California with her husband and son; and Corky—my poor darling Corky, was managing somehow, going through a divorce. She had tolerated the physical abuse from Jason, thinking that all his promises of "I'll never do it again," were sincere. But when he abused little Tiffany, she knew that divorce was the only answer. She paid a high price for what I believed was my fault. After all, if her home life had been more stable, she would never have been attracted to Jason in the first place. Ray was physically handicapped from injuries he sustained in the big World War II. The after effects were severe gout in his hands and feet, making walking painful, even with the use of a cane. Somehow, by taking care of some of his physical needs, compensated for my feelings of guilt for having married again during a time when I knew in my heart of hearts that I should have made some personal growth instead.

For two months it looked as though my life would finally settle down to normal—as I perceived as normal.—a husband, a home, and the husband out working every day (Ray was a car salesman) and me playing the part of a suburban housewife. The fact that Ray seemed to be quite uninvolved with me did not bother me—or raise any question about his love for me in my mind. After all, hadn't it been Ray who had pushed so hard for this marriage? I was too busy preparing for a wonderful Christmas— Charmy, Allen and Casey were flying in from California and Corky would come with Tiffany. I would have my whole family together. I could hardly wait.

Now when I browse through my photo albums and look at the smiling faces of my daughters and their babies on that first Christmas, I can still remember the gratitude in my heart at that time. Alas, it only lasted less than three months. A few days after the new year (1981), Ray had a massive heart attack. For six months the doctors told me he would not make it till the next day. Muttie's doctor from Canada informed me the same. I traveled back and forth, expecting each trip to find my mother or my husband to be dead when I returned. But—again—reality demanded my time, diverting my full attention from the life and death situation I was facing. Ray had insisted to handle all our finances, claiming he wanted to protect me from any worry and I had gladly accepted. Now I was suddenly faced with stacks of bills I didn't even know existed. Ray had convinced me before the marriage that he was financially secure—he had showed me deeds of property and other financial holdings. Not wanting to appear mercinary, I had only glanced at these papers—now I discovered them to be of no value. Yes, he had owned these rentals at one time, but they had been sold many years ago. The truth was, not only did he not have any assets, he was deeply in debt. What to do—sell the house to get at least my $30,000 down payment back and move into a small apartment, get a job and try to clear up some of these debts I guessed was the best way to proceed. Alas, when I attempted to put the house on the market, I discovered that it had been purchased by Ray as a single man. Of course, I remembered, "he had insisted we buy a house before we were married." How could I have been so totally trusting? So stupid? The picture became only too clear to me when I entered the hospital room to confront him with these financial matters, only to find Emma, the girl he had been dating before we were married, sitting at his bedside, holding Ray's hand.

I returned home devastated. As I sat in my beautiful blue velvet chair, looking around the attractively decorated living room, feeling like a total failure and idiot, I remembered that the suitcase was still in the trunk of my car for I had gone straight to the hospital after returning from the most recent trip to see Muttie—she was now in a semi-coma and had not even recognized me.

Slowly I made my way down the few steps from the living room of my split level home—ha! my home—what a joke, to the entry to retrieve my suitcase with the intention of taking a long bublebath after unpacking and enjoying a good night's sleep before facing the next day. Charlotte, my good friend and next door neighbor met me by the car. "You poor thing, running from your sick mother to your stick husband every day. How can you even stand it?"

A little bit of sympathy is all it took for me to lose control. I fell into her arms, sobbing. "Charlotte, that's not all; I just found out Ray is just using me." The insistent ringing of my telephone interrupted us. "Let it ring," I said. "I don't give a damn right now who needs me. I'm sick of being needed."

Charlotte guided me into the house and up the steps. "Here; sit down while I answer this thing." It must have rung twenty times by now— "maybe it's something important." I paid no attention to what Charlotte was saying into the receiver but I knew what she was about to tell me as she walked toward me, her face pale, eyes filling with tears. Quietly I asked, "Is it Ray or Muttie?"

"It's your mother's doctor. I think you better talk to him, Aggie." Suddenly I was calm and in control as I listened to the doctor tell me, "Your mother went in her sleep, Mrs. ___ She did not suffer, just never woke up. She will sleep peacefully till Jesus wakes her with the sound of the trumpet in that promised day when He will appear again in the clouds as He rose up from this earth long ago. You will then be reunited with all your loved ones, including your dear mother. I'm sorry about your loss, now let me know if I can be of any help to you." I held onto the receiver a long time listening to the dial tone, thinking how much comfort those words held—how glad I was at this moment that Muttie had insisted on a doctor who belonged to the same faith as she—a doctor who now had been able to comfort me because of his faith. "Thank you, Jesus," I said quietly as I hung up the phone.

"Gary," I said quietly to myself. "I need to call Gary." The crisp, efficient voice of Gary's secretary informed me that her boss was "in conference" but would return my call as soon as possible. How often, I now remembered, had I made the same statement while working at the state offices, never giving a thought to the need of the caller on the other end of the telephone wire.

I started re-packing my suitcase, becoming irritated as I discovered I had nothing suitable to wear to the funeral. Immediately I chided myself silently, "Aggie, how can you put so much emphasis on clothes at a time like this, your mother is dead—dead—dead—and you're worrying about what dress to wear?" The words echoing in my mind sounded strangely like Muttie's with her heavy German accent. The phone interrupted my thoughts. "Is this the call I've been expecting, Aggie? Is it finally over for Muttie?"

"Yes Gary," I spoke into the phone, angry that I was separated from my brother by the long wire. "Yes, it's over—do you want to fly to Seattle and I meet you at the airport to drive up to Abbotsford together, or do you want to meet me at the nursing home?" I asked.

"Well, Aggie," came the reply, "I wasn't planning to come up for the funeral. What possible good would it do? Muttie is dead. I can't help her any more, and you can make the funeral arrangements without me, I'm sure. You know, of course, I'll take care of the cost. Just send me the bills."

I was trembling but I was not going to show him how vulnerable I felt and how deeply his decision hurt me. Instead of saying what I felt, 'Gary, you're right; Muttie doesn't need you any more—but I do, please come for my sake'. I just said icely, "Of course I can take care of everything by myself—just wanted to let you know."

After a quick conversation with Ray's doctor, I was on the freeway heading north with the doctor's words ringing in my ears—"Of course you have to go bury your mother but don't stay any longer than necessary if you want to see Ray alive. It's a miracle he's hanging on as long as he has already."

As soon as the necessary arrangements were made with the funeral directors, I headed for the nearest shopping center to search for a suitable dress for myself, feeling guilty the whole time that this seemed to be the most important thing on my mind at this time when I should be grieving. But I was obsessed, rushing from one store to the next. The dress had to be just right—it had to have long sleeves—it had to tie at the neck—it had to be just the right shade of rose, and most of all, it had to be silk—not a blend or look alike but genuine 100% silk. I heard Muttie's voice from the long ago past, "Oh, to be a lady and wear real silk in a lovely shade of rose."

Mission accomplished! I had the whole holiday weekend in a lonely motel room to wait for the funeral. I drifted in and out of sleep, unaware of whether it was day or night. At long last I heard the organ playing as I stood at my mother's casket, looking down at her wearing the beautiful rose colored silk dress I had spent so much time selecting. Somehow the fact that I had searched for a dress for myself and ended up selecting one for her, started to make an impression on my mind as I looked down at her. My mother's image would change to have a likeness of me and a strange calm came over me—I could feel the peacefulness of death surrounding me. I longed to be in the satin lined bed myself—I felt one with her—I felt peace.

* * *

At home again, the weight of the harsh reality of being solely responsible not only for myself but for a sick man I was married to in name only—who had plunged us both into financial disaster, started to cause me to tremble. I went to church on Sabbath morning to find solace for my pain. During an old, familiar hymn I remembered the times I had stood next to Muttie, singing in church. The words in the hymnal blurred as my eyes filled with tears. I noticed church members glancing in my direction. Swiftly I fled from the scene. I headed for the phone to call Muttie for help as soon as I entered the house—then I remembered, the realization that I would never be able to call her again settled in the pit of my stomach. Overwhelmed with a fear far beyond anything I'd ever experienced, I sank to the floor; "Lord," I prayed, "I need you; I want to have faith in You but all I know about You is that You have disappointed me in the past.

I want to love You, but all I know about love is that it hurts to be loved. I want to feel your presence in my life, but I can't trust you. Please, please, God, if you are up there in the universe and care about Your children, show me some sign that You exist—anything—as long as it will leave no doubt in my mind, and I will believe."

Nothing happened. I stood in the middle of my beautiful kitchen, thinking that soon I would lose this too, and God was nowhere. Feeling empty, I turned the key in the ignition, "Might as well enjoy the car while I still have that," I thought to myself. Heading toward Salem was the easiest decision to make. I had made the trip so many times I didn't have to pay attention—I could just set the car on "automatic pilot" and let my thoughts wander.

Pouring out my heart to Betty, where I usually found myself on Sabbath afternoon, she said, "Aggie, I know you didn't drive here today from Portland for a sermon from me, but let me read to you from this book, "Desire of Ages,—in fact I was thinking of you as I read this just a few minutes before you came."

I was grateful for my friend at this moment, realizing how often she had listened to my woes and how tiresome it must have become, but she never showed anything but compassionate love for me. I listened to her read from the Chapter 34, "Tenderly He bade the toiling people: Take My yoke upon you, and learn of Me; for I am lowly in heart and ye shall find rest unto your souls." Yes, I thought, that's what I need. "Rest for my soul."

She continued reading, "In these words Christ is speaking to every human being, whether they know it or not, all are weary and heavy laden. All are weighted down with burdens that only Christ can remove. The heaviest burden that we bear is the burden of sin. If we were left to bear this burden, it would crush us. But the Sinless One has taken our place— He has borne the burden of our guilt. He will take the load from our weary shoulders. He will give us rest. The burden of care and sorrow also He will bear. He invites us to cast all our care upon Him; for He carries us upon His heart."

Betty looked up from the book, pleading with her eyes—my words pierced the silence, "Betty, that's what I want from the Lord, but He isn't making Himself known to me the way He has obviously done for you and countless other Christians—what am I doing wrong?"

"I don't know, Aggie," Betty answered, "but I do know that He loves you for He loves all His children."

We sipped herbal tea mostly in silence, then Betty spoke with determination in her voice, "Aggie, you know I love you and it is difficult for me to do or say anything that will hurt you. I know how much you are hurting already, but I have observed something in your life that might contribute to your struggle to bring Christ into your life in such a way that you can trust in Him. May I speak to you frankly?" She didn't wait for my answer. "It seems to me," she continued, "that you are willing to accept Jesus only on your terms—you go to Him when you need Him and expect Him to solve your problems the way you expect them to be resolved. Why don't you give your heart completely to Him, willing to take out of His hands whatever He gives."

"Betty," I said, "I don't know how. I have experienced so many disappointments from so many people who professed to love me, I learned from these experiences that I am the only one I can rely on."

"Oh, Honey, but look at you; you are breaking under the load. What have you got to lose—you have put your trust in so many wrong people, why don't you give your Heavenly Father a chance?"

We parted with my words, "I need a sign that He knows I even exist before I can plunge into that dark hole of blind trust," repeating itself in my ears as I merged into the freeway traffic to return to my empty home—and God was preparing the sign I needed for He knew I was ready to trust Him."

* * *

Convinced that I would soon lose my home, I decided to make use of the fireplace while I still had it to take the chill off the October air with it's ever present Oregon drizzle. Watching the flames lick around the logs, slowly consuming what once was a living tree, my thoughts floated over my past, bringing tears as I remembered my mother's recent death. Feeling the need to talk things over with her, but realizing I would never be able to do that again, I decided to look through some of the boxes of her belongings I had stored away in the closet. Slowly I sorted through some of the old books and various "important" papers she had saved over the years, feeding them to the greedy flames in front of me. "Oh, Muttie, you saved every letter I ever wrote you," I mused to myself. Then I spotted the red cover of my personal phone directory of many years ago. Why in the world had she saved it? Crazy old women—I read through the listings of friends long forgotten, and people I had lost track of—mostly on purpose in a never ending pursuit of leaving the past behind and making a new start. On the inside of the back cover, a folded piece of paper, yellowed around the edges, was neatly paper clipped. I unfolded it carefully—a prescription written in Dr. Shower's handwriting—my memory snapped to attention—of course; it was the pills for nausea during my first pregnancy I was unable to fill because I lacked the $5.00 for it. I turned cold—my hands trembled as I read "Thalidamite"—Oh, my God—Charmaine could have been born without limbs had I been able to afford the medicine. I had blamed God at the time for my misfortune—I could now see the

265

blessing He had bestowed. I fell to my knees in front of the fireplace; my face on the floor, I sobbed out my gratitude to the Lord, remaining in this position, feeling secure in His hands. When I rose, the fire had died and I was a new person—reborn by the knowledge that God loved me in a way I had been unable to comprehend, but was now ready to accept. How many times had I been saved miraculously, never giving thanks because I was unaware of anything but my misery. As I stood up, I would face the future with confidence. The need to "know" was diminished—I was able to trust. The sense of emptiness I had experienced for so long was slowly replaced by joy in the ordinary things of every day; colors seemed brighter—music was soothing—a neighbor's smile and "Good morning" as we met by the mailbox was special. I became filled with a sense of wonder at all the wonderful things I had missed during my long journey of self discovery. Pain and sadness were still a part of me, but I was now willing to acknowledge the feelings instead of denying them and by facing them they became less scary.

One of my monsters of reality that needed to be faced was how I could support us and be home to care for a totally dependent, sick husband at the same time. I learned that by constant communion with my Heavenly Father who had become so real to me when He had revealed Himself to me by giving me the sign I needed, life became so simple. I poured out my problem of the moment, then waited for His answer by observing whatever open door would present itself and walking through it with confidence. I felt His protective presence when I received a phone call from a church member, asking for my help. "Aggie," the voice on the other end of the line said, "I know this elderly man who had a stroke and has no one to care for him but needs to be released from the hospital—he is not in need of total nursing care and therefore does not qualify for a nursing home."

"How can I possibly help?" I asked. "I have my hands full with Ray." That's when the text in Romans 8:28, "All things work together for good to them that love God," became meaningful. A short time later I received my State License to operate an Adult Foster Care home, and with some remodeling to comply with regulations, I had five patients to care for besides Ray. The income far surpassed anything I could have earned in the clerical field and I was able to continue making payments on the house.

* * *

In spite of repeated predictions from the doctor of Ray's health status being so critical that I could not expect him to live more than three to six months, Ray not only lived but with care his health slowly improved to the point where he was able to undergo triple bipass surgery after five years of being in the hospital more than at home, and when he was at home, requiring almost total care—at times needing to be fed, using the bedpan and having bed baths.

During these years, although caring for five sick elderly foster patients, besides Ray, I grew spiritually and became totally content in the humble service of caring for others. The fact that I was completely housebound gave me the opportunity to read and study the Bible and other uplifting material after all my charges were asleep—usually by 8:00 p.m. Slowly I got in touch with the person I was created to be—instead of the person I had created—one who was taught to please everybody. I gained self-respect and overcame my low self esteem. As I treated myself more kindly, I was able to love others more. My relationship with Corky became especially meaningful and I looked forward to Sunday mornings when I hired a caretaker for a couple of hours in order to have brunch at a nearby lovely restaurant that featured European pastry. Tiffany was a toddler and always drew compliments—and what Grandma doesn't thrive on comments like, "Oh, she looks just like you."

Corky had paid the consequences of her teenage rebellion when she had to divorce Jason because of his abusive behavior not only toward her but also Tiffany when she was just an infant. I was thankful that the experience had led her to God and back to the church I had raised her in. We had long, deep discussions about our deep love for God and each other. I always returned home refreshed and uplifted.

* * *

Ray not only survived the bipass surgery, but made a complete recovery from all the other ailments related to the heart problem which had caused his disability. After two months of recuperating, he returned to his job as car salesman full time. During his long illness, I had hoped that he had come to care for me—even if for no other reason than gratitude. And indeed on the surface, that seemed to be true, but as time went on and I saw him repeatedly taking advantage of me, mostly in the area of finances, I was forced to confront him on several occasions about him sabotaging our security which I had built with the foster care business. I was appalled at his bold lies in the face of evidences. Slowly I realized that I served only one purpose in Ray's life—and that was to supply his insatiable appetite for money. When I discovered that he was still seeing his girlfriend whom, he had told me he had separated himself from when he met me, I knew this was not a marriage but an exploitation. After much soul searching, prayer and a few sessions with Dr. Howard, I calmly told Ray that I was filing for divorce and he would have to find himself another place to live.

Ray then exposed a part of himself I'd never seen before. With a viciousness unlike his usual good humor, he overturned furniture, throwing anything in his way, even pushing one of my foster care patients against the wall—all the while screaming obscenities at me.

Amazed at my own calmness, I diffused the situation by apologizing in order to stop the tirade for the sake of my patients. When he had regained his composure, he gave me an ultimate threat: "If you ever get a bright idea like this again, I'll ruin you forever." To my questioning look he added, "All I have to do is call the State and report to them how you abuse and sedate these old people and you'll be finished." I walked out to the swing on the gazebo. I had the gazebo built, surrounding it by a rose garden and cement walks for my residents. Instead, it had become my hide-away. Secluded by the grapevines covering its latticed walls, it was my place for prayer and meditation. I did not cry, as I sat there alone. I realized I could not lose a marriage or husband I'd never had. A voice within me urged, "This man is capable of anything—

get out before it's too late." I heard Ray's words again—"I'll report you to the State—and then other lies I'd heard coming out of his mouth repeated themselves. He was such an accomplished liar he was completely believable. How many times he convinced me with his sincerity. I could not take the chance for such vicious and false accusations against me.

* * *

Once again I found myself on the road with my possessions in a small U-Haul trailer, heading for a new beginning. This time the destination was Pendleton, Oregon where I had found a position as assistant manager of a retirement home. What had persuaded me to take this job was the perk of a small efficiency apartment in the complex and meals in the dining room, plus all utilities paid. I would not have any responsibilities but the job. I was looking forward to the freedom from the mundane everyday struggles connected with running a household.

As is usual in Oregon, it was raining on my arrival, making the unloading somewhat difficult. Finally at 10:00 p.m. I fell into an exhausted sleep in my furnished, single bed. It felt strange having my arms dangle over the side of the bed no matter what position I laid in. I promised myself I would get used to this too—what mattered was the inner peace and serenity I felt as I fell asleep.

Around 2:00 a.m. I woke up with a start—I was shivering under the thin blanket provided but it was more than the cold I felt in my body—it was a strange feeling of loneliness, not like the panic attacks I had experienced in the past, but a feeling of abandonment. Immediately the thought came to me "Turn to your Father." I didn't even bother to kneel for prayer—I needed to connect with my source of strength immediately. "Dear Father," I prayed, "I need You. Somewhere in the Bible it says that You will be a Father to the orphan and a husband to the widow. I qualify and I claim Your promise-I need your presence and I need it right now, Lord. I don't want to feel this distance. I need Your reassurance that you have not rejected me, dear God, because of the divorce that is about to take place. You know I sincerely tried to make it work. I know that my sin was in marrying Ray without turning to You for counsel first. But you know how weak my faith was at that time. Lord, I beg you—show me that you have forgiven me."

I laid there for some time, watching the moon move across the sky through the window. Then ever so gently I felt a warmth surrounding me like two loving arms holding me. I knew at that moment that I was in the presence of God and I had nothing to fear for the future. "Thank you, Lord," I whispered as I drifted off into a blissful slumber.

* * *

Not having the financial resources to fight Ray in court for my original investment in the house I had worked so hard for to keep from losing during his illness, I watched as he moved his girlfriend in to enjoy the fruits of my labors—but not for long—two years later he died suddenly of another heart attack.

I felt no bitterness for I knew I had married him for the wrong reason as well as he had used me—I had been only too willing to walk into that trap because I had needed love so desperately. And being able to see that clearly now I felt only relief to be free of this desperate need.

Daily I counted my blessings as I went about my duties. Although I had endured much pain and experienced many losses, I had emerged triumphant. In the process I had found myself—the real me—and I was able to love that "me." And I was being loved by others. Gary, who had returned to the United States with his family and was now living in Washington, D.C. did not call often—after all—we were living in two different worlds. But the bond of love was present—I knew I could depend on him to be there for me if I should need him.

My daughters were a source of pride and joy— in spite of the tumultous circumstances I'd had to raise them in, they were responsible adults—successful in their chosen careers and concientious mothers themselves but taking time in their busy lives to always keep in close touch with me and never failing to show me their love and appreciation. This was expressed again on this particular birthday of 1986—two months after I moved to Pendleton; Charmie remembered me with one dozen yellow roses—my favorite; and Corky had chosen a beautiful simple card with one yellow rose on the cover. I will always treasure it—it read, "You are not only my Mother—but my very best friend." Yes, I was finally content, peaceful, happy and felt secure—knowing I had my Father in control of my life. But still feeling the need for the love of someone special I did id again.

He was 6 ft. 2" tall with wavy hair, a military erect posture who got every one's attention when he entered the church—and he chose me. He had been widowed recently and every single woman in the congregation was hoping to become the next wife of this pillor of the community—church elder with a sterling reputation. I felt so unworthy when he preposed—and every day thereafter. He treated me like the fallen devorcee who had to be put in her place.

We lived by the church rules and I could never measure up. I worked tirelessly in the legalistic church system to earn heaven, but fell short daily. I also fell short of working my way into my husband's heart. He felt guilty for marrying a devorced woman and there was nothing I could do to change my past.

After seven years of marriage I sat alone by his casket the day before his funeral, praying for peace, but none came. I felt empty once more. "I've worked so hard to be saved, Lord. I can't do it anymore."

My life's journey has had many twists and turns after I officially left the church. I've never rejected the Lord and I missed the church felloship but I knew that following the law to the letter was not what God wants from His children.

Eventually I ended up in a very small community, where I found the peace I'd been searching for. I learned about the danger of church doctrines. I don't have to work at all at being saved—or loved by God. Jesus Christ did it all for me. I am saved—not will be saved after I live my life precisely by the rules. Once I confessed to be a sinner and accepted His sacrifice for my sins I was saved—period—forever. Once God accepted me as His child, nothing or no one can separate me from Him.

MY WAR IS FINALLY OVER.

Photographs

At age two in the communist daycare. I am in the bottom row, center, wearing a cap. My brother directly above, top row.

At age three, smiling with tears in my eyes

Age four, with my brother.

A feast with my family, proudly serving white bread
reserved for special occasions.

Family gathering in front of our little house.
Me, holding my kitten, with my little cousin,
standing next to the tree. Parents in background.

At age twelve, wearing the lace collar I made
when I learned to cloeppeln (bobbin lace making).

Three years after the war ended, sitting in front of a cell block at the Flossenbuerg concentration camp, converted to living quarters for refugees. Wearing clothes donated and shipped by Americans.

1951 - Still living in makeshift shelters created from
bombed-out buildings. My brother and me.

1952 - Waiting for our daily meal at the immigration
camp in Munich. I am in the bottom row, center.

My mother and me (left) on the long-awaited
train ride to Bremen to board the boat to U.S.A.

Nine days of sea sickness - the price to enter the promised land.
My brother, patting me on the head to comfort me.
We arrived at Ellis Island in New Yorrk March 4th, 1952
on the army transport ship "General Mui"

June 1952 - An all-Americanized Agathe

1952 - Cleveland OHIO.

Summer of 1952 - The all-american family.
My brother's $40.00 De Soto and all of us, dressed in clothes,
bought with our first pay checks. Living the good life.

At age 23, with my two precious little girls.